HARD DOG TO KILL

CRAIG HOLT

WILD BLUE
PRESS

WildBluePress.com

HARD DOG TO KILL published by:
WILDBLUE PRESS
P.O. Box 102440
Denver, Colorado 80250

WILDBLUE PRESS is registered at the U.S. Patent and Trademark Offices.
ISBN 978-1-947290-35-8   Trade Paperback
ISBN 978-1-947290-34-1   eBook

Interior Formatting by Elijah Toten
www.totencreative.com

HARD

DOG

TO

KILL

PART I

CHAPTER 1

I SAT IN my boss's opulent office, waiting to hear what atrocities Frank and I would be ordered to perpetrate next. It was hot, and rain lashed the tin roof of the former monastery in hissing waves. Out in the Congo jungle, bugs and night creatures whirred and screamed.

I was folded into a too small chair of oxblood velvet and black lacquer, balancing a tumbler of whiskey on my knee. My pistols jabbed me in the sides through the Kevlar. Beside me, Frank guzzled Johnnie Walker Red and laughed at Zhou's lame jokes, seemingly unbothered by the low chairs, the muggy heat, and the very real possibility our tenure as private security contractors was in jeopardy, thanks to his latest outburst. Eager as I was to be free of Mister Zhou, I knew that after all Frank and I had done in the service of Zhou's diamond mining operation our employment was likely to end with a literal termination.

Zhou made a point of excluding me from the conversation, and since Frank's braying laughter seemed to please the little bully, I kept my mouth shut. To calm myself, I calculated the overhead on a live water cattle ranch outside Del Rio, Texas, which I'd found listed for sale, price reduced, on the internet. As a boy I despised ranching, but after ten years of killing I'd come to see beauty in the peaceful routines of farm life. If it weren't for my obligation to Frank, I would have gone back to Texas years ago.

Feeling eyes upon me, I looked up to see Zhou's sneer. "Am I right?" he asked.

"I was distracted by the rain," I said.

"I said maybe I can't trust you to find this man who betrayed me."

That got my attention. "One man?"

"An engineer. He walked into the jungle with four mine laborers three days ago."

"You doubt we can track and capture a few civilians?"

"Too many mistakes. No focus." Zhou pointed at me rather than Frank.

I clutched my untouched whiskey and waited for Frank to come to my defense. Instead, my friend and partner gulped his liquor and checked out his reflection in the dark, rain-splattered window. Apparently, he didn't see how dangerous it was for us to lose face with a tyrant like Zhou.

"I've done everything you asked, without question," I said.

"You don't want to quit?"

I opened my mouth, but couldn't muster a response. I should've assumed he tracked my online activity. Though my farmland research was innocent enough, Zhou considered anything but slavish dedication to The Company as an act of sabotage.

Frank looked away from his reflection to frown at me. "You're bailing out?"

The plan had been to take Frank with me, though I hadn't shared this with him yet. "Don't be stupid."

"Yes," Zhou said, "Who else pays so much for broken-down men?"

"There's no better soldier than me in the entire Congo." I struggled to keep the anger out of my voice.

"You aren't a soldier anymore," Zhou shot back. "You are a watchdog – a big, ugly watchdog who doesn't behave." He laughed at his own joke.

This carried the unpleasant sting of truth. I took a deep breath, struggling to calm myself.

Frank chuckled along with Zhou. In our ten years as soldiers and mercenaries, I had never seen him kiss ass so hard. Maybe he understood the situation after all.

Zhou slapped his desk. "Example! Uvira mine. You did nothing!"

He had wanted us to open talks with the striking miners by shooting their spokesman. "I was negotiating," I said, my guts coiling tight as my pulse ticked upward.

"Those fucking guys," Frank said through a yawn. "They went back to work real quick after I beat the shit outta that lippy bastard."

"Not acceptable," Zhou said to me. "I say shoot; you shoot. No questions!"

Frank pointed a finger at me. "Bang!"

Zhou trained his own chubby finger on my head. "Bang! Bang!"

I hurled my glass against the wall and jumped to my feet.

Zhou shrank in his chair as I stepped toward him.

"Stan!" Frank's shout stopped me. I turned. He had his gun – a real gun this time – pointed at my heart. "What the fuck?!" he said.

I took a step back from the desk and drew a deep breath. "We're the best team for the job," I said to Zhou, as calmly as I could. "Let us prove it to you. We'll have your man back to you in a few days."

With Frank's gun trained on me, Zhou recovered his swagger. He frowned, gesturing toward the door with his whiskey. "I will think about it. Now go away. I need to talk to Frank."

My common sense collided with my outrage, leaving me frozen in front of Zhou's desk. Frank staggered over and put a hand on my shoulder. "Easy, big fella," he whispered. "I got this."

Frank's drunken assurances brought me little comfort, though he could be a charming son of a bitch when it served his purposes. Thanks to my loss of control, I'd have to trust in his growing rapport with our shit heel boss. I forced myself to leave the room, and slunk downstairs like the chastened dog I was, clenching my fists and growling.

My departure was a poor tactical decision. Not only did it further diminish my credibility with Zhou, it also left me outside, staring at the pelting rain like a fool, watched by the smirking Afrikaner guarding the front door. I needed to be alone with my fury, but couldn't stray too far. I had serious reservations about my partner's skill as a contract negotiator, and feared he'd need my support.

Frank was a bit like a pit bull—loyal and eager to please, but damn near impossible to control. As his handler, I often shouldered the blame for his brutality. Zhou even faulted me for the mess in Mbuji, where Frank beat the mine manager to death with a crack hammer and torched the compound, costing The Company millions.

When Frank befriended me back in basic he was superficially crude, but beneath the thin veneer of macho posturing and dumb jokes was a generous and reliable friend. The last ten years of war had shifted the balance in him. That good man receded from me as Frank armored himself against the horrors we witnessed and, increasingly, perpetrated. As his violence intensified, I became less of a friend to him, and more of a concerned ward trying to save Frank from himself.

Yet now Frank sat in the parlor swilling cheap liquor and chit-chatting, while I endured a soggy exile.

I pulled out my tattered copy of *David Copperfield,* hoping to read until my rage subsided enough for me to return to the meeting.

I am, despite my early departure from the Texas public school system, an avid reader. During my years as a military man I always kept several books in my kit for those terrible still times stuck in the bush, awaiting orders. Now I was more likely to read while languishing outside a brothel, waiting for Frank to finish with some big-assed whore – stuck, you might say, in bush of another sort.

Frank said reading anything other than mission briefings was "fucking pointless," though when he was down with malaria he asked me to read aloud to him, and seemed to enjoy my recitation of *Lord of the Flies*.

The guard smirked at me as I paced on the stone front steps of the monastery, clutching the thick book in my fist and muttering the things I wished I'd said to Zhou.

I turned on the grinning South African. "I don't appreciate you gaping at me like that."

He leveled his gun on me. I was often greeted this way in the Congo. "It's my job to keep an eye on any *loskops* hanging around."

"I'm taking a break from my meeting with Mister Zhou."

"You're prancing around on the porch like a *moffie*, *bruh*."

I struck him in the ear with my book. He crashed into the door in a clatter of gear. When he tried to stand, I dropped him with a blow to the temple.

Perhaps I'm not yet ready for diplomacy after all.

I opened my book with shaking hands and leaned against the open front door. I was done looking like a fool for the night.

A few minutes later, Frank lurched down the stairs. I could tell when he saw me, because he went quiet and tiptoed toward me in a drunken attempt at stealth. I let him come on until I smelled Johnnie Walker breath and felt the burn of a knife at my throat. "You're already dead," Frank growled in his Batman voice.

I slipped a hand between his wrist and my throat, and nutted him with a boot heel. "I told you to use the pig sticker when you're slicing a gullet. That giant blade of yours is unwieldy."

Frank laughed and fell over the unconscious mercenary, full of drunken mirth. "I get a point for that ambush. You didn't do shit until I had a knife at your throat."

"I thought you wanted a hug."

"Just admit I got you."

"If you need affection, just ask. I'm here for you, little man."

Such was the level of our discourse.

Frank pointed at the South African. "The fuck happened?"

"He fell victim to his own arrogance."

Frank struggled to his feet. "Jesus fuck. I just cleared things up with Zhou. You kicking the shit out of his monkeys ain't helping."

"You seemed to enjoy your time with the boss just fine," I said.

"I did it for the team, asshat."

"Someone had to fall on that whiskey grenade."

"You could just thank me for saving your job."

"My appreciation expresses itself as sarcasm."

Frank slapped an arm around my shoulder. "That's why I love ya, man. You're always funny, even when you're sad."

Sad? "This is your mess." I elbowed him in the ribs, knocking him into the doorframe. "And I'll let you know when I need to be psychoanalyzed."

He rubbed his side, smiling. "Why you got a stick up your ass?"

"Why does Zhou always blame me for your mistakes?"

"You think too much, Stan. That shit'll get ya killed."

I didn't have the energy to point out that in our line of work, death would sniff us out whether we were thoughtful or not.

"So, did your charm offensive save the day?" I asked.

Frank pointed at the fallen guard. "Unless you killed that fucker and got us fired, we got the mission." His smile fell. "I just ain't so sure we want it."

CHAPTER 2

WE TRUDGED THROUGH the rain along the compound's single paved road, which led from the monastery past rows of poorly-built prefab buildings to the helicopter landing pad and a huge Quonset hut warehouse at the far end of the camp. The sturdiest structure in the whole place was the fifteen-foot fence surrounding the property, topped with razor wire and punctuated by blinding sodium lights. Between that and Zhou's heavily armed, multi-national security staff, the enclosure always looked to me like a prison camp guarded by UN peacekeeping force rejects. To the east lay the grubby beaches of Lake Tanganyika, across which most of The Company's diamonds were smuggled out of the country. Half a mile to the south was Kalemie, a single dirt high street lined by crumbling buildings abandoned by the Belgians almost fifty years ago, and hemmed in by a mass of mud and tin shacks. To the north was a forsaken wasteland of scrub brush, elephant grass, and acacia thorns. To the west, the land rose quickly into ranks of high mountains bisected by the Lukuga River, which fed into the Congo somewhere in the deep jungle.

Out of habit, I counted the guards as we walked through the compound; one at each hut, a man every fifteen meters around the fence, six in each corner tower, and six more at the gate. Forty in all, each armed with a poorly built Chinese QBZ-95 rifle and a couple flash-bang grenades. Thirty-nine men, assuming the idiot at Zhou's front door was still compromised. We could take them if we had to, even with Frank half drunk.

At the end of the block, just in front of the warehouse, we came to the hotel-cum-bar-cum-restaurant-cum-dispensary. Importantly for Frank, this was also a whorehouse.

"You plan on telling me about the assignment or what?" I asked, chafing at the new sensation of Frank holding the intel.

"All in good time, motherfucker. First, we drink." He patted my head. I slapped his hand away.

Frank slammed the bar door open, grinning hugely as we entered the white plastic world of plinky Korean pop music and yammering Chinese contractors. His smile spoke of home and hearth, a return to the bosom of family, even as men and women alike shrank in on themselves at the sight of us, avoiding eye contact.

"Hey, fellas!" Frank shouted. While I hung back in the doorway, scanning for threats out of habit, he strode toward the bar, slapping men on the back with his hairy paw, winking at the few whores who dared return his gaze.

Frank was a handsome son of a bitch in a swarthy Italian way. He was tall and strong like me, but lean. He also had all his hair, which I envied. The disconcerting thing about Frank's good looks was that when he smiled, he appeared to have more teeth than the average man. I suspect his toothsome visage had inspired the rumors about our taste for human flesh.

My own teeth are of normal size, though somewhat unevenly distributed in my mouth. With my smashed-in nose and the terrible scars all over my head, I've never been accused of being pretty, but my dear departed mother once told me I have kind eyes. On the rare occasions I confront my reflection, I bare my teeth and ask *is this the face of a cannibal?* I think not.

Frank, though, well...

Satisfied at the lack of weapons and other soldiers, I caught up to Frank and guided him to the far side of the U-shaped bar, where we had a clear line of sight to both doors and no one behind us. I left the safeties off both my Glocks.

"Has Zhou forgiven me for your latest mistake?" I asked. As I sat down, I reached over to unclip Frank's pistol and release the safety.

"He seems all right with me," Frank said, still leering at the hookers.

"And me?"

"He thinks you wanna buy a pig farm back in Texas or some shit." Frank chuckled, poured himself another shot.

"Zhou doesn't know everything." *It was cattle.* "You genuinely believe he doesn't want to get rid of us?"

Frank sneered at me. "You going through puberty again or something? You seem kinda emotional."

I slugged him in the arm, harder than I intended. "This isn't Blackwater, Frank. They won't just fly us to another country when our mistakes outweigh our usefulness."

"You got an active motherfucking imagination, buddy." Frank flexed his hand on the arm I bruised. "Like a... what do they call it? A *persetution complex.*"

"Perse*cution* complex," I said.

"Whatever."

The pretty Chinese girl behind the bar approached us, settling her expression into a perfect mask. "You drink tonight?"

Frank laughed. "*Do I drink?* Fuck, lady, do I ever *not* drink?" He slapped my back. "And my pal here needs a beer worse than I need to get laid. Maybe you can help us both out."

"Two Budweisers, please," I said, wincing in silent apology for my partner.

Her Chinese name was Yingchun, but, for reasons I never understood, she chose the western name Rebecca. When we were alone, I called her Yingchun.

"Whoa!" Frank grabbed Yingchun's wrist as she turned. He scanned every bottle on the shelf, still clutching her. "Gimme that Midori instead, would ya?"

Frank only ordered off the dust-covered high shelf in the compound, forcing Yingchun to climb onto the counter in her sequined miniskirt to retrieve the obscure and hideous liquors. Thus did Frank waste hundreds of dollars for a glimpse of panty.

He made a great show of tipping Yingchun two dollars, and poured us both a shot of syrupy green liquor.

He raised his venomous-looking drink. "To Sergeant Stanley Mullens, a stone cold killer."

Ah, hell. Frank's compliments generally preceded bad news, stinging insults, or gunfire.

"About this mission you're so hot to take," he said.

I drank the shot, and my stomach clenched around the syrupy glop. "That was the worst beverage I've ever put in my mouth."

"You drank banana beer in Gashora."

"That was a concoction born of necessity and limited ingredients. This here is like a mean joke. Pure liquid cussedness."

"I'm the Supervisor on this one." Frank rapped his knuckles on the table, as though there was some need to punctuate this point.

A lengthy silence ensued as I considered the implications of that statement. Frank was a highly effective killing machine as long as I pointed him in the right direction, but only a fool would think he was cut out for leadership, and Zhou was no fool.

"Commanding Officer of a two man army," I finally said.

"I didn't ask for it or nothing. It's what Mister Zhou wants."

"And if he wanted a kiss and a cuddle?"

"Very fucking funny." Frank's nostrils flared when he was irritated. "He says lack of leadership caused all the problems with the last engagement."

"Bad intel and a dozen Interahamwe soldiers with RPGs caused the problems, in case that escaped your attention."

"Zhou don't see it like that." Frank fidgeted, scraping at the label of his beer. "Says you're losing focus."

"That engagement cost me several pints of blood and six weeks in Nairobi recovering from surgery." I had taken a round to the shoulder and finished off the Rwandans with my left arm hanging useless at my side. Frank was so stoned during the ambush that he fumbled re-loading his weapon, and missed his targets repeatedly. His sloppiness nearly got us both killed. All of this was in my report, making Zhou's decision to elevate Frank above me all the more questionable. Frank put his hand on my neck, cajoling. "So, the job…"

I recoiled from his grip so hard his drink spilled. "Your pay grade go up along with your security clearance?"

Frank brought another shot of green slime halfway to his mouth, put it back down, and drank half his beer. He drummed his fingers on the table. "You'll make the same as always."

"And you'll make more."

"Not my call, Stan. Anyway, I ain't gonna cry for a guy pulling down three hundred thousand a year."

"It's the principle of the matter that chaps me." We were in the Congo because of Frank's poor impulse control, which had also gotten him drummed out of the army. Later, he got us fired from private security work with Blackwater by shooting the Iraqi Vice President's bodyguard. Zhou's company was the only outfit willing to overlook Frank's transgressions.

"Boohoo."

I counted to ten, breathing deeply like the shrink back in Jalalabad suggested. When that didn't slow my surging adrenaline, I drank my beer in one go, then snatched Frank's beer and drained it as well. I watched Yingchun moving gracefully behind the bar until the urge to shoot Frank subsided. "Zhou calls me a white devil."

"You call him a fat bastard. To his face."

My beer buzz came on, rendering me philosophical. "My employer fails to appreciate the Stanley Mullens product. My mockery is a defensive response to the sting of his disrespect."

"I understand about ten percent of the shit that comes out of your mouth."

"Understand this. We've worked as equals for three years. You treat me like a subordinate now, this partnership will end. And poorly at that."

Frank nodded. "That's fair."

"Nothing fair about it. I'm just warning you not to ride this horse too hard."

The futility of ten years of soldiering pressed in on me, crushing me from all sides. I nodded at Yingchun, who placed another Budweiser in front of me. When I slipped her twenty dollars she offered the ghost of a smile and a small tip of the head, which revived me somewhat.

Frank, assuming our matter was settled, produced a wad of damp, curling files from his shirt and slapped them on the bar. "Intel on our objective. Meet the sad fuck we're about to terminate."

I flipped through the life of a Zimbabwean national named Tonde Chiora, now reduced to a thick stack of printouts—his birth certificate, report cards, medical history, employment records, photos, and Facebook posts.

There were notes, poorly translated from Chinese, about the whereabouts and habits of all his known associates. I knew his favorite color (green), his sexual history (limited), and his religious affiliation (Christian/animist, a uniquely Congolese mash-up of conflicting faiths). Chiora and several of his men had been called back to headquarters from the Lodja mine, and had slipped out of the compound after a heated meeting with Zhou. Chiora and his men were last seen heading west out of Kalemie on the trail along the Lukuga River.

The investment The Company had made in gathering this much intelligence suggested that Zhou had an intense interest in capturing the poor bastard. The only things conspicuously absent from the files were an explanation of his crime and his specific whereabouts. All we knew was that he had done something to anger our employer, and he had taken one of the only passable trails west into the jungle, at about the time Frank and I were destroying the Mbuji mine.

Usually, Frank and I went up against other mercenaries or marauding thieves, men who were at least as deadly as the two of us. I found nothing in the mission briefing to imply that Chiora belonged in that dubious company. The difference between good guys and bad guys was always blurry in the Congo, but this mission seemed particularly unfathomable. *What could an engineer have done that justified sending monsters like us after him?*

I shuffled through pictures of our target, a skinny fellow with big eyes and a nervous smile, which he flashed in every picture. He hardly looked capable of causing The Company any harm. Still, like many stories in the DRC, Chiora's would end with a brief introduction to Frank and Stan, and our famously terminal attentions.

The mission briefing mentioned nothing of the standard support protocols, either. No other men were assigned to the mission. We were on our own for transportation. Zhou was telling us to walk into the jungle, and not come out until we had killed our man.

Apparently my confusion about the mission showed on my face. Frank slapped me hard on the back. "Problem, soldier?"

"This doesn't even tell us what Chiora did wrong, or where he is, exactly."

"He headed toward the Congo. There are maybe three real trails between here and the river. We'll figure it out."

"It also says Chiora is a lapsed Methodist who has taken up voodoo, which makes no sense."

"You afraid he's gonna put a curse on you or some shit?"

"It seems unlikely Zhou would hire a devil worshipper."

Frank smirked. "Zhou would hire Satan, Hitler, and Charles fucking Manson if he thought they could get diamonds out of the ground."

"It's a dangerous policy is all I'm saying."

"Fuck man, he brought us on board. You can hire all the psycho killers you want, long as you control 'em."

"But Zhou failed to control Chiora, and now he wants him dead." Given our recent failures, I couldn't help but wonder if Frank and I might end up sharing Chiora's fate, with some flunky putting bullets in our brains. While I found myself strangely unmoved at the prospect of my own death, my bone-deep urge to protect Frank kicked in.

The first time Frank saved my life, I had been captured by Al Qaida soldiers in the Korengal Valley. Frank ran into the field of fire and killed the four men hauling me away, taking several bullets in the process. Later, in Fallujah, an IED hit my Humvee, and Frank was nearly killed standing over me to return fire on the insurgents swarming the wreckage. From that point on, my own life had been spent trying to save Frank—usually from himself. The debt I owed him knew no limit. It made for a goddamn exhausting life.

I tapped the files, which I had re-organized into a neat stack. "So, Commander, what's our plan?"

"Collect the package, bring him back to Zhou. Fuckin' simple."

"Wrong answer," I said. If I was going to save Frank from Zhou, he had to embrace the seriousness of our situation. "We're following Chiora into a trackless jungle crawling with heavily-armed criminals from ten different countries, not to mention locals who would kill us just for a bag of rice and our boots. I assure you, there's nothing simple about this."

Frank chuckled. "Nobody could wear your fucking boots. Your goddamn feet are like pontoons."

I slammed a fist on the bar, silencing the other patrons. "This isn't standard operating procedure. We won't be dropped in with a support team, and extracted when the mission is over. The Company has clearly withdrawn its support, and we're being sent into the deep jungle with incomplete intel. If we aren't killed by the Mai-Mai with their poison arrows and curses, it'll be the Hutus, The DLRC, or the goddamn Congolese military. If we get past all that, there are also a hundred diseases that could have us bleeding out through every orifice. The goddamn air here can kill us."

He scratched absently at the label of his beer. "Take it down a notch, Sad Sack."

I drained half my beer. "We leave in the morning. I'll organize our kit, but you damn well better get to work on a mission plan."

"Okay already. Jesus." Frank slumped, chastened.

I threw an arm over his shoulder, and shook him gently. "I appreciate you covering for me with Zhou. It's the mission that has me angry."

Frank grinned. "You almost went bat shit on him."

"It was touch and go for a moment there."

"Woulda been epic." My berserker rages ranked high on his list of favorite entertainments.

"It would've gotten us killed."

He ordered another round. We drank in companionable silence as I did mission prep in my mind and Frank scrunched up his face in a drunken parody of deep thought.

He finished his beer and smiled. "I got it."

"A plan?"

Frank spread his arms wide. "We don't do nothing."

I smiled. "That's your stroke of genius? A double negative?"

Frank rolled his eyes. "If shit's as bad out there as you say, the fucker'll be dead in a week."

"And if he doesn't die? How do we explain it to Zhou when Chiora pops up in Kinshasa or Nairobi?" We couldn't afford to sit around idle. We at least needed to get out of Zhou's sight for a while.

Frank slumped. "Shit."

"You'll think of something," I said, forcing myself to sound optimistic.

Frank finished off his beer and mustered a weak smile. "Sure. We'll be fine."

"It's been a long time since we've been fine." I stood up from the bar, and nodded to Yingchun. "Good night, miss."

Yingchun dipped her head slightly and put her hand over her heart. That was our signal to meet in her tiny room later, for what she called *small consolations*. I called it pretending we were a couple so Frank and the rest of the men in the compound would leave her alone.

I waved goodbye to Yingchun and left Frank at the bar, staring suspiciously at a shot of vile liquor and contemplating, I hoped, how to become a real soldier in time to save his own life.

CHAPTER 3

AS PART OF my phony relationship with Yingchun, whenever I was in the compound I slept in her room a few nights a week. Sometimes we talked. She told me about her kids back home, and her plans for moving them from Nan Huh to Kunming, where there were more jobs. Some nights I prattled on about my dream of returning to Texas. I also wasted a fair amount of time lamenting the ugliness of the work we did for Zhou.

Mostly we played chess—me badly, and her well. So, while people thought we were screwing, I gave myself a headache trying in vain to protect my queen.

I slept poorly in Yingchun's little bed, but I didn't mind. I liked waking up to the sound of her breathing, her tiny body warm against my back.

Although our relationship was a lie, we had developed something that felt almost like friendship over the years. Sometimes, when I was very drunk and she lay curled against me, I could very nearly convince myself she saw me as more than a friend.

When Yingchun got to the room the night before my mission, she warned me that Frank had gotten shamefully drunk on Midori, beat up one of the company engineers, and finally passed out on top of a hooker in the ladies' bathroom. The woman nearly suffocated under his weight, and it had taken two men to lever Frank off her.

Yingchun frowned as she set up her portable chess set, the magnetized pieces snapping into place on the board.

"You shouldn't be friends with him," she said. "He is dangerous."

"There's a good man in there," I said, keeping my eyes on the chessboard.

She put her hand on my chest, just over the dog tags I still wore for no reason. "In here, a good man," she said. "In him, I think no."

I wasn't sure I agreed with her in either case.

Thanks to Yingchun's warning, I wasn't surprised that I had to wait a spell in the misty pre-dawn darkness outside our quarters the next morning. Still, I stared fruitlessly for nearly an hour into the stagnant fog cloaking the compound, fuming about Frank's failure to start his first command sober and on time.

Gear clattered to my left. I pointed my Glock into the haze. Someone retched, and I holstered my sidearm. Frank hove into view, squinting, his face a greenish echo of the previous evening's Midori.

I executed a crisp salute. "Good morning, Commander, sir!"

"Fuck you."

I stood at parade rest, chest out and eyes on the invisible horizon. "While you were indisposed I prepared our gear, sir! But progress will be slow with all that on our backs, sir!"

"Motorbikes," Frank said, rooting in his flak jacket pocket. He produced a few pills, gulping them without water. Frank traveled with a mobile pharmacopeia of potions, pills, and powders, occasionally falling quite low when the medicines ran out. I worried about him using his body as a chemistry experiment, but one didn't address such concerns with Frank. To keep the peace, I looked the other way while he ate poison.

He led me through the fog to one of the compound's numerous freight containers, which listed in the mud where the helicopters dropped them around the warehouse. Once the pills had their desired effect, Frank became something of a dynamo, chattering happily about the virtues of Congolese prostitutes and his enthusiasm for hitting the trail.

We would, he said happily, *gut this fucker, Chiora.*

My first mission had been to defend America against terrorists. Frank and I had come a long way since then, and mostly in the wrong direction.

Frank found the container he was looking for and swung open the doors to reveal a pair of motorcycles. One was a shiny new Bajaj Boxer, 125 cc's at best. The other looked like a plastic replica of a motorcycle that had been abandoned in a field many years ago. A faded decal on the tank said TVS Max, a brand of bike I have yet to encounter anywhere else in the world. Frank, of course, assigned me to that questionable vehicle.

"These aren't motorcycles," I said. "They're gas-powered toys."

"Everyone uses this kind of bike to get around here. They'll be fine."

"The Max will rot in the jungle. Maybe one hundred miles from where we stand now, if we're lucky."

"Fuck that. We'll catch up to Chiora in like two days. He's on foot."

"As we will be shortly, when my bike breaks down."

"These things are bulletproof. They build shit right in India."

"India is known for tech industries, Bollywood, and spicy food, not high-performance machinery." I shook my head. "And only the one bike is from India. The other looks to be homemade. By idiots without thumbs."

"Grab the gear."

"The chain of command brings order to our mission once again." I retrieved our equipment from the bunkhouse, strapping huge packs onto myself, front and back. I didn't share Frank's optimism about finding Chiora quickly and had taken the liberty of stocking food, medicine, weapons, and ammo for a multi-week reconnaissance, along with several gallons of gasoline in a variety of yellow plastic containers. I didn't anticipate needing our M4 carbines, night vision goggles, explosive charges, or the numerous grenades I'd slipped into the outer pockets of each rucksack, but the years in Afghanistan and Iraq taught me the value of pessimism in mission planning.

As a way of protecting my sanity, I also packed a half-dozen books. The occasional escape into other worlds was well worth the extra pounds.

Frank muttered about the weight of his packs, but, out of habit, he did a quick inventory and a status check of his M4 before hefting the one hundred-pound load onto his back.

We mounted up and puttered through the compound, our motorcycles sagging beneath our gear, our huge bodies hunched over to fit between rucksacks and handlebars. The Max rattled and belched a cloud of blue smoke that stunk of raw gasoline and oil.

The guards we passed averted their eyes as though confronted by wild dogs. The huge front gate rolled back on its tracks with a rumble, and we rolled into the gaping mouth of the Congo.

We climbed up and away from the stillness of Kalemie, heading west and leaving the fog behind. Under a star-burdened sky, we passed local women with bundles on their heads and wooden hoes in their hands, plodding out to work their meager fields. Small birds launched from the tall, dewy grass and shrubs, wings flashing in our headlights, showering us with icy water. I experienced a strange tranquility, disconnected from this dangerous new mission.

Regardless of the hazards ahead, it felt good to escape the vile politics of Zhou's compound. It felt like I had moved Frank at least a few steps away from mortal danger—at least for now.

In the equatorial regions, dawn more or less jumps out at you. One minute you're scoping the dark brush for heat signatures with your infrareds; the next minute you're blinking, eyes naked, into the glare. It's unpleasant, being ambushed by the day like that, so it was that morning. We rode from the darkness into the light in the time it took to cross the ravaged bridge over the Lukuga River.

Once we crossed the river, we left the rutted mud track optimistically referred to as the "N5 highway" and turned left onto a smaller path into the bush. From there we relied on our handheld GPS and our years of experience navigating the Hindu Kush and the deserts of Iraq.

By midday we had covered just over eighty miles, and I had repaired three flat tires on my motorcycle. Popping out the back inner tube the first time, I discovered it was warty with old repairs.

"There's more patch on this than there is tube," I said.

"The guy in the bar told me the bike was in good shape."

"It's nothing like that, as anyone could see at first glance."

"Bitchin' ain't gonna fix it."

"It wouldn't kill you to admit a mistake from time to time, sir."

With each successive flat, Frank became more irritated with me, as though I was popping the tire on purpose. We were like a married couple that way; the person proven right was always the villain.

Frank's pills could only overcome so much. He vomited several times along the way, staining the jungle with lurid green bile. Every time we stopped for repairs, I suffered both his ill humor and the stench of metabolized alcohol oozing from his pores.

Between pit stops we covered ground at a good pace, surfing the muddy ruts of the trail and skirting the puddles. This was particularly important, as one couldn't distinguish a few inches of brown slop from a trench deep enough to swallow a bike.

In my youth on our Texas farm, I spent a great deal of time bombing through the pastures on an antique Honda 250. Frank had never ridden a motorcycle before, but despite lack of experience and the torments of his self-inflicted illness, he was a natural, downshifting rather than braking when appropriate, throttling up just enough to dodge branches and rocks. Physical tasks from volleyball to murder came easily to Frank. I begrudged his athletic gifts almost as much as I did his perfect goddamn hair.

We stopped on the trail for lunch, in a patch of thicker jungle where pale, vine-decked trees rose above an impassable tangle of bushes and giant ferns. To atone for my irritability, I shared some of the excellent Congolese coffee Yingchun had put in a thermos for me. Frank took this with a rueful smile that indicated a truce. I listened for approaching motorcycles or foot soldiers, but heard nothing aside from screaming birds and the reverberating static of bugs.

As we sipped our coffee in the deadening heat, something moved in the bushes to my right. My heart thrummed, assuming it was a snake. I have an almost phobic fear of snakes. When I made out a human figure crouched in the shadows, I sighed in relief, even though humans are, by far, the deadliest creatures in the Congo.

"I believe we have a lunch guest," I whispered.

Frank nodded over his coffee. "Two meters. At three o'clock from your right shoulder." He already held his Glock.

"Hold on. He might have intel."

Frank chuckled. "Yeah. Maybe he's got a fucking bag full of diamonds for us, too."

"Let me talk to him."

"Fine, get your intel. I'll be sure to plug the fucker after he jabs you full of frog poison."

"Racist."

"Dumbass."

I stood, holding my hands out from my sides, and turned to the mottled gloom beneath the trees. "We aren't your enemies," I said in Swahili, French, and English. Languages come to me the way marksmanship came to Frank. I didn't realize this was an exceptional skill until the army went cuckoo over my ASVAB scores and foolishly tried to make me an intel analyst.

"We won't hurt you if you come out slowly," I said. "We're looking for a friend. We will pay you for information. And we have food to share."

The dark shape moved. I slipped a few steps farther into the jungle. My eyes adjusted to that shade, revealing a woman cowering in the leaf litter. More accurately, I saw the ambulatory remains of a woman; the thing before me was little more than ebony skin fit loose over a rack of bones. She wore a shift of threadbare cotton, no shoes. I had seen thousands of these wraiths over the past three years.

"Food?" I said, again cycling through my languages and pantomiming. "Are you hungry?" In the Congo, most folks preferred food over cash.

The woman spoke in a dry whisper, repeating a single phrase in several languages. "Please," she said, "don't rape me."

"I'm not a rapist," I assured her, but when I reached out, she backed farther into the bushes.

I cut a rough figure, being over-large in all ways, with vast but shapeless farm boy musculature, a heavy brow, and a head mangled by a Fallujah IED. My shaved scalp no longer sits quite right on my skull, and the exposed scars are unpleasant. I wasn't surprised that the woman expected the worst of me, but over time one grows weary of people's fear.

"I'm trying to feed you, God damn it," I said in English.

I turned to see handsome Frank grinning, his gun pointed right at me. "How's the interview going there, buddy? Winning hearts and minds?"

"It's a woman. She's afraid we will rape her."

"Is she hot?"

"Christ on a cracker, Frank. Hold your tongue for one damned minute." Frank said these things mostly to get a reaction out of me, and I couldn't help but oblige.

The woman broke from the bush, running away from us and up the trail the way Frank and I had just come.

I caught her, twisted her arm behind her back, and trapped her against me with my free hand. She smelled sourly of shit, and her breath was like crypt vapors. I could actually see her heart knock against her thin dress, as though the tattered cotton were the only thing holding her together.

I said to the woman, "We won't hurt you. Understand?"

She nodded. "Yes. Okay. Okay." She spoke in French. "Give me food, water."

"When I release you, move slowly. My friend is easily spooked, and he's quick with his weapon." I loosened my grip.

She collapsed next to the trail. I handed her an energy bar and a water bottle. She drank the water greedily, but looked at the wrapped energy bar as though I had handed her something as useless as a pair of dirty underpants.

"What'd you say to her?" Frank asked, always uncomfortable when I spoke other languages.

"I apologized for my friend's shithead behavior," I said, unwrapping her energy bar.

"Miss," I shifted back to French. "Do you live near here?"

"I come from Mukumbo," she said, keeping her eyes on me as she sipped the water.

"You're far from home."

She shrugged. "Men came to our village. They killed my husband and took my sons. I ran. I am running still."

"Who were they?"

She shrugged. "It does not matter."

"I'm sorry for your loss," I said, sticking to military protocol for questioning civilians. I counted to five and continued. "Have you come into contact with a man called Tonde Chiora?"

Much to my surprise, her face lit up. "The man who hands out diamonds!"

"Excuse me?"

"People say Mister Chiora is a great man. If you are poor, he gives you a diamond. He fights the rebels, the soldiers, and the *mzungu*."

I tried to keep my expression neutral, though I chafed when locals called us *mzungu*, which in Swahili means *person who wanders without purpose*.

Frank tapped my shoulder. "What's the deal?"

Keeping my eyes on the woman, I said, "She's heard of him. She talks about him like he's Santa Claus, Robin Hood, and Jesus Christ rolled into one guy."

Frank gasped. "Holy shit. They're *not* the same guy?"

I held up a hand to silence him and turned back to the woman. "Where did you hear of Chiora?"

"Niemba. He was there some days before me," she said. "They say he went to Mukumbo, to fight the bad men who burned our village."

"How many men were with him?"

"He came with only a few men, but many from our village joined him to fight."

"Thank you." I turned to Frank. "He already left Niemba, heading north."

Frank pointed at the woman, who sipped from the water bottle. "I ain't drinking out of that bottle again. Ever."

"She can have it." To spite Frank, I put some cash and food from my rucksack into a bag and set it on the ground next to the woman. "For you," I said, crouching beside her, "in thanks for the information."

"Please do not rape me," she said.

"What the hell are you doing?" Frank said. "That's our shit."

"We have plenty of gear—which you would know if you had helped with mission prep."

"I order you to take back that food, motherfucker."

Was Frank already attempting to pull rank? I leaped up, turning on him so we were nose to nose. Frank smelled more rancid than the Congolese woman.

"I took it out of my kit," I growled. "If I go hungry, it will be no business of yours."

"If you ain't combat effective, you put me at risk."

The bushes rustled. Where the woman once sat there was nothing but the bag of supplies, the water bottle, and the unwrapped energy bar.

Frank found the woman's disappearance hilarious, but I couldn't share his amusement. If we couldn't detain a lone, starving woman, what would become of us when we caught up to our enemy, who apparently had a growing band of supporters?

CHAPTER 4

WE MADE GOOD time on the trail. The land opened up as we sped along the north bank of the Lukuga River, through miles of abandoned cotton plantations, now overrun by elephant grass taller than a man and crested with seed tufts that bowed gracefully at our passing. Our speed made the heat bearable, the humid air washing soft against my face.

We encountered only one other soul, a gray-haired and leathery soldier in a ragged uniform, camped out on the north bank of the river at a spot where the road from the south intersected our own via the impassable remains of a bridge. What was left of that crossing moldered in a papyrus swamp, and I couldn't imagine anyone trying to cross the decaying ruins of that span. The man guarded it all the same, sheltered beneath a scraggly acacia from the cruel heat.

At the sound of our bikes, he leapt out from beneath the tree and commanded us to stop. I obeyed, in part to ask if he had seen Chiora, but also to find out what this emaciated man in the tatters of a uniform thought he was accomplishing.

Frank was of another mindset. He swerved as though to run over the guard, forcing him to dive into the reeds.

"I'm sorry," I called out to the man in Swahili. "We won't hurt you."

The man spoke from the shelter of the grass. "How can you say this when your friend just ran over me?"

"That was my…" *What the hell* was *Frank?* "We work together. He thought you meant us harm."

"What kind of an idiot is this man? How could I hurt him when I have no gun?"

I couldn't help but like the old guy. I got off my bike and pulled a pack of Marlboros out of my kit. "I have American cigarettes for you if you answer some questions."

The man poked his head through the grass, eyes narrowed. "Do you also have matches?"

I smiled. "Better." I pulled a green disposable lighter out of my vest. "You can have it."

The man broke into a broad smile and stepped out of the reeds. He accepted the cigarettes and shook my hand. "I am Captain Baraka Kasali. I am in charge of this bridge. Welcome."

"Stanley Mullens, United States Army, retired."

Baraka took an appreciative whiff of the Marlboros before opening the pack and lighting one. He took a deep drag, his eyes closed with pleasure. "Ah," he said, exhaling smoke. "This is a good day. Please, let us sit." He gestured toward the acacia tree.

In the shade he politely offered me one of his cigarettes. When I refused, he smiled with relief and insisted I sit on the upended log he used for a chair. Baraka crouched on his haunches before me.

"My partner and I are looking for a Zimbabwean man named Tonde Chiora."

Baraka frowned. "That one is a bad man."

"You've seen him?"

"Three days ago. He took my gun."

This was a far cry from the saint the woman in the bush described. "Did you attack him?"

Baraka chuckled, ejecting plumes of smoke. "My friend, I have not had bullets since 1975. What could I do? Throw my gun at them?"

feel like a sweaty, miniature Matterhorn. We labored too hard for idle chitchat and were therefore left alone with our own thoughts. At least, I was. I had never seen any evidence that Frank was the thinking type. I always envied his ability to get into a zone when we were at our labors.

Without Frank's blather to distract me, I worked fruitlessly to build a psychological profile for Tonde Chiora based on our intel and the reports we heard from the locals. In Afghanistan and Iraq I enjoyed great success profiling our black ops targets, and I was often able to track them down swiftly by anticipating how they thought. In Chiora, however, I found myself chasing an enigma. His files held nothing to indicate that he was either the saint spoken of by the homeless woman or the violent rebel described by Baraka. For all that Zhou had given us, we knew almost nothing useful about the man we were hunting. Not knowing the motivations and tendencies of our enemy added a new level of uncertainty to the operation; there was no way to predict what Chiora might do.

We rode through the heat of the day and stopped for a late lunch in the steaming shade of a giant banyan tree. While I gnawed on energy bars and read a book, Frank lit up a joint. After he had taken a few tokes, I put the book down and said, "I cannot shake the feeling that there is something the files aren't telling us about Chiora. What did he do to anger Zhou so completely?"

Frank shrugged. "I think he stole some kind of tech or something. Like blueprints or some shit like that. You can ask the perp himself once we got him."

"The perp? Now you're using police slang? Do we find ourselves deputized into law enforcement at this late stage of our careers?"

"We're more like… justice," Frank said, smiling lazily. "Just ask Chiora why all this shit came down on him. He'll know."

"I find prisoners reluctant to open up to me. There are trust issues."

"You don't need to strain your head worrying about why the guy is in trouble. No point worrying about doing the right thing, when you always end up pulling the trigger. You gotta pick a spot, brother."

It's uncomfortable to be seen so clearly by a drug addled killer. Rather than address Frank's insight, I changed the subject. "It never ceases to amaze me, the way so many men fall foul of Zhou."

Frank took another hit and gestured with the joint. "Here's the thing, Stanley. Zhou is a Boss. Capital B. It's human fuckin' nature to wanna take a shot at him."

"He lives in a fortress lined with money, men, and guns. Not even the finest sniper in the United States Army could get a shot at him."

"The Boss is always at risk."

"Wait. *He's* at risk?" I said.

"Safe people don't hire guys like us, fucknuts."

"Ah, the poor, helpless Mister Zhou. I do pity him so." The idea of Zhou all shivery with fear inspired me to song. "*There is a fat and wealthy businessman,*" I sang in my Lonesome Cowboy voice, all high and querulous.

"Making fun of the fat guy. Not cool." Frank muttered, grinning.

"*He has guns and go-o-o-old to spare.*

"*But he gets scared, and hides behind a fence. A-all of his henchmen are there.*"

"No wonder I'm your only friend."

I poured my heart into the chorus. "*Our boss is... he-elpless, he-e-elpless. Helpless helpless he-elpless!*"

Frank gave in and grinned. "Shit. I know that one."

"Neil Young," I said.

"A cowboy like you."

I took it as a compliment. "A Canadian, in fact, but I admit he seems to share a cowboy's longing to leave home and seek new vistas."

"Deep fuckin' thoughts for a hit man," Frank said.

I failed to notice the warning tone in his voice. "We're both cowboys in that way," I continued, philosophically. "It's the same yearning that led you to leave New York and choose the military life."

"Choice had nothing to do with it." Frank's voice lacked his usual bravado, and he spoke with such finality that my questions died in my throat. He tossed his unfinished joint into the bushes, started his bike, and drove away. By the time I could organize my gear and go after him, he was far ahead, nothing but a dark shape fading into the gloom.

CHAPTER 5

BY NIGHTFALL, WE had reached thicker cover. The path veered away from the river, and our pace slowed to a miserable crawl. The trail devolved into a tunnel, almost overtaken by the riotous growth of creepers, palms, and thorns. We labored over ground complicated by a slimy jumble of stones and twisting vines. We passed no other man or woman in that gloomy and difficult place. Though I doubted we would stumble upon Chiora and his followers so soon, I couldn't shake the feeling of being watched by some malevolent force.

Having left the river it was easy to believe we had wandered off course, and as the day wore on Frank checked his GPS with increasing frequency. I double-checked our route myself when Frank wasn't looking, and let him believe the course corrections I made were his idea.

With darkness about to fall, we made camp under the gigantic trees with buttress roots that fanned out in all directions. The structural supports were so large and flat that you could have cut a slab out of one to form the wall of a good-sized room. I tried several times to engage Frank on our mission and the deepening mystery of Chiora. When he answered at all, he did so in grunts and gestures, like a caveman in Kevlar. I considered apologizing for bringing up his past, which was always a sore subject for him, but could see no reason to beg his forgiveness. I silently made our meal, oppressed by the deep jungle and Frank's moodiness.

I preferred to sleep in a hammock while bivouacking in the Congo, to keep myself clear of the loamy ground with its myriad creeping, slithering killers. That night I strung my rack sack between two of the outsized banyan tree roots, pleased by the serviceable nest I'd created. I wouldn't be comfortable, but I thought I'd at least be safe.

As I lay sweating in my cocoon beneath a shroud of mosquito net, looking up through the gaps in the trees to a night sky burdened with stars, I pondered how to catch up to our target and regain Zhou's trust long enough for me to finish planning our final escape from the martial life.

I passed a night of fitful sleep, and awoke in the morning with a snake coiled on my heart, a huge thing that must have weighed fifteen pounds, its fat body intricately patterned with triangles and rectangles of buff, garnet, and brown.

For a long moment, I believed I was still in the clutches of a bad dream, but it was horrifyingly real. When I stirred, the snake lifted its powerful head to regard me, and I saw two spikes pointing up from the tip of its snout like tiny rhinoceros horns. *Gaboon viper*, I thought, remembering my obsessive research into African serpents. It was the last coherent thought I had for some time.

I would be lying if I told you my reaction was manly in any way. I flailed and shrieked, flapping my arms and tangling myself in the mosquito net. The startled snake shot out and bit my cheek.

I arched my back as the fangs sank into my face, and we tumbled out of the hammock, the hot venom pumping into my bloodstream. I fell on top of the beast, stunning it. The commotion roused Frank, who leapt up, and, without hesitation, pushed me away and hacked the serpent into several writhing segments with his giant knife.

Frank tossed the chunks of snake away from me and rolled me onto my side. He grabbed the antivenin in his kit, drove the needle into my neck, and slammed an EpiPen into my leg. Epinephrine sent my already-thrumming heart slamming wildly in my chest as Frank pushed several pills into my mouth.

"Whaddzzit?" I asked, my tongue and lips huge and unwieldy, my teeth chattering.

"Swallow while you can, dumbfuck!"

I did so with some difficulty, and he dumped water into my mouth.

Tossing the bottle aside, he drove his huge knife – still dripping with snake gore – into my swelling cheek, making a rough cross below my right eye. I had little time to regret the addition of another scar, because Frank was already sucking blood from my cheek. I wanted to tell him sucking venom only worked in movies, but my mouth no longer worked.

Frank sucked and spit repeatedly. As I fell into a scrambled kind of unconsciousness, I saw him spewing a last great mouthful of my blood onto the snake's remains. My thoughts were dreamlike and disorganized, but I remember being disappointed to think the last thing I saw on God's green earth would be Frank's blood-smeared face.

I drifted in and out of consciousness, my dreams lurid and populated by serpents and my waking moments strangely euphoric. Frank left me where I fell, shoving his sleep pad beneath me as a nod in the direction of my comfort.

My entire face felt pillowy and enormous, and I could barely force my eyes open when Frank roused me to push another handful of pills down my throat. For once I was glad, as bliss chased the pain from my body, for his chemical lifestyle.

Frank lit fires around me—to keep the snakes away, I suppose—as though I was a sacrifice on a pyre. Once, I awoke to see him feasting on what appeared to be a length of spit-roasted snake, which nauseated me terribly. The beast had, after all, been marinated in my blood.

At last, after what felt like weeks of pain and nightmares, I woke up for real and sat upright, propping myself on arms that felt leaden and strange. The swelling in my face reduced my eyes to slits, and even my ears throbbed hotly. I itched all over.

Frank was watching me. "The hero returns!"

"How long have I been out?"

"Couple days. You should see your fuckin' face."

"I disagree."

"Zhou ain't gonna be happy about the delay," Frank said, like some disappointed father.

"Then he should not have sent me on a suicidal snipe hunt in the deep jungle, with a junky ape for a commander," My self-control had apparently been burned away by the fever.

Frank glared, jaw muscles flexing, but didn't respond. After a lengthy silence, he dug into his kit and produced a handful of pills. "Take your medicine."

"Which ones are for the poison?"

Frank removed two pills from the pile and shoved them into my hand, leaving six others in his palm.

"And the rest?" I asked.

"Pain and whatnot," he said, avoiding my gaze.

Good Lord. What had I taken already? "You keep those," I said.

"I'm thinking you wanna take 'em. That cut on your face don't look so good."

I reached up to touch where Frank had performed his misguided operation. Coarse thread ends poked up like cactus spines, rough stitches straining to contain the swollen skin. "You'd best get me a mirror."

Frank chuckled as he handed over the small signaling mirror. "I didn't do so good in sewing class."

Holding the mirror with shaking hands, I saw that Frank had stitched me up with thick black line, in uneven loops that puckered the skin. *More scars.*

I also discovered a rash of red bumps covering my face and neck. I assumed it was some reaction to the venom. The overall effect wasn't flattering.

"You kept me among the living, and that's the main thing." I attempted a smile, which came out rather wobbly.

Frank shrugged. "Saving your ass is like my fucking hobby."

"At least this time you didn't have to take a bullet to do it."

"No shit, right?"

This was the third time he had pulled me back from death's edge. Rather than repaying my debt to Frank, I kept increasing my obligation to him.

My soul seemed to hover just to the left of my body. My head ached at the temples. Fumbling to put the mirror in my pocket, I noticed my hands were covered in red welts just like those on my face. Even through the fog of poison and drugs, I made the connection.

My relief at surviving the snakebite dimmed considerably.

"Did you put any bug juice on me while I was indisposed?" I asked.

Frank chuckled. "Nah. I didn't rub you down with scented oils, either. Busy keeping you alive and shit. I figured the skeeters were sucking the poison out of you." Frank's transformation from killer to nursemaid wasn't entirely successful after all.

Every mosquito bite in the Congo is like Russian roulette with two of the chambers loaded, so high are the chances of the little blood suckers carrying some dread disease. Suffering as many dozens of bites as I had was like playing Russian roulette with a machine gun. The only question now was *which* horrific ailment coursed through me. Sleeping sickness? Dengue fever? Malaria? Ebola? I dug into my own med kit and took four different kinds of antibiotics, hoping one of them might fight the poisons coursing through me.

Despite my weakness and bone-deep body aches, I stumbled around organizing my gear, possessed by a new mania for escaping this place and finding Chiora.

Frank stayed seated, watching my bumbling efforts. He had done nothing to keep our camp in order while I was unconscious, nor did he lift a finger to help me pack up. My obligation to Frank for, yet again, saving my life fought with my urge to slap him for being so stupid.

"Two days snoozing, and you're in a big fucking hurry all of a sudden?" he said.

"Snakebite and sickness have dampened my enthusiasm for jungle living. Pack your goddamn gear."

Frank jumped up and shoved me. "You ain't in charge."

"Someone has to be, and I guarantee isn't you."

"This is how you thank a guy for saving your goddamn life? Shit, I should have let you die," Frank snapped.

I put my arms through the straps of my pack, staggering as I hefted it onto my back. "Consider it a missed opportunity."

We spent the balance of that difficult morning silently nurturing our grievances, petulant children that we were.

In any case, I lacked the energy for conversation. Rocks, roots, and bogs made riding impossible, and pushing the motorbike was rough sledding for me. My whole body felt strafed and hollow, and the TVS Max, which had previously seemed laughably small, appeared to have tripled in weight. I alternated between shivering and boiling alive, though I couldn't tell if this was the result of the snake's poison, Frank's medicine, or perhaps the onset of a hemorrhagic fever that would end with me bleeding out through the eyes. Frank followed along behind, grumbling about the slow pace and cursing at rocks and roots.

We continued on toward Mukumbo, but I had no thought of the mission. Day after day, I focused all of my energies on surviving. My fever waxed and waned on a twenty-four hour cycle, each recurrence more debilitating than the last. By the fourth day the fever—or rather, the hallucinations brought on by the fever—cut short our progress.

At one point I swerved off the trail to avoid running over a winsome maiden in elaborate Victorian garb. It didn't occur to me in the moment that a lady in heavy taffeta and whalebone corsets was more than unlikely in this steaming wasteland.

"What the fuck!" Frank said, when he came back to find me lying in the brush.

"Malaria," I said, for that's what it was. I was strangely ashamed of my newfound penchant for misfortune.

"Fuck, man. We don't have time for this shit."

"Behold! The CO rediscovers his sense of mission."

"Half dead, and you're still a prick."

By nightfall, his irritation gave way to real concern. He kept an eye on me as he set up camp for the night, checking my temperature, and encouraging me to eat some food. I suspect he felt some twinge of guilt, having exposed me to half the mosquitoes in the Congo. I lay in the mud, shivering and trying in vain to make a blanket out of giant leaves and saw grass.

Throughout the terrible night I passed in and out of consciousness, suffering visions of myself twisted in razor wire and vines, and of murderous clowns in full regalia.

Their shrill laughter sounded just like Mister Zhou. Frank spent the night preparing hydration fluids and propping me up while I drank. By morning, my fever cycled down once more, but a headache like shrapnel in the brain remained.

"You good to go?" Frank asked, handing me what was surely one of our last bottles of clean water.

"I wouldn't describe myself that way, no."

"Map says there's a village up ahead. Might be a doctor or something."

"That or a battalion of rebels, or Chiora and his men lying in ambush. I'm past the point of caring."

"Good. I'll use you as a shield if we get into the shit."

CHAPTER 6

WHEN THE DEEP forest gave way to small patches of cultivated land, I sent Frank ahead on foot to scout the village while I pulled my motorcycle into a patch of five-foot-high cassava plants. I lay shivering on the red dirt, looking up through the imperfect shade of the purple-green leaves.

Frank returned in twenty minutes, chuckling to himself. "That place is like the land of the living fucking dead."

"You saw no evidence of Chiora?"

"Unless he's a hundred years old now, that fucker's long gone."

"Did you speak to anyone? Did you ask about him at least?"

"I was in kind of a hurry to make sure my partner hadn't been attacked by monkeys or some shit. Ask 'em yourself, if you manage to not die."

Entering the village, I was struck by the splintered and ramshackle look of the huts, and the exceptionally benumbed demeanor of the few villagers who materialized to stare at us.

Frank's description was accurate. The emaciated inhabitants were hollow-eyed and shambling things, and my guts twisted uneasily at their dead-eyed stares. Had I not been so entirely undone by fever, I would have climbed aboard my motorcycle and put as much distance as possible between myself and those grim shadows. Instead, I asked for a doctor.

No one spoke, but a naked, big-bellied toddler wandered off, presumably to retrieve the physician.

The locals gawped at us for some time before I put my finger on the other unsettling thing about the place.

"There are only babies and old people," I said to Frank. "Toddlers and the decrepit."

"And that guy," Frank said, pointing to an emaciated young white man being led toward us by a couple of children.

"You're the fucking doctor?" Frank asked the wild-haired and bony man, who was wearing nothing but mud brown underpants.

"I'm Robert," the man said, plucking nervously at his tattered briefs. Frank and I turned to leave, and the young man clutched at our shoulders. "I can help! I can help!"

I shivered despite the heat, my pulse throbbed in my skull, and my hips ached terribly. I needed help. Yet as my fever spiked, I saw a corona of darkness around the fluttery little man before me.

"You don't yet know the nature of our problem," I said, squinting in sunlight that scintillated and fractured into shards of stabbing pain.

Robert giggled and covered his eyes with one hand. "Wait-wait-wait. Lemme guess." He rubbed his chin and furrowed his brow as though consumed by deep thought. Then he whipped both arms out wide. "Malaria?"

We acknowledged the truth of this, grudgingly. Robert bowed and danced a little jig. He was a strange bug indeed.

"If you aren't too consumed by other obligations, do you reckon you could find the time to help me?" I said, as calmly as possible.

Robert ceased cavorting and pantomimed deep concern. "Yes, terrifying white man, I can. And I will."

Robert led us into a half-collapsed hut near the center of the village and crouched behind an incongruous, hard-sided Samsonite suitcase. He dug through piles of moldering clothes, small bones, and bits of junk. From time to time, he glanced at us over his shoulder and waggled his eyebrows. His shoulders bunched occasionally, as though he fought back hilarity, or perhaps stomach cramps. He produced a rust-damaged first aid kit, and the rummaging continued on a smaller scale.

Though Robert's antics were superficially comical, all I saw was desperation. Ten years of war taught me the difference between silliness and bat shit crazy. The fellow before me was far past daffy. I couldn't help but wonder how long the man had been here, and if perhaps this was the fate of any outsider who tried to carve a life out of the Congo.

Frank was getting antsy. He reached for his Glock just as Robert shouted "Ta-da!" and wheeled around to wave a giant oblong pill in my face.

"That's a pill," I said.

"A magic bean," Robert replied.

"Jesus Christ," Frank said.

Robert patted Frank on the cheek, like a mother soothing a child. I was surprised Frank didn't cut off the man's hand and choke him to death with it.

"What kind of pill?" I asked, slumping to the floor as I resigned myself—once again—to death.

"Cures malaria," Robert said confidently. "I think."

Frank grabbed Robert's throat and squeezed. "What is it, Daffy?"

Robert gurgled and shrugged. "I forgot?" He actually scratched his head in thought, even as his face purpled. "Could be Fansadar. Might be the cyanide I copped off the Israeli guy from the UN."

"You have a suicide pill?" Frank asked, letting go of Robert's throat.

"Well, duh!"

"And you keep it with your goddamn malaria medicine?" Frank turned to me. "Don't take it."

"What option do I have?" I held my pill up to Robert. "Think, son. Will this one cure me or kill me?"

Robert eyes lit his grubby face. "Only one way to find out!"

I took the pill and leaned back against the wall. Soon, the darkness around Robert expanded until it filled the room and overtook me.

I AWOKE, WHICH was a surprise. Even more remarkably, I felt a bit better.

Frank leaned over me. "Can I kill him?"

Robert hunched in a corner of the hut, humming "Nearer My God to Thee," an old hymn I recalled from childhood visits to the Pentecostal church. A frightful purple bruise reduced Robert's left eye to a slit.

"Was that necessary?" I asked Frank. "Him saving my life and all?"

"Fucker wanted you to kack out. I took a leak. Came back and he was squatting on your friggin' chest."

"Not worth a blow, I'd think."

"One hand over your mouth, one hand holding the suicide pill."

"Well, all right then."

I couldn't summon any outrage. My headache still dogged me, though the fever had broken. The days of venom and sickness left me weak limbed and aching. I sat up, and a wave of dizziness broke over me. When it passed, I saw the somnambulant villagers crowded around the mouth of the hut. All of them, grannies and tots alike, held weapons: rocks, clubs, and even a few battered old machetes with twine handles. Their eyes fixed on Robert with grim anticipation.

This wreck of a man was some kind of leader to them.

I turned to regard my dubious savior, who in turn cocked his head to peer at me through his good eye. He did seem disappointed to see me so recovered.

Frank handed me a water bottle and an MRE, which I ate with relish, still locked in eye contact with the poor white man, whose previous foolishness had been replaced by plain old Helter Skelter, bug-eyed insanity.

The food reignited my sense of mission, and made me eager to ask about Chiora. Given Robert's instability, I needed to work into the interrogation slowly. Once I gained his trust, I could gather intelligence.

"So," I said, making an effort to sound friendly and sociable, "How did you come to be the medicine man of this wilderness?"

Robert remained unnaturally still. "Doctor? No. I'm the shepherd of this flock."

"Hoo boy," Frank said.

I was worried Frank's sarcasm would keep Robert from telling his story. Or, worse, that the so-called shepherd would set his tattered band of Christian soldiers against us.

Robert's gaze didn't leave my own, though. The story rushed out as though a great pressure had been released, the words tumbling over each other.

He had grown up in a place called Index, Washington, and came to religion out of a desire to escape playing soccer in the rain. He stayed for the donuts, and grew into a man of deep faith and limited options, living in his parents' basement. The idea of mission work in Africa appealed to him because of the promise of warm weather and an escape from the tedium of working in a convenience store.

Despite months of training, the realities of deep jungle mission life proved a rude awakening for Robert. The heat crushed him, the food made him sick, and his dank, dirt-floored hut smelled of urine. The villagers treated him kindly and were quick to laugh, but they showed little interest in his ministry.

Their response to his first service confused him. As he sweated in the middle of the packed-earth communal area, putting forth the word of the Lord with all his might, people laughed uproariously. Later, they told him that instead of saying, "God is great!" in Kiswahili, he had shouted, "God is well endowed!" Nothing he said thereafter was taken seriously.

After some months of this—and the heat, and the bugs, and the vile manioc paste called *fufu*, and the diarrhea— Robert began to have decidedly un-Christian thoughts about his flock. He indulged lurid fantasies of the whole congregation going up in flames. His sermons became nightmarish dilations on the theme of eternal torment.

The villagers loved it.

Robert's faith rotted away in the heat of the Congo.

"A while back I got hit with some kind of fever," Robert said. His agitation had given way to slump-shouldered dejection. "I couldn't do anything but lie around and sweat. I thought I was going to die, but the kids brought me boiled water, and the mamas took turns spoon-feeding me *fufu*. They even cleaned up when I, uh, soiled myself. I felt bad about wanting them to burn in hell."

He worried at a stone stuck in the packed earth.

"That ain't the end of the fucking story," Frank said.

Robert shook his head. "I repented of my evil desires. But, uh, it was too late. About a month ago, my fever got so bad I passed out. I woke up to find the Mai-Mai destroying the village. They looted everything, killed the men with machetes, and raped the women and girls. They smashed babies against the ground until their heads broke open. The bodies piled up in front of my hut until they blocked my view. When the Mai-Mai finally found me they just laughed, and left me here with my sin and my shame." Robert sniffled and wiped away a tear.

"That's a terrible story," I said, just to fill the awful silence.

Robert broke into a crazy grin. "That's when I knew."

"Knew what?" I asked.

His good eye went wide. "That I was in hell."

"Aw, for Christ's sake," Frank said.

"The only way this place makes any sense," Robert said with a thin-lipped smile, "is if it isn't supposed to make any sense."

"*That* makes no fucking sense," Frank said.

"Hang on now, Robert," I said. "You said everyone died, yet there's a group of people right outside this hut, very much alive."

Robert shook his head. "Only a few of the old ones are from here. The rest are replacements."

"What do you mean?" My headache gained strength. I couldn't tell if it was sickness, or just a response to the oppressive grimness of Robert's story.

"They just appear out of the jungle. The newly-damned." The wild-eyed gleam had returned. "These people pay attention. They know I'm right about the evil we fight against."

Frank jumped to his feet, holding his Glock. "So leave." There was only so much blasphemy even his latent Catholicism could stand.

"You don't just walk out of hell," Robert said.

Frank pointed to our bikes. "Rent a motorbike, numb nuts."

I felt the need to play peacemaker, lest Robert sic his minions on us before I could ask about Chiora. "Frank, I believe the young man is speaking metaphorically."

"He's dead fucking serious. Look at him."

Robert's good eye fixed on me, solemn as murder. I turned back to Frank. "Point taken." I took a deep, shaky breath. It seemed increasingly likely we would have to fight our way through Robert's flock of emaciated ghouls, and I had no stomach for it. In any case, I knew Frank would handle whatever killing became necessary.

"I think you could leave if you wanted to," I said to Robert in what I hoped were soothing tones. "We have traveled these seven days unimpeded."

"Aside," Robert said, "from the serpents and pestilence."

"Okay, when you put it that way it does sound like a series of trials. I admit there have been hazards." The man's moments of lucidity were more unnerving than his insanity. "We have survived though, more or less unscathed."

Even Frank raised his eyebrows at that, silently considering my scarred face and sickly pallor. I ignored him.

"There's no survival or death here," Robert said, "only torment in its many devious expressions."

Frank cocked his gun. "So it's all good if I blow your brains out."

Robert shrugged. "You would just be doing your job, and it would only increase my punishment for another eon or so."

"What do you know of our job?" I asked. Had Chiora and his band had stopped here, and did they know we pursued them?

The question amused him. "You are of this place."

"We're strangers here, just as you are," I said.

Robert laughed so hard he actually rolled around, slapping the dirt, something I had never seen a man do in real life. The villagers outside seemed galvanized by this, as though he was experiencing some sort of holy possession rather than just losing control. They clutched their feeble weapons more tightly.

Robert calmed down enough to say, "I might deserve to be here, but you two *belong* here."

Until that point, I viewed Robert with a level of sympathy. But his words struck a sour chord, rankling as they did against my sense of fundamental innocence. I had, after all, gone into the military out of necessity. It was the United States government that honed the killer in me, and then loosed it on the enemies of freedom. Later, it was my loyalty to Frank that entangled me in the dubious world of private security. And it was Frank's mistakes again that brought us to the Congo, where threats multiplied in a wilderness of mirrors, and words like *right* and *wrong* lost their teeth.

I jumped up, angry beyond reason at the scrawny fool, fists aching to crush his skull. "You saw the evil in this place and you rolled in it like a pig in shit."

Robert clapped at my performance. "Thus spoke Frankenstein."

That stopped me like a punch to the chest.

The villagers shouted their approval, egging Robert on with catcalls and ululations, creating a hellish din.

"You have mistaken us for some other men," I said, but my voice shook.

In certain parts of the Congo, people ran my name together with Frank's and whispered about us as one terrible monster. I always denied an association with the legendary figure. Once people realized who we were, the pitchforks— metaphorical and literal—tended to come out.

Robert laughed, and his feeble minions cheered. "Predicting your arrival was the only true thing the false prophet said."

"False prophet?" I had to raise my voice above the weirdly excited villagers.

"Tonde Chiora. The man who came spreading lies about riches and glory." Robert frowned and looked to his flock. "He was a bad man."

"Bad man!" the villagers shouted.

"When was he here?" I asked.

"We cast him out," Robert said.

"You killed him?" Frank asked, glancing for just a moment from the crowd to Robert.

Robert looked only at me. "The people didn't need his lies. We're the innocent, and we cast the stones. He fled into the deeper darkness."

"Cast the stones!" the villagers shouted.

I wasn't enjoying Robert's call and response sermonizing, but I needed to know where Chiora went. "Where did he go?"

Robert smiled at his crazed minions before turning to me. "Toward the Big Smoke downriver, where all evil flows."

"Kasongo? Kindu?" I asked.

Robert shrugged exaggeratedly. "It doesn't matter."

Frank tapped me on the shoulder. "Can I kill him, or do you want to do the honors while I start on the clown posse here?"

I looked at the man rocking back and forth in the dirt, whipping his followers up to murder in the name of his twisted god. The villagers clapped and jeered, shaking their sticks at us. "I don't believe he's earned that kind of mercy."

The villagers shouted louder, on the verge of attacking. Robert leered at us, his good eye now hooded with blood lust.

Frank said, "We going out the front or the back?"

I looked at the crones and children thronging the tiny doorway. "The back, I think. I would like to avoid infanticide if I can."

"Infa-what?"

"I don't feel like killing babies!" I shouted over the din. We strapped on our packs.

A child no older than four hurled a golf ball-sized stone that grazed my head. A red flash of pain lit my skull.

"Motherfucker!" I kicked the child in the chest and pulled both pistols, firing once at the feet of the mob.

Frank withdrew into himself the way he always did in a fight, regardless of the enemy. He kicked Robert in the head, knocking the crazy son of a bitch out cold.

Despite our four guns pointed at them, the horde rushed the doorway.

I turned and crashed through the back wall of the hut with Frank right behind me, still cackling.

The motorcycles were surprisingly unmolested by the villagers. Even more shockingly, the TVS Max spluttered to life on my first kick of the starter. Small rocks, weakly thrown, pelted me as I shot into the jungle.

I assumed Frank was right behind me, but over the blattering whine of my bike, I heard the crisp *pop pop pop* of his pistols. I looked back to see four children and a couple of old women on the ground, presumably dead, and the rest scattering into the bush.

And Frank, striding into the jungle after them, his face a blank mask.

I turned away and kept riding.

CHAPTER 7

WE RODE THROUGH the sweltering day without speaking. Whenever I glanced back at Frank, he grinned and flipped me off, as though he had spent the morning tucking into a hearty breakfast with friends rather than gunning down a crazy man's followers. Frank appeared able to wipe his mind clean of even the most horrific scenes. Probably it was just the drugs.

My day, however, was poisoned by thoughts of Robert's perverted faith and his flock's willing embrace of perdition; I couldn't get past the sick logic of it all. He said *you don't just walk out of hell.* But surely a person could fight their way out if it was important enough to them? I tried to imagine some other ending to our time in that village, but my visions of leading the oldsters and children out of the darkness were laughably unrealistic. Instead, I fled while Frank shot children in the back. To chase that vision from my mind, I recited Eliot's "The Waste Land" out loud, shouting poetry over the din of our motorcycles.

A few hours down the trail, we stopped at the edge of some nameless stream to eat, since my appetite had come back with a vengeance. I read *Blood Meridian* and kept one eye out for enemies while Frank napped. I was still weak despite having filled my belly, and I had to prop the book on my pack to keep my hands from trembling.

When Frank finally woke up, I said, "You get Robert?"

Frank shrugged. "Couldn't find him."

"You shouldn't have wasted time killing babies and grandmas," I said, surprising myself.

"Anyone trying to kill us is an enemy."

"Cut off the head and the body stops moving."

"They were assholes."

"We shoot every asshole we meet, we will be out of bullets in a week."

Frank turned away to fuss with his gear. He tightened several straps with unnecessary violence and said, "You really think Chiora's all the way to fucking Kindu?"

"He could be in Kinshasa, Burundi, or Rwanda by now." I felt oppressed by the gloom and heat of the jungle that surrounded us for so many miles. "We have no choice now but to press on toward the Congo River. Unless he cut east toward Uvira, which is unlikely, he will have used the river to make time."

"If you hadn't gotten sick we'd have the little shit by now," Frank said.

"And if you would have done your job instead of shooting people for sport, Zhou wouldn't have devised this fool's errand in hell." My patience for Frank's recklessness was worn thin by an exhaustion that was more than physical.

"Seriously? You think I got us into this shit?"

"You always seem to be the one emptying his gun into someone's belly."

"At your fucking orders."

"You acted on your own back there," I said, stunned to have Frank question me this way.

"You didn't seem too broken up about it, neither."

Before I could defend myself, Frank started his bike and raced into the shadows.

For much of the afternoon we rode a tortured path through foliage so dense I turned on my headlight in order to see the trail. So monotonous was our journey that several times I panicked, thinking we had crossed over the same fetid stream more than once.

When I could hardly hold the bike upright, I told Frank we had to stop for the night. He grudgingly agreed, but only if we could find some sort of village in which to sleep. We had underestimated the amount of fuel we needed, and he hoped to find some place to top up our supply.

After an unbearably long time, the heavy cover gave way to patches of cassava and corn as we approached another village. Again, I sent Frank ahead on foot to scout the village. As I waited for his return, I noticed the acrid scent of a bush fire had replaced the swampy jungle smell.

When Frank returned, I said, "All clear?"

He laughed. "Literally."

His response didn't make any sense to me until we rode into a recently burned clearing that used to be a village of several dozen huts. Nothing remained but blackened earth and charred circles of ash, the scorched outlines of former dwellings. There were no cook pots or clothes, no weapons, tools, or toys—none of the detritus of life. In a few more weeks, the jungle would cover this human stain with grass and vine.

Suddenly Frank tensed. He cocked his pistol and stepped lightly and quickly to the shelter of a patch of giant bamboo. "Look."

I followed his gaze straight back from the trail to a hut set apart from the rest, hunched in the shade of the brooding forest. The mud walls and thatched roof were untouched by fire. Wicker baskets and clay pots framed a door covered by woven reeds. Firelight, which we had somehow not seen before, flickered through gaps in the walls.

I pulled out one of my Glocks, which, in my weakened state, seemed to have tripled in weight. I was obliged to hold it with both hands to keep it from shaking.

"Damn it, Frank," I whispered. "Did you scout the place at all?"

"Fuck you. I didn't see it."

"How is that possible?" I asked. The hut was three times the size of a normal Congolese dwelling, virtually impossible to miss.

"Dunno," Frank said. "It's like it wasn't even there before."

"Why would a single home be spared?" I asked, more to myself than Frank.

"So you could have someplace to sleep?" He forced a quiet laugh.

"I don't like it." Darkness began to fall with typical equatorial quickness, but I had the unnerving impression that the strange hut had chased the light away.

The woven grass door swung open to reveal a wizened old man with a large black and green feather stuck in his hair, a slash of white paint across his face, and a necklace; at our distance, all I could make out were shapeless black lumps. He wore nothing but an oversized red T-shirt, which I later saw to be from a George Michael concert tour, circa 1993. He leaned on a large staff, the top of which was festooned with small white spikes that looked, in the fast-dimming light, like tiny seashells.

This was clearly a *marabout*. A witch doctor.

He turned without hesitation to where we hid in the dark, and waved us forward.

"Lucky you." Frank, surprisingly, began to push his bike toward the hut. "It's a medicine man."

The old man's dead-eyed countenance chilled me even across the clearing. He turned back into his hut without waiting to see if we would follow.

"We should leave," I said.

Frank shook his head and kept walking. "He's one old guy. How dangerous could he be?"

Despite my misgivings, I grabbed my bike and followed, trudging toward the strange hovel.

Inside it was unnaturally gloomy despite a good-sized cook fire. When we reached the doorway, I put a hand out to stop Frank. The room was perhaps twenty feet across, full of all manner of macabre bric-a-brac. Gourds, lengths of chain, and ancient plastic bags full of God knows what hung from the ceiling. Other strange items dangled in the flickering shadows. Nearer at hand, the woven floor mats were almost entirely covered with burlap sacks, crude boxes, and piles of bone. Grass screens created shadowed corners. One nook contained a nest of okapi pelts. By local standards, the place was a palace.

The old *marabout* sat on a tiny three-legged stool near the fire and made an elaborate show of ignoring us.

"I vote to move on," I whispered to Frank.

"Fuck that. It's dark."

"This is not right."

"You wanna snuggle with snakes again? C'mon. We ain't looking to move in permanently."

I stayed where I was. "I say we keep going."

The old man barked at us in some guttural language, gesturing to the two stools across the fire from him. I couldn't imagine that one such as him often received company. The arrangement struck me as suspicious.

Frank said, "I think a night indoors would be out-fuckin'-standing."

"I'm the one who is sick, and I want to keep on."

"Don't be an asshole. You can't even lift your weapon."

I looked down to see that my gun was, two-handed grip and all, pointed at my foot.

The man shouted again, waving his leathery hands at the night, the door, the fire. His eyes reflected no light.

"Look," Frank said, "the old fart is excited to have company."

But will he let us leave?

It didn't matter. I was too tired and ill to keep going. When Frank shoved me toward one of the stools, I didn't resist.

The old fellow had set a rack over the fire, and a clay pot bubbled atop the flames. He stirred some viscous liquid with a stick, and I caught a pungent whiff of meat that smelled like smoked pork. Nobody in this part of the Congo had meat. I recoiled from the smell, and vowed not to let that foul broth pass my lips.

"That smells great!" Frank said, brassy with attempted charm. "My buddy here is kinda sick, and we could use a home-cooked meal." When the man didn't respond, Frank said to me, "Me think him speaky the tribal *mumbo-jumbo*."

"I don't need words to understand," the man countered in Kiswahili. He speared a hunk of meat from the pot and stuffed it in his mouth. His voice was like rocks falling down a well. I translated.

"Right!" Frank said. "No offense, sir." He gestured to the cluttered hut, aping appreciation. "I can see you'd have to be pretty sharp to have such a swanky place out here."

I translated as best I could, tamping down the unctuous tone.

The old fellow carefully placed his stick across the top of his pot and chewed his supper, staring at us. His craggy face was vividly ugly in the fire's dim glow, his eyes like chunks of charcoal.

"I know what you are," he said at last. He nodded toward our guns.

When I translated this, Frank became himself once again, leaning forward and seeming to take on size. "Oh yeah? Who's that?"

The old witch doctor said, "You are hunters of men."

"Tell him he don't know shit," Frank said to me, apparently having understood the man without any translation.

"The air behind you is crowded with death," the old man continued. "Angry souls."

It was stupid, I know, but as I interpreted this for Frank, I fought the urge to look over my shoulder. Frank just smiled. His voice was smooth and quiet. "You think maybe you're gonna join 'em pretty soon?"

I didn't have to translate that last. The old man spit into the fire, jabbing a finger at Frank. "You are the one who should fear death."

"What'd he say?" Frank asked.

I was weary of all this posturing. "He, too, is a man of violence, but of a different sort, I think." To the witch doctor I said, "I'm too tired to play at death tonight."

To my surprise, the man smiled. "You need strength for the trials ahead. Sleep there." He pointed to the nest of furs.

"And you?"

"I must work. In the morning I fade."

I assumed I heard him wrong, or that my Kiswahili was a bit off. Drained as I was, I had no energy to pursue the question.

Frank continued glaring at our host. "What the fuck is your deal, anyway?"

Though I didn't interpret Frank's question, the old man went stiff and still. "Your spirit's song is like the scream of rats in a fire. It burns my ears and blackens my heart."

This I translated dutifully. The two men stared at each other, communicating deep violence through their gazes, mirror images of vile intent.

Eventually, the old man resumed his meal. Frank produced a bag of jerky, and the two sat across the fire from each other, masticating with intent. If they were not such frightening people, their face-off would have been comical. Even for them, it was difficult to look tough while chewing.

I lifted a hand to the old man to distract him from Frank. "Have you heard of a Zimbabwean leading a group of young men through these parts?"

The old man nodded. "I gave him strength."

This woke me up a bit. "How so?"

"I made bullets useless against his men."

I explained this to Frank, who sneered. "Yeah, right."

The old man took another bite of stew and turned to me, ignoring Frank. "He's more than a man now. You should not oppose him."

"We aren't necessarily enemies," I said. Much as I wanted to deny it, the old man radiated a foul energy that made my scalp prickle.

"You wear the false face of a child," he said to me.

A child? "Excuse me?"

The *marabout*, his eyes still locked on mine, pointed a bony finger at Frank. "This one is no friend to any man."

"Can I beat some answers outta this fucking guy, or what?" Frank said, before I could demand an explanation.

I held up a hand to shush Frank without looking away from the witch doctor's dark eyes. I tried to smile, though I was dizzy and dry mouthed, eager to end the old-school psychoanalysis session. "Since you made Chiora invincible, I'm sure he wouldn't mind you telling us where he's traveling."

"He takes his power from the great river now, drawing men and riches to himself as he draws the poison out of the land."

To Frank I said, "I was right. Chiora is on the Congo, heading downstream."

"Crusty the Clown told you that?"

"Not in so many words."

"Can I pop him, or do you wanna keep playing twenty questions?"

I had to give the old bastard credit; he had Frank figured out. "I prefer to wait for someone to do something wrong before I kill them."

Frank bristled. "Yeah, you're a real fuckin' saint."

His disdainful tone caught me off guard and brought the heat to my face. "There's no reason to kill him."

"Who the fuck would miss this guy?"

"He's a strange duck, but he has given us food and shelter," I said. "And I have had enough of death for one day."

"You're turning into a damn old man."

"Be that as it may, I need to sleep."

Exhaustion overwhelmed me so suddenly and completely I wondered if the *marabout* had somehow managed to drug me, though I hadn't taken food or drink from him. I crawled onto the low bed and found myself face-to-face with the spiny head of his walking stick. It wasn't crested with shells, as I had first thought, but with hundreds of human teeth. Despite my horror, I put my faith in Frank standing vigil and slipped into sleep.

Dreaming, I saw the hut as it was in real life. I stood in the doorway, watching myself twitch and sweat. Frank leaned against the far wall, holding his pistols, snoring with his mouth half open. The old man rose from beside the fire, whispering in some forgotten tongue. His gravelly voice grew louder as he stepped toward my sleeping form, moving his arms back and forth as though pulling a rope. A black snake emerged from my navel, pushing its head between the buttons of my sweat-soaked shirt and flowing through the witch doctor's hands and into his own belly. When the tip of the serpent's tail disappeared into the old man's navel, he turned and leaned over Frank, chanting and huffing until the snake coursed from his mouth into Frank's, filling

Frank's mouth and distending his throat without making him struggle or gag. My dreaming self screamed from the doorway.

I awoke in my own body to find the cabin as dark as I had seen it in my dream. Frank still snored against the far wall, and the witch doctor sat harmlessly by the fire, gnawing on something that looked for all the world like a human finger.

I drifted back to sleep with the realization that the shapeless lumps of his necklace were likely dried tongues, possibly human. I couldn't muster the energy to wonder.

CHAPTER 8

THE NEXT MORNING I woke up from a dream of violence. The hut was empty. I heard heavy steps just on the other side of the mud wall, and then Frank stood grinning in the doorway.

"Hey, you're not dead," he said easily. Last night's tension had vanished.

"Not yet, and no thanks to you." I looked around. "Where's the witch doctor?"

Frank shrugged. "Fucked off somewhere." His grin widened. "Probably after he put that shit on your head."

I touched my forehead and came away with a smear of brick red pigment. I pulled out the signaling mirror and saw the crude outline of a hand with the palm just above my eyebrows, the fingers stretching up over my bald pate. My mouth went dry and my guts roiled at the thought of the old bastard placing his paw on me while I slept.

Frank laughed as I cursed and rubbed away the stain. Then he produced his toothbrush and set about his morning hygiene rituals as though this were a day just like any other. As if a cannibal wasn't going to come through the door at any minute.

I felt dizzy, and my limbs were hollow and insubstantial as balloons. The room stunk of ash and greasy meat, the morning air was hot and muggy. Perhaps Robert was right about this being hell.

Frank said the maps showed another good-sized village a few clicks off the main trail, deeper into the jungle where we might be able to top off our fuel supplies enough to make it to Kindu. Given my enfeebled condition, he suggested I stay behind and gather my strength while he found more gas.

"You just take another little nap while Daddy goes to work," he said.

I flipped him off out of habit. Much as I loathed the idea of remaining in the hut, I was still too lightheaded to safely operate a motorbike. I agreed to wait behind.

"Do you think the old man will return?" I asked.

"I think I scared him off."

The *marabout* didn't strike me as a man to scarper at the sight of common killers like Frank and me. I figured he would return, but, in the light of day, I also felt better able to deal with his particular evil.

Despite Frank's nearly constant abrasiveness, and the way our friendship had frayed of late, I still felt a twinge of panic when he disappeared into the forest a few minutes later.

Alone in that scorched village, I ruminated on how we might catch up to Chiora. If we could only catch our prey, we could return to the world of the living. Robert was wrong; a man could walk out of hell, even if the road would be long and perilous.

"The only way out of it is through it," I said to the stillness, quoting my estranged father.

I dug out my copy of Poe's collected works and read for an hour or so. The book turned out to be a poor choice for someone who had spent the last few days with men who spoke convincingly of hellfire and voodoo. Halfway through *The Tell-Tale Heart*, I tossed the paperback into my kit, convinced I heard the witch doctor's laughter over a child's screams.

"Steady there, Stanley," I said, jumping to my feet. My strength seemed strangely returned.

The coals from the previous night's fire still glowed, so I decided to make myself a good breakfast. I pulled apart two of the old man's stools, the legs of which were perfectly sized for a cook fire. Figuring I could pay him for the furniture I destroyed, I continued vandalizing his hut. I sliced off some of the wicker floor mat and used that as tinder. Soon enough I had a little blaze going, and I set about preparing a bit of the oatmeal I saved for special occasions.

I wolfed down a massive pile of the treat and couldn't have enjoyed it more if it had been an entree at a five-star restaurant in Houston.

I headed outside to scour my pan, and something in the doorway caught my eye.

Strung across the entrance was a garland of dried human hands in various stages of decay—all with the fingers lopped off at the last knuckle, all of them strangely small.

Moving closer, I saw an order to them, from pitch-black old leather and bone on one side to fresh skin on the other. The last hand was particularly tiny, its foreshortened fingers reaching toward the floor. It appeared to have been added only within the last few days.

A child's hand.

Had Chiora bartered a child for the old man's protection?

Ants blackened the wrist, working busily at the clotted blood.

Bile burned my throat and my own hands tingled with the urge to lash out. I screamed as I tore down the string and tossed it out of the hut.

The evil garland landed at the feet of the *marabout*, who stood in the blazing sun pointing his staff at me, chanting in an unnatural voice that buzzed and rumbled too loudly for one man. His muttering seemed to incite the birds and bugs to whine and shriek in a rising panic. The dissonance grew louder, deafening as a firefight. My blood pumped hot and fast, and my body sang with terrible power. A scream tore from me.

I charged the old man, ripping the tooth-headed staff out of his hands. He didn't run or defend himself, but kept chanting as I swung the cane down on his skull.

The blow stove his head in, spraying me with blood. His body dropped to the scorched earth. I levered the staff out of the gory mess of bone and brain, howling and flailing at his corpse, alive with righteous fury until finally the ironwood staff snapped with a report like a gunshot.

The late morning heat walloped me as I stood panting over the mutilated body, soaked in blood and sweat, my hands still tingling as though electrified. Bugs and birds alike were silent. The blackened earth of the village baked under the sun, and the air seemed freighted with fire.

I spit on the body, wondering if whatever curse he had put on us could live beyond him, or if, with his death, his evil just uncoiled and spread into the world at large. I stayed there with my pistol in my hand for half an hour, just to be sure the witch doctor didn't reanimate. Finally, the fiery sun drove me into the shade of the hut.

Stepping inside, I bumped my head on a plastic bag hanging from the rafters—a sack full of little finger bones, small enough to have come from children. I moaned aloud.

A feverish inspection of the shack revealed all manner of human anatomy strung on ropes and secreted away in plastic bags and wicker baskets. Wooden boxes of skulls, strings of dried hearts, femurs stacked neatly like kindling. I puzzled for a long time over a loop of yellowish cord, finally understanding it to be a coil of human intestine. A rattan screen hid large piles of smoked flesh.

I stumbled into the sun and vomited. Standing with my hands on my knees and strings of drool unspooling from my mouth, I noticed once again the pile of hands. Determined to erase the *marabout* completely, I tossed them back into the witch doctor's lair and dragged the old bastard's body inside, dumping it over the cook fire. His corpse burst into flame as though filled with kerosene. I pulled a half-burned stick from the fire and touched it to the pelts, the walls, and the rafters. As the hut crackled and roared, billowing black smoke, I intentionally stood too close to the blaze, burning away the witch doctor's evil. The conflagration stunk precisely like the previous night's stew.

The hut reduced to a mound of ash surprisingly quickly, leaving only the *marabout*'s charred corpse, blackened but intact, with his lips peeled back, leering at the sky. I traced the mark he made on my forehead, wondering how deeply I might be infected with his malevolence.

I grabbed my tiny bar of soap from my kit and stormed into the jungle in search of water. I needed to wash away the witch doctor's blood. The GPS indicated that we were near the Lualaba River, also called the Upper Congo. Heading west through thorn bushes, vines, and lianas, I came to the river's edge.

Even this far inland the Lualaba was nearly a kilometer across, a languid, red-brown smear pressing seaward. There was no babble of water on stone, no cooling breeze, just the mighty river moving unheeded through the heart of Africa.

I stood on a narrow shelf of slimy clay, several hundred meters long, recently strafed of vegetation by higher water. I was strangely heartened by this humble patch of open ground and by the sight of the river itself. The oppressive feeling from our run-in with the witch doctor lifted.

Then the crocodile attacked.

The beast shot from the river in an explosion of spray and scrabbling claws, fifteen feet of prehistoric killing machine with a gaping, tooth-jagged mouth aimed directly at my torso.

I leapt to the side just in time, and rolled to my feet with my gun already in my hand. I fired six shots into the crocodile as it spun toward me. The bullets hit it randomly in the front quarters, the belly, and the tail. The wounds only enraged the beast. It lashed back and forth, snapping and thrashing in the mud as I blundered backward down the beach, slipping in the muck as I pushed another clip into my gun.

Fifty feet away I stopped, my fear twisting itself into the berserk rage of battle. I squared up to the crocodile, planted my feet, and roared. The killer turned toward me, its sides heaving. I bellowed again, and the crocodile responded with a terrible, mouth-gaping hiss.

A man with even an ounce of sense would have run into the jungle. Instead, I charged, screaming as I put twenty rounds into the maw of the beast.

Its mouth snapped shut with the unique finality of death, as though someone had cut the power to a machine.

I put another clip in each pistol and approached the motionless croc. I spit on it, and emptied both guns again into the top of its head. My hands shook, and my legs could barely support me. My entire body thrummed with fear. I looked out across the river, wondering what other horrors its beauty might hide.

I took a few steps down the length of the crocodile, heading mindlessly toward the water. I needed to sit, and, for lack of a chair, I flopped onto the croc's broad back.

Examining the sinewy length of the creature, I felt a twinge of regret at having killed an animal that had survived so long in this place.

I patted the croc's forehead. "I'm sorry about all this," I said, "truly." I drew a shaky breath and put my head in my hands.

I was still sitting on the back of the crocodile when Frank stormed out of the bushes with his guns drawn. Seeing him, I realized I was weeping.

CHAPTER 9

FRANK PULLED UP short at the sight of me.

"The fuck is going on?" he said. "I let you rest while I take care of business. I come back, and the fucking hut is burned down, there's a barbecued stiff in the ashes I'm pretty sure is the witch doctor, and you're just gone. Your bike is there, but your shit has all been rifled through. I'm thinking the Mai-Mai or some other assholes nabbed you. By some goddamn miracle I think to check down by the river in case they dumped you in the water, and here you are, just…" He grabbed his hair with both hands, consternation getting the better of him. "What the fuck *are* you doing?"

I took a deep breath and wiped my tears away. "I'm weary of all this killing."

Frank's look spoke of deep concern for my sanity. "You had a pretty busy morning of it, what with roasting the old guy and going bat-shit on the crocodilian."

"The crocodile attacked me. And the old man…"

Frank laughed. "You ain't gotta explain nothing to me. I'm glad the fucking monster is dead. I woulda killed that old fucker if you hadn't. Dude gave me the creeps."

"Frank, the man was a cannibal. He killed children and used them in his vile rituals."

If Frank cottoned on to the fact that the stew we had watched the man eat so happily last night was made with human flesh—that the rumors of his cannibalism had come so close to being proven true—he showed no sign of it. "Yeah, there you go. Good fuckin' riddance."

I looked across the river, tracing the progress of a clump of water hyacinth. "Death follows me. It's just as the *marabout* said."

Frank sat down beside me and gave me a manly slap on the back. "So. Croc jumps you, you shoot crocodilian. Can't beat yourself up for wanting to live, right?"

"I was cursed long before we met that cannibal."

"You gotta get over that shit. If that fucking guy knew so much, why's he the one got beat to death and thrown on a fire, while you're off kicking a sea monster's ass and whatnot? Think about it. If you hadn't come along and popped this fucking croc, he probably woulda killed a couple hundred Congolese mamas and babies before he finally kacked out."

Frank delivered another stingingly affectionate blow to my back. "Nope," he continued, "Far as I can tell, you deserve a fucking medal. These people should be kissing your huge-ass feet and putting on a goddamn parade. Stan Mullens! Fuckin' hero of the jungle!"

I couldn't help but smile through my tears. "That's the longest speech you have ever given."

"Desperate times, my man."

We watched the river in silence for a while. Finally, Frank cleared his throat. "Why are you sitting on the goddamn croc?"

"No chairs."

Frank pursed his lips and nodded. "Huh." He looked at the bullet-riddled crocodile, the pulpy crater where his brain used to be. "How many times did you shoot him?"

"Enough to finish the job."

Frank heaved a great sigh and kicked the unyielding crocodile. "Jesus Christ."

Regrets large and small crowded my mind. "Frank, do you think there's such a thing as personal transformation?"

Frank grimaced. "You mean like getting totally fuckin' ripped?"

"I mean, can a man change who he is, and how he interacts with the world?"

"Oh. Right. Gotcha." He frowned. "Are we talkin' about you?"

I couldn't meet his gaze. "We could be."

Frank's laughter rang through the jungle. To change the subject, I asked him how he fared with the search for gasoline.

"It's all good," he said, still chuckling.

There was obviously more to the story. "Good in what way?"

"Let's just say you and me both got in some target practice this morning."

No one and nothing is safe in this place.

Frank decided we should have a souvenir of this eventful day, and he set about hacking the claws off the crocodile while I made my way back to the ruined village.

I re-packed my gear and mounted the motorcycle. My gaze was drawn to the witch doctor's blackened corpse, sprawled across the ashes. A thick column of smoke still rose from his grinning mouth.

Frank emerged from the brush some minutes later, carrying four huge and bloody crocodile feet. He followed my gaze, and walked over to spit on the smoldering body. He turned and smiled, pointing at the charred body. "That's what I call a personal transformation, Stan."

CHAPTER 10

MY BIKE RESPONDED poorly to its long rest, belching a particularly thick blue-black cloud upon starting, and failing to idle properly as we left that cursed place. Throughout that day, the Max stalled with more than usual regularity, as though it absorbed the sickness that had so quickly left me.

I finally stopped in the steaming dark of the heavy jungle, at a point where an even rougher path cut off into the darkness, so I could tinker with my motorbike's air intake. "This bike is about done for," I said.

"When it actually dies, we'll talk. Until then, just deal with it."

I pointed down the smaller trail. "How far down is the village?"

"No idea. I got what I needed just a few clicks in."

"You just bumped into some people willing to sell you gasoline?" I asked, sitting up.

Frank shrugged, looked away. "Something like that. Doesn't matter."

"You said you also got some target practice," I said.

Frank started his bike. "We're burning daylight."

"What if I wanted to talk to these good Samaritans?"

"Wouldn't be much of a conversation." He revved his engine. "But if you're all hot for a field trip, let's go."

I turned down the smaller path.

We traveled for another dark and difficult fifteen minutes to a small clearing, little more than a widening of the trail, where I met the men from whom Frank procured his gasoline. Or more accurately, I came across their mortal remains.

I counted six freshly killed corpses scattered across the trailside grass. Frank told me the story of their demise while rifling through their surprisingly new clothes, a task which he said he had put off earlier due to concern for my safety.

"This muscle-bound fucker was the hard case. I tried to buy some gas from him, but he wanted to rip me off. Had a real mouth on him, this guy. Starts barking at me about jurisdiction and shit. I figured *fuck it* and shot him in the face. His buddies all bailed out like a bunch of pussies. That's why they're all spread out like this."

I marveled that Frank's inner voice could muster nothing more profound than *fuck it* when confronted with life-or-death dilemmas. I couldn't decide if he thought too little, or if I thought too much.

Perhaps we're both incorrectly wired in some important way.

Frank squatted beside a small body. "How old do you think this little guy is? Was."

I looked into the wide-eyed face of a boy with strong cheekbones and smooth skin. Bile rose in my throat as I pictured the small hands strung up around the witch doctor's door. "Too young to be shot in the back for a couple liters of gas, I reckon."

"You've seen the shit kid soldiers do around here," he said. "Anyway, he shouldn't have been on patrol with a bunch of assholes."

"Patrol?" My stomach clenched.

"Government pricks from the sound of it. Guy didn't speak a lotta English." Frank kicked the boy in the ribs. "Patrol's over now, soldier. At ease."

"You killed five government men and a boy for a bit of gasoline?" I asked, as calmly as I could.

Frank turned on me. "What the fuck? You'd rather walk to Kindu from here?"

"You didn't have to do it."

"You didn't have to get sick."

We spoke with exaggerated calm, but growled like dogs.

"I didn't choose to be bitten by a snake, or near killed by malaria."

"So now the malaria is my fault? Or are we gonna blame the snake?" He shook his head with a forced laugh.

"This isn't about blame," I said, my voice shaking. "I'm talking about choices."

Turning to the scattered corpses, Frank said, "News flash, fellas! You were actually killed by a snake that tried to face-fuck my partner here a few days back. Fate's a real bitch."

"I'm just saying I regret them having to die like this. It's a waste." I bent down to close the dead boy's eyes. "You dispense death too freely, Frank."

I ignored the voice in my head asking how much I did to stop him.

"Shit happens." But Frank wouldn't meet my eyes. "They shouldn't have tried to rip me off. Fifty bucks a liter, they wanted to charge me. Laughing like they had me over a barrel."

"Petty officials in this place like to lord it over the helpless. You know that. Still…" I ran out of words to express my loathing for Frank. For myself.

"Did you at least learn anything about Chiora?" I asked.

"We were busy negotiating."

I rubbed my face hard with both hands to keep from screaming. "So. You run into a group of men from the town where our target is rumored to be holed up, and it doesn't occur to you to find out what he's doing, who he's with, and whether or not he's still there?"

"What's your fucking problem? Without the gas we'd never get there."

"Frank, if you were going to shoot them anyway, you could have at least learned something before you executed them."

He shrugged. "Game time decision, coach. Heat of battle and whatnot."

I forced myself not to bellow in his face. I wanted to pound his head into a tree. "Do you even want this mission to end, Frank?"

Instead of answering, Frank went back to turning out the dead men's pockets. From the big man's shirt, he produced a fat cloth bag. Opening it, he smiled. "Holy shit. Diamonds. A fuck-ton of 'em. Want some?"

The fight went out of me. "Leave them," I said.

"I order you to take some."

"Take them for yourself or just leave them. And don't play the commander card with me."

Frank secreted the diamonds with his pills and potions, and his earlier discomfort disappeared, leaving me to marvel at how easily money seemed to quiet Frank's conscience. He told me he had stashed more of the fuel in the bush, and we made our way into the deeper shadows to find another half a dozen liters of gas. Farther into the weeds still lay a twisted and burned pile of metal. I recognized three motorcycles. Any one of them would have been an improvement on the rattletrap I was driving.

I pointed this out, and Frank's temper flared again.

"Great fucking idea, Stan. And when we rode into Kindu on government-issue bikes, how you think that woulda gone?"

"Smarter to pawn their diamonds there?" I asked wearily. "Will we pretend that despite appearances we're miners?"

"We're done talkin' about this."

"I believe this is one of those topics that'll refresh itself indefinitely."

We started up the bikes to head for Kindu. My TVS Max rolled ten feet and died in a cloud of smoke.

CHAPTER 11

KINDU WASN'T AN attractive town.

After so much time wandering in the wilderness, Frank and I had built it up in our imaginations to be a shining sanctuary. In living fact, it was a crumbling memory of a city, full of grubby buildings melting into the jungle and potholed roads devoid of traffic aside from the incongruously clean UN Land Cruisers. There were motorcycles as well, all of them similarly whitewashed and plastered with blue UN initials.

The presence of so many peacekeepers put my pulse up a notch. Security contractors were less than popular with the international community in general, and there were rumors that Frank and I might be on their radar as potential war criminals. If that was the case, they would be well within their jurisdiction to send us off to The Hague or some other such place to stand trial. However, the stories about us tended to be so exaggerated that no one could rightly identify us except our victims. And they kept their own counsel in the sweet hereafter.

UN forces were, of course, not our only conceivable adversaries. Every civilian could be one of Chiora's new followers, ready to impress the little big man by killing his enemies. I realized that in one sense, at least, I had become like a Congolese local; I no longer felt safe in town.

We arrived late in the afternoon as the sun plunged into the jungle, so I assumed our only decision was whether to get a hotel and get off the streets before dark, or take advantage of the remaining daylight to question folks about Chiora. Frank, on the other hand, couldn't decide whether he should do some whoring immediately or sell his diamonds first.

In the end, his lust for money won out. Despite my protests, we walked up Kindu's red dirt main street as amateur traders rather than soldiers, scanning the crumbling concrete buildings for customers instead of informants.

Diamond buying operations in the Congo are easy to identify; their shops are exceptionally beat up on the outside, and very well stocked inside. In places like Kindu, a fellow doesn't want to advertise his prosperity to every passing malefactor.

At the hour of our arrival the townsfolk were busy boarding up against the night, so Frank banged on the battered steel doors of one-story hovels while I faced the street, glaring at anyone who had the temerity to come within fifty meters of us. At the fourth concrete shack, Frank hit his jackpot. A gray-bearded gentleman of Indian extraction opened the door.

"You buy diamonds?" Frank asked.

The old fellow smiled and wobbled his head in a way that might have meant yes, but could have meant no.

"Come in! Come in!" he said in singsong English. "You are most welcome."

Frank stepped into the dark shop. I followed, flicking the safety off my gun and pulling the door shut behind us.

Waiting for my eyes to adjust to the gloom, I breathed in the particular musty smell of African stores – cornmeal, mothballs, stale biscuits, and perfume-scented laundry soap. Jugs of purified water and cheap plastic buckets cramped the entrance. There was a tub full of cassava flour, shelves of cookies, and tinned food I suspected had been there since the Belgians ran off in 1960. Bolts of colorful cloth, piles of worn pants, and rumpled shirts lined the back wall. A modest pharmacy of pills and plasters labeled in Chinese covered most of the front counter. Among the medicines, I noticed a soda pop called *Orgasm*. I was even more shocked to see a dust-covered tube of toothpaste called *Darkie*, which featured the cartoon face of a grinning black minstrel. I wondered how the locals felt about that one.

"My name is Nithya," the shopkeeper said, smiling in the darkness. "You are so very welcome." He turned to the back door and shouted, "Sunalini! Generator!" From the back came the *gururr, gururr* of someone yanking a starter cord, and a generator spluttered to life. A single orangey bulb came on, casting more shadow than light.

"Now," Nithya said, turning back to us, "what can I do for you?"

Frank said, "I told you. I wanna sell diamonds."

"Right, right, right." Nithya reorganized his Chinese pharmacopeia with darting hands. "We can talk about that, certainly, but should we not begin with some provisions? You are on a long journey, no?"

"How much do you pay," Frank whispered, "for motherfucking diamonds?"

"Fair price, of course. Fair price." The shopkeeper's smile tightened. He thrummed his fingers on the counter. Frank didn't return his smile.

The old man glanced at me. "You are a man with appetite. Are you hungry? My wife makes the best chimp curry in Kindu."

"You keep that foulness away from me," I snapped.

I didn't realize I was moving toward Nithya with my fists clenched until Frank stepped between us, grinning. "Stanley don't eat monkey."

Most village markets sold primates for meat, displaying them skinned and whole so that they looked exactly like human corpses. The sight, obviously, offended me deeply.

The old man shrugged. "Clearly he eats everything else."

I forced myself to continue nosing around in the shelves, looking for an opportunity to change the subject and question the shopkeeper about Chiora. I pointed to the can of *Orgasm*. "You sell much of that?" My attempt at a conversational tone still came out harsh and loud.

"That is my last one. Good energy for the balls!"

Frank slammed the bag of diamonds on Nithya's counter. "How much?"

The lights went out.

"Damn it!" Nithya shouted. "Generator! Generator, goddamn you!"

A woman's voice muttered in another room, and the motor came back to life.

Nithya's eyes lit up. He hustled over to throw the lock on his steel front door, enforcing it with a length of rebar. "This is a great amount of riches," he said when he returned to the counter. "Where did you unearth them?"

"Oh. Yeah," Frank said, his eyes seeking mine. "We, ah..."

"Lodja," I said. "We're partners in a mine down Lodja way."

The old man looked us over, and I'm sure he didn't for one second believe me. "I see. Well then."

"Speaking of diamond mining," I said, turning away from Frank's glare, "you hear of a fellow named Tonde Chiora come through here, recruiting for a diamond mining outfit?"

Nithya's smile disappeared. His eyes darted to the door. "He is a bad one, that man."

Thank goodness. Chiora might be worthy of our violence after all.

"How so?" I asked.

"He came into town with a crowd of men and boys, talking all sorts of nonsense about getting rich and taking back Africa from the foreigners."

"That does not sound like such a bad thing," I said, in order to draw him out.

Nithya sneered. "In case you have not noticed, I myself am a foreigner. I didn't wish to be strung up by the mob."

"Mob?"

"This Chiora, he went into the bars and made speeches. He got the people very excited, I tell you. He had them crying for justice, which here means blood. There were rumors, you know, of him calling up the old religion. Dark things, very dark."

"Curses and shit?" Frank asked, suddenly paying attention.

Nithya did his yes-no head wobble again. "His men wore *gris-gris* pouches around their necks." He held his thumb and forefinger a couple inches apart. "Little leather bags full of totems. They claimed to have gotten them from the most powerful *féticheur* in the region."

Frank chuckled, slapping me on the back. "Somebody should tell 'em there's no more juice in their voodoo sacks."

Nithya looked from Frank to me. "I do not understand you."

"Is Chiora claiming to be Mai-Mai, then?" I asked, ignoring his curiosity. As glad as I was to have killed the *marabout*, I didn't care to be advertised as a murderer.

"His men dress as Mai-Mai, but it's all for show. They bullied people into joining their gang or whatever it is. The little fellow, Chiora, called it a cooperative diamond mine." The Indian sniffed at the term.

"He terrorized people into a profit-sharing scheme?" I asked, incredulous.

"He made it sound as if the old gods would ruin their lives if they didn't join him. Many did, and the many who didn't brought him gifts instead—machetes, guns, bullets."

I looked at Frank to see what impression this news made on him, but he had lost interest, his face pinched with impatience. "Chiora's got guns, whatever." he said. "Can I sell my fucking diamonds now?"

Turning back to Nithya, I said, "Where are they staying?"

"They left, finally, several days ago," Nithya said. "And thank goodness. Those boys were very bad for business. Very, very bad."

"Where were they headed?" I asked.

Nithya waved impatiently toward the jungle, the river, the dark night. "I didn't run out to ask them, you know. They could be going to the diamond fields, to the city, or to the black hell from which they came." Nithya had worked himself into a lather. "All I care about is that they're gone, and I'm not dead. That is the main thing, don't you think?"

"Good talk, fellas," Frank said. He leaned over the counter and pulled the string on his bag of diamonds, dumping them onto the counter. "Can we do some motherfucking business now?"

Nithya's attention was lost to the glittering stones. He scratched his puffy gray beard a long time. Finally, his smile returned. "I cannot buy this whole mountain, but I can relieve you of a select few."

He and Frank settled into negotiations while I wandered the store, stewing about Chiora. He seemed to take the pulse of each community and employ whatever method of persuasion was most likely to work in that environment. The man drew solutions from the soil itself. I shuddered, recalling the *marabout*'s claim that Chiora drew power from the river.

After some minutes of muttered conversation, Nithya turned to the back of the store and screamed, "Sunalini! Strongbox!"

A young and very ugly woman draped in an emerald sari appeared from the back room. She had protuberant eyes, a shockingly large nose, and a downy mustache that did little to increase her feminine appeal. I was frankly amazed to see that she was pregnant.

She hustled over to Nithya, plunked a key on the counter in a way that spoke eloquently of disdain, and scuttled out of the room.

Nithya saw my expression. "She preferred Uganda."

Frank seemed happy with his negotiation. He smiled and tapped out a happy beat on the counter. "That your daughter?"

Nithya's smiling mask cracked briefly. "Clearly she's my wife."

"Wow," Frank said. "So she's gonna have your kid?"

Oh my.

The shopkeeper stopped counting out Frank's money. "Who else would impregnate my wife, I ask you?"

"I'm not sayin', I'm just sayin'..." Frank grinned.

"You are very impertinent."

I stepped between them. "How is it the two of you came to live in Kindu?" I asked.

The mercurial old fellow forgot his irritation. "So much potential here!" he said, as though the Congo was on the very brink of becoming a global economic powerhouse.

Stanley, you are looking at the most hopeful man in the world.

"Sir, we're looking for a place to stay," I said. "Someplace secure."

"Yeah," Frank said. "Someplace with real good hospitality, know what I mean?" He slapped the poor shopkeeper's back. Frank's backslapping habit, which for ten years seemed harmlessly stupid, was beginning to wear on me. I thought I should start kicking him in the shin every time he did it. Or perhaps stabbing him in the throat.

Nithya pretended the blows to his back were not painful. "There's a young woman named Claire who accepts lodgers. Turn right out of the shop. After the fourth building you will find her gate."

"Do you know if she has any rooms available tonight?" I asked.

Nithya looked at me as though I were dumb as a mud fence. "Who else would be there?"

"Someone who sees all the potential in the Congo," Frank said, thankfully with a straight face.

As a conciliatory gesture, I bought several packets of cookies called *Eat Me Now*. Walking our bikes the short distance to the guest house, I said to Frank, "That man is doing surprisingly well."

"I would puke if I had to screw that chick."

"You should avoid antagonizing people all the time."

"Says the guy who almost kicked a shopkeeper's ass for offering him some fuckin' soup. Shit, I'm just being honest."

"You are being unpleasant. We'd both have less stress in our lives if you didn't go out of your way to make enemies."

"What do I got for stress?"

"You take all those pills to escape your fear."

Frank's cocky smile disappeared. "I got pain."

"Pain has many faces."

"Whatever."

We pushed on in silence.

We found the lodge tucked behind a gratifyingly high cement fence, and were grudgingly admitted by the young African woman named Claire. She spoke in monosyllabic whispers, as if in deference to the night dark of the jungle. She was apparently economizing on both candles and conversation. In the darkness, she was nothing but a roundish shadow who took two nights' payment in advance before pointing to the main building across the yard, and disappearing into a little gatehouse built against the fence.

I walked the perimeter and did a room–to-room sweep of the ruins of the main building, a two-story structure so decrepit that even the concrete was rotten and pulpy to the touch. At one time, an elegant balcony had run the length of the building. All that remained was a ragged line of post stumps dangling from the roofline and poking up from the ground like rotten teeth in the mouth of a gray giant.

Humble as our accommodation was, I still relished the opportunity to sleep indoors for the night. Since only one of the six rooms we saw was habitable, we were forced to share. This was something I'd hoped to avoid, given my increasing irritation with Frank. At this point, we needed space from one another.

The damp bed stunk of mildew, so I made do on the floor, taking special care to fully enshroud my space with the bug net. I didn't care to endure more mosquito bites.

Frank flopped without concern onto the rank bed and stared up at the bugs massing in the light of his headlamp. After a time he flicked off the light, humming tunelessly to mask the sound of his rooting around in his medical kit.

This was a disheartening turn of events. My anticipation of a restful night collapsed. I pulled out my book of Eliot's poetry to distract myself, but soon enough Frank's mood swept upward on a chemical wind, and he decided to find a bar. He invited me to go along, and much as I wanted to avoid watching Frank drink himself into violent stupidity, I believed he needed protection. I also thought I could gather more information about Chiora from the locals. Drunks often make the best informants.

Babysitting Frank in his drunkenness, I admit, was also better than being alone in our dank cell with its smell of dry rot and molding earth. There are times when the only sound lonelier than the forced hilarity of drunk people is the thump of my own heartbeat in an empty room.

CHAPTER 12

WE WOUND UP in a roofless shack strung with colorful Christmas lights, overlooking the rapids on the Congo. Pounding dance music competed with the thundering water for auditory dominance. The ensuing debauchery earned me nothing but a bad hangover and an increasingly baffling picture of Chiora.

Lifeless as Kindu was, the disco was crowded with an uneasy mix of shamefully drunk men from the UN—Pakistanis, Uruguayans, some bellowing Australians—hitting on the scantily clad local girls, and the town's young men brooding in the corners. The presence of the peacekeeping forces made me nervous, but Frank was laser focused on the women. He brushed off my concern about the soldiers, claiming that our civilian clothes would allow us to blend in, and then hit the raw timber dance floor.

I pulled up a chair to a table full of young local men. In Swahili, I ordered everyone a round, making myself instantly popular. After ordering a second round, I asked about Chiora. They bombarded me with contradictory opinions. Talking over each other in their eagerness, some described him as a savior of the Congo, while others said his men were bullies and rapists. A dapper young man lifted his silk shirt to show me bruises he claimed to have gotten from Chiora himself when he refused to pay the exorbitant price the Zimbabwean wanted for his diamonds. I heard that Chiora had taken control of the biggest diamond mine in the Congo, and that he was planning to take down the government with a combination of weapons and voodoo.

It was as though they were trying to confound me.

As the beer flowed, some of the young women joined us, and the stories grew more fantastic. I heard tales of Chiora healing the sick with a touch of his hand, and of him cursing a man who subsequently succumbed to a terrible fever and died. One woman claimed his men raped local girls in broad daylight, while another said Chiora himself provided her with a powerful charm that struck her rapist impotent. Whatever people believed about Chiora, they believed it so vehemently that the conversation devolved into a heated argument that nearly came to blows.

The evening became hectic, what with all the shouting, the music, and the young women showering me with attention because they smelled money on me. I didn't realize how drunk I was until I had an out-of-body experience, wherein the sober Stan stood back and watched drunken Stan grinning stupidly amidst a throng of shouting Congolese men and women. A girl in a bright red dress hung off my shoulders, whispering in my ear. Frank was nowhere in sight.

Return to base! My thinking self shouted. *The mission is compromised by liquor!*

I lurched upright, scattering my newfound friends, and stormed clumsily out of the bar with my pistols drawn.

I staggered back to town under the flat light of the moon, the air soft and warm against my face. Below the rapids, fishermen's poles and nets cut black lines across the shimmering water, and clumps of water hyacinth rocked in the current, their white blossoms luminous in the moonlight. Half hidden in darkness, Kindu was enchanted and almost beautiful. Anything seemed possible. I saw myself solving the mystery of Chiora and buying that ranch in Texas, starting a new life far away from people like Frank and Zhou.

The sober part of me looked down from the treetops, shaking his head at my folly.

The next morning I awoke on the floor several feet away from my bedroll, a pistol in each hand and my mosquito net wound tightly around my left leg, along with most of my clothes. My head throbbed cruelly, and my mouth was a gluey pit. Glancing at the bed, I was relieved to see Frank had made it back alive, though I could have done without the sight of his naked, hairy rump.

I untangled myself from my clothes and stumbled over to the doorway, wearing nothing but my grimy briefs, to stare at the coming day. A truck labored down the road beyond the lodge's high fence. After the silence of our weeks in the jungle, it was like a song of civilization, and it lifted my spirits a small way out of the depths.

The compound was heavily planted with beans, tomatoes, and cassava. A few scabby chickens wandered about. A movement in the gatehouse across the yard caught my eye, and I saw Claire's face receding into the shadows of a small window. I was thus reminded of my almost-nakedness. I went back into the room to check on Frank, who looked much worse than I felt.

"Kill me," he said, when I shook him.

"I'm not one hundred percent myself, though I suspect I will live."

"Shower," Frank croaked. "Tell the woman I need a shower."

"It's unlikely she has that technology."

"Tell her to build it if she has to. Gotta get the stink off me."

"I'm sure Zhou would be well impressed to see his squad commander in such a state."

"Fuck off. Tell the lady I can pay whatever. See if there's a masseuse in town."

"You are still drunk if you think you will find such luxuries in this place."

"Then bring me a hooker with strong hands. And hurry."

"I will look into getting you cleaned up. Nothing more."

I found our hostess under a thatched awning beside her little house, pounding cassava flour in her outdoor kitchen. This consisted of a cement fire pit with a grill and an attached work surface worn shiny by years of labor. Two colorful plastic buckets full of murky water sat off to the side. I wondered if she purchased the pails from the optimistic Indian fellow with the ugly wife.

I had not really taken notice of our hostess in the dark of the previous night, but in the daylight, I saw she was young, smooth skinned, and generously curvaceous through the buttocks and bosom. I admired the way her sturdy shoulders flexed while she worked the cassava. Her hair was a sight to behold, the strands woven to stand straight up in tall, unlikely, pencil-thin spikes with tufted tops. I suspected she only achieved this effect after meeting us. The hairdo was her way of gussying herself up for company.

I sucked in my belly and cleared my throat, determined to make a good impression. She looked at me the way many locals did, eyes dull and contemptuous.

"Good morning," I said in French. "My associate is feeling poorly, and is desperate for a shower or bath."

"We bathe in the river," she said in a voice so quiet it was as though she couldn't deign to spare breath on me.

I blanched, thinking of my last visit to the riverbanks. "Aren't you afraid of crocodiles?"

The woman continued pounding cassava.

I soldiered on. "I myself had a run-in with a crocodile quite recently. I'm lucky to be alive."

Silence. She didn't so much as nod or raise an eyebrow.

Stung by her indifference, I produced a grotesque amount of money and thumped it onto her table. "Money is no object. My friend needs to clean up *tout de suite*."

She stopped pounding and stared at the wad of bills. Finally, she set her pestle down and peeled several notes from the stack. The look she spared me was heavy with disdain. Still, I felt the need to warn her about the risks of coming into contact with Frank.

"My friend lacks my charm and good nature, and he's irritable today. Help him clean up, but show him a touch of respect."

"He will be clean," she said.

She tucked the money into her skirts, and bent to take up her cassava. As she leaned over, her loose top gapped open to reveal her full breasts, nipples and all. She remained in that posture for some time, scooping flour into a pot, unaware of her display. The flash of skin flustered and thrilled me, and I took my ferocious erection as a sign that my health had truly returned.

She went inside her dim little home without another word, and I whistled a happy tune as I strolled back across the yard to retrieve my pistols.

I knew I should gather more intel regarding Chiora's whereabouts, but my night of dissipation robbed me of the energy for proper soldiering. Instead, I decided to go see if the old Indian fellow had any Alka Seltzer or some other hangover remedy.

I scanned the street thoroughly before stepping out of Claire's compound. As I walked down the potholed road toward Nithya's shop, past mounds of refuse and rows of rundown cement buildings, I viewed every man, woman, and child as a potential enemy. My suspicious gazes were met each time by empty masks, as though I were a wind-blown leaf or a piece of furniture.

At Nithya's shop, I found his mustachioed wife sulking behind the counter. So palpable was her unhappiness that I found the bottled water and antacids as quickly as possible, lest I become infected by her negativity.

As I pocketed my change, the woman spoke up. "The stitches need to be removed. Immediately."

"Excuse me?"

She pointed to a spot below her right eye, corresponding to my snakebite. "The flesh is healing around the stitches. If you don't remove them now, they will rot inside. Infection will surely follow."

I had not considered the need to remove Frank's rough sewing. His bad work had become a part of me. "Thank you, ma'am. I'll take care of that directly."

"I was a nurse." She shrugged. Her rueful smile transformed her face into something almost lovely.

There are hidden depths to all of us. I vowed to be more kind to hirsute women in the future.

Back at the lodge, Claire came pounding out of our room just as I mounted the porch. She clutched one of the colorful buckets in front of her, sloshing water all over her. She stopped to glare at me, breathing as if she had been in a foot race.

"Are you all right, miss?" I asked, though I had seen many women leave Frank's company in such a state and could imagine what had befallen her

By way of answer, she launched a barrage of profanity in French and Swahili, the likes of which I hadn't heard since pulling shrapnel out of a fellow soldier's guts. So vehement was her diatribe that I missed much of it, but she definitely suggested that Frank should have his testicles cut off and shoved down his throat. This was shocking talk from a young lady.

"I'm not like him," I said, disgusted by my pleading tone.

Claire stalked off across the yard to her own dwelling, tossing the tub against a wall as she disappeared inside. I quietly retrieved her tub and set it in its accustomed place in the cookhouse.

Returning to my room, I saw that the door was still half-open. Frank's voice came from inside, low and deferential. *He must be on the phone.* I crept a bit closer.

"Don't worry," he said. "I got this. We're in Kindu. We'll have him in a couple days, tops."

The screeching response was audible even ten feet away. *Zhou.*

Frank said, "Stan's under control, sir. It's just he can hardly find his dick with both hands. He's been sick, like, the whole fucking time. I'm keeping him focused on the mission, though."

Apparently, having Frank in charge meant having him cast aspersions on me to our boss. I should have either walked away or stormed into the room to confront him. Instead, I froze, flushed and ashamed.

I backed off the porch in a crouch, and continued to walk backward all the way to the main gate, rubbing frantically at my face and growling. I punched myself on the side of the head several times, as though trying to dislodge the memories of all the times I defended Frank's mistakes and protected him from himself. I stood at the front gate with my eyes closed and my hand on the door, trying to control my rage.

There was nowhere for me to go. I couldn't question civilians about Chiora in such a state, for fear of crushing someone's skull if they annoyed me. For lack of another destination, I drifted to the middle of Claire's corn patch and stood there for a long time, rustling amongst the dry stalks. The Army shrink in Afghanistan said I should visualize my negative thoughts leaving my body every time I breathed out. So, standing amongst the dead corn, I huffed and puffed for all I was worth. This made me dizzy, but no less miserable.

I caught movement in the shadows of Claire's house and thought that she might be sympathetic of my tales of Frank's perfidy. At the very least, I could show her how different I was from him. However, I couldn't muster the courage to approach her.

When I grew weary of gnawing on my grievances and trampling Claire's plants, I returned to the room.

I stomped up the porch, making a ridiculous amount of noise, humming to myself and clapping my stupid hands.

"Frank!" I called, too loudly. "I picked up some antacids and a bottle of water."

I tried to sound casual, but my throat was constricted, and my voice came out pinched and weepy.

Frank sat on the bed, wearing nothing but a pair of briefs. He held his pants in his hands and was running the zipper up and down, up and down. His eyelids drooped, and his smile was mindless.

He had clearly taken more than antacids.

"Hey, Stanley. Wassup?"

My body buzzed with adrenaline, and I regretted my inability to shoot him – or leave him, or do anything intelligent.

"Feeling better?" I asked.

"Still hung over. I just don't care anymore." He held the pants out to me, his eyes full of wonder as though presenting the baby Jesus himself. "Zippers are fuckin' amazing."

"It's difficult to feel safe under your command."

Frank blinked unnaturally slowly, his lids staying shut too long. There was a large and dented metal bowl next to the bed, and I wondered briefly about its purpose.

He grinned sloppily. "At ease, fucker. We got us a nice, mellow mission today… no problem."

"This Chiora fellow won't capture himself. When are we leaving?"

Frank let his eyes slide shut and stay that way. "I ain't goin' anywhere for a while. Won't kill us to chill out here. Get some laundry done and whatnot."

"Yes, *sir*. Departure at oh-laundry-hundred, sir."

Frank propped his eyes open enough to look at me. "What's your problem?"

"Nothing I cannot solve on my own time. Contrary to public opinion, I *can* find my dick with my own hands."

Doped as he was, Frank caught my meaning.

"You were spying on me. When I was talking about you."

I said nothing. There was nothing I wanted to say.

Frank sat upright, struggling to organize a response. "You got it… you got it all wrong."

He leaned over, and casually vomited into the bedside bowl. His face was sweaty and sallow when he looked back at me, but he smiled. "Almost yacked on my pants. That woulda been bad."

"We can talk later."

"Nah, we're good. I'm just sick. Look. That stuff I said don't mean nothing."

"Not to you, clearly. To me it means damn near everything."

I left him without another word. Emboldened, I went outside again and crossed directly to Claire's kitchen space, where I found her making *fufu*. I was encouraged when she looked me in the eye when I said hello and responded in a clearer voice. Perhaps she had heard me talking to Frank and decided that the enemy of her enemy was her friend.

"Do you, by any chance, have a hand mirror?" I asked.

"I have a large one inside."

"Excellent. With your permission, I would like to use the mirror while I remove these stitches."

Claire examined my stitches and clucked in disappointment. "Who did this to you?"

I pointed to my room across the yard.

Her face hardened into a sneer, and she turned away. "Follow me."

I noticed for the first time that she wore no shoes. Almost no one in that place could afford footwear, but I was strangely touched at the sight of her naked feet padding across the packed earth.

I followed, squeezing myself through the small doorway and into Claire's home. Cool as her initial response to me had been, I felt as though we had bonded over our mutual disdain for Frank, and I was giddy at the privilege of being invited into a woman's inner sanctum.

CHAPTER 13

THE ONLY PREVIOUS times I had been in Congolese homes had been in the line of duty, chasing enemies into cramped huts and shooting them from the doorways, or locking them inside so that they might be immolated. The only real exception to these flash-bang domestic experiences was the time I spent in the witch doctor's hut.

I had not, in other words, taken the time to get a feel for Congolese domesticity. In Claire's life there were no frills. No couches or coffee tables, no pictures hanging on the walls. It was an unlit gray box with a wooden chair in the middle of the floor. A row of shelves along one wall held a couple of plates, some stacked cassava roots, a bowl full of greens, and a lidded cook pot I believed to be the source of a faint but foul fishy odor.

Habituated as I was to scanning rooms for potential danger, I glanced into the corner behind the door and caught a nasty shock. A figure, goggle-eyed and four feet tall with his tongue sticking out, hunkered in the dark space. I had my gun out before I realized he was, in fact, a wooden carving of a man, his body bristling with rusty nails, scrap metal, and shards of glass. Bits of twine wove through the figure's spikes, which were also hung with lengths of chain and burlap rags.

Claire didn't seem surprised to find me heavily armed and quick to fire. "That is Nkisi Nkondi. We call upon the *nkondi* to hunt down bad men and bring vengeance upon them for their crimes."

"You believe in that kind of thing? Evil spirits and such?"

"In this place, it is wise take help where you find it." Her eyes brightened with what might be mischief. "It is interesting that he caught you, I think."

Heat rose to my face. "I believe I got the jump on him."

"And yet you are afraid."

"I have not had good experiences with Congolese spirituality."

"Has it had a good experience with you?"

I thought back to the witch doctor's crushed skull, the burned hut. "Where is this mirror?"

Claire took me into a second room, which abutted the compound wall and had a stale, smokehouse smell. The tiny-screened window was positioned in such a way that smoke from the cook fire must roll into the room. There was a crudely hewn bed frame covered with a colorful blanket featuring the face of the Congo's former dictator, Mobutu Sese Seko, complete with his leopard skin hat. A hand-carved bedside table and matching straight-back chair occupied the darkest corner of the room. Below the window was an entirely anomalous art deco vanity with a large oval mirror, its clean lines and elegant carved details as out of place here as a spaceship would be in my father's barn.

This is where she does that stuff to her hair. The idea of her sitting here, alone, to prettify herself in that strange way broke my heart.

Claire shyly twisted at a piece of her shirt. "It is not like a house in America."

"It's a fine room," I said, casting about for something to praise. "Very comfortable."

"Are people very rich where you come from?"

"Many are, though it does not do them any good that I can tell."

"I would like to be rich," she said. "I would know how to be happy."

"I imagine you would," I said, looking out the window.

Silence stretched out between us. Finally, Claire told me to sit and guided me to the chair. It was shockingly heavy, made of ironwood or some such hefty timber. I dragged it before the mirror and sat.

I was confronted by the disappointing sight of my overlarge self in the mirror. My trek through the jungle had not been kind to me. My sallow skin hung loose on my face, black circles ringed my eyes, and the stitches formed a black snarl across my cheek. I looked like I had been *rode hard and put away wet*, as my father liked to say.

I had to look away.

I took the field first aid kit from my vest and laid out the tiny scissors, tweezers, alcohol swabs, and the tube of antibiotic ointment. Claire stepped out of the room, and returned with a bowl of water.

"It has been boiled," she said.

Claire watched me fumble, trying to get my thick fingers to work the tiny scissors, for a moment before clucking impatiently and taking them from me. She tipped my head back, and I felt the weight of her pressed along my side. I had to cover my lap with the med kit to hide my enthusiasm for that simple contact.

Claire snipped at the heavy stitches and pulled the black string from my face. It burned a little, and the rotting smell of the thread was shocking, as though I was already dead inside.

I made a face at the stink, but Claire continued working without reaction, carefully laying the foul strings on her vanity. Tilted back as my head was, I managed to catch a glimpse of this tableau in the large mirror – a great, scarred hulk of a man with an antennae-haired Congolese beauty at his shoulder, attending to his ruined face. *This is your life, Stanley.* I nearly laughed then, imagining myself at a high school reunion explaining how I spent my time.

After Claire removed the stitches, she dipped a rag in the boiled water and wiped down my cheek. "You have many scars." She released me, stepping aside.

Checking the mirror, I saw that Frank's crude work left me with an angry red welt shaped like an upside-down cross; it angled across my face from near the jawbone to the outside of my eye, and was ringed with uneven red dots. It did nothing to enhance my appeal.

"Why were you cut there?" Claire asked.

"Snakebite," I said. "Frank sucked the poison from the wound."

Claire frowned. "That does not do any good."

"I realize that. I was in no position to point out the mistake."

I handed Claire the alcohol swabs, and she gave my face a vigorous buffing. My eyes watered at the pain of it. Finally, she dabbed the antibiotic onto my wounds and cradled my face, tipping my head from side to side to examine her work. This intimate contact left me dizzy with lust, but Claire seemed unaffected.

"Tell me more about you," I said, to break the tension.

Claire let go of me and looked toward the door. "I am from this place. What else can I say?"

"But I'm interested in you. You have to share a little bit with me."

"My family always lived here. My grandparents and my parents worked at this lodge."

"Where are your parents now?"

"They have passed." She looked down, again worrying at the hem of her shirt.

"And how is it that a pretty girl like you lives all alone?"

Claire looked to the door again. "My husband was killed by the Mai-Mai – or perhaps the RPF, or the Ugandans, or Interahamwe." She shrugged. "It is hard to tell them apart sometimes. They took my son. He was only a little boy, nine years old."

"So he might still be alive."

"Death would be better."

"How can you say that?" I couldn't imagine a mother who would wish her son into the grave.

"Do you know what life is like for child soldiers? What they do?"

They do the same kinds of thing that I do, but not as efficiently.

Claire swept the stitches onto the gauze pad, and led me outside to her kitchen space. She threw the trash into her cook fire, where it raised a brief, unholy stench.

"That man," she said, pointing her face at the lodge while she put a pot of water on the fire, "He's your friend?"

"We have worked together for a long time," I muttered, choking back a new surge of anger at his betrayal.

"You are very different from each other."

"He saved my life, and we have been like brothers for a long time. He gets me into a terrible amount of trouble."

"He is a bad brother. It is better for you to leave him," Claire said. "And where is your real family?"

"I'm from Huntsville, Texas. I grew up on a cattle ranch. There's a university in the town, and also a penitentiary. It allows a person to see the full range of life's options on a daily basis." *Stop babbling, Stanley.*

"You speak of the place, but not of your people."

"My mother passed some years back, and I had no siblings. My father and I more or less forgot how to look at each other once Mother was gone."

"But he is alive?"

"Last I heard." We had not spoken since I signed on with Blackwater, five years ago.

"I think he must miss you."

"I left under poor circumstances. He was ashamed of me."

"All parents take pride in their children."

"He might have been proud while I was in the military, but he couldn't make sense of my current work. I've been led down a bad path."

"We cannot be led if we don't follow."

My cheeks warmed uncomfortably. "That may be. But until something changes, there's little to say between us."

Claire went inside briefly and returned with the covered pot. She removed the lid and I saw the source of at least some of her home's stink – a mass of the tiny dried fish the Congolese inexplicably call Thomsons. She put a small pile of these on a plate next to a glob of *fufu* and handed it to me. "What are you and your friend doing in Kindu?"

"You might say we're in private security."

Claire looked between the lodge and me. "I asked what you are doing in Kindu."

I pointed to the lodge. "I'm looking for a colleague who has gone missing, a man by the name of Tonde Chiora."

Claire's face twisted with disgust. "That one causes a lot of trouble."

So do I. "What makes you say so?"

"He came here dressed as a healer, making big promises to the men and boys around town. 'I will make you rich,' he said. 'I will save the Congo.'"

"What's wrong with that?"

Claire harrumphed, so full of disdain that I admired her even more. "He spoke like a *mzungu*. Big words that mean nothing. If people said anything against him, he pretended he could turn the old gods against them."

"A bully," I said. Once again, Chiora was willing to become anything to get his way.

"That one wears the old gods like a mask. His only god is money." She arched an eyebrow at me. "You should find better friends."

I couldn't have agreed more. "We work for the same people. Or used to. He cheated our employer, and we have been sent to…well… retrieve him."

Claire went very still, then set the bowl on the counter with shaking hands. "You and that Frank are the monster people speak of, the Frank-and-Stan."

Damn.

There was nothing to say, but I felt compelled to try. "There's more to me than people realize."

"In the stories you are one man with two faces. Now I see." Claire's voice trailed off. She went inside, shutting the door behind her. She didn't reappear, and after a time I left her in peace.

CHAPTER 14

HOPING TO REKINDLE some sense of purpose, I headed out into the infernal afternoon heat of Kindu to see if I could learn more about Chiora's whereabouts.

Kindu was eerie in its weed-grown suggestion of former glory. The rutted and puddled high street took me past the commercial buildings, with their faded paint and hand-lettered signs, and into the residential neighborhoods. The streets were lined with a hodgepodge of tin-roof shacks, traditional mud huts, and squatter's hovels made of scrap wood, cardboard, and bits of tarp. Each home had a garden plot out back, with pale green corn and purplish cassava planted among crowding vines and trees. In front of the houses, trash piled up to form tightly packed middens, some of which reached the height of a man. Feral dogs rooted through the stinking mounds while big-bellied children, some in ragged shirts or the remains of shorts, but many naked, played king of the mountain on the refuse. Seeing me, the urchins shouted, "Bye-bye, *mzungu*! Give me money!" which seemed to serve as a sign for their parents to disappear. I saw not a single adult as I canvassed the neighborhoods.

The futility of my mission, stacked as it was on top of three years of fruitless wandering in the heat and ugliness, oppressed me. I turned back to the river, as much for its relative cool as for any information I might gain.

At the dock, I struck up a conversation with the Uruguayan crew of the UN gunboats. They were tasked with patrolling the river between Kindu and Ubundu, where Stanley Falls forms a rocky barrier between the upper Congo and its lower reaches. Their boats – sleek cruisers with padded white seats and powerful engines – were as incompatible with the surroundings as everything else the UN dropped into the Congo from on high. They looked better suited to a cocktail cruise in the Mediterranean than combat operations on the upper Congo.

At first, I was uncertain about talking to the peacekeepers, but those bored young men were no threat to me. We talked about the heat and the regrettable limitation of dance clubs in Kindu, and I learned they were awaiting clearance to head out in search of one of their boats, which had recently been stolen.

"Stolen?" I asked.

"We are not supposed to talk about it," a baby-faced fellow named Luis said, "but a gang of Mai-Mai killed Claudio and Milton when they were on watch three nights ago, and they took one of the gunboats." His eyes welled with tears.

"I'm sorry to hear of your loss." I looked out across the river to spare him embarrassment.

"We will catch them, and we will kill them," an older fellow named Emilio said. "But it's stupid that we have to wait all this time for clearance from the goddamn United Nations."

It had to be Chiora. The move had what I had come to recognize as his flair for the dramatic. I couldn't prove it, but I was certain my prey had taken the gunboat. If I could somehow get aboard the UN chase boats, I could gain some ground on Chiora.

Despite the terrible breach in protocol our presence on the boats would represent, I was hopeful that these novice soldiers would allow it. The loss of their comrades to an untrained force showed their tragic lack of discipline. Also, not one of them so much as asked how a scar-faced white man in body armor ended up in Kindu. This last was sloppy soldiering indeed. I had witnessed too many cases in Afghanistan where chatty civilians engaged a battalion in friendly conversation long enough for insurgents to set the coordinates for mortar rounds.

Clearly, these smiling youngsters had never seen that kind of combat, nor had they learned from their previous disaster. Instead of treating me with appropriate suspicion, they invited me to join them for a lunch of steaks and French fried potatoes, flown all the way to the Congo by the Uruguayan government. I can say for a certainty that South American beef is far superior to *fufu* and bony little fish.

As we talked and ate in their dockside compound and sucked on our Primus beers, a huge vessel eased into view around the bend in the river. It loomed over Kindu like a harbinger of the modern world, all sharp angles and broad, clean-swept decks. The bright red side of the ship was printed with *SacOil* in white letters, and its appearance shattered the typical stillness of the Congo.

The whole city surged to life, with people rushing to the dock like ants to spilled sugar. In minutes, the shoreline was packed with locals carrying dented jerry cans, empty water bottles, and steel buckets. Children jostled and cheered around the adults, who greeted each other with smiles and laughter while jockeying for position at the water's edge.

"Petrol," a young deckhand said. "The barge is here once in the month."

A phalanx of UN trucks moved through the crowd, horns blaring as they scattered the line. We watched as the ship was tied up, and dozens of peacekeepers began to fuel their own tanker truck and vehicles, and then go on to fill dozens of cans.

I did my best to look Uruguayan. Blending in is not my strong suit, but I need not have bothered, for the crowd kept its collective back to me, fixated on the barge and its combustible contents.

When the UN group moved off, the locals surged forward.

An older woman shrieked, and I turned with the rest of the crowd to see a young boy in red shorts and a bright orange shirt trying to wrestle away her mama-shopper. Those closest stepped in. Someone tripped the boy as he fled toward town, another kicked him. The horde closed around the thief, beating him.

"Mob justice in the Congo," the Uruguayan skipper said with some admiration. "Swift and merciless."

My sympathies were with the boy. What could he have possibly expected to find in a poor old woman's purse? How desperate must he be to attempt such a heist in broad daylight?

I turned away from the horrible thrashing and said goodbye to my hosts, politely turning down an invitation to meet them later at the riverside bar.

On the long, sweaty walk back to the lodge, I braced myself for a confrontation with Frank, but I found him out cold, still in his underpants. While I had patrolled the city and gathered vital information, he had spent the entire day on a chemical holiday.

I got a bucket of water from Claire, who treated me more warmly than I might have expected, and managed a sponge bath for myself out behind the cassava patch. When I returned the bucket Claire told me my dinner would be ready shortly.

"I didn't realize meals were included with our room," I said, trying to cajole her into trusting me.

Claire gave me a timid smile. "Well, it is not. I will need one American dollar."

"I can pay you two," I said. "The service here is excellent."

She rested her hand on my arm, and her touch blazed there. "You are a funny man."

"I have my moments," I said.

The evening passed without incident, and the next morning, Frank was back in control of himself. I had asked Claire to prepare some of our oatmeal and a bit of fruit, since the lodge contained no kitchen or cooking facilities, and she did respectable work on the food. Frank wolfed his breakfast while I sipped the last of my coffee. I had vowed to lose weight, reasoning that my new scar would be less stretched and pronounced if I burned off a bit of my farm boy weight.

Frank acted as though things between us were normal. "Remember when I got buried alive outside Baghdad?"

I chafed at the attempt to dredge up the bonding moments of our past. "Chiora is heading downriver."

Frank stopped eating. "No shit?"

"While you enjoyed your spa day, I interviewed some of the UN soldiers. He stole one of their gunboats."

"Ain't it kinda stupid to grill the UN types, what with the 'crimes against humanity' rumors and whatnot?"

I ignored his antagonism, just as I had ignored his attempt at friendship. "Chiora and his men will be headed to Kisangani."

"The UN fuckers told you that?"

"It's the only city between here and the next rapids. Where else could he go on a boat?"

Frank jumped up and paced the room, his brow furrowed in a parody of deep thought. "Then we gotta get to Kisangani like, right the fuck now."

"That's why I got us on the patrol that's going after Chiora tomorrow," I said calmly.

Frank nodded, pretending to consider. "Yeah, okay. Let's do that."

"If you aren't too busy napping," I said, weary of him play-acting at leadership.

Frank spun toward me, fists clenched and snarling. "What's your fucking problem?"

Claire came in at that moment, bustling around the room to retrieve the dishes.

I turned away from Frank to bid her a good morning and compliment her hair. She had removed her crazy spikes and loosed her hair into a bold and springy Afro that framed her face fetchingly. She favored me with a beaming smile.

Frank fairly shouted good morning and winked at her, putting on a great show of swagger even as his voice crackled with throttled rage. Claire pretended to be blind and deaf to him. She fussed around me instead, frowning when she picked up my mostly-untouched breakfast.

"But Mister Stanley," she said in Swahili, "did I make the porridge incorrectly?" She put her hand on my shoulder as she spoke.

"No, ma'am. It's perfect. I'm simply on a diet."

"A what?"

It occurred to me that the idea of limiting food intake on purpose wasn't a luxury many folks in these parts indulged. "It's hard to translate," I said. "On second thought, I'll have breakfast after all." I dug into my porridge.

She smiled. "It's good for you to eat, Mister Stanley. You need your strength."

Frank looked back and forth between Claire and me, his eyes following her as she left the room. He turned back to me, leering. "You banging her?"

"There's more to life than bumping and grinding," I said.

"Really?" Frank's laugh was a nasty bark.

"I will confirm our passage on the UN boat and do some more recon." I watched Claire walk across the yard, admiring the grace of her movements, the alluring way her hips rolled and swayed.

Frank followed my gaze, and waggled his eyebrows at me. He had an irritating way of reading me sometimes. "Recon?"

"Repeating what a person says doesn't move a conversation forward."

"Are you blushing?"

"Your leadership style leaves much to be desired." I walked out into the blazing day, dogged by the sound of Frank's raucous laughter.

CHAPTER 15

FRANK TOOK IT upon himself to visit the Uruguayans and confirm our ride downriver. I spent a few hours packing my gear, trying to jettison excess equipment now that we wouldn't be traveling by motorcycle. I was happy to be clear of the TVS Max. That humble vehicle carried a curse, which oozed up from the seat and compromised the rider's fortunes.

Frank returned to the room and handed me a beer. I accepted his peace offering but didn't open it. I continued packing while he sat on the bed, guzzling Primus and cleaning his M4. "Those Panamanians are good guys," he said in a brittle attempt to chitchat.

"Uruguayans," I said.

Frank flushed but didn't rise to the bait. "You know those guys got steaks and beers flown all the way from Central America?"

"South America."

"What are you, a fucking geography teacher?" Frank shook his head and changed the subject. "We gotta sell the bikes. I figure we'll keep the money, tell Zhou they fell in the river or something." Our boss was a stickler for expense reports, which was absurd given the amount of money he skimmed from The Company himself. Prior to our arrival in the Congo, Frank never seemed to care much about money. Since we started in Kalemie, though, he had become a man after Zhou's heart, always looking to gain excess cash despite our huge salaries and the windfall of his stolen diamonds.

My bitterness only grew as I considered that Frank would make a fair bit of money off his bike, while I would be lucky to gain anything in return for my wretched and spluttering vehicle.

Hope is a hard dog to kill, though, so I spent a foolish hour in the courtyard in front of Claire's kitchen, washing the motorcycle so that I might trick some idiot into paying good money for it. I sweated in the blazing sun while I tried to erase all evidence of the bike's hard life.

Claire watched me from the shade with lazy fascination. She said little, and I began prattling on like a fool to fill the silence. I talked about Huntsville, and my mother's fatal car wreck, and my first taste of combat in the Hindu Kush. I talked about how cold it got in the mountains of Afghanistan, and how I'd gone numb after an Afghani sniper took out my sergeant as we stood talking about football. I described the breathy *thwip* of the bullet as it passed an inch in front of my face before entering his eyeball. He was a Chicago Bears fan.

I described, in regrettable detail, the Rorschach pattern of the sergeant's blood, brain, and bone on the stone wall behind me. "His last words," I told Claire, "were 'Eli Manning is a fucking pussy.'"

Nothing I said inspired any reaction, but I kept throwing coins into that well. Even as I tried to hide my motorcycle's scars, I flaunted mine to this silent stranger.

When she stood up abruptly and walked into the house, my feelings were well and truly hurt. The slamming and bolting of the door seemed particularly cruel.

Then I felt Frank's blade against my neck.

"Dead again, Chatty Kathy."

"Look down."

I had my knife against his testicles.

Frank released me with a chuckle. "You girls have a nice little gossip session?"

"What exactly did you do to her?"

Frank showed his teeth. "You can't please everybody."

"She seems to dislike you intensely."

"Let's go sell our bikes."

We set out into the city, riding our motorcycles without gear for the first time. Unburdened, even my rattling death trap seemed full of zip. I was almost able to enjoy the ride.

Old Nithya and his wife had no use for motorcycles, so we made our way to an open market described as the commercial heart of Kindu. It turned out to be a desolate patch of packed earth no bigger than a basketball court, with a handful of women languishing in the sun before their meager goods. One had a small pile of bleached cassava root; another offered a few threadbare blouses from China. The only man had a skinned chimp. He cowered at my murderous glare.

Frank clapped me on the shoulder, and I flinched. "Stanley," he said, "I ain't optimistic about finding a buyer here. But I got an idea." With his usual knack for commerce and his baffling lack of self-preservation instincts, he guided us straight to the UN base.

Like all UN outposts in this country, the Kindu compound was an anomalously clean and orderly collection of container buildings. In the crumbling, organic context of the Congo, they were as something dropped from outer space: cool, white, and utterly *other*.

Such a sight should have been refreshing after weeks living rough in the bush, but instead I found the place obscene. Perhaps I was jealous that the denizens of the scrubbed and ephemeral world had access to toilets.

I watched Frank banter with Pakistani soldiers who guarded the compound gate, charming them with his easy smile. He shook their hands and swaggered back to me, vastly pleased with himself.

"We're good," he said. "We'll meet 'em tomorrow morning before we get on the boat. They'll give us four hundred bucks for my bike, and fifty for yours."

"Two hundred twenty-five each then," I said, to be difficult.

"You're being funny again."

"I should have negotiated myself. As it stands, I'm being ripped off by the Pakistanis and my CO."

Claire made herself scarce throughout the last evening before our departure. I'm normally very efficient at organizing my kit, but my progress was slowed by the constant need to step outside and see if she had returned from whatever mysterious errands she must be attending to in town.

Frank teased me mercilessly for *going gopher*.

As night fell, I peeled off a one hundred dollar bill from my sizeable stash and put it inside an extra mess kit, with the idea of presenting it to Claire. I envisioned her using the plate and cutlery daily, thinking of me as she broke her fast.

Frank caught me putting the gift together and laughed at my chivalry.

"You're wasting your time, fucknuts," he said.

"It's no business of yours."

"First off, she's got her own fucking plates. They're bigger. Better to hold giant wads of that glop they eat."

"And second?" I asked.

"It's stupid. She's already got enough money."

"How would you know? I say she will appreciate it."

"Wrong again. Besides, a hundred bucks is too much. Leave her ten bucks and she'll live like a queen in this shit hole."

"You are jealous that she's fond of me." I couldn't look him in the eye as I said it.

"Oh yeah? You swept the massage lady off her feet? You should take her home to meet your pops. I'm sure he'd be real happy you brought home such a sweet and innocent little girl."

Massage lady? "You are a spiteful son of a bitch."

"She's pure as the morning dew, all right. A bona fide African maiden."

For fear of attacking Frank, I stepped out of the room and was disappointed to see a candle flickering in Claire's little room.

Why hadn't come to see me? Had she heard Frank's foul talk? I couldn't imagine what she would do with herself in that barren space. Did she simply stare into the old mirror and wonder what she might have been and done if she lived somewhere else?

The porch shifted under Frank's weight. "There he is, folks," he said in a carnival hawker's voice, "The Great American Lover, gazing at the moon and writing love songs in his head. Will he get the girl? How much will he pay for a taste of that sweet local honey?"

I marveled at my reluctance to kill him.

When I ignored his goading, Frank stepped into the yard to inspect our bikes. He fiddled needlessly with something in the guts of his Boxer. I saw that he opened his mouth to speak several times before finally saying, "We're gonna bivouac in the bush again these next few days," he said. "No more kicking back in luxurious hotels."

"Fine by me."

"I'm saying, if your fragile constitution gets the best of you, I gotta carry on with the mission. You know, alone."

Aha. The truth is out. I snarled.

"*My* fragile constitution? I have survived a snakebite and malaria. You couldn't even handle a night out at the bar."

"Yeah, whatever. We've all had malaria. Let's just agree that we've had some unexpected stuff come up," Frank said. "We're past that now, and we're going to be all about the mission from here. All right?"

"I won't take any guff about my supposed frailty."

"Sure, yeah, good."

He ceased tinkering with the motorcycles and looked back up to the full moon, which seemed too large, too low in the sky, bathing everything in angular gray light. I had not noticed it before in my preoccupation with Claire and Frank.

Just to show Frank I didn't care what he thought, I crossed the moonlit yard and set the plate with the money on Claire's doorstep.

I lay awake much of the night worrying that some nocturnal creature might abscond with my gift, or that—worse!—Claire might find it in the morning and think it was from Frank.

In the steamy gray dawn, we mounted our motorcycles one last time. Before we pulled out, I noticed Claire's face outlined in the tiny window. She sported her crazy antennae hairdo again, and she clutched the hundred dollars to her chest. When she beckoned me over, my heart leapt in my chest.

"Mister Stanley," she said, "this money…"

"It's a gift," I said, fidgeting and avoiding her gaze. "I will be honored if you keep it, and think of it as a sign of my deep regard for you."

Claire nodded. "I see. But Mister Stanley, it is from 2001."

"And?"

"It is too old. I can only exchange bills from 2006 or later."

This wasn't the appreciative farewell I pictured. Blushing furiously, I dug around in my money belt until I located a sufficiently fresh bill. We made the exchange, passing the notes through a hole in her screen. Claire didn't even deign to come into the yard for me.

When I got back on the bike, I saw her put a hand over her heart. She nodded solemnly, then stepped back into the shadows of her lonely room. I made an effort to be happy with myself for having left her the money and pictured her using it to have a real window put into her house.

My folly was all the more painful for having played out in front of Frank, who I knew would remind me of it regularly so long as our partnership lasted.

CHAPTER 16

FRANK LED THE way off the road and through a gap in the thick jungle a hundred yards from the UN compound. We drove into a vine-strewn patch of ground, bumping over angular stones before coming to a stop in the muggy shade. Given the scale of the place, I assumed we were in the ruins of some grand old structure.

"Why are we hiding in the bushes?" I asked.

"Buying bikes off mercenaries ain't exactly UN policy, numbnuts."

I took in the wall of thick trees that formed an amphitheater around our hiding place. "I have a bad feeling here."

"You got a bad feeling about every place."

"I'm usually right."

We waited. I got off the bike and wandered away from Frank. Despite taking care on the uneven ground, I still tripped over an unexpected rock.

I scuffed the clinging vines and weeds off the offending lump and discovered it to be a gravestone, the rock blackened and the words illegible under mildewed growth. The name might have been Italian.

No wonder this place felt haunted.

I was struggling to make out the inscription when I felt a gentle pressure at my hip, and spun on my heels to stare down the barrel of my own sidearm. It was held by a scrawny and badly bruised young boy, the purse snatcher from the docks. I went pale with the shame of having a child get the jump on me.

He was still dressed in ragged red shorts and the bright orange jersey of the Houston Dynamo soccer team. Despite his small size, the boy seemed perfectly comfortable with the weapon, and I took him to be a veteran of such ambushes. His eyes, like so many of the children in that place, were deadly serious. I believed him to be perfectly capable of murdering Frank and me if we didn't tread carefully.

"Frank," I said in what I hoped was a soothing voice, "it appears we made a new friend." To the boy I said in French, "We don't mean you any harm, young man."

"People tell me that every day. Then they beat me and take my *fufu*."

"We hate *fufu*. Honestly and truly."

"It does not matter. I have no *fufu* for you to steal."

"Why the fuck did you give that kid your gun?" Frank asked.

"He took it on his own initiative," I snapped.

Frank sighed. "What are you two yacking about?"

"We're talking about *fufu*, and the fact that neither of us has any."

"Hurry up and shoot the kid or something. The Pakis should be here in a minute."

I had no stomach for murdering the poor waif. He was clearly near starved. "I have biscuits if you want them," I said. "I bought them from that nice Indian shopkeeper."

"That man beats me every time I go into his shop."

"Is it because you steal from him?"

Frank strolled over to us, as though casually interested in our conversation.

The boy's eyes flicked to Frank briefly before turning back to me. "That filthy Indian should not hit me. He is a bad man."

"That's no fault of the cookies, which I have right here in my pack." I pulled out the *Eat Me Now* biscuits. The boy's eyes went wide with food lust.

Frank snatched the gun and pistol-whipped him smartly on the head. The boy collapsed onto a gravestone, unconscious.

Frank handed me my sidearm. "You didn't tell me you had cookies." He took the whole package as his reward for saving my life, falling on them with his usual piggish appetite.

"Save some for the boy. I promised I'd share them with him."

He laughed, spewing crumbs. "I mighta killed the little bastard."

"He's alive, but I doubt he'll be gone when the Pakistanis get here."

"If he ain't armed, I don't care."

I checked the boy's pulse, taking up his thin wrist between finger and thumb. The bones were delicate, birdlike. I was surprised he could hold my gun so steadily, but imagined such skill was born of necessity.

The child awoke with a gasp, feeling my hands on him, and scrabbled back across the graves. He took in Frank gobbling biscuits and me leaning over him with my gun firmly in hand. There was no fear in his eyes, only wariness and a bone deep disappointment.

"You hit me," he said.

"My partner did that."

"It was a trick then."

The blow left a neat rectangular welt on top of the boy's shaved head, splitting the skin. A minor rivulet of blood ran down the right side of his skull, coagulating just above his ear.

He touched the bruise, wincing. "You never meant to give me biscuits."

I snatched the remaining half bag of cookies from Frank and tossed it to him. "I'm a man of my word."

The boy stood, wobbling a bit, and moved a few feet farther off. He lowered himself gingerly onto another weed-grown headstone. I pulled a bottle of water from my pack and set it beside him, moving slowly so that I not frighten him.

"How do I know it's not poison?"

"Because I don't care enough to poison you," I said. "I lack the motivation for murder."

"I might call the soldiers and tell them you attacked me."

I couldn't help but admire his craftiness. "You'll be disappointed with their response."

The boy sighed and looked at his knees for a while. He still hadn't touched the cookies. "I'm tired of people hitting me."

"Perhaps you should not steal from them?"

"I am not a thief."

"You were when you grabbed that old woman's purse, which is why that crowd beat you yesterday."

He shrugged, unabashed. "I was hungry. I have to eat."

"There's no point in defending your motives. Once you do people wrong, your own hard luck story is no longer interesting to them."

I told Frank about the boy's resentment at being hit. Frank laughed. "Tell him he's fucking lucky he just got popped in the head. I shoulda fucking shot him."

"Your friend has a voice like a monkey," the boy said.

"That's intentional." I decided I liked the boy.

"What did he say?" the boy asked.

"Nothing, really. The noises that come out of his face rarely have any substance."

The boy grinned at me and finally fell on the cookies with savage intent. He finished them with shocking speed and guzzled the bottle of water. Less than a minute later, he vomited it all back up.

He stared at his mounded puke as though he might just give it another go.

Frank shook his head. "No, no, no. If he even touches that shit I will blow his brains out."

I dug the second bag of cookies out of my pack and told the boy to go easier this time. To ensure a measured pace, I handed him half a cookie at a time, counting a full minute on my watch between servings. I doled out water in a similar fashion. This seemed to work, for though I could hear the boy's guts roil with complaint, he managed to keep the food down. After ten minutes of this, his demeanor took a turn for the better.

"Are you soldiers?" he asked.

"We were, once."

"What are you now?"

"Private security functionaries." This line of questioning didn't lead anywhere useful. "How is it your parents allow you to run loose, stealing purses from old ladies and pulling guns on innocent men?"

"My mother was killed by a Ugandan soldier the last time they came through."

"Why?"

"She had a bicycle."

After all I'd seen, I still grieved a world where possession of a bicycle could be one's undoing. "And your father?"

"He left a long time ago. He went to Kinshasa to get a job. Once he gets rich, he will come back for me, and we will live together in one of the great houses on the river."

This child was utterly alone in the world. He would live and die by his wits, such as they were. I translated the facts of this youngster's situation for Frank.

My esteemed colleague shrugged. "Sucks to be him."

"How long will you be in Kindu?" the boy asked me.

"We leave for Kinshasa as soon as we conclude our business here."

"What is your business?"

"At the moment, selling these motorcycles."

The boy clapped his hands and smiled. "If I had such a machine I could be rich." Childish imagination lit his eyes. "I could provide a taxi service and go deep in the bush to hunt. There would be so many ways to make money."

I wanted to point out that if he could afford a motorcycle, he would already be rich by local standards, but I stopped myself. I saw no need to ruin his brief happiness. That would come soon enough.

The Pakistanis finally arrived. At the sight of strangers, the boy fell into my shadow, keeping me between him and the soldiers at all times. It felt good to be sheltering a child in this way. As the UN men handed over the cash for both bikes, I had a flash of inspiration.

"My bike is no longer for sale," I said.

"What the hell?" Frank said.

"I'm selling it to this young man." I pointed to the boy.

"What the screaming hot fuck is wrong with you?" Frank was angry beyond reason.

The Pakistanis couldn't have cared less. I gave them their fifty dollars back, and they drove away on Frank's Bajaj with a cheerful wave.

"You owe me twenty-five bucks, asshole," Frank snapped.

"Take it out of the two hundred you owe me for the other bike."

"That's not the deal."

The kid pulled on my sleeve. "Why is the giant monkey angry?"

"I gave you my motorcycle."

The boy narrowed his eyes at me. "What do you want for it?"

"It's a present. Like the cookies."

"Those cost me a bruise on the head."

Frank poked me on the chest. "You can't give away mission-critical equipment without my approval."

"That joke wasn't funny to begin with. Time has not improved it."

Frank snarled, red-faced. "What are you now, Mary-fuckin'-Poppins? Mother Teresa? Quit playing the saint."

"Why does one small act of kindness upset you so much?"

"We're soldiers, cockwad. You gotta get your edge back, or you're gonna get yourself killed."

I whispered to keep myself from shouting. "If I make a friend or two along the way, it does not make me less of a soldier."

"Friend? Like that bitch back at the hotel?" Frank's laugh was a sharp bark. "You know, she *gave* me the action you paid a hundred bucks for and didn't get."

I opened my mouth to say I wasn't paying for sex, but I couldn't think of what I *was* trying to do with Claire. Instead of defending myself, I stood with my mouth agape.

Frank was relentless. "It was her idea. She said the bath was five dollars. A happy finish was twenty bucks. I took the happy finish, but she was kind of a wet fish. I told her it was only worth ten bucks, and she took it—you know—personally."

I couldn't begrudge Claire wanting to make money, and there was nothing new in Frank's revolting behavior. Still, my blood pounded through my body, and my hands tingled with the urge to break something.

The boy tugged on my sleeve.

"What?" I snapped, glaring at him.

"I have decided I will work for you," he said with a smile. "I can be your bodyguard."

I turned my back on both Frank and the boy, and began the long walk to the river.

Despite my repeated efforts to send the boy away, he strapped our gear to the balky motorcycle and acted as our porter. Thus, what would have been a silent walk to the gunboat was dogged by the boy's chatter and the rachitic splutter of the TVS Max. It wasn't pleasant to move in a blue haze of exhaust, but I couldn't convince the boy to turn off the motorcycle, so thrilled was he to have a combustion engine under his control.

As we approached the waiting boats, Frank cast a hard glance the boy, then at me.

"No way he comes with us. He knows that, right?"

"I will speak to him about it."

We found the Uruguayans mounting Belgian-made general-purpose machine guns on the boats, three per vessel. Those belt-fed monsters could fire up to nine hundred rounds per minute.

Those will put a hole in someone all right.

The Uruguayans looked up from their work to wish us a cheery good morning, but their friendliness couldn't penetrate my grim mood. Frank threw his gear on board the lead boat and moved to help with the guns.

I turned to the boy. "Time to go home. Thank you again for not shooting me."

"I'm glad I didn't kill you," he said. "You are a good man."

"I can think of a few folks who would disagree," I said. "In any case, off you go." I made a shooing gesture, flapping my hands like someone urging a dog away. Although I immediately regretted this, the boy seemed not to mind.

"I cannot be your bodyguard if I'm sitting here and you are off down the river."

"It's not my place to invite you onto a UN vessel. Now go."

In my agitation, I raised my voice, and the boy shrank into himself. "It would be a bad thing to lose my job so quickly," he muttered.

I wondered how a person might measure failure in an environment so void of success.

With cynical precision, the boy tried another tack, turning on a deep frown. "Please, mister. I need your help."

"You look like a UNICEF commercial."

The boy dropped his performance, which made him look more desolate. "I do not want to lose my friend."

"You're better off being clear of me," I said.

The boy just stared at me, large eyes silently daring me to leave him. I shoved money in his hand—maybe thirty dollars—and got on the boat. I refused to look back.

Frank was busy impressing the Uruguayans by hefting one of the machine guns with one hand and pretending to open fire on Kindu. I wanted to be as far from him as I could, and the only thing that kept me from switching boats was knowing I would have to face the boy again on the dock.

One of the things that preys on the minds of combat veterans is that survival is predicated on the arbitrary intersection of a million insignificant actions. The difference between life and death can be something as small as leaning over to tie a bootlace just before the sniper fires, or stopping to pee one step in front of a land mine. Or, in my case that day, staying on the boat with my obnoxious partner because I couldn't face a lonely boy.

The very randomness of fate often drives soldiers clear around the bend. At the very least, it convinces most of them that if there's such a thing as God, he's the kind of fellow one wants to avoid.

The peacekeepers cast off the ropes. We pulled into the sluggish current, and I turned back to shore at last. The boy raised his hand in farewell.

"Okay, boss!" he shouted over the rumble of our engines. "I will see you in Lowa!"

My God, I will get this boy killed yet. Lowa was a hundred and fifty kilometers from Kindu.

Frank leaned against his pack in the bow, smiling at me as we powered away from the dock. "You're turning into a fucking one-man humanitarian organization, Stanley."

"It wasn't my intention."

Frank chuckled, "This is the Congo, dumbass. Nobody gives a shit about your intentions."

PART 2

CHAPTER 17

I SPENT NO small amount of time on the boat that morning dreaming up elaborate scenarios wherein I saved Frank's life in the face of terrible odds and multifarious enemies, thus freeing myself of my debt to him. Despite the vividness with which my mind painted the heroic scenes, my imagination failed me when it came to picturing the life I'd live after I unyoked myself from Frank's traveling circus of death. All I could come up with was vague images of smiling women, quaint houses, and grazing cattle. In that sense, I was like the fellows who wrote the Bible—stronger on the fire and brimstone than on the sweet hereafter. My failure to achieve any real mission planning for life after Frank made me restless. I worried about how boring happiness looked.

Traveling by boat, however, eventually lulled me into a more serene state of mind. I watched the terrible jungle slip past and wondered at how picturesque such a deadly place could look from a safe distance. The shades of green were infinite—bright and waxy banana leaves, olive-green reeds, emerald palm fronds, yellowed grasses. A kingfisher swooped and glided along the water's edge, its gray and blue plumage vivid against the crowding foliage.

The heavy breeze pushing against my face rendered the heat tolerable. I escaped happily into a book by a man named McCarthy, about bad men adrift in the North

American wastelands. I was relieved to find myself reading about relatable people.

I should have been standing watch for Chiora and his men, but after our overland travail, I felt as though I was on vacation. I tried to imagine myself on a pleasure cruise, even if my fancy vessel was cramped, bristling with guns, and stank of man-sweat.

Content and sleepy, I left Frank in the bow and climbed onto the roof of the wheelhouse. I slathered myself with sunscreen, plopped a wide-brimmed hat over my face, and fell into the deepest sleep I had experienced since my last night in Yingchun's bed. Despite my baffling flirtation with Claire, I felt a twinge of nostalgia for my situation with Yingchun. I wondered how she was getting along without me, and if, perhaps, I was wrong about the pragmatic nature of our involvement. Lazing on the UN boat, I half convinced myself I could rescue Yingchun from her lonely life.

Mostly, I wanted to be in the company of someone—anyone other than Frank—who at least pretended to be my friend. I drifted off to sleep happily picturing myself back in her charmless room, playing chess in companionable silence. I awoke what must have been hours later to the sound of cannons. Instantly alert, I rolled into a crouch with my pistol in my hand, my heart hammering in my chest. Someone laughed, and I looked down to the back deck where one of the Uruguayan crewmen grinned at me.

"*Tranquilo, gringo.*" He pointed back over his shoulder.

Upriver, a wall of black clouds moved toward us, flickering with lightning, dragging a thick curtain of rain.

"You heard only thunder," the Uruguayan explained.

I was still considering his words when the wheelhouse window exploded in front of him. A split second later, the distinctive crack of a gun broke the air.

I wheeled to see what must have been the missing UN speedboat plowing toward us from downriver. They fired an

RPG at our second UN boat, which had turned sideways in the current. The rocket hit near their stern, igniting the fuel tanks and blowing the bodies of all aboard into the river. All of this took perhaps three seconds.

Chiora's men opened up with machine guns as I dove into the bow of our boat, where we'd stored our bags, to assemble my M4. Frank had already put his weapon together. The Uruguayans scrambled for their own guns, too busy staying alive to react to our firepower.

The killer in me awoke with a roar as I pushed the clip home.

Finally!

There's no high quite like battle. It's a plain goddamn thrill, and there's no other way to replicate it in this life.

Bullets pinged and flashed off the deck, spidering the remaining glass on the wheelhouse. Unable to navigate from inside, the captain fearlessly climbed to the second console on top of the cabin.

These are men worth protecting.

Sighting down the barrel of my M4, what I saw on our enemy's boat made no sense. Chiora's men had painted faces and feathers in their hair. Several of them wore dresses and lipstick. The man on the bow-mounted machine gun was decked out in a wedding gown. Chiora himself was nowhere in sight.

The Uruguayans returned fire, shooting in disciplined, short bursts. The enemy rained bullets, screaming curses. Frank and I sighted through a gunwale, picking men off with our M4s.

RPGs sizzled over our heads and detonated in the river, throwing up a disappointingly small spray of water. The boats circled in the wide river, taking each other on broadside. A high caliber round hit our bow gunner, just a few feet away from me, in the face. The back of his head blew open in a puff of pink mist. Frank used his corpse as a gun rest.

Within seconds, the other UN gunners were also undone by the sheer volume of enemy fire.

We were doomed without machine guns.

I ran to the stern and took the gun, strafing the enemy boat. Bullets snapped past me as we rocked and bucked over the rebels' wake.

From this vantage, it was clear we had inflicted far more damage on them than we'd taken, if I didn't take into account the first boat that was destroyed. Due to their greater numbers and those goddamned RPGs, though, we were by no means out of danger.

Bullets stitched a path across the water straight for me, and I hit the deck. From my prone position, I saw our captain take an RPG in the back, which blew a chunk of him onto the throttle. The engines roared, rolling me across the blood soaked deck. We slammed across the water at full speed, and plowed into the river bank.

The impact hurtled me into the body of a dead Uruguayan. The engines screamed in protest, then expired with a bang.

Our enemies cheered. The Uruguayans all appeared to be dead. Frank had disappeared, but I heard gunfire from the shore that sounded like his M4. Things would end poorly for me if I didn't find cover. The boat was well sunk into a tangle of broken branches. I gathered my gear and unpinned one of the mounted guns. I hefted this and a crate of belt-fed ammo, and jumped into the sucking mud of the riverbank.

I followed the sound of Frank's weapon to find him sheltered behind a pirogue at the river's edge, holding back the cross-dressing pirates. We smiled at each other, and he nodded at the machine gun.

"Good thinkin'."

"I thought so."

He held up a grenade launcher. "Look what I found below decks."

"Hooah."

The fight between the two of us was forgotten. The battle had wiped out the uncertainties of our relationship. This was what Yingchun never fathomed about my connection to Frank. Who else could understand these most vivid and vital moments of my life?

Bullets slapped into the pirogue and sprayed us with slivers of wood.

"You hit?" Frank asked.

"I don't think so. You?"

Frank shook his head.

The rebels motored toward us, ululating and laughing.

Frank clicked an oblong round onto the end of grenade launcher and snapped open the sights. "Hello, beautiful."

Frank smiled as he fired, blowing a ragged hole in the bow of the approaching boat. The vessel nosed down, slewing sideways in the water. The rebels' cheers turned to screams. Perhaps a dozen of them made it into the river before it capsized completely.

I put the giant machine gun to my shoulder. The monster in me took great pleasure in shredding those men as they bobbed in the water.

The last pirate alive was the fool in the wedding dress. Seeing all his partners in crime dispatched efficiently, he stopped swimming and turned back to us. "I surrender!" he shouted in French, Lingala, Swahili, and English. He tried to put his hands in the air, but dipped below the surface. He emerged, spluttering, and begged us again not to shoot him.

"Was Tonde Chiora on the boat?" I shouted in French.

"No," the man answered. "We're Kufi's men."

Kufi? I had not heard of Kufi before, but I figured he was the master of yet-another fiefdom in that wasteland.

"Why are you on the boat Chiora stole?" I asked.

"Chiora came to Kisangani. He paid us…," the man dipped below the surface, came up coughing, "…and Kufi gave the order."

"Why did he send you?" I asked.

"He said…" the man gasped, catching his breath, "…an enemy of the Congo…sent a two-headed monster…to thwart the will of the people."

I translated all of this for Frank, who chuckled. "He sounds like he's reading from one of your fucking books."

"Mister Chiora is trying to mix a little Marxism with his voodoo," I said.

Frank pointed his gun at the man treading water. "Ask him why he's wearing a fuckin' dress."

I asked the question, and the man frowned in exasperation. "I didn't have a uniform."

"Where'd he get it?" Frank asked. I translated.

"From a woman in Kinshasa," the man said. "She won't need it any longer."

I shot him in the head.

His body floated up, the white dress billowing around him. I poured bullets into the corpse until it sank from view in a swirl of blood and white satin.

I translated his last words for Frank.

The storm that had been following us finally arrived, unleashing a torrent of rain.

CHAPTER 18

FRANK AND I took shelter in the ruined UN boat, hunkering under the canopy in the company of the dead. Rain pounded down as though the very sky were enraged by the sight of so much violence to so little purpose.

My heart throbbed and jumped, and my blood bubbled with joyful fury. I have heard meth addicts describe the terrible vividness of their experience similarly.

The sight of the dead Uruguayans scattered across the decks made me want to act out my vengeance anew, but that wrath had no outlet and spun back on itself, leaving my legs twitching and bouncing.

Frank rooted through his pack and found an MRE, which he dug into with gusto. "What is *up* with the dresses?" he shouted over the hammering rain.

"I'm more interested in this Kufi fellow," I said. "He mustered a hell of a force against us. There's also the problem that Chiora knows we're pursuing him. We cannot take him by surprise." My voice trembled slightly, but I knew I needn't be embarrassed. Frank was deep in his own head, meditating on the battle as he always did.

"Lipstick, eyeliner, and everything." He shook his head. "That's fucked up."

I tried again to bring him back to what mattered. "People at the UN will blame us for this. We should bury our friends and destroy the boat somehow. It won't clear our names, but it will slow down any search."

Frank belched and tossed his lunch garbage into the river, which always irritated me. "We got some C4. Can't we just chuck the guys in the river?"

"Some respect would be appropriate."

"You bury 'em while I blow the boat, then. Gimme your C4 and grab their weapons and ammo. I put half my bullets into those cross-dressing clowns back there."

The rain stopped as abruptly as if a switch had been thrown. I still shook, but the urge to tear my own skin off had eased. I dragged the bodies into the bush, stripped them of their guns and ammo, and used my trenching tool to dig shallow ditches in the clay. It was difficult work in the heat, with the blood-colored soil clinging to the shovel. Sweat ran into my eyes, and the last of my battle euphoria spent itself on this duty.

I put the last man to rest and looked down on their punctured and bloody bodies. I felt compelled to say something, but found myself not up to the task.

More dead friends.

I considered it fair that we would be blamed for their deaths. The *marabout* I killed was right. There was, well and truly, an army of the dead trailing along in our wake. I was about to apologize to the men when Frank came up and slapped me on the back.

"Boom-boom time," he said, his eyes alight with the boyish thrill of impending explosion.

I pushed ten or fifteen yards into the bush and sat down behind a low hump of earth, but Frank shook his head as he walked past me. "You're gonna wanna get a little more distance."

We took shelter behind a giant tree some fifty yards away, and Frank pushed the detonator. The blast rocked the earth, and a fireball mushroomed up into the sky. Mud and debris splattered on the trees and bushes.

Frank whooped. "Get some, fuckers!" He grinned at me. "That was fucking awesome!"

We returned to the river to find the boat reduced to a twisted black skeleton of metal poking up from the river. As an added bonus, the soil thrown up by the blast covered the bodies almost entirely. I finished burying the men and shouldered my pack, which was now heavy with ammunition issued by the United Nations.

"Where are you going?" Frank asked.

"Kisangani. Chiora sent those men after us, and I find myself more motivated than ever to get this job done."

"That's like three hundred klicks."

"We should get moving, then."

"I told myself after the Korengal valley I wouldn't march anymore."

"This won't be the first promise you have ever broken."

We walked through the heat of that day, following the path parallel to the river, in a gloomy world of huge, buttressed trees and washed-out bridges over minor tributaries of the Congo. We checked the GPS occasionally, to make sure we hadn't strayed too far from the water. For a long time we shouldered our way through a dense forest of giant bamboo, where we finally had to make camp for the night.

The giant stalks cut easily with machetes, but it was impossible to find flat ground on which to sleep. I rigged my hammock in the bamboo, but Frank worked at his bed for an unreasonably long time, dragging his huge knife along the soil line as though shaving a titan. By morning the new shoots were already poking into his back, such was the riotous fecundity of that place.

Our legs ached from the previous day's efforts, unaccustomed as we were to marching anymore. It became clear to me that we would run out of food well before making it to Kisangani. I kept my own counsel on that matter. Fearless as Frank was in battle, he was easily upset by the idea of going hungry.

I was greatly relieved, then, to emerge from the dark jungle and discover a stately, albeit crumbling, brick building before us. An officious looking old man in a threadbare uniform sat in the shade of its sagging awning. He seemed unaware of our approach.

"What the fuck is this place?" Frank asked.

I pointed out the tracks running past its far side. "We appear to have found a train station."

"Holy shit. We can take the train to Kisangani." We whispered, though the station and its lone attendant were some seventy-five yards off.

I glassed the building and its surroundings. Although the tracks were visible, weeds had grown up between the ties, and the rail itself was corroded and twisted.

"Don't get your heart set on it," I said.

We argued then over whether or not to approach the man.

"Fuck it," Frank said. "Just shoot him."

"That would severely limit our access to information about the trains," I said. "I doubt the schedule is available online."

As punishment for being a smart aleck, I was ordered to approach the old man alone, while Frank covered me from the bushes. This made me anxious. Frank wasn't an exceptionally attentive person, and I told him so. He seemed genuinely hurt by this.

"When have I let you down?" he asked.

I laughed out loud.

Frank said, "Fuck you."

When I glassed the building again, the oldster had disappeared from view. He was off, I assumed, on one of those seemingly-directionless errands Congolese folks often perform. I emerged from the jungle and walked up the slight rise, calling out to the old man in several languages.

Typical of buildings in those parts, the closer I got the worse it looked. I mounted crumbling cement steps to find the station windows devoid of glass and the awning timbers porous with ant tunnels. Despite the decay and vandalism, there was an incongruous absence of debris on the cracked floor.

I poked my head inside the old waiting area to find it in a similar state of tidy degeneration. There was no sign of the man. I began to doubt the evidence of my senses and wondered if this ghost station had a phantom attendant.

This childish fear was allayed only when I looked behind the old ticket counter and found that someone had clearly made a home in that sad place. A pair of men's shorts and a much-laundered shirt were neatly folded in a corner beside a pair of shoes so tired and old that the uppers were held to the soles by neat twine stitches. A bag of cassava flour hung from a peg on the crumbling wall. The bed frame had, in lieu of a mattress, an ingenious weave of grass fronds. It didn't look strong enough to hold a man, and I couldn't help but test it by pushing down with my hand. It had plenty of give, but felt reassuringly sturdy.

This was a monk's cell, showing all the signs of a meticulously organized life of service. "But in service of what strange god?"

Someone pushed a rifle barrel into my back, saying in French, "Who are you talking to?"

I raised my hands and heard a gravelly old man's laugh. My relief at confirming that the man I'd seen was among the living was outweighed by his gun and his cackling. He jabbed me painfully in the thigh with the business end of the gun, and I made as if to turn on him. "If you look at me, I will shoot the eyes out of your skull, *mzungu*," he said.

"There's no reason for guns and threats. I mean you no harm."

He poked me again, which sent a stab of pain up my leg.

"Perhaps I mean to harm you for trespassing on government property," he said, chuckling. He was a smug old son of a bitch. I was well and truly tired of being ambushed by amateurs. And Frank had allowed this to happen.

"You are one of Kufi's men, come to collect tax. Is that not so?" he asked.

"I don't even know this Kufi. Even if I did, I wouldn't travel all the way out here to collect money from an abandoned train station."

This earned me another poke in the leg. I sucked in a breath, my hands tingling with the urge to throttle the old bastard.

"Abandoned?" the old man said, "I have maintained this station since the time of the Belgians. I won a commendation for cleanliness and service."

I took in the silence and rot all around. "And when was this?"

"Nineteen fifty-nine."

Though I was generally sympathetic to the duty-bound hermits I occasionally ran across in the Congo, this old man struck me as nothing more than a thwarted tyrant. "When was the last train through these parts?"

"Twenty-seven years, one month, and twelve days ago."

I received another poke, this time in the kidney, and the fiery pain sent my heart racing. My adrenaline surged.

"Tell me about Kufi," I said through gritted teeth, my body thrumming with anger.

The pressure of the gun eased slightly. "How can you not know him? He is the *bwana* in this region. His men range very far. Whenever they come here, they tear up my home and take my *fufu*. If they find me about, they demand tax." He jabbed me in the back again. "And I think you are one of his men. I saw you with that other bastard."

He was sharper than I had realized.

"That's my traveling companion," I said smoothly. "He stepped into the bushes to relieve himself. We're heading to the diamond mines near Kisangani."

"White men only work as managers and overseers in that place. You are no managers." I heard him shuffling as he turned to peek out the door. "And how is it you come on foot, with no supplies?"

"Our boat was caught on a sandbar, and our supplies lost along with it. We swam ashore."

"Ha! You would be wet if you came from the river. I have caught you in a lie." He jabbed me in the leg again, pushing so hard I feared the gun would pierce my skin.

A twig snapped outside. The old bastard turned to look. I snatched up the rifle and turned it on him.

He jumped from the platform with surprising agility for such an aged creature. I pulled the trigger, but the gun was, of course, empty.

Before I could draw my pistol, Frank stepped into the man's path and put a bullet in his chest.

I ran, gimping on my abused leg, to where the fool twitched and flopped. My thigh and my side throbbed fiercely, and my blood, free from the restraint of gathering intel, was electric with fury. The man tried to breathe, but no air issued from his mouth; instead, red bubbles gurgled up from his chest.

He was dying already, but, in my rage, I didn't care. I stomped on the man's ribs until they snapped, and his vital organs were reduced to a slurry of gore, covering my boots with gobbets of liver, heart, and lung. It wasn't the station master's goading that had me so upset. It was the years of pain and violence, and the crushing sense of all the mistakes I'd made to wind up in that terrible place. But you can't vent your frustration on abstractions, and the old guy's petty cruelty gave me an easy place to point my anger. The rational part of me recoiled even as I destroyed his corpse, but still I howled and stomped on his body.

Frank stood to the side and watched. As usual, he waited quietly for my rage to ebb, though through the haze of self-loathing and adrenaline I heard him laughing.

When it was over, I stalked off into the jungle with no destination and no purpose, other than to get clear of my rage. Frank called to me, but he didn't follow. He knew better than to come after me when I reached this point. Fury raced through my body like poison to throb in my temples and knot my stomach. I huffed and growled, heartsick and ashamed to find myself succumbing to my animal self again so soon. Deep in the gloomy forest, I put my forehead against the smooth bark of a tree and reached out to squeeze the trunk with all my strength. As the frenzy crested and broke, I turned and slid to the ground, beating the mulchy, bug-ridden soil with my fists. After a time, I drew a deep, ragged breath, stood and howled at the festering Congo.

I dropped my trousers and twisted around to get a look at my leg, finding several perfectly circular purple bruises where the station master had poked at me. The sight of these welts enraged me afresh, and I considered returning to the clearing to smash his head in.

I decided that after I crushed his skull, I would use the machine gun from the boat to macerate his remains. The logistical concerns about wet boots and wasted ammunition distracted me from my murderous intentions, however, and I finally decided against further desecrating the fool's corpse. I clutched my skull and squeezed my eyes shut, struggling to contain the crazy violence that so shamed me when reason returned. Slowly, my heartbeat eased, and I came back to myself.

I looked up to the dark canopy and let out a deep, cleansing sigh. Then, noticing that my pants were still around my ankles, I began to feel foolish.

I refastened my trousers and trudged back toward the station, hollowed out and headachy but no longer furious. As reason returned, I worried that such an insignificant old fool could cause one of my outbursts.

Frank and I decided to shelter in the train station, as it had all the advantages of good cover, solid walls, and high ground. Since we had been attacked already, we counted ourselves as marked men who should remain alert for other incursions. We also opted to keep a regular night patrol until Chiora was captured.

Frank was always very careful with me after one of my murderous episodes, and that night was no exception; he put the McCarthy book *Blood Meridian* in my hand, and encouraged me to read aloud while he prepared dinner. He listened attentively to McCarthy's description of the Sonoran desert, and afterward he was full of friendly conversation and funny stories. He even offered to take the first watch.

I agreed readily. My head ached fiercely, and my body was a leaden thing; these were the inevitable after-effects of my rage. Once Frank donned his night vision goggles and went outside, I settled in to sleep.

I scrutinized the station master's bed, calculating whether the delicate-looking web of grass could support my bulk. Finally, I lowered myself upon it inch by inch, and was impressed anew. It sagged and stretched, but held me firmly off the ground. The way the fronds supported me was surprisingly comfortable. I smiled at the ingenuity of it before feeling stricken by a brief pang of regret at having reduced its maker to a pulp of blood and bone.

He should have been a mattress maker instead of a petty tyrant.

I slept well after that.

Frank didn't wake me for the change of watch, allowing me the entire night to convalesce. I woke in the brightness and bug noise of dawn, and had a moment of panic, worrying that he might have been killed in the night.

Rushing outside with my M4, I followed the sound of a huge splash in the river. I crashed through the bush and came to the water's edge just as Frank burst out of the river, whooping with joy. He climbed out, naked and seemingly unaware of my presence, and scrambled up a tree that leaned out over the water. Once he reached the first branches, he leapt into the river again with a joyful shout. I sat to watch him splash around.

Was he singing?

He hadn't been drinking and didn't appear to have dipped into his pills. I was reminded of times when he would clown around with the other men during basic training. While the rest of us treated the trials and humiliations of military life as a punishment, back then Frank always had the air of a man enjoying himself. His energy and good humor were infectious; every man in our battalion considered him a close friend and ally.

A month into our deployment in Afghanistan, though, I found him in our quarters, reading a letter. I was stunned to see he was crying, his face ashen.

I asked what happened, but, as I approached, he jumped up from his cot and backed away, shouting, "Get the fuck out!" As I backed out of the hooch, Frank put a lighter to the corner of the paper.

After that, he became withdrawn and cruel even to our fellow soldiers. If someone greeted him the wrong way, he went at them with his fists flying. He instigated firefights while on patrol. He lived for battle, and didn't care who he called enemy.

I asked him countless times what dread news had upset him so, but he never would tell me. In time, even asking the question caused him to lash out. Frank had stepped from the light into the dark, and he didn't seem to have any interest in so much as looking back to where he'd come from.

So I was sad in a way to see him playing around in the languid water, with morning sun shining on his shoulders and the deep jungle crowding around him. It reminded me of what he had been.

When I stood up, Frank saw me. He laughed and waved. "Mullens!" he shouted. "Check it out!"

He scrambled back up the tree, executed a perfect swan dive, and was swallowed neatly by the murky current. He emerged grinning and proud.

Frank's happiness continued through breakfast, rendering me conversely maudlin. Of course, he teased me for this, and brought me to laughter by doing a clownish impersonation of me in my rage the day before, all stomping feet and pounding fists.

"I'm the Vanilla Gorilla!" he bellowed.

We were chuckling at my folly when the boy from Kindu wandered out of the jungle along the train tracks, bloody and bruised anew, and noticeably without the motorcycle.

He stumbled past without appearing to notice us. We followed him down to the river, where he splashed water into his mouth, then passed out on the muddy banks.

CHAPTER 19

THE BOY REMAINED unconscious for several minutes. Frank grew impatient, and against my protests picked up the sleeping child and heaved him into the river.

The boy came up spluttering, yet he smiled as he waded out of the river. "You have baptized me," he said, which made me cringe despite my lack of religion. He leaned down and paddled a bit of water into his mouth. "I have a terrible thirst."

"What happened to you?" I asked.

"I bought some fuel with the money you gave me, and began my journey downriver to meet you. It was very exciting to fly down the trail on my motorcycle, and I was very proud. Then I met four men who blocked the trail. They asked me if I had seen two white men who carried many guns."

"What did you say?"

"That I had seen no such men. They told me they would give me money if I helped them find you, but I told them again that I had not seen any white men. That's when they kicked me and hit me with their guns. When I woke up, my motorcycle was gone. I walked through the night hoping to find you and warn you."

When I translated for Frank, he found this hilarious. "You could make a real project of this little bastard."

I turned back to the boy. "Did these men say who employed them?"

"Back by popular demand, the Stanley Mullens home for wayward hookers and lost orphans," Frank continued.

I punched him in the thigh. "Repeating jokes doesn't make them more amusing."

The boy said, "They said it was Kufi who would pay me if I helped them. He's in Kisangani. I wonder if Kufi might have seen my father on his way to Kinshasa."

"From what I hear, Kufi is not the kind of man who would take an idle interest in passing strangers," I said. "I think your father would count himself lucky if he escaped this man's notice."

To Frank, I said, "Kufi seems to be taking Chiora's jungle fatwa very seriously."

"Chiora's a fucking Muslim?" Frank asked.

"No, I think not. I just don't know what else to call it."

"It's a hit, stupid." Frank's New Jersey accent came through broad and brassy. "The fuckin' guy put out a hit on us. Every dumb fuck with a gun between Goma and the coast is gonna be tryin' to put us down."

"Unless," I said, "we kill Kufi."

Frank grinned. "Nice. A side project. Now you're fuckin' talkin'."

I shook my head. "The necessary removal of an obstacle between ourselves and Chiora."

The boy returned to the water's edge, rinsing the clotted blood from his numerous cuts and bruises. I told him about the bed and the sack of cassava flour back in the station, and suggested he lay low there and regain his strength for a while before heading home. This confused him.

"I'm your bodyguard. I have to protect you."

I explained the boy's interest in carrying on with us, but Frank shook his head. His joke only went so far. "No fucking way. The first time it was funny, but that's it."

"Please," the boy said, catching Frank's tone. "I have saved you once, and I can save you again."

Frank shook his head. "No means no, shit stain."

The boy appealed to me with his big-eyed poster-child look.

"You are safer on your own," I assured him.

He cried, and Frank pulled back as if to hit him. I restrained Frank, who stormed off into the brush.

I had trouble looking the boy in the eye. "We aren't the kind of men who need looking after." I said, "The farther you run from us, the safer you will be."

I could well have saved my breath, for the child was too far gone into his self-pity to hear. At last, fearful I might pummel him myself if I heard more of his bawling, I took him by the arm and marched him back up to the train station. There, I shoved another twenty dollars into his hand.

"This is enough to get you back to Kindu if you can avoid having your skull stove in by the next passing stranger. I suggest you feed yourself, get a good night's sleep, and go home."

He stared at the money.

"Go back to Kindu," I said to the boy. "Talk to the Indian shopkeeper's wife. See if you can get a job running errands there. She's ugly, but there's a good person behind that mustache."

Finally accepting that I meant my refusal, the boy nodded solemnly. "I will try. I will be a good man thanks to my benefactor."

I began to like him a little bit once again. "Stick to the edge of the trail, and if you see anyone coming along—and I mean anyone—hide yourself."

"What if they have food to share?"

"They won't share it with you. They'll hit you on the head and take your money. I'm trying to help you, do you understand? I made an investment in you, and if you don't listen to me I will take that money right back."

The boy fell silent. I showed him the cassava flour and the cook pot, and instructed him to get a meal going before he grew too weak to cook. I climbed down from the station to the train tracks.

"Good luck, young man." I said, raising a hand in farewell as I turned away.

As I caught up to Frank at the edge of the jungle, I turned back.

The boy stood rooted to his spot on the platform, waving both his hands, a brave smile on his face and his whole body lumpy with bruises and bony joints. "Thank you!" he shouted. "I will make you proud!" His head was entirely too large for his body. He looked like some kind of fool alien crash-landed on a hostile planet.

Frank scoffed, but I couldn't help but be impressed. Despite everything, the boy was still determined to make something of himself. A fellow could do worse.

CHAPTER 20

WE FOLLOWED THE train tracks downstream, assuming the railway would offer some advantage over hacking through virgin rainforest. We were mostly wrong in this assumption. The jungle had overgrown the line so completely that the track itself had warped and buckled. We tripped over railroad ties pushed up by roots and stumbled into holes where the soil had washed away in rainstorms. Vines, bushes, and stripling trees blocked our path. I marveled at the gamey smells of the jungle. That gross abundance of life stank of death.

The stationmaster said a train had come through just twenty-seven years previous, but I couldn't countenance that possibility, so complete was the return to nature.

Frank took refuge from our labors in his medical kit, zombifying himself with pills, his joyful innocence of the morning replaced by drugged somnolence. So far gone was he that when I accidentally let a branch snap back in his face, he took no more notice of the bleeding cut than he would have of a falling leaf.

Our interaction with the boy, who I suspected was doomed despite my best efforts, left me strangely agitated. I had refused to learn his name for the same reason I never named cattle back on my father's ranch, but he still had infected me with his foolish optimism. Throughout that long, hot day, I found myself once again imagining a future far away from soldiers, jungles, and death.

"Have you ever heard of Svalbard?" I asked Frank, after hours of silence.

"What?"

"In the Arctic, up above Norway. Snow and silence. There are polar bears, which are dangerous but also majestic. I'd like to see one."

Frank frowned as if I had soiled my pants. "Whoop dee fucking doo."

I marched double-time, seized by my increasingly manic desire to finish the Chiora assignment. Perhaps he was still in Kisangani with Kufi, and we could take out both men at the same time.

By afternoon, we reached a small village built astride the defunct tracks. Round huts, packed red earth, and the brooding quiet I had seen so often in Congolese villages.

"They will have heard of us," I whispered to Frank. "We need to go around."

"Fuck that," Frank said. "I ain't hacking through the jungle again."

"Would you rather fight your way through the village?"

Frank smiled.

Wrong question.

Sooner or later Frank would start massacring innocent civilians just to avoid extra mileage. Skirting each riverside community was untenable.

"We have to get back on the river," I said, hefting my pack and moving off, away from the village.

"Yeah?" Frank hissed, but he shouldered his gear and followed. "You got a fucking yacht tied up at the marina?"

"Fishermen," I explained. "We're safer negotiating with a small group. A whole village might overwhelm us, but we can take a handful of men swinging paddles."

As I expected, at the banks of the Congo we found a group of four young men from the village, resting in the shade near a collection of rough pirogues. They were surprisingly blasé about seeing two heavily-armed American men appear out of the bush, and when we offered to pay them to ferry us downriver they happily agreed. It appeared that not everyone had heard about the bounty on our heads.

Their leader, a young man named Moyo, told us to wait just a moment while they collected what they needed.

The supplies for a long journey turned out to be long-handled paddles with spade-shaped blades, and little blocks of *fufu* wrapped in glossy green leaves. Nothing more. I felt a twinge of shame at our massive packs, the sheer technological excess we dragged around with us.

Within minutes, the men had a ten-meter long, high-sided dugout in the water. Frank and I climbed aboard awkwardly, and we pushed out into the current.

"We need to be in Kisangani as soon as possible," I said.

Moyo nodded. "We can take you as far as Boyoma Falls, at Ubundu. You can find other boats below the falls.

"How long will it take to get to Ubundu?" I asked.

Moyo furrowed his brow and stared into the brown water as though divining the future there. "Two days. Maybe less."

"I will pay you double if we get there in one."

Moyo smiled, and the boat surged forward. "We can do this."

CHAPTER 21

FOR ALL THE fishermen's efforts, the day passed slowly. The paddlers talked amongst themselves in Swahili, bantering and laughing quietly. They fairly danced up and down the length of the delicate pirogue as they worked their paddles. When Frank or I so much as stretched our legs, we set the whole boat rocking. The best way for us to help our mission was to stay out of the way.

Exposed as we were out on the river, the sunlight bore down on us cruelly. Even in Iraq, I never experienced the sun as such a vengeful force. The crew seemed impervious to the solar onslaught, but I cringed beneath the shade of my wide-brimmed hat and repeatedly splashed my arms and face with bath-warm river water.

I spent the afternoon praying for the relative cool of evening. To distract myself from the swampy hot grotesquerie of my body, I dug into a book called *Tell Me a Riddle*, which had been recommended by a depressive priest at the base in Baghdad. I had to stow the book after an hour, as its tales of loss and regret were some of the saddest things I had ever read, and I didn't want to cry in front of Frank and the other men. I made a mental note to lay in a stock of light comedies next time I found myself at a bookstore. Frank would tease me for adding more weight to my kit, but without the refuge found in books I'd surely lose my mind.

Instead of reading, I counted the stroke rate of our riverine chauffeurs. After the first couple of hours, the men took turns putting down their paddles and wolfing down their awful *fufu*. It seemed like an inadequate snack for such hard work, but when I offered energy bars, the men frowned and pursed their lips in refusal. There's surely no accounting for taste.

In the late afternoon, their pace dropped off. Moyo said, "We must stop. We must rest."

At the next break in the wall of foliage, they nosed the pirogue into the shore and went off to buy more *fufu* in a village. Frank and I secreted ourselves in the bushes, weapons in hand, for fear that they might alert bounty hunters.

However, the men returned in minutes with a lump of *fufu* the size of a rugby ball on a large banana leaf. They joined us in the shade of a kapok tree and attacked their meal. They ate with the same quiet focus with which they paddled, pinching off a mouthful with their fingers and garnishing it with a tiny fish dipped in chili oil. When Moyo noticed me watching, he offered me a bite again. I accepted just to be friendly. The fufu smell—something like rotting cheese and wallpaper glue—always triggered my gag reflex, and the Congolese hot chili paste seared my mouth. Still, I pretended to relish the treat, and gave the crew a weak thumbs-up, eliciting smiles all around.

Frank said, "Kiss ass."

After our fuel stop, the crew returned to their task at full power and full voice. Moyo sang a refrain, and the others picked it up. The men's voices were not polished, but they were deep and expressive and rang from bank to bank on the broad river. The effect was mesmerizing and strangely heartbreaking. I don't believe it's an exaggeration to say it was one of the most beautiful sounds I have ever heard.

It occurred to me that this was the first time in three years I had moved at the pace of the Congo River, rather than roaring across it in a motorized vehicle, or struggling beside it on foot. I wasn't foolish enough to think I belonged there, but, for once, I didn't feel so much like an intruder. Looking back, I see that time on the river as the closest to peace I would get during my entire sojourn in the Congo.

At the time, though, most of my energy was spent lamenting the damn heat.

We seemed to be making good time, but it was hard to tell on the river. As the sun dropped toward the jungle, I became anxious.

Moyo saw my distress and reassured me. "Don't worry, my friend. We will get to Ubundu by nightfall."

He left off singing to engage me in conversation, telling me about the river, the tribes thereabout, and what it was like to live there.

"The river is everything here," he said. "It is our highway, our market."

"It's full of crocodiles and snakes," I said.

"And tiger fish and Thomsons, as well. There's much more good than bad, I think."

"I'm not sure I agree."

"You look with *mzungu* eyes, only seeing the bad in it."

His hopefulness shamed me. I had become not only the pampered traveler, but also the mean-spirited and impatient one.

As we talked, a man named Kago dropped his paddle to the floor of the boat and collapsed.

In response to what must have been my panicked look, Moyo said, "He has fever. It is nothing to worry about."

I thought a fever in the Congo was exactly the kind of thing a fellow should worry about, but I held my tongue.

There was no shade to protect Kago from the fierce sun. He didn't drink anything. He just fell fast asleep in the muddy water sloshing around at the bottom of the boat. I offered to paddle in Kago's stead, but the men chuckled and politely refused. I would compromise their balance and the rhythm. I spent the rest of the late afternoon needlessly fretting about poor Kago and the possibility of making Ubundu in time.

River traffic picked up as the shadows lengthened. We passed dozens of pirogues making their way upstream, clinging to the bank where the current was weak and the shadows offered a respite from the sun. Most seemed to be fishermen or taxis carrying women in colorful *pagnes*, bringing their wares back from the market in Ubundu.

Each time we passed a boat, the river rang with shouts of *Mzungu! Mzungu!* Frank and I clutched our pistols, expecting attack by Kufi's men, but few had the temerity to approach us, and those who did paddled away quickly at the sight of our guns. Moyo and his men ignored our weapons and didn't ask any questions about our purpose.

To avoid bounty hunters, Frank and I took to slouching down and covering ourselves with our foul bedding, sweltering in our own stench.

Late in the afternoon, we approached a boat with a small dog in the bow, standing proudly over a butchered antelope. Moyo expressed delight at the sight of fresh meat and steered us over to them. He bought a blood-soaked quarter of antelope wrapped in leaves.

The hunters were two tall and muscled fellows, shirtless and arrogant. As Moyo handed them a wad of francs, one said in Lingala, "Why haven't you slit their throats?"

Moyo and his men went still. Moyo pointed to me. "That one speaks Lingala."

"And," I said, pointing my Glock at the fool's heart, "he's armed."

Frank had been almost dozing in the heat, but he roused at the sound of my voice and shot upright, waving his pistols around. "What the fuck? Should I kill 'em?"

The hunters drove their paddles into the water with gusto, getting away from us as swiftly as they could.

"You are late to the party as usual," I said.

"Whatever." Frank was asleep again within minutes.

The gamey stench of the antelope meat sickened me, but it energized Moyo and his men. We made fine time, their paddles churning through the brown water while I breathed through my mouth and checked my watch obsessively. Frank snoozed.

We arrived in Ubundu just as the sun plummeted below the horizon. Though it was a town of only thirteen thousand, it sat at the head of Boyoma Falls, so I expected to see some sign of commerce, or at least some lights on the shoreline.

Such expectations are bound to be disappointed in the Congo.

Moyo pointed to a dark shore. "There is Ubundu."

I blinked. "I see nothing."

"It is in front of you, even though you are blind to it." Moyo was right, of course, but I couldn't trust a city that lurked in the dark that way.

In the gathering darkness, we approached a broken pier sticking out of a wall of jungle. The only evidence that we had reached our destination was the sound of the rapids off to our right. Up to that point in our journey, the Congo had moved in languid silence. In Ubundu, the huge river gathered itself to roar over the rocks with a terrible power.

Moyo whispered, "This is the harbor. Ah! And there is a soldier on the dock."

The moon broke through the clouds at that moment, and in its sharp light I made out a dark figure moving toward us, the barrel of his rifle gleaming in the moonlight. He was small, no more than a boy.

Avoiding people in uniform, even if they were kids, was a good self-preservation strategy in the Congo. Moyo, I'm sure, feared a shake-down for "taxes." My own fears went deeper, assuming as I did that government officials, even pint-sized ones, would know our reputation, or about this new bounty on our heads.

I had no interest in killing a child, or – more likely – watching Frank put a bullet in his heart, so I developed a plan. When we bumped against the low pier, I leapt out of the boat, barking orders.

"Who are you? Where is your commanding officer? And why—why! —aren't you saluting?"

The gunman snapped to attention. He saluted.

"That's better. I have a mission in Ubundu right now. See that my men aren't disturbed. Is that clear?"

"Sir!" the boy nodded.

"At ease." I turned to Moyo and whispered, "We need a place to sleep tonight. I have no idea where to go." The boy's superiors would make an appearance at some point. I wanted to be well clear of that place when they did.

"Follow me." Moyo picked up my pack, which had to weigh at least half of what he did, and marched into the darkness.

Frank, who had watched all of this in a daze, picked up his own kit and stumbled into line behind us. "What's the deal?"

"Shut up and march," I said.

For once, Frank did as he was told.

In the angular moonlight, we made our way along a thickly overgrown track between two banks of dense vegetation. Still, there was no evidence of a town. Tall trees lurked overhead, creating a tunnel into which we blindly stumbled. I wasn't in the mood for pratfalls, so I lifted my feet high to avoid tripping on the web of roots and tendrils underfoot.

We left the riverside and the roar of the cataracts. Sweat poured down my back in the muggy heat. Fireflies glimmered and swirled in the shadows.

Once we were well clear of the boy soldier, Moyo said, "There is a priest here. A monastery. They take in lodgers sometimes."

Under one particularly thick clump of vegetation I could just make out a carved stone Madonna, keeping her lonely vigil over the jungle.

This place is beyond your help.

"What?" Frank said.

"I was just thinking."

"You're doing it out loud."

"Better than not at all."

I was reassured by Frank's irritability, as it indicated his slow return to full consciousness. I was unsure how long the boy soldier would remain baffled by my bluster, and I needed Frank ready for battle in case the child alerted his superiors.

We labored up a hill, grunting with each step as we hauled our feet out of the sucking mud. I distracted myself from the climb by picturing a clean monk's cell with screened windows and a real bed. I even allowed myself to imagine a fan in that room, spinning merrily and rendering the thick night air bearable. This was how reduced my fantasy life had become.

After a few minutes, we came to an area where the undergrowth had been cut back. Buildings loomed out of the darkness. Moyo called into the night, his quiet voice clear as a shout. For several long minutes no one answered, and Moyo called again.

Finally, a human shape emerged from the darkness. I gripped my pistol, but the figure turned out to be the housekeeper.

After some negotiation with Moyo, the shambling old man said, "You can pass the night here, but the cost is three United States dollars for each person. It is four dollars if you wish to eat breakfast."

"If there's coffee with that breakfast I will gladly pay you five," I said, rendered goofy at the idea of dropping into a clean bed.

My weak attempt at jocularity was lost on the housekeeper. "So you want breakfast."

Moyo was eager to rejoin his friends. I switched on my headlamp and turned away from the housekeeper to dig out payment for the paddlers. I decided to give him four clean fifty-dollar notes. This was more than four times the price we agreed upon, but I was impressed by Moyo and his men. I thought they would do good things with the money.

Moyo didn't respond to my largesse. He simply turned the cash over in his hands, as if doubting the reality of it. My generosity clearly troubled him, though I couldn't tell if it was embarrassment at having been overpaid or disappointment that he didn't charge this idiot American a higher rate.

"Is that all right?" I asked.

"Yes. Yes," he said softly.

"You seem surprised."

He shrugged. "You could have just killed us instead of paying."

"I'm not that kind of man," I said. "Anyway, it's bad policy to kill the people who help you."

"It is as you say then. Thank you."

Moyo turned on his heels and disappeared down the trail, my awkward thanks dying in the air behind him.

If the definition of insanity is doing the same thing repeatedly and expecting different results, the Congo had surely made me crazy when it came to making friends.

The housekeeper led us to an outbuilding. The door opened with a squeal of protesting hinges, and I heard the unmistakable scuttle of cockroaches in the musty-smelling dark. The cozy bed and cooling fan of my dreams were nowhere in sight. Still, a concrete floor was a step in the right direction. I fell asleep shrouded in my bug net, smiling at the thought of a hearty, home-cooked breakfast. Hope does spring eternal in the minds of fools.

CHAPTER 22

I AWOKE TO the sound of nearby drums, a deep, throbbing rhythm like the heartbeat of some dread giant.

BOOM ba-dah BOOM ba-dah BOOM.

I tumbled outside, still mostly asleep, and found the source across the courtyard, in front of a large brick building badly in need of tuckpointing. Windows would have also been helpful, but of those nothing remained but bug-eaten frames and a few shards of broken glass. A scarred bronze plaque identified the ruins as Saint Joseph's Church, built in 1952.

The drum was a six-foot length of hollow log, nearly waist high on me, with a slit down the center. The old housekeeper pounded on it with impressive vigor for a man of his age. When he saw me, he ceased abruptly, flashing a sheepish smile.

"We have no bell," he said.

"The drum seems to do the trick." As I pointed at the instrument, I noticed the Glock in my hand. I next realized I was shirtless, having stripped down during the night to combat the infernal heat. The housekeeper must have taken in the gun and the scars, because he hesitated. But in the end he kept his own counsel.

"Breakfast will be in the rectory when you are ready." He put down his drumsticks and disappeared into the church.

As I crossed back to our shack, I took in the other humble buildings scattered across the property, all of them in a state of crumbling disrepair. A chaos of rampant jungle growth covered the grounds between the structures, surging up against the buildings in places.

My sleepy mind snagged on the idea that the Garden of Eden was pulling down the house of God.

Back in the room, Frank was awake and cleaning his guns. "You were raised Catholic," I said.

"What of it?"

"This is a Catholic Church."

"I was hoping for a different kind of whore house."

I didn't let him deter me. "Will you not go to confession?"

Frank frowned, his eyes fixed on his weapons. "Why would an innocent guy like me go to confession? My soul is pure as the driven fuckin' snow. It's God who has some motherfucking explaining to do."

I had tapped a raw nerve. "And what sins do you want The Almighty to atone for?"

"Stanley, I don't even know where to begin."

That was all I could get out of Frank. We cleaned ourselves up as best we could, which wasn't much at all, without the benefit of running water. Frank's body odor was like chicken soup, with a bitter tang to it that put me in mind of lions marking their territory. The smell was a frontal assault on the nostrils. I assumed that I smelled similarly gamey, if not worse.

When we entered the rectory kitchen, I tried to convince myself that the priest's obvious dismay was the result of our smell. I knew in my heart, though, that it was the sight of two gun-carrying white giants in his own kitchen that caused him to drop his fried banana.

"Ah," he said in English. "You are..." his voice trailed off. He put his trembling hands on the table.

"Ready for breakfast!" I said, too loudly and with forced affability.

"Good morning," Frank said, shaking the man's hand. "Didn't catch your name."

"Father Nzuzi." He spoke with a thick accent. "Welcome." I had never seen a man so disappointed to share his name. He didn't ask ours.

We sat down and thanked him profusely for his hospitality, such as it was. The grand meal I anticipated turned out to be banana fried in palm oil; it was gluey stuff sure to worsen the constipation I suffered in the Congo whenever I wasn't racked by explosive diarrhea. Nevertheless, I ate everything on my plate and complimented the housekeeper generously.

Our charm assault seemed to ease the priest's mind somewhat, but he was clearly still uncomfortable with our presence.

"This is not a safe place," he said, skipping past our small talk and looking seriously into my eyes. "You must leave as soon as possible." His concern was clearly for himself, but I couldn't fault him for that self-interest. If I were a decent person, I wouldn't want folks like me and Frank hanging around my house, either.

"This is an awful place where awful things happen," he continued, warming to his theme. "If they find you, they will kill you."

Frank flashed his teeth at the priest. "Who's *they*?"

Father Nzuzi looked around, as though checking to make sure no one was spying on him in that lonely place. "There are many dangers here. The Mai-Mai, the government, gangsters under the command of..." he dropped his soft baritone voice to a whisper, "Kufi."

Frank blew a raspberry. "That fucking guy again."

Nzuzi looked terrified to have even mentioned Kufi, as though saying the name would summon the regional devil himself. "I lock myself in at night. I hear terrible things. Sometimes I hear guns. Other times the only sound is the victims' screams. That is when they are using white weapons."

"White weapons?" I said.

"The ones that do not make a sound: machetes, spears, knives, clubs."

Frank smiled. "Not to worry, Father," he said. "Me and Stan here, we're the most badass white weapons to ever hit this fucking jungle."

I smiled at Father Nzuzi, trying to look harmless and humble.

But Frank continued. "We're like the fucking *nuclear option* of white weapons."

This didn't seem to comfort the priest, who looked like he might cry. "There is no law here, and without law you have chaos. Kufi's men kill for no reason. If they see you, they kill you. There is no point to it. Perhaps they do not like your clothes. Maybe you smiled at them. Or didn't smile. They just make a decision, and you are dead. They kill, and they know they will never face judgment."

"Not even by God?" I asked.

Nzuzi's brow furrowed. "I believe that he has let the devil have the Congo."

"That's a surprising thing for a priest to say," I replied, trying not to show how much his response troubled me. I had dismissed crazy Robert's talk about the Congo as hell on earth as the ramblings of a lunatic, but to hear it from what appeared to be a genuine man of the cloth unsettled me.

"How else can you explain the many forces of evil in this place? I have heard of things even worse than Kufi. In the east there is a kind of monster, a pale, two-headed beast the people call Frankenstein. It can kill you by looking at you. It eats children and leaves whole villages in ruins."

A blush heated my scarred cheeks. "That sounds like a bogeyman," I said, "a made-up creature."

"He is real. The spawn of Satan."

Frank looked like he was going to laugh, but my hackles went up. "I think you're a little quick to judge. I'm sure this Frankenstein has a perfectly good reason for what it's doing. There are two sides to every story."

"The devil himself was cast out of heaven because he loved God too much," the priest said with a shrug. "Knowing the reason behind his foul deeds does not make him less evil to me."

We finished the meal quickly, and in silence. My pulse raced, but I had nothing else to say to the cowering priest.

In his urgency to be well clear of us, Father Nzuzi was extremely helpful in facilitating our departure. He went so far as to arrange our passage to Kisangani with a group of International Rescue Community aid workers who had delivered medical supplies to Ubundu the previous day.

The four men from the IRC looked like any other gang of Congolese tough guys as they rolled into the church grounds on their clattering Yamahas, but the priest assured us they were good and reliable people.

When it became clear we would make the one hundred kilometer journey as passengers, Frank balked. "I ain't ridin' bitch all day."

"You'd rather walk?"

"Can't we just kill them and take the bikes?" Frank whispered, smiling as innocently as if he had just suggested stealing a pack of gum from the corner store.

I glanced at Father Nzuzi. I would be embarrassed to prove so quickly that the rumors of Frankenstein were true. "I for one would like to take a break from murder."

Perversely, even as I said that, some dark part of me thrilled with the scratchy urge to punch the cowardly priest in the face.

I'm truly a man divided.

Frank gave me a questioning look. "Everything all right there?"

"Just get on the goddamn bike."

Frank did as he was told, laughing at my consternation. This was a particular genius of his, this ability to cooperate with such insolence you felt he'd thwarted you entirely.

As the bikes clamored to life, I said to Father Nzuzi, "You're wrong about that Frankenstein fellow. He can change. He will change." I had to shout to be heard over the revving motorcycles, and my optimistic thought came out sounding like an empty threat.

CHAPTER 23

UBUNDU WAS A thick jungle complicated by dwellings, but once we got past the town we returned to the full rainforest, with trees so high the details of the canopy were lost to the naked eye. Lower, but still far above our heads, ran a crisscrossing matrix of ominous boughs as thick as steel girders.

The drivers were fearful and didn't speak to us, and the long, uncomfortable day dragged on in silence. They responded to my questions with the fewest words possible. Even when we stopped to eat, or pour gas from old plastic water bottles into the bikes, the men avoided our gaze. When they looked at me at all, it was to glance furtively at my pistols. Without the distraction of driving or conversation, time slowed to an excruciating crawl.

Finally, late in the evening, we sped out of the darkness and into a rush of light.

Kisangani was a disorienting chaos. In an instant, I was surrounded by tall buildings, wide roads, crowds of people, and actual moving cars. We were not even in the central part of the town, I knew from the maps, having come out on the west bank, across the river from the main city. Still, I was dazzled by modernity of a scope I had not seen since my last leave some six months previous. I had spent a lonely week in Kampala at the decadent Serena hotel, fending off whores in the bar, drinking too much espresso at Café

Pap, and reading for hours in my room. In Kampala I had hidden from the city. In Kisangani, such escape wouldn't be possible.

Docks and crane gantries glowed in the evening light. The teeming motorized pirogues on the river seemed glamorous and strange to me. On the far side of the water, a few incongruous high-rise buildings pierced the sky.

I experienced an almost religious appreciation for the advances of civilization, and for mankind's capacity to establish this kind of order in the chaos of the jungle.

Frank was equally moved, in his own way. He clapped his hands. "Let's kill this dirtbag Kufi and get some ass."

We bid farewell to our taciturn chauffeurs, and, for once, I found it easy to avoid over-paying.

A scrappy older man with a dugout canoe ferried us across the river, and we walked toward the center of the city. Hoping to avoid being identified too quickly, we stuck to the shadows of four-story buildings from the fifties, now blackened by mold. Our efforts to remain unnoticed proved fruitless, as we found ourselves pushing through a swarm of aimless pedestrians, muttering old drunks, young couples holding hands, swaggering young men laughing at nothing, and cripples dressed in rags, whispering for alms and clutching at the legs of passersby. We were the only white men in sight, and nearly a foot taller than anyone else on that street.

Still, though, nobody called us out or opened fire.

In the gaps between buildings, hefty women guarded rickety tables of everything from cell phone chargers to chewing gum. Their wares were lit by tin paraffin lamps the size of coffee cups that bathed the passing crowd in weak orange light.

I asked one of the scowling street vendors which was the best hotel in the city, and she pointed straight down the road, her eyes still on me. "The Palm Beach."

When I thanked her she nodded, still frowning. "My dear, do you need some batteries, maybe a T-shirt for your girlfriend?"

"I have no girlfriend," I said.

Her broad smile caught me off guard. "You could try me. I'm very good."

"Ah. Umm. Well…" I stammered. Ready as I was to be attacked, I had not anticipated a sexual frontal assault.

Frank approached and slapped my shoulder. "The fuck is wrong with you?"

"This young woman is offering me much more than a hotel recommendation."

Frank nodded, appraising the woman. "A big girl. Nice."

I turned to the market lady. "Thank you, ma'am, but not tonight. Perhaps later?"

She turned her smile up a notch. "My name is Martha. I'm always here."

I admired her salesmanship, but, after my interaction with Claire, I had little stomach for the complexities of dealing with women. I executed an awkward little half bow and headed toward the hotel.

As we approached the center of town, Kisangani revealed itself to be like a long-abandoned movie set, a flimsy façade quickly succumbing to the elements.

I scanned the area restlessly, still expecting an ambush as we passed the Falls Hotel, a ruin where prostitutes paraded along a rickety second-floor balcony, shouting lewd offers in French, Russian, and English. Frank didn't feel the same need for vigilance as I did, and he shouted back to the hookers, assuring them he would be back to sample the merchandise. This raised a bawdy cheer.

My hand drifted to my pistol as I nudged Frank and pointed out the dozen or so arrogant, well-armed men lounging around the entrance to the brothel's main floor bar. They looked familiar, tarted up with makeup and elaborate coiffure just like the men on the boat that attacked us, their hair sculpted into strange geometric architectures.

"Those will be Kufi's mongrels," I said. "It would be wise to indulge yourself elsewhere."

"Fuck that. I ain't gonna let a couple lady boys scare me away."

"I won't pretend to be surprised," I muttered. "But I'm damn tired of having my nights end by dragging you out of some whore's bed or helping you fight your way out of some bar."

"Then leave me the fuck alone."

"It's not that simple, and you know it."

"Do I?"

Afraid I would succumb to his goading and end up in a fistfight on the streets of Kisangani, I clamped my mouth shut and double-timed it toward the hotel, leaving Frank trailing after me.

My frustrations disappeared when I got to my room at the Palm Beach Hotel. By American standards, it was a ratty and depressing dive, full of grungy carpets and stained walls. It cost seventy-five dollars a night, less than I would pay for a Motel 6 in Houston. They could have charged me five times that amount, and I would have paid for my private room with a smile.

While Frank went off to debase himself at the Falls Hotel, I rejoiced in the air-conditioned room and a hot shower—four showers in a row, actually. The Congo had insinuated itself so deeply into my pores that it wasn't until the final scrubbing that the water stopped running off me as rusty brown as bush tea.

Thus cleansed, I looked at myself in the mirror. The new scar on my face stood out, livid and harshly pink, on my sun-browned face. On the plus side, our long trek across the jungle, along with snakebite and illness, had burned off some of my fat. While I didn't look lean by any means, I had lost quite a measure of the upholstered quality that was my normal state.

I patted my newly-solid belly and flexed my muscles, putting on a bit of a show for my reflection. *Surely the right woman could find something here to love.*

Though it was only seven in the evening, I put myself to bed, reveling in the threadbare sheets and the sagging mattress. I feared I was too giddy with luxury to fall asleep, but I was nearly out before I finished that thought.

I awoke to the sound of my watch alarm in the darkness. Reluctantly, I swam back to consciousness from a profound sleep. It was one in the morning. Where was I? Not knowing didn't bother me much. I breathed in cheap detergent, mildew, and bug spray for long minutes, listening to the effortful whir of the air conditioning. I felt clean and cool, ready to face what came next.

Finally, I roused myself fully and went out to the Falls Hotel to rescue Frank.

Kisangani's high street was even more crowded at two in the morning than it had been earlier. The nice young couples of the early evening had been replaced by reeling drunks, but the cripples and street vendors were still there. Pushing through the thronging late-night pedestrians, I questioned again the value of saving a man who would surely end up getting me killed. Still, I didn't hesitate, walking straight to the heavily guarded entrance of the Falls Hotel.

The men at the entrance decked themselves so heavily with pistols, knives, bandoliers, and grenades that I wondered how their legs didn't simply buckle under the weight of it all. The biggest of them, a sinister-looking giant with bulging eyes, was also the most heavily made up. He had splurged on false eyelashes and dangling earrings of ruby and diamond.

They looked at me without the slightest glimmer of concern when I appeared out of the darkness in front of them. They were a type I had met many times before in lawless places, both fearless and stupid. They continued enjoying their beers and joints, though I saw their fingers slip to the triggers of their AK-47s.

I took the muscle-bound man with the fancy earrings to be their leader and addressed him with a polite nod. "Good evening."

He sneered and rose to his full height, which was only a few inches less than mine. "What do you want, *mzungu*?"

"I came to retrieve my friend, a large *mzungu* like me."

The man grinned. "You are his errand boy?"

The rest of the thugs chuckled. I took a deep breath and exhaled slowly, easing my heart rate back down. I ignored the tingling in my palms. "Have you seen this man?"

The thug stepped aside and jerked his head toward the open doorway. "He's with Kufi."

I took another breath to calm myself.

And another.

Kufi's men roused themselves to surround me, and one of them pushed me down the hall toward my enemy.

CHAPTER 24

KUFI'S MEN HERDED me unceremoniously through a crowded bar that reeked of spilled beer and cloying perfume. Whores in short shorts and halter tops shook their asses to a Werrason song called *Lelele, Lelele* blasting through blown speakers. I was relieved to see the bar held no other cross-dressing goons. If I had to shoot my way back out, I could use the crowd to my advantage.

They pushed me through a door at the edge of the bar and moved down a dark corridor. Without witnesses, Kufi's heavies jostled me and cuffed my head with casual precision.

Here are men I could enjoy killing.

The thugs pushed me through another door and into the bright lights of Kufi's inner sanctum.

Readying myself for a fight, I scanned the room. Scattered amidst the gaudy, overstuffed couches, stacks of weapons and ordnance, and tables littered with drugs and liquor, I counted another eight armed men and a dozen languid whores of various sizes and shapes. The air was thick with pot smoke. Chiora was, disappointingly, nowhere in sight.

The men inside Kufi's chambers appeared even more drugged than the ones outside, which was to my advantage. The hookers were more of a wild card, as you could never tell if they would run screaming at the first sign of a fight or pick up a weapon and come at you like harpies. But here, even if the women attacked, I liked my odds.

Frank lounged on a couch in the middle of the riot of contraband, staring up at his reflection in the mirrored ceiling. When I glared at him and hooked a thumb toward the door, he chuckled. "Uh-oh. Mom's pissed at me." It was a lark for him to get drunk with the man Chiora sent to kill us. If we survived, he would repeat the story of this adventure endlessly.

Frank's smile widened as he pointed to the man sunk into an outsized and lumpy purple armchair next to him. "Look, Ma. It's Kufi!"

Frank giggled while I took in the great warlord, who stared back at me with hooded eyes, a glass of pink champagne in one hand and a spliff the size of a cucumber in the other. He was a tall, handsome bastard, so lean and muscled I assumed he abused steroids. I felt a pang of jealousy for the son of a bitch's good looks, and took an instant dislike to him.

The warlord didn't know who I was nor why I had come, but he showed not the slightest interest in my arrival. He certainly didn't extricate himself from his giant chair to shake my hand.

The four thugs who brought me down the hall flanked him, glaring at me.

On the coffee table between me and Kufi, amidst the piles of pot, pills, and what I assumed was cocaine, a line of perhaps a dozen iPhones were set out with military precision, facing the warlord.

By way of greeting, I said in Lingala, "You only need one of those phones."

Kufi spoke in English, adopting a weary, professorial tone. "I receive many calls. I know what kind of person is calling depending on which phone rings." His baritone voice was hypnotic, languid and musical.

The man was using the army of phones to fluff himself up a bit. I found this childish and somehow despicable. Despite Frank's warning look, I said, "You can set different ring tones for each caller and get the same result. It's simple." I reached for the phone.

Kufi swatted at my hand. "Do not touch them!"

I jerked back as though bee-stung, hating myself for responding to his command.

To Frank, he said, "Everyone wants to play with my phones. It bothers me immensely."

"I was trying to help," I said, but Frank nodded sympathetically at his new friend. I decided to hate this Kufi person in earnest.

Kufi barked an order I didn't hear, and a stooped old woman entered through a side doorway. She lugged a huge tray of ice, which she attempted to use to refill the champagne bucket. This work was too much for her flabby arms, but Kufi's thugs pointed their guns at me when I moved to help her. Of course the crone tipped over the champagne and dumped her tray, spilling ice, champagne, and water across the table and herself.

Kufi lunged, shouting and throwing his champagne flute at her. It bounced off her sagging bosom and shattered on a rhino horn. She didn't even flinch, but shuffled out of the room without complaint, her eyes cast down.

"My mother," Kufi said, "has become worthless in her old age."

The thugs laughed at this, and I breathed deeply to contain my rage.

Even Frank's smile tightened. "Easy Stan," he said quietly.

Kufi's men noticed the undisguised hatred in my eyes and muttered amongst themselves, gesturing at me.

Frank seemed to notice that the worm had turned. He continued to smile, but he put down his champagne glass.

"I'm just wondering," he said, "since all of you dress like chicks, who gets to be on top?"

The enraged men reached for their guns and took a step forward, looking to their boss for approval, which didn't come. Kufi just laughed. They stood down.

The large one with the false eyelashes pointed at me. "You will soon know that I'm more of a man than you."

"That's a flattering offer," I said, "but I don't have time to develop that kind of relationship."

Kufi kept laughing. "You are a funny man. Will you stay in Kisangani for long?"

Frank answered for me. "We move around a lot, but with such a welcome I bet we'll come back through here again now and then."

The thugs understood English, and fairly growled at the news of us popping back into town. The big one said, "You cannot surprise us, white man."

"You don't think so?" I asked, winking at them. I thrilled at the idea of shooting my way out of that hateful place.

Frank belched prodigiously and arched his back to scratch his ass.

The old woman returned, lugging a platter burdened with a giant fish, fried whole and surrounded by potatoes, onions, and tomatoes. I again moved to assist her, and this time Kufi himself ordered me, quite sharply, to stop.

"It is her job," he said.

She struggled across the room, her arms shaking, and dropped the tray on the table in front of her son and master. She wiped her trembling hands on her smock and limped out of the room.

My hands ached with the urge to throttle Kufi. I said, "You shouldn't treat your mother this way."

Kufi shook his head. "Taking care of me is her greatest joy."

"I didn't see any happiness in her. She must be shy about smiling in front of strangers."

The warlord sneered. "Whether she is happy or not is none of your concern."

"I'm not concerned, particularly," I said, my voice tight with rage. "Just making an observation."

Kufi abandoned his smile. "You are not amusing anymore."

The whores started to slip out the door. The goons snarled and muttered.

Frank said, "Before this gets ugly, are you gonna pay us for killing the croc, or what?"

Kufi stared at me for some time longer before reaching behind himself to grab a small bag of fine gray cloth, which he threw onto the platter of fish. It landed heavily in the grease.

"Why," I asked Frank, disappointed to feel the tension leaking out of the room, "is he giving us money?"

"Apparently that big old bastard crocodilian you killed ate more people than Jeffrey Dahmer, and our pal Kufi had a bounty out on its head."

Frank grabbed the loot out of the fish tray as though blind to the offense of it.

He pulled open the drawstring to reveal a shining haul of Krugerrand, South African gold coins. He took out about a third of them and put them in my hand. I decided to waste that bounty even more quickly than normal.

To Kufi, I said, "You value human life so highly?"

The man gave me a blank-eyed smile. "I wanted the beast's hide, but your friend produced enough of it to prove the monster is dead." He waved to the claws that I now recognized on a table beside him.

I looked him in the eye. "Another monster will always come along," I said quietly, "bigger and meaner than the last."

Kufi stared murder right back at me. "I will kill him, too."

"You didn't kill this first one," I growled.

Frank laughed too loud. "He's got a point there, big guy."

Kufi shouted toward the hall a third time. I braced for more henchmen, and possibly gunfire. Instead, the whores rushed back in, giggling and playful. Congolese pop music flowed around us, too loud and seemingly out of nowhere, filling the room with lilting guitars and falsetto voices.

The whores cavorted about us, sloppy with drink and drugs, pantomiming flirtation and lust. They worked hard, these girls, acting out curiosity, domination, childishness, or severity as they tried to guess our proclivities. One of them thought it enticing to stick her bulbous rump in my face and smack it savagely with her own hand.

The girls depressed me, but Frank looked as though he had stumbled into the Promised Land. His earlier antagonism faded, and I saw his appreciation for Kufi's lifestyle growing minute to minute. Here was a model of all my partner hoped to achieve in this life, should he live long enough to make the vision real. I could imagine Frank here, barking orders from a treasure room full of writhing, ass-slapping whores, while his minions waded through blood in pursuit of enemies near and far.

Kufi must have thought I wasn't adequately aroused by the women. "You don't like Congolese women?"

"I like them just fine, thank you."

Frank said, "Stan's got a thing going with a Chinese chick, but he took a run at a local girl just a few days ago."

Kufi ignored him, his eyes fixed on me. "Perhaps you are snarling and muttering that way because you cannot handle your liquor."

"I handle my liquor as well as the next man."

"You are offended by my joint? The smoke burns your pale eyes? Shall I open the window that you might breathe more freely?"

"I don't require any assistance."

"Then perhaps in America it's acceptable to growl at your host." He turned to Frank, who was hidden by a girl in a bright red teddy straddling his lap. "I visited America once. New York. I didn't like it."

Frank leaned around the whore, spilling his drink on her. "What took you to the States?"

"Business. It ended poorly. I intended to sell raw diamonds to the merchants there, but it is difficult to step off a plane with a bag of diamonds in your trousers and find a jeweler who will work with you. I wasn't prepared for the confusion such a place can create in you. After many terrible days of wandering in the lights, I sold the jewels to a white man in a basement. I was young and ignorant then, but I know now this man gave me a very bad price. Very low. I do not remember his face, but this one had a rash on his arms, which he scratched at constantly." Kufi looked from Frank to me. "Do either of you have a rash on your arms?"

"Have you seen us clawing at ourselves?" I said.

"I was not looking at you closely. Pull up your sleeves and show me."

"I will do no such thing," I said.

Frank pulled his hand out of a woman's panties and waved Kufi off. "Relax. We ain't got no psoriasis or nothing."

Kufi turned to me. "You won't prove it, though?"

I snapped. "I would rather cut my own arm off than do your bidding."

Kufi said to Frank, "He was funny at first, but then he changed."

"Good cop, bad cop," Frank said. "We take turns."

"You are much better company than him."

"Where was this guy who ripped you off?" Frank asked. "Downtown? One of the boroughs?"

"It was a place called Yonkers."

"Fuckin' Yonkers."

"You know it?"

"Whether I like it or not, yeah," Frank said. "Lots of shitheads in Yonkers."

"This man had a copper beard and a stoop. Beady eyes."

"Oh, you're talkin' about Itchy O'Connor."

Kufi sat up. "You know this man? Are you certain?"

Frank nodded. "Everyone knows Itchy."

"Itchy?" I said, doubtfully. "Really?"

Frank glared at me.

Kufi took a deep hit off his joint, nodding. "Itchy O'Connor," he whispered as he exhaled. "Does he still live there?"

"Oh yeah," Frank said. "Nobody ever leaves Yonkers. You go back there, and you'll find that Mick bastard sitting down at Murphy's pub, drinking a Guinness he paid for with your diamonds. He's probably there right now, laughing his ass off about the time he ripped off that dumb Congolese guy."

"I cannot forget that man," Kufi said. "I will flay the terrible skin off his arms. I will cut off his feet, and he will watch me take a bite of his heart as he dies."

I couldn't help but scoff at this melodrama. The logistics of gnawing on a man's heart prior to him expiring were unworkable.

Kufi didn't see my reaction, however. His anger had inspired him to step out of the room to piss.

"Is there such a man as Itchy O'Connor?" I asked Frank.

"There was until I whacked him twelve years ago." He shrugged, but with one sentence Frank opened the biggest window into his past I had ever seen.

"You killed a man in Yonkers? Why? What had he done?"

"I been fightin' since my nuts dropped, one way or the other." A whore flopped onto his lap and whispered in his ear. He smiled at her, his urge to confession forgotten. He said to me, "We'll hole up here for a while, get some R and R. Kufi got us free rooms, girls included. All you can eat. Ha!"

Frank's past would have to wait. "This is no place for us to sleep. We need to learn what we can about Chiora and carry on."

"Fuck that. I got needs."

"Kufi, you remember, has been hired to murder us."

"We're the ones who cause trouble. He should watch out for us."

"It's not a question of who initiates the conflict, and the ending is never guaranteed. I want to finish the job."

He shook his head. "Sorry, my man. The Italian pink stallion rides tonight."

Kufi came back into the room, still tucking his member back into his fatigues. "Ah. Frank and Stan are making plans."

I turned to Frank. "You told him who we are?" I had assumed, stupidly, that Frank had the good sense not to expose us within a few minutes of meeting our enemy.

Frank waved his champagne glass. "How the fuck could he not know it was us?"

Kufi laughed, spewing gouts of pot smoke at us. The hookers cavorted and purred, laughing on cue. Apparently the warlord didn't care to kill us immediately.

"Kufi, you badass motherfucker!" Frank shouted, his features twisted into an exaggeratedly earnest look, "How did you get up and running in the warlord business?"

This was all the invitation Kufi required. He spoke about his rise to power at some length, with Frank encouraging him shamelessly. His story was both pompous and vague, but I took that he had been a soldier in Kabila's army and turned to small-time hustling to supplement his pay. In the early 2000s, when the country descended into a free-for-all of competing armies, Kufi leveraged his connections and his exceptional ruthlessness into the jungle empire we now found ourselves entangled in.

Kufi and Frank's banter bored me, so I abandoned my vigilance and focused on downing a bottle of the sour champagne. The women continued swirling about me, taking a special interest in breaking through my indifference. They tickled and teased me, squirming in my lap until my little soldier stood at attention. Then they laughed at me and turned back to Frank and Kufi.

As the champagne did the devil's work on my brain, the girls became indistinguishable from one another in a way that was at once exciting and nightmarish. I tried to question the hookers about Chiora, but they ignored me, and as drunkenness overwhelmed me I quit caring so much about my objective.

Kufi and Frank appeared to be deep in conversation, but really they were each talking to themselves. They would have been just as happy speaking into a mirror. Frank made fun of my snakebite; Kufi extolled the virtues of the AK-47 over the M4.

Words upon words upon words until I hated them both in equal measure.

These two men wish only to crawl up their own backsides. The image disturbed me, but it at least killed my erection. I belched stomach acid.

At some point I switched to Johnnie Walker, downing glass after glass. Turning my glance away from the crowding whores, I saw a new girl in a corner, looking out at the night.

She was thinner than the others and not dressed so provocatively. Despite her unhealthy skinniness, I found her hauntingly beautiful, with high cheekbones and full lips. Her hair was plated into braids, which she pulled back into a heavy ponytail. She turned from the window and looked at me, revealing almond-shaped eyes of an unearthly golden color.

Full of liquor and its attendant false confidence, I invaded her privacy with stares until she had no choice but to acknowledge me. This she did with a smile that could only be described as pitying. I smiled back, and she shook her head at my folly. I told myself I only wanted to question her about Chiora, but the sober part of me knew I was succumbing to my old habit of doomed attractions.

The golden-eyed girl moved toward the door, but, as she picked her way past the loot and the whores, she kept her eyes upon me. After she left, the door remained ajar, and I continued staring at it.

"Who was that?" I asked Kufi.

The warlord looked up from a pile of cocaine, his nose festive with powder. "Who?"

"Hoo-hoo!" Frank said.

The hookers laughed too hard.

I stumbled out of the room and found the woman standing just outside the door. She didn't evidence any particular joy or surprise at the sight of me. She seemed accustomed to having men trailing blindly in her wake. As she stood, kneading her hands together, I found myself imagining how stunning she would be when she returned to health and put some weight back on her graceful frame.

Trying to get clear of foolish romantic notions, I shook my head like a dog getting out of the water, and crashed into the wall. The woman looked at me with quiet alarm.

In English I said, "Speaking for myself, I don't think that room was a good place for decent people."

She didn't respond, and though I should have assumed from this that she spoke no English, I was too drunk and marble-mouthed to use French, or to stop talking. "My partner has a way of sniffing out trouble. He's like a truffle pig that way. He can root out dubious treasures underground. I follow him to make sure the bad men he unearths don't cause him undue harm. That Kufi back there," I said, swinging my thumb in a loopy arc back toward the parlor, "is a bad seed."

Her eyes traveled from scar to scar across my head and face, mapping my damage. She smiled slightly, as though remembering something that used to make her happy.

"Are you a whore, too?" I asked, shocked at my own bluntness. *God damn the tongue-loosening effects of liquor.*

"I am General Kufi's business manager," she said in English, with no hint of anger.

"Do you stay in one of the rooms here?" I blushed. To my relief, the woman smiled.

She produced a cigarette, and when she fumbled with the wooden matches I took one from her and struck it against my teeth, as though to impress her with my skill in the tavern arts. The sober part of me shouted *Stanley, you are a boob!*

The woman contemplated me coolly, as you might a bad painting or a raccoon splattered onto the freeway.

"You're hard to read, miss."

"How is that?"

"I can't tell if you like me or hate me, if you are happy or sad."

"I am sick."

"In what way?" I asked, though I could already guess.

"The forever way," she said with a triumphant smile, as though she found the whole thing amusing. I couldn't take it lightly, though, and became angry at her gallows humor.

"You want to die, is that it?"

Her smile collapsed. "Are you always so stupid?"

My face stung, so great was my embarrassment. "Not always. Liquor makes me vomit words. Please forgive my impertinence."

She didn't respond, but at least she didn't seem to simmer with resentment.

In my drunkenness, I decided to press on with my flirtation. "What are your plans for the rest of the evening?"

"There can be no plans here. At night the streets are not safe."

"If I didn't know better," I said, fluffing my ego like an idiot, "I'd think you were waiting for me out here."

"You don't know anything."

I felt the need to argue my point. "You stared at me as you walked out, and you left the door open. It was a clear invitation to rendezvous."

"You don't understand."

"Most of the time, no. But I think I got this one right."

One of Kufi's cross-dressing mongrels clicked off his safety down at the end of the hall. I hadn't noticed him there, but he had been listening to us for some time, I thought. I found his unsmiling stare ominous.

In French, he said to the woman, "You should return to your room."

"Are you the general now?"

"I work for the general."

"As do I. And I am entertaining his guest," she said.

"You should not do that any longer, unless you want trouble."

"And from where would this trouble come?"

"From Kufi himself."

"Hey," I said to the thug. "Leave the lady alone. Go."

The man froze, then reached up to fiddle with his dangling earring. He turned at last and retreated down the hall.

The woman shook her head. "That one is like a shadow, following me everywhere. I lock my door at night."

"Are you Kufi's woman, then?"

She pointed back to the vile parlor. "He is not a man who chooses one woman." Seeing my disappointed frown, she continued. "We are not together in that way. Once, it was possible perhaps, but not now."

Frank's uproarious laughter came through the door. He sounded particularly idiotic when he laughed.

"I don't believe I like Kisangani," I said.

The woman stepped closer to me. Did she long for my embrace? No, she wanted to share a confidence. "I heard the men talking about you and your friend," she said. "Kufi is only letting you live because he wants to learn how to attack your employer. He wants to know how many guards they have, and where are their weaknesses."

"He's welcome to it."

She rolled her eyes. "They will kill you the minute the general has the information he needs. Normally they drink and bother the girls until very late, but tonight they are sober and watchful. You should be careful."

"I'm too drunk for careful."

"There is more than one bounty on your head. Kufi cannot resist."

That got my attention. "How do you know there are any bounties on my head?"

"The general confides in me. A man named Chiora offered a reward. A Mister Zhou also put a price on your heads, just two days ago."

"Heads, plural? Both of us?"

She nodded.

My concerns about Zhou were well founded, but that thought brought me no comfort. Frank would take this poorly. He admired Zhou.

The woman grabbed my arm. "You should go back to the parlor. You must stay near Kufi for now."

"Another minute in there and I would kill Kufi, but I'm too drunk to fight all of his men now. I'll go back to my hotel."

"He knows where you stay. It would not be safe. Come, I will find you a good place."

She led me down the hall and up a set of sagging stairs. At the end of a musty and dark corridor, she produced a key and opened one of the old hotel doors. I followed her in creeping silence, imitating her soft steps and careful movements.

She ushered me into the dark room and closed the door behind us. She took me by the shoulders, touching me for the first time, and placed me in a corner like a piece of furniture. She turned to leave.

"Wait," I shouted with drunken concern, my voice echoing in the stillness. "What about Frank?"

"I will work with the other girls and make sure he stays safe tonight, as well."

"What's your name?" I asked.

"Nadine."

"That's a beautiful name."

"Stay still, and stay quiet."

I was utterly blind in the darkness, but followed the sound of her progress; her light steps, her hands opening the drapes, the drag of the curtain rings on the bar. I felt coddled and protected, and was touched by this strange woman's decision to hide me from danger. I decided I liked Nadine very much.

Dim moonlight revealed a hotel room like any other, with the exception that everything in this place was forty, perhaps fifty years old. I scanned the chipped coffee table top, listing chairs, and threadbare covers on a sagging bed.

Nadine glanced around. "This is the room Katherine Hepburn stayed in when they filmed *The African Queen*. For many years it was preserved as a tourist attraction, even after there were no tourists."

"It's a miracle you were able to maintain it."

"When Kufi took control, I hid the key so that the men could not destroy it like they did everything else. He does not care enough about it to kick in the door or change the locks. I come to tidy up every week. I dust, change the linens, and spray chemicals to kill the insects."

"Why?"

She ran a finger along a table checking for dust. "It's good to have someplace clean in the midst of so much that is rotten."

I nodded, thinking of Nadine's illness. I was afraid I would weep for the sadness of it all if I didn't change the subject.

"Why are you helping me?"

She looked out the window. "The more power Kufi gets, the worse it is for the people in the city. I think maybe it's time for a change."

"You want me to kill him?"

She sighed, running a hand down the drapes. "That is up to you."

"And you think Frank and I could outwit his whole army?"

"I hope so."

I tried to tease her again. "It's clear you have passionate feelings for me."

Her sad look collapsed into a frown. "In that you are mistaken."

I waggled my eyebrows, playing the clown. "It's clear as day. You are in the grip of an all-consuming love that's crashing over you, wave after wave of it until you don't know up from down. Believe me, miss, I see it all the time.

It's my curse; each time I walk through town I leave a trail of broken hearts and unrequited love. I grow weary of women throwing their brassieres at me." I dropped onto the narrow bed, vamping like a bikini model.

Nadine managed a smile, but wasn't so taken with my charms that she cared to stay with me. When she put her hand on the door to leave, I redoubled my lascivious posturing. The ancient bed squealed and creaked.

She started to lose patience. "You must stop making so much noise, you foolish man. The soldiers sleep just beneath you."

I wasn't going to woo this woman. Catching myself on the verge of falling pointlessly in love yet again, my alcohol-soaked mood swerved into darkness. "I don't give a rusty rat's backside about those fools. They can't hurt me."

Nadine rushed over to grab my shoulders, whispering sharply, "Hurting people is all they do. They are killers."

My throat tightened against a wave of self-loathing. "We have that in common, then."

"Are you proud of this?" She dropped her hands from my shoulders and stepped away, her golden eyes wide with alarm.

Seeing the disgust in her eyes, years of dread and frustration boiled in my guts. I hated seeing my ugliness reflected in someone else's gaze. As so often happened, my shame gave way to resentment, and boiled over as rage. My murderer-self awoke with a surge of adrenaline. I threw my head back and bellowed like a gorilla, terribly loud in the small room, rebounding off the tatty furniture and bare walls.

Three times I drew breath and emptied my lungs.

Nadine escaped out the door, locking it from the outside once she was safe in the hall. I lurched across the room and slammed back the bolt, throwing the door open so that there would be no barrier between me and Kufi's men. Let them kill me here, in Katharine Hepburn's room.

I drew both my guns and flopped onto a musty chair to await what I assumed was my final battle. I couldn't decide if I wanted to laugh or weep.

My pulse pounded crazily, blood coursing through my body as I sat with the guns cocked and pointed at the door. I looked forward to going out in a blaze of gunfire and bloodshed, but after several minutes of waiting my bloodlust ebbed. I began to feel sleepy.

Some minutes later, I realized that my attempt to call death to my side had fallen on deaf ears. Kufi's men were either out drinking, despite Nadine's warning, or were too accustomed to tortured screams to rouse themselves to respond. I hauled myself out of the chair, swayed and moaned in the middle of the room for a while, then collapsed sideways onto the bed and passed out.

CHAPTER 25

I LURCHED AWAKE just before dawn, soaked in sweat. My stench was so profound that even I was offended by it. I was still fully clothed, but neatly arranged on the bed with my head on the pillow.

When my hangover and I finally turned toward the door with an idea to exercising the caution I had forsaken the previous night, it was already shut and dead-bolted. I wondered if my unconscious mind took these precautions, or if Nadine had returned in the night to lock me in for both her safety and my own.

"You are still drunk if you think that woman came back to help you," I croaked, my voice rumbling like a bag of rocks.

I dragged myself to the window. Leaning heavily on the frame, I looked out at the street, bustling even at this hour. Hawkers walked past, selling everything from Chinese-made blouses to bananas. One lean youngster jumped from pedestrian to pedestrian, offering a single brown belt he dangled from his finger. On the far curb, a long line of people used the pavement's edge to sharpen their knives, doing their small part to hasten the road's decay.

A large plinth across the street, clearly built for some monumental statue, was now a monument to hygiene; it held a water spigot from which local women filled buckets and the hotel's whores scrubbed their underpants.

Farther down the street, I saw a thin woman in a threadbare dress who looked familiar, though I couldn't place her. She drifted through the hectic crowd like a phantom, without destination, as though her mind were elsewhere and her feet moved of their own volition. Even as I struggled to remember her, the familiar stranger disappeared into the crowd.

The woman from the trail. That she could wander, weak and penniless, the hundreds of kilometers from Kalemie to Kisangani, and get to the city in the same time we did, struck me as a miracle. If my own situation had not been so urgent, I would have followed her to ask what kept her going.

At that moment, though, a man bellowed in anger somewhere, snapping me out of my drunken reverie and reminding me of my predicament. I slapped myself to knock out the alcohol fumes, checked my pistols, and went to look for Frank.

I used my signaling mirror to check the halls for an ambush, but found the hotel silent in the early light. I crept along the passageway and down the stairs unnoticed.

Pausing at the door to Kufi's inner sanctum, I saw the man himself asleep in his chair, his head thrown back and mouth agape. He still clutched a spliff in one hand and a champagne flute in the other, a fascinating expression of his commitment to his vices. He looked as though he would be out for several more hours.

A curvaceous whore slept naked on the floor beside him, sprawled out on her back. Her plump face was disturbingly childlike in sleep, and I paused to stare at her nudity; her large breasts and belly lifted and fell with her breath. Her exposed sex shocked me, the tangled muff was smeared and mashed, and the puckered folds looked somehow ridiculous, yet my fool penis still stirred in my pants.

Frank, however, wasn't in the parlor. This sent me back upstairs to search the rooms.

In a long and musty smelling hallway, I found one of the other hookers slumped on the floor, awake but decidedly green around the gills, as my father used to say. A sheen of sweat slicked her forehead. I felt a twinge of sympathy for what was clearly a bear of a hangover. Her breathing came shallow and uneven.

I asked if she could tell me which room held my friend, but instead she labored to her feet, saying, "It's not my job to chase down white men. Find him yourself."

My sympathy for the woman disappeared. I watched her stumble down the corridor, bouncing heavily off the wall every few feet. She bumped into one of the doors, and I heard Frank on the other side, cursing the noise.

When I knocked on the locked door and called out to him, he snarled. I refused to leave, though, and finally he appeared, shamelessly naked, his skin gray and waxy. His room looked as though it had been the scene of some great battle. There were clothes everywhere, the drapes were pulled down, and the mattress lay on the floor behind the toppled bed frame.

"What the fuck?" he said.

Kufi's voice came from downstairs, an angry barking.

"We need to get out of here," I said. "The bounty on our heads recently doubled, and Nadine says Kufi is eager to collect."

"Nadine?" Frank's eyes were not focusing.

"The golden-eyed woman from last night," I hissed. "Now let's go, damn it."

"Did you make this chick up?"

"Frank! Zhou has ordered us killed. We need to get clear of this place right now."

"Fuck. Wait. Slow down." Frank rubbed his face and tried to blink away his confusion. I tried to slow down. He needed to understand this.

"It appears we've fallen irrevocably out of favor with our employer."

Frank stared, uncomprehending. "Zhou? No fucking way."

"Surely you knew it would come to this at some point," I said, my eyes darting up and down the long hallway. If Kufi was awake, his men would be, as well.

Frank's mouth fell open, and his shoulders slumped. He looked, for all his size and fearsome strength, like a lost little boy. "But Zhou likes me."

"It does not matter who likes you if you're dead," I said, shoving him back into his room. "Get your goddamn pants on."

"I'll talk to Kufi," he said, his eyes darting, his focus returning. "We partied last night. He'll change his mind about it after we talk."

"He was working you for information about The Company. You talk to him now, and he'll put a bullet in your skull."

Frank thought on this for a while, my certainty breaking through the fog of his hangover. Finally, his wounded look gave way to an angry sneer. "Fine. Fuck 'em," he said, slapping me on the shoulder. "Let's kill somebody."

"That's the spirit." The thrill of battle tickled up from my toes to the top of my head.

Frank staggered about, collecting his scattered gear. He leaned down with a groan to root about in the sheets, pulling his underpants from underneath a statuesque whore I had not noticed before.

When he was dressed, Frank went to the window and scanned the street.

"What's our play?" I asked him, hoping to buoy his confidence by giving him a sense of control.

"If I wasn't so fucking sick I'd wipe those guys out right now." He turned to me. "What about you, big guy? You ready to kick some ass?"

"Hooah."

He looked out the window again and grunted. "Ah, shit. Here it comes."

I joined him at the window and saw Kufi's large whore, now clothed, talking to the big, elaborately-jeweled henchman. The man listened, squinting as he dragged on a joint. When she stopped talking, the man nodded and turned his gaze to the hotel. He caught us staring at him.

Instead of opening fire, the killer below blew a stream of smoke in our direction and walked toward the hotel, smiling.

Frank shook his head. "What is it with guys and their fucking jewelry around here? I mean, earrings? Jesus." I scanned the street but saw no more of Kufi's men. I assumed many of them were already gathered under our window, hidden by the balcony.

Frank rubbed his eyes with the palms of his hands. He smiled. "Let's just waste Kufi and shoot our way out, Butch and Sundance style."

"They didn't survive that adventure," I reminded him. "I don't think we could take on his entire gang with just our pistols. A stealthy retreat to retrieve the rest of our weapons is the thing. We can collect our gear at the Palm Beach, and deal with Kufi once he tells us where Chiora has gone. When that's done, we will leave this city as quickly as possible, and set off after Chiora."

"We don't have to go after him no more, though," Frank said.

"He set both Kufi and Zhou on us. I feel compelled to pay him a visit."

Frank nodded, smiling. "It's funny. You look like a fucking goof, but there's a lot going on in that big ugly head of yours."

"That was the worst attempt at a compliment I've ever heard."

Frank reefed open the window, splintering the bug-eaten frame and releasing the musty smell of rot that's always near to hand in the Congo. "We'll go down shooting if we gotta, but first I need to get the taste of puke out of my mouth." He scanned the length of the veranda, and stepped onto the sagging timbers. "We'll slip out of here like we're already ghosts."

We're already ghosts, I said to myself as we crept out onto the decrepit balcony.

CHAPTER 26

WE SNUCK ALONG the gallery for a few steps before realizing that our attempts at secrecy were foolish. We were, after all, strolling along an open walkway above a crowded street in broad daylight. Kufi's men would either spot us or not.

Reaching this conclusion in silence, we ceased tiptoeing. Halfway to the end of the building, Frank paused. The pungent tang of marijuana drifted up to us. Through the gaps in the slats at our feet, I saw a loose knot of Kufi's men smoking and laughing, decked out once again in makeup and women's clothes.

"That whole tranny thing is just totally fucked up," Frank muttered.

"I believe consternation is the desired effect," I whispered back. "You need to get over it."

Frank pointed at the leader. "If we end up in a fight, let me have that bastard. I guarantee you the other ones will bail once he kacks out."

We turned the corner of the balcony before dropping back down to the street. To my great surprise, no one tried to stop us. We marched double-time to the Palm Beach.

The cool of the air-conditioned lobby made me shiver. The young fellow at the front desk flashed us a tight smile. His eyes skittered away from us.

"Ah," he said, fidgeting with papers, "you are back!"

I was too caught up in my own plan to be suspicious when he pulled out his cell phone and turned away. And that's why I was standing in Frank's room, waiting for him to finish packing his gear, when the earringed leader of Kufi's men burst into the room with three other murderers in drag.

They had us dead to rights, their poorly oiled AKs pointed casually at our beating hearts. Their only mistake was that they didn't shoot right away.

"You are going on a trip?" The big one asked in English.

"Yeah," Frank said. "We're heading to the Canary Islands. Heard the chicks there sunbathe with their tits out."

I wasn't sure what Frank's next move would be.

"General Kufi is looking forward to killing you personally."

"*General* Kufi," Frank said. "You learn to speak English just so you could be his little lap dog? You wipe his ass after he shits, too?"

"There will be a great ritual. We will capture the power of the *mzungu* demons."

"If," Frank said, "the demons don't fuck you up first."

"You do look a bit anxious, friend," I said.

The thug snarled. "You think I'm frightened by the terrible Frankenstein, but you are just drunken men who talk too much. It is me the people should fear. You should also be frightened, for soon I will tie you to a pole and hack off your feet and your hands. You will beg for death, but before I let you die, I will cut off your genitals and stuff them in your mouths. People will feast on your ugly white flesh."

"You are one sick puppy, Chief," I said.

Frank smiled, as calm as a man washing his hands before a Tuesday dinner at home. "Here's why I ain't worried about you, buddy." Frank counted the points off on his fingers. "You're cocky, you're slow, and you're stupid as fuck. Worst of all, you're shit scared of us, so even if you do squeeze off a round, you're gonna shoot wide and high."

The thug tried to laugh, but let out a small yelp instead. "Last night you consumed huge amounts of alcohol, pills, and cocaine. I saw this all happening, and I decided I would avoid everything, even beer, so I would be ready when the time came to capture you. Now that time has come. I'm ready. You will die slowly, watching as I make a meal of your flesh."

"Give it a rest," Frank said. "We both know you fake that cannibalism shit just to freak people out. Besides, you already had your last meal; you just didn't know it." My hands buzzed and twitched with the wild joy of battle coming upon me.

"You are all talk," the man said.

"Jesus." Frank squinched up his face as though the man had farted. "Are you sure you want that to be that last thing you say? Ever? This is your last shot at coming out with something cool."

The man shook his head. "I will continue talking for many years. I will tell my wives, my children, and my grandchildren that I am the man who destroyed the white monster Frankenstein."

Frank nodded. "That's more like it. It's pretty fucking funny, too—you know, in light of what comes next." He cracked his neck and turned to me. "Whaddya think?"

I said, "Bingo."

Frank and I opened fire.

Each of the men took at least three rounds to the chest. None of them fired a shot. They fell in a row across the thin and filthy carpet in a spreading pool of blood.

"Well," I said in the ringing silence, "there you have it."

Frank laughed. His hilarity was contagious, and soon the two of us were doubled over, giggling like little kids.

The small, wiry soldier was still breathing. He struggled to speak. Even with the rage of battle still hot in my blood, I felt a tug of conscience. Perhaps I should ease the man into the next world by staying at his side.

When I knelt beside him, he blinked rapidly, looking around in wide-eyed confusion.

"Am I shot?" he asked in Lingala.

"Yes, sir," I said.

"I cannot feel my legs."

"They're not as firmly attached to you as they used to be. Your spine is shattered, just above your pelvis. These guns we carry aren't pea shooters."

I'm poorly-suited for hospice care.

"What about the others?"

"Right beside you, also well aerated."

"Are they alive?"

"Not even close, no."

"Can I be saved?"

"Only by Jesus, if the Christians are to be believed. But there's no doctor who could put you back together. You're all broken up, Humpty Dumpty like." I cringed to hear myself.

The man gurgled pink foam. His chest heaved spasmodically, then settled with a bubbling sigh. I assumed that was the end of him, but he spoke again. "This wasn't my idea. I said we should wait for the others."

"You were clearly right to feel that way."

"Fiston wanted to play the big man. He thinks someday he will replace Kufi."

"That seems unlikely."

"Fiston was very angry with you for mocking our jewelry, the way we dress."

"That doesn't matter now, though it's a bit of a shame you will die looking so foolish."

I'd hoped that we would speak of important things, but instead we were chitchatting about fashion. "Well, um, goodnight."

"Hello? Is it night already?"

"You should relax. Think about happy times in your life or something."

"I did not want to do this!"

"Just stop talking." A heaviness settled on my chest. I would relive this moronic conversation for the rest of my days.

He made a strange huffing sound, *urgh, urgh, oof,* and that was the end of him. I was glad of the silence.

"What did he say?" Frank asked.

"He said it was a bad idea to attack us."

"No shit. What did you say?"

"I said goodnight."

"Goodnight? Are you fucking serious?"

"I don't generally engage my victims in small talk. I found myself tongue-tied."

"Thank God for *Bingo*, right?" Frank said.

I agreed. It was a plan we came up with clear back in Fallujah, but had not previously put into effect—a safe word that put everyone but the two of us in mortal danger.

Frank was still chuckling about this when someone in the hallway said, "Hello? Is it done? Shall I take them away?"

Frank ducked into the bathroom. I tucked myself behind the door. When the man from the front desk poked his head in, I grabbed him by the neck and pinned him face-down on the bloody floor with my knee in the center of his back.

"Frank," I said, "I believe I trapped a rat."

Frank stood over the whimpering man. "You thought you were gonna make a little extra money today, huh?"

"I had no choice!" The man said, spitting other men's blood.

"We always have a choice in this life," I said, "though sometimes it's difficult to see which one is best."

Frank nodded. "Deep thoughts, Stanley. You're a regular fucking philosopher today."

The man wept and squirmed in the gore. My stomach roiled, but I held firm.

Frank said, "Time to say goodnight."

I tightened my grip and turned the man's face straight down into the carpet. He thrashed, and I was obliged to use my other hand to keep him down. Bile rose in my throat, and tears filled my eyes. But I didn't loosen my grip until the body went still.

CHAPTER 27

FRANK FINISHED PACKING his gear. My own kit was already organized, so I spent the time washing the mess of blood off me as best I could. After a futile attempt at spot cleaning, I emptied my pockets and stepped into the shower fully clothed.

The water ran muddy red for long minutes, and I was disturbed by how perfectly it matched the color of the river outside the window. Even after my thorough rinse, the towel I used to dry myself came away blood stained. I spent more time than was necessary chafing at my gore-soaked clothes and cursing the blood that seemed to be replenishing itself, to the point where I began to worry that I'd been wounded somehow.

I became, briefly, quite frantic.

This irrational fear and the shaking hands were both after-effects of the fight, which hit me only occasionally, usually after close combat. Knowing this and getting over it are very different things.

Frank found me in the bathroom and frowned. "You're doing that thing again."

"I know it." My teeth chattered.

"It's fucking weird."

"I thank you to mind your own goddamn business."

"You ain't done it in a while is all."

The banality of arguing with my partner lifted me out of my strange inward spiral. I took a deep cleansing breath, and blew it out horse-like, lips flapping.

"Are you ready to finish this thing with Kufi?" I said.

"Fucker was gonna cut my dick off," Frank said, jamming the last of his gear into his rucksack. "That shit cannot be forgiven."

We gathered up the dead men's weapons and left. The front desk was, of course, empty as we passed, so I put our room payment in an envelope and set it behind the counter. Frank found this ridiculous, refusing to accept that one crime does not excuse another.

Bristling with guns, grenades, and ammunition, we strolled through the sewer stench of Kisangani as though we were just two friends out for a morning constitutional. Thanks to the crushing heat, the broad streets were less crowded than they had been the previous night, giving the city a somber, forsaken feel. Those who were wandering about stuck to the meager shade offered by flimsy tarps over market stalls and balconies clinging to the sides of moldy buildings.

The smell of bad meat dogged us, and I thought we might be walking through the butchers' quarter until it occurred to me to lean over and give Frank a sniff. I instantly regretted this.

"You should have washed the blood off yourself," I said.

"That's why we wear black."

"You smell like a corpse."

Frank took a deep whiff of himself. "Ah! Nothing like the smell of dead guys in the morning."

As he spoke, the sidewalks cleared of pedestrians and shopkeepers alike, all of them pouring away into the shadows without a word. In moments the street was still and quiet, with the only sounds the distant barking of a lone dog, and the creak and rattle of our gear.

Without pausing to discuss it, we moved swiftly to opposite sides of the street. Frank tucked into the entrance of a clothing store. I took cover in a market stall amongst tall sacks of beans, dried corn, and manioc flour. Each of us swept the street through the sights of our M4s.

I huffed two quick breaths as my heart rate skipped upward. I did a mental run-down of my ammo count, congratulating myself for including grenades in my gear.

Fifteen or twenty of Kufi's men, wearing their distinctive ragtag scraps of military uniforms, silk blouses, and makeup, strolled into sight. Every one of them carried a gun in one hand and a lit joint in the other.

Frank shouted, "Yo, assholes!"

The stoned thugs stopped and raised their weapons. We each hurled a fragmentation grenade and a flash bang into their midst.

After the grenades did their work, we stepped back into the open and finished off the staggering, baffled soldiers.

We picked up guns and more ammo off the bodies, as well as an unexpected pair of grenade launchers, and continued our march to the hotel. The crowds didn't return to the streets.

Frank said, "We're on a roll today."

"That was a very tidy bit of killing."

"I love my job."

I grinned. "Things will be more difficult at the hotel, partner."

"Get some!"

We approached the hotel under cover of the rickety market stalls, and crept into position behind the marble plinth and watering hole. Across the road, a couple dozen of Kufi's men clustered around the hotel's entrance. Another five stood on the balcony. Despite their vigilant poses, not one of them noticed our approach.

We fired the grenade launchers, decimating the gang at the door—and doing a fair bit of damage to the door itself.

The survivors staggered about blindly, screaming and firing at nothing. Frank put them down with short bursts from his M4. I picked off the balcony guards.

Frank grinned at me. "Nice shootin'."

"You were mighty efficient, too." I knew I was smiling, as well.

Frank slapped me on the back, and we double-timed across the street to find Kufi.

Inside the hotel, we encountered a few stalwart stragglers, who popped out from behind couches firing wildly from the hip. Frank made a game of shooting them precisely between the eyes.

Kufi appeared quite disappointed to find us knocking politely on the door of his treasure room, covered as we were in the blood of his fearsome army. He didn't speak or move, but glared at us like a petulant child.

"Keep your hands where I can see them, and sit here on the floor," I said. "Failure to comply will result in your immediate termination."

He sat cross-legged on the floor, the very picture of dejection.

I nudged Frank. "General Kufi seems to have lost his stuffing."

"This is the real deal right here, Stan," Frank said. "The minute I met this guy I knew he was full of shit."

Frank strolled over to Kufi, casually putting the barrel of his rifle against the man's forehead. "We wiped out your guys, chief."

"Also a man at the hotel," I added.

"Right, and the dumbshit at the hotel. But that was his own fault for being a fucking rat. So anyways, all that's on you."

"I'm not afraid of you," Kufi said, his lip trembling.

"That just shows how fucking stupid you are," Frank said. "You could have just let us move on through, but you went and fucked everything up. You know why? Because you're a fucking small time punk. A bully. You. Are. Nothing."

I found it hard to believe Frank didn't see the irony of berating Kufi for bullying. Did he really see himself as morally superior?

Hell, did I?

Frank paused to admire the room with all its accumulated wealth. He emptied a bowl of uncut diamonds into his duffle bag. This seemed to calm him. I didn't share his obsessive love of diamonds.

"Now, me and Stan here," he said, "We're the real deal. You think you're a stone-cold killer. But me and my partner are death, motherfucker."

Kufi stared at a spot on the far wall. I followed his gaze to see what so captivated him in these final moments, but it was one of the few bare spaces in the room. I looked back at the man; the great Kufi took a shaky breath, fighting back tears.

I slipped my M4 onto my shoulder and strolled over to Kufi until I stood over him with my crotch pressed gently against his shoulder. He turned his head away but remained otherwise still. "Look at me, son," I said.

Kufi didn't turn his head.

I grabbed his jaw and wrenched his head around until he faced me. "There you go," I said. "Now, where is Chiora?"

"I...don't...know," he grunted, his voice throttled by my grip.

Still clutching his jaw, I punched him several times in the eye with my free hand, opening a broad cut above his eye.

"I didn't hear you," I said, squeezing his chin so hard I felt his teeth move. Blood poured down the side of his face and over my hand.

"Kinshasa!" Kufi shouted, spraying blood.

I let go of him, wiping my hand on his shoulder. "Doing what?"

"Buying equipment. Getting government clearance for his mine."

Frank sat on the edge of the desk, just off Kufi's other shoulder. "Where's the mine?"

Kufi slumped. "Somewhere in Kasai. Near Tshikapa."

Frank nodded, looking to me. "So we go to Tshikapa?"

"Only if he's already there." I tapped Kufi on the head until he looked up at me again. "When did he get to Kinshasa?"

"Four days ago. They took a plane."

"And how long," I asked, "will it take him to get his equipment and his documents in order?"

Kufi sneered. "How would I know this?"

I drove a finger into the wound above his eye. He screamed and writhed in the chair, but knew better than to lash out.

Frank chuckled. "Wrong answer, douchebag."

When I released him, Kufi panted and moaned. Words rushed out of him. "If he can bribe the right people, it will be quick. Otherwise, it could be a week, or longer."

I patted Kufi on the shoulder. "That could have all been so much easier." Turning to Frank, I said, "Sheppard will track him down before he can get out of Kinshasa."

Frank nodded. "Dude is fucked."

Mike Sheppard was the closest thing we had to a friend in the Congo. Our former gunnery sergeant in Iraq and Afghanistan, he was the man who got us our gig with Blackwater, and subsequently with The Company after Frank got us fired. A bookish man like myself, Sheppard treated me with a gruff friendliness, and he seemed to find Frank amusing. Still, I wasn't sure that our shared history would protect us.

"As are we, now that Zhou has taken out a contract on us."

Frank shook his head. "Sheppard wouldn't fuck with us. Would he?"

"We'll have to convince him to look the other way," I said.

"Or," Frank said, "pay him off with some of Kufi's loot."

"I'm not sure he's the kind to be paid off."

Frank shrugged. "Then we'll kill the fucker."

Was it really that easy for him?

Kufi squirmed in my grip. "Chiora told me he has help in Kinshasa. A military man who works for Mister Zhou, who has agreed to protect him from The Company. He arranged this a long time ago."

Frank grinned and jumped up from the desk, patting Kufi on the head. "Now that's some useful shit, right there." He turned to me. "You hear that, Stanley? Chiora turned Sheppard. We're all good."

"We don't know if it's Sheppard," I said.

Frank shook his head. "Yeah we do. Who the fuck else could it be?"

He had a point. Sheppard was the toughest hombre in the Congo, aside from me and Frank. If you needed protection, he was your man. My spirits rose, thinking I wouldn't have to fight my old friend.

Frank turned back to Kufi. "So here's your punishment, asshat. The price you pay for being a fucking prick." Seeing that Kufi's mind had wandered, Frank punched him in the side. "Are you listening, shitball?"

Kufi nodded, wheezing, and struggled to right himself.

"You're going to carry all your shit out into the street and leave it out there for the good people of this burg."

"I'll be damned," I said.

Frank turned on me. "You got a problem with the order, soldier?"

"None at all." The irony of Frank playing Robin Hood wasn't lost on me.

Kufi saved me from Frank's ire by saying, "I won't do it."

Frank said, "You do it, or I will pistol whip you like a bitch."

Kufi said nothing. Frank flipped his gun around so he held the barrel. He popped the warlord smartly on the head. Kufi flopped onto his side, clutching his scalp and making a high keening noise.

This coward was the most feared man in the region.

Blood pulsed from between Kufi's fingers. I marveled at the sheer quantity of it. Was there an artery in the head that I didn't know about?

Frank yanked the man upright. Kufi stared at us in a peevish way that I think was meant to seem defiant.

Frank said, "You've got work to do. And if you don't get on it right fucking now, I will jack you in the head another couple times. *Capiche?*"

"You cannot take it all."

"We're burning daylight, asshole."

"The people will steal everything I earned."

"Suit yourself." Frank clipped Kufi twice more on the head.

Kufi hit the floor, crying out and flopping.

I said, "You are choosing between the possibility of life and the certainty of death, you fool. I suggest you take the former."

Frank shook his head and said to Kufi, "Stan talks funny."

Kufi stood, wavering slightly. He leaned over to pick up a crystal vase, but flopped backward onto his couch. "I need whiskey. Cocaine. I cannot work like this."

Frank brought the requested medicaments, and I tracked down some hand towels and a basin of water, so that the former warlord might clean himself. In my search for toiletries, I found the hotel eerily silent, seemingly emptied of its prostitutes and sycophants.

Buoyed by chemicals, Kufi regained some of his former dignity. He took the bowl and towels from me, and went to work cleaning himself. This he did with all the care of a man heading out for a night on the town with his lady friend. I was impressed with the way he regained his self-control and wondered what he might be meditating on to have made the change. When I asked him, he looked up from his ablutions.

"I'm thinking about my mother," he said.

"Your mother?"

"If you leave me with enough money, I will take care of her."

After seeing how he cared for his mother when he was rich, I found it hard to believe he would treat her properly now that he was poor.

"I ain't leaving your sorry ass with nothing," Frank said.

"So we're leaving him with something?" I said.

"He don't get shit."

"To 'not leave someone with nothing' is a double negative. It means you will leave him with something."

"Don't be an asshole, Stan."

"You have a bad habit of double negatives."

"Eat me," Frank said. "That clear enough for you?"

Kufi said, "You argue like old women in the market."

Frank cocked his arm back as if to strike, and Kufi fell silent again.

Kufi said, "I want to make a clean break from the Kufi that I was, and become a new Kufi, with a clear mind and an open heart."

"Your name sounds really stupid when you say it too much," Frank said. "Kufi, Kufi, Kufi. Sounds like Goofy."

The man dropped his rags in the bowl of water. His movements were exaggeratedly slow, and his jaw muscles flexed in his effort to ignore Frank's goading. "You defeated me too easily. I deserve to be stripped of my power. However, I believe that I can make a good life for myself if I address the mistakes I made in the past."

"You can't go back in time," I said.

"But I can do good things."

"Nope," Frank said, grinning. "You can't."

I shoved the warlord. "We have work to do. Get a move on."

Kufi rose to his feet and reached for a pile of guns.

Frank knocked his hand away. "No guns, sunshine."

Kufi chose a rolled-up rug, which he dragged through the long hall and set out on the empty street. He shuffled back inside, the very picture of dejection, and returned with a large Chinese vase, which he set next to the carpet. He was starting with the items he valued least, working his way up to what folks at home called *the big ticket items.*

Frank told me to set up watch at the front door. "Shoot him if he does anything stupid. I'm gonna set us up with more of a nest egg. You think diamonds or gold?"

I told him I already had substantial savings, but if he was going to make the effort, gold would be best. As Kufi plodded back and forth, Frank filled a wicker basket with gold pieces. Halfway to the door he grabbed another handful of diamonds and shoved them in his pocket, as though unable to help himself.

The people of Kinshasa appeared at the edges of street, peering from behind buildings and poking their heads around corners. Seeing Kufi's wealth piled up next to the dead soldiers in front of his hotel, they were quickly emboldened.

The little boys were the first to come close, slinking along the edge of the road, dashing forward to pluck up a piece of cutlery or a crystal vase before sprinting out of sight. I thought of the crows back home, picking at the carcass of a dead bull.

The success of the urchins encouraged the adults. The crowd grew, creating a perimeter perhaps fifteen meters off. Every time a boy's raid went unpunished, the crowd inched forward. As the mass of locals grew to the hundreds, the air buzzed with hostility. People began muttering and shouting insults when Kufi stepped outside. When he dragged out a case of cognac, a collective sigh of wonder arose from the crowd. Someone threw a rock, which thumped off Kufi's shoulder. He winced and turned back inside. I called for Frank, but got no response.

A young man rushed the pile of loot and grabbed the cognac. He dashed for the corner, but the crowd enveloped him, and a fight ensued. Just as this fracas played itself out, the warlord returned to the street, slump shouldered, with a canvas sack the size of a grocery bag.

Another rock hit him in the center of the chest, and he looked out at the massed citizens, his one-time subjects, with tears in his eyes. He untied the top of the bag, and dumped a pile of diamonds at his feet. The crowd roared as one, and fell upon him in a crush of grabbing hands.

The wave of people poured over Kufi, kicking and pummeling him with rocks. He had no fight in him. His body lay motionless in a slick of blood.

The crowd stormed the hotel.

I fled upstairs, calling for Frank as I ran.

The whores I had thought long gone rushed down the hallways, throwing clothes into shoulder bags, their teasing smiles replaced by grim masks of fear. Below us, glass crashed and wood splintered. A whiff of fire seared my nostrils. I caught sight of the hung-over girl from earlier that morning, and had a flash of panic. I had not yet seen Nadine. I grabbed the prostitute by the arm. She struggled and clawed at me.

"Have you seen the girl with golden eyes?" I asked.

"She has gone to the hospital. Let me go!"

I squeezed her arm tighter and glared. "Which hospital?" I heard the crackle of spreading flames and gunfire, the clattering conversation of death. Someone screamed.

The whore kicked me in the crotch, and I hit the floor. She stood over me. "What is wrong with you, chasing a girl at a time like this?!"

"I wanted to say thank you," I gasped.

The whore screamed and booted me in the side. She burst into a nearby room and jumped out the window. Damaged and endangered as I was, I admired her dramatic flair.

I looked up to see Frank standing over me. "You make friends everywhere you go," he said.

"This plan has gone awry," I croaked.

Frank shrugged. "I've seen worse."

He helped me to my feet, and we left through the window the woman used. Once again, no one paid the slightest attention to our departure. The mob seethed around the hotel entrance, locked in an orgy of greed. Despite the fact that some young men had armed themselves and were shooting anyone who attempted to enter the lobby, wave after wave of people launched themselves into the breach in the desperate hope of striking it rich. Bodies lay all around.

I threw an arm over Frank's shoulder. "Well, partner, shall we go find this Chiora fellow?"

"Fuck yeah."

"We could just walk away," I said, thinking of the ranch in Texas, "leave the Congo, and start a whole new life."

"Nah. That asshole Chiora turned Zhou on us. We're gonna find him, and I'm gonna make what happened to Kufi look like a fucking birthday party."

I would like to say that I at least hesitated to point Frank toward yet-another enemy. But after the day of gunfire, blood and screams, I felt my dreams of the bucolic life could wait while my partner and I enjoyed one more adventure.

I grinned and clapped Frank on the back. "Kinshasa it is, then. We can catch up with Sheppard, and finish things with Chiora."

I gave no more thought to what came next.

Frank and I walked away as the building consumed itself. Black smoke billowed into the sky. Rounds cooked off inside, crackling like firecrackers and punctuated by the deeper clap of grenades.

Several blocks from the hotel, we came across an old taxi driver sitting in his scrap heap of a car, listening to a soccer match. Shouting over the scratchy, blaring speakers, I negotiated a ride to the airport.

We made our way to the bleak terminal unmolested. The dusty, garbage-strewn departures area of the building hadn't been updated since the 1950s. It was unlit and nearly void of people, aside from a few bored soldiers and a gaggle of haggard-looking Americans in safari pants.

None of the ticket counters were staffed, but I located a UN official (a surprisingly tiny and brisk Nepalese fellow) in a dark corner, and I bribed our way onto a Doctors Without Borders flight to Kinshasa. After just an hour or so of watching a UN freight plane disgorge an enormous helicopter out of its hold, we walked across the dusty runway and onto an incongruously new Bombardier turbo prop, in the company of the khaki clad, shell-shocked American physicians.

Frank and I, still riding the high of the battle, were amused to find ourselves sitting in the midst of earnest physicians, bristling as we were with instruments of death and reeking of blood and cordite. Many a furtive glance was cast in our direction. I gave them each a polite nod.

Frank glared at a wiry blond lady. "The fuck you lookin' at?"

After that, the only sound was the engine roar as our plane made its shuddering mad dash for the sky.

PART 3

CHAPTER 28

NDJILI AIRPORT IN Kinshasa is the waiting room for hell. Shockingly hot and painted in the horror-show pink of the Congo's TIGO telecom company, it teems with lost, wild-eyed souls being herded to and fro by cruel imps sowing fear and confusion. Endless lines lead nowhere. Piles of suitcases are whisked off to warehouses, where contents are sorted and then sold in the markets by beefy, big-bosomed women known as Heavy Sisters. The arrival hall rings with panicked cries for help in French, Lingala, English, and Swahili. Documents disappear for examination, never to return. The air is soupy with the stench of anxious sweat, fried food, and sewage.

Its confounding horrors struck me as a fitting place for the next phase of our so-called mission.

Frank and I grabbed our bags straight from the belly of the plane and pushed through the shouting crowd, not far behind the American doctors from our flight. The head of the group was an irritatingly handsome man from Palo Alto who spoke French with a snooty accent and wore his linen shirt unbuttoned to the last rib.

"Stay quiet and do as I say," he told his group. "I'll handle this."

The underpaid and gleefully corrupt Congolese airport workers must have smelled the American dollars, and they began to descend from all directions. The first guard to reach them barked in Lingala at the man's face, demanding their passports. He responded to the doctor's unctuous greeting by ordering his flunkies to search the group's bags.

The Californian grew impatient. He grabbed the guard's shoulder and was quickly hustled into a side room, leaving his associates teary-eyed and helpless. All of this took less than a minute.

Frank and I kept moving past the frightened doctors, muscling easily through the crowd. Few officials approached us, and those who did were turned away with a whispered promise of violence or the application of a few gold pieces.

They asked for our papers at the final checkpoint. We presented a quarter-ounce Krugerrand instead. There followed a veritable flurry of stamping, and we stepped out into the rank air of Kinshasa.

Our direct transit through the airport took perhaps five minutes, though it felt like hours. Most people, I was told, didn't get through the maze in less than three hours, and generally they escaped unencumbered by their luggage.

As the hawkers and cab drivers thronged around us, offering everything from transportation to bubblegum to heroin, I looked back through the grimy terminal windows to see if the doctors were making progress. I couldn't see them, and suspected their good intentions were of no help there.

Kinshasa, a city of some nine million souls, made Kisangani seem like a mere hamlet by comparison. The scope and intensity of it assaulted my senses. While I gaped at the thronging mass of people, Frank engaged the services of a surprisingly dapper cab driver. The young man wore pointy-toed lavender slippers, the most impractical shoes I could imagine in that environment. He also wore gold-framed glasses with oversized, round lenses, and kept an elaborate Meerschaum pipe clenched in his teeth. These accents set off the rest of his outfit—high-waisted jeans printed in a fleur-de-lis pattern and carefully cuffed, and a billowy, purple silk shirt buttoned to the neck. His hair was cropped tight, with patterns shaved into the sides like miniature crop circles. He was the only man on the street who managed to avoid sweating in the stunning heat.

"I'm The Colonel," he said in English, shaking my hand languidly.

"Colonel of what?" I asked, more bluntly than I intended.

The driver shrugged gracefully. "Just the Colonel."

"I don't give a shit if you're the president," Frank said. "Where's your fucking car?"

We had decided on a direct approach with Sheppard. We wouldn't be able to outmaneuver him and all of his men in their city, and so we might as well throw ourselves on his mercy—or fight him—right up front.

The dapper Congolese fellow sashayed over to a venerable Russian car, a Lada that reminded me of a pop can repeatedly crushed and painstakingly pulled back into shape. He didn't offer to carry our bags, and he didn't hold the door open for us. I had to admire his bravado.

"Is it worth it?" I asked the cab driver as we got in. "All the effort you put into your getup?"

The Colonel sighed. "I'm a *sapeur*. This is more than fashion. It's an act of rebellion."

Frank said, "Bullets would be cheaper."

"I don't expect you to understand."

"Then you won't be disappointed," I said. "But please, I'm curious. What is a *sapeur*?"

"It stands for *Société des Ambianceurs et des Personnes Élégantes*," he said.

"So," I said, confounded by the translation, "It's a club for men who dress nice?"

"Fairies," Frank said, sneering.

The Colonel rolled his eyes. "We dress, *and act*, like gentlemen at all times."

I wanted to know more, but Frank had that look that threatened violence if we didn't start moving. I gave Sheppard's last known address to the Colonel. It was still written on the scrap of paper our brother in arms gave me when he invited me to drop by for beers my first week in the Congo.

The Colonel's eyebrows went up when he saw what was written. "Your friend is rich."

"His employer is, yes." Frank and I laughed at the realization our gunnery sergeant had gotten rich. Then again, we were two grunts walking around with a bag of gold and diamonds.

Crushed into the back of the spluttering little car, I quickly lost my bearings in the chaos of Kinshasa. I had never been there before, having slipped into the Congo overland via Uganda three years ago. Since then, Zhou had kept us busy in the mining regions of the east, while Sheppard and his crew handled things in Kinshasa. I couldn't reconcile what I saw here with the Congo I knew. Here, paved roads were jammed with traffic, skyscrapers strained toward the sky, and an endless parade of shops offered imported goods from all over the world. In a country where most people had nothing, everything was available in Kinshasa.

The idea of searching for Chiora in that mess made my head swim. What if Chiora or Zhou sent a team after us? How would we spot our enemies amongst this crush of humanity? A dull pressure built at my temples. I could only hope Sheppard had indeed been turned, and we could work with him to decide what to do next.

The Colonel narrated our ride for us in his lazy drawl. He pointed out the long central arterial of the city, The Thirtieth of June Boulevard, which he described as "the longest independence avenue in Africa." We passed the house where post-independence leader Patrice Lumumba ran the government for a short time before being, as The

Colonel described it, "assassinated by the Americans." He then directed our attention to the crumbling Twentieth of May stadium that had hosted the 1974 "Rumble in the Jungle" boxing match between Muhammad Ali and George Foreman.

"You guys ever give stuff a real name, or you just always go with a date?" Frank asked.

The colonel remained unflappable, as though his snappy clothes protected him from insults as well as the grubbiness and disorder all around him. He smiled. "They want people to remember the important moments in our history."

"How's that working out?" Frank said.

The Colonel tipped his head to the side, thoughtful. *"Comme ci, comme ça."*

My head ached. Each city block assaulted my nostrils with the miasma of car exhaust, ripe garbage, fish, rotten meat, urine, and excrement. Car horns blared, and every time traffic bogged down and stopped, a horde of people surrounded the car, begging or trying to sell us Chiclets, lottery tickets, pirated CDs, and unnamable snacks. They thrust grubby hands into the car, into our faces, forcing us to roll the windows up almost completely. Then they shouted at us in a patois of half a dozen languages while we sweltered in the close quarters.

I kept my hands on my pistols, in case one of them turned out to be a bounty hunter.

My breath went shallow. I felt as though the car were shrinking, crushed under the swarming mass of bodies outside.

"Colonel, can you tell these people to step away?" I said as we languished at an intersection.

"I can tell them to fly to the moon," The Colonel said, his calm smile reflecting in the rearview mirror. "I can threaten to beat them or run them over with my car. But they will not stop asking for help. You are white, and therefore rich, and therefore an opportunity that must be exploited." Even his speech was stylish. I liked him.

Frank said, "Where are the whores?"

The Colonel's mouth turned down at the corners. "Offer any one of these people twenty dollars. You will have your whore."

Frank laughed uproariously at this. "I like Kinshasa."

I said, "I think that's a rather unfair statement about your countrymen, Colonel."

He shook his head, still respectful but no longer smiling. "I think you don't know what it's like to be poor in Kinshasa," he said. "There is no hope here. Government officials line their own pockets. Soldiers and police must steal to survive. The schools are abandoned. The hospitals are houses of death. Would you not sell whatever you have?"

We sat in silence as he drove for a few minutes. The Colonel finally turned to me, smiling. "Would you like some music?"

Without waiting for an answer, he punched a button and the car filled with lilting, joyful guitar music. He told us it was the local star named Werrason, and I was confounded anew. The music had nothing to do with the city, which had nothing to do with the rest of the country, which had nothing to do with me.

A wave of something like homesickness washed over me. Sweat stung my eyes. I flinched at the sound of gunfire. A woman screamed. The crowds swirled and pressed around us. I looked over to see Frank smiling.

CHAPTER 29

MY DISORIENTATION BECAME complete when we approached the walled neighborhood of The Company's compound. Armed guards stepped in front of us, but they relaxed when we flashed our Company credentials. When we pressed a wad of US dollars into their hands, they smiled and waved us through a cast-iron gate and into an exclusive riverfront community.

We rolled past curving cul-de-sacs that led to large houses, well-tended gardens, and shiny new cars parked in driveways. It could have all been lifted from a high-end Houston suburb. The house The Colonel stopped in front of had beige stucco walls, a tile roof, and a border of flowering plants.

The only reminders that we were in the Congo were the uneven line of bullet holes pocking the stucco of the garage wall, the heavy front door kicked off its hinges, and what looked like a smear of blood on the door frame.

My guts roiled as I scanned the area for Chiora's men or Zhou's assassins.

Frank drew a deep breath and released it slowly. "This is fucking interesting."

The Colonel took our cash and drove away quickly, his studied cool forgotten in his haste.

We quickly checked the grounds, which were empty, hid our bags in the garden, and approached the house with guns drawn.

Frank knocked on the unhinged door on our way into the marble floored entryway. "At ease, motherfuckers. Anybody home?"

There was no response. Everything was perfectly in order, but slightly askew. We found the living room spotless and arranged for entertaining friends, if you overlooked the slashed-open couch, the bullet holes in the TV, and the coffee table spider-webbed with cracks leading in to the blood-stained impact point of someone's skull.

The entire house presented the same conundrum, as though someone went to great lengths to put everything back where it belonged, but made no effort to mask the evidence of a terrible battle. We cleared the first floor and made our way up the stairs. We found bloodstains scrubbed inexpertly from the carpet just below an oak handrail gouged by a machete blade. On the upper landing, near a vent blowing icy cool air, I found the overlooked tip of a white man's finger, covered by a swarm of tiny black ants.

"Things ended poorly for our associates," I said.

"No shit."

We went room to room, finding neither friend nor foe. In what we thought was a closet, we discovered a bank of video monitors, showing live feeds from every corner of the property and every room of the house. All was silent and still.

In the master bedroom, which featured the largest bed I had ever seen, we found a leather cigar case full of Vegas Robainas from Cuba, with which Sheppard always traveled.

I picked up the cigars. "This was Sheppard's room."

"You're a real Sherlock-fucking-Holmes today." Frank snatched the cigars out of my hand, fumbling awkwardly as he tried to shove them in his vest pocket, his concern about Sheppard rendering him clumsy. I couldn't recall ever seeing him so anxious.

"There were—what—eight Company men here? Unless Chiora had sixty or seventy well-trained and heavily armed soldiers, there's no way they should have taken it."

"They woulda had to shell the place," Frank agreed.

"But this assault was all room to room." I studied the broken leg on the bedside table.

"They were inside the compound before the fighting started."

"Even though there are cameras all over the yard, and likely a twenty-four hour watch in place."

Frank chuckled. "Fuck me. An inside job."

We were wrapping our minds around the implications of this when we heard the soft shuffle of footsteps downstairs. We slipped down to the security center at the end of the hall, and discovered that the intruder was a rotund cleaning woman. She rooted around in the closet, collecting her bucket, mop, and basket of supplies.

Here, then, was the answer to the house's tidiness.

We silently trailed the woman to the recreation room at the far end of the house. She dropped to her knees with a heavy sigh and began to scrub gore from the floor grout between a pinball machine and a venerable old Pac-Man video game. Both machines had been riddled by bullets.

On her knees, with her massive rump in the air, she hummed as she worked. Frank and I watched her for a while, mesmerized, I suppose, by the metronomic sway of her titanic buttocks in a lemon yellow skirt. Finally, Frank cocked his pistol.

"Ay!" The woman shrieked, throwing her hands in the air and spinning around, still on her knees, to face us.

"Who the fuck are you?" Frank asked.

The woman gaped at us, wild-eyed and uncomprehending.

"What are you doing here?" I tried French.

"I am cleaning. Obviously." Despite her fear, there was still some pepper in her.

"Mopping up blood," I said. "Did it occur to you to wonder why there's so much blood to clean?"

She rose slowly to her feet and put her hands on her hips. "I was told not to ask questions. So I don't ask."

"Men died here."

"Men die all the time. It is what they do." She knotted the rag in her hands. "And women clean their messes."

I explained all this to Frank.

"When did the shit go down?" he asked.

The woman shrugged when I asked, avoiding my gaze. "Maybe two days ago," she said. She pointed her rag at us then. "Do you work for The Company?"

I acknowledged that we did.

"So you can tell the big boss I expect extra money for the extra work."

"For all he knows, you aided the attackers," I pointed out. "Perhaps you should be glad you aren't killed for being a spy."

"How dare you accuse me!" she said, pretending at outrage.

"How dare you use the death of our friends as an excuse to demand a raise," I said.

"These men were no friends to anyone."

"They would disagree," I said.

"And can you prove you have a right to be here?" She waved the rag in my face. "Perhaps you are the enemy."

"Hey!" Frank said to me. "Unless this bitch has something to tell us, I'm gonna put a bullet in her head."

The woman needed no translation to understand Frank's intent. Her defiance gave way to dull-eyed sullenness, a mask that contained resignation and disgust in equal measure.

"You are bad men," she said.

"We're men like any other," I said. "And if you help us, no harm will come to you."

"And if I don't?"

"Men aren't the only ones who die. Now, tell us everything you saw and heard in the weeks before our associates disappeared."

"I saw men consume many bottles of beer, and I saw men watching naked ladies doing unspeakable things on the television. I saw these men living like pigs. Smoking, drinking, and carrying on terribly."

"You describe soldiers taking their leisure," I said. "I assume that there were always a few men guarding the facility?"

"Yes. One outside by the gate and one by the river. Another watching the computers."

I explained all this to Frank. He had me ask the woman exactly what state the house was in when she found it emptied of men.

The woman looked everywhere but at me, twisting the rag in her hands. "I found a big mess. A lot of blood and broken things. I think these men were punished by God Almighty for their sins."

"As you will be," I said, glowering at her, "sooner rather than later if you keep talking about God instead of telling me what happened. Were there any bodies?"

She hesitated a moment, eyes darting. "I told you," she finally said. "There was blood and broken furniture. There were bullet holes."

"Did you call the authorities?"

This made her chuckle. "Do I look so foolish to you?"

"That's not an answer." Her constant tugging and kneading at the rag grated on my nerves. Just as I thought this, Frank snatched it out of her hands and threw it behind the pinball machine.

Tears welled in the woman's eyes. "It is possible that one man lived."

"Possible?" I asked.

Her gaze dropped to the floor. "I heard a sound in the garden. Someone whispering."

"Who was it?"

"I would like to go home now."

"You work for The Company, remember? We will tell you when you are done. Did you see the man in the garden? Did you help him?"

"He is not here."

"You're skilled at not answering." To Frank I said, "There was a survivor, but she won't tell me who it was or where he is now."

"Tell her to make us some lunch," Frank said.

I automatically opened my mouth to translate this, but hesitated. I turned back to Frank. "I don't believe that will help us divine the man's identity or his whereabouts."

"I'm fucking hungry."

When informed of our desire for a midday meal, the woman mustered a bit of her former resistance. "I am paid to clean."

"Today you cook. I assume there's food in the larder, or did you steal that after you helped our enemies escape?"

She brushed by me, frowning. "I am not a thief."

We followed the woman down to the kitchen and sat at the bar as she prepared us a perfunctory meal of fried river fish and potatoes. While she banged pots around, I looked out the windows. The broad lawn sloped down to the river. The Congo was so wide here that the other bank was lost in the distance. At the water's edge, a tall, gated fence topped with razor wire separated the property from a long dock.

The whole situation confounded me. If Sheppard was helping Chiora, who would attack the house? Who could bring this vengeance down upon the members of

The Company? The cleaning woman had a key, which made her what the TV detectives call a prime suspect. Her unwillingness to talk about the possible survivor put her in an even worse light.

Still, I had little stomach for killing her. It was too easy to picture her surrounded by children and grandchildren, sharing hugs and sage advice.

Frank, on the other hand, might murder the woman for the simple crime of having born witness to our presence.

The food she set before us was quite satisfying, despite the lack of care or seasoning with which it was prepared. Weeks of MREs and *fufu* allow a man to appreciate life's small comforts.

Afterward, belching palm oil and sipping on a Primus, I picked up the theme of the wounded man in the garden, asking her what she said to him.

The woman's resistance abandoned her at last, and there was a clear plea for mercy in her eyes. "It was Mister Sheppard," she whispered.

Frank recognized the name, and his gaze snapped to the woman. "Sheppard made it?" he asked me through clenched teeth.

I asked about Sheppard's fate, but the woman didn't answer for some time. She stared out the window, the picture of dejection. Frank flexed his hands and glared.

I said, "Miss, you need to answer our questions if there's to be any hope for you."

She wiped away a tear. "He was the only good man here."

"That may or may not be the case," I said, "but I won't be able to determine that unless you tell me what happened after you found him."

"He didn't drink, and he didn't watch the naked women. He spoke to me kindly."

I said, "Mister Sheppard was a particular friend of ours as well. Can you tell us anything else that might help us know what became of him?"

Her glare was like ice. "I don't believe he would be friends with people like you."

Heat rose to my face. "You should not be so quick to antagonize us."

Frank clapped his hands in front of her face, loud as a gunshot. "Where. Is. Sheppard?"

When I translated, the woman shook her head. "You will kill him."

"Miss, I'm not asking you to trust me. But you need to work with us, or things will go poorly for you."

She turned her chin up. "Why should I believe anything such a one as you would say?"

"Because I'm telling you the goddamn truth!"

Frank tapped me on the shoulder. "I know just enough to be really pissed off, Stan."

There was nothing for it. I told him the woman wouldn't cooperate.

Frank smiled, putting a hand on her shoulder. "Okay," he said. He punched her in the belly so hard it threw her back against the cupboards. She collapsed and lay on the floor, gasping for breath. When she finally gained her feet again, she stared at us with the dead-eyed fury of the doomed.

Even Frank usually didn't go for inflicting violence on unarmed women. I felt the ghost of her pain in my own stomach.

I encouraged her again to tell us where Sheppard was, and ensured her that no further harm would come to her or to Sheppard if she did as she was told.

At first I wasn't sure she heard me, but then she released a moaning sigh. "Mama Yemo."

"Who is Mama Yemo?" I asked.

"It is the hospital, also called Kinshasa General," she said. "I took him there. If he lives, that's where you will find him."

The woman closed her eyes and bowed her head, entirely convinced she was about to meet her maker. I was duly impressed with how calmly she confronted it. Frank, of course, longed to put a bullet in her head, but I convinced him that she was no enemy to us.

As I followed him out of the broken house, I turned to look back at the cleaning lady. She sat there in her yellow skirt, rocking gently back and forth and staring out at the river. I wondered what she saw there.

CHAPTER 30

MAMA YEMO HOSPITAL sat in the northeast part of Kinshasa, near the edge of the city center. A low-lying structure of crumbling cement, it was ringed by a tall iron fence that appeared more substantial than the hospital itself.

As we approached, Frank put a hand on my chest. "You sure we want to go in there?"

"Is Chiora still in Kinshasa, or is he already out in the bush?"

"How the fuck should I know?"

"I rest my case." I patted Frank's shoulder and headed toward the gate. "Intel, Frank. The difference between attack and defense."

"Fuck you," Frank said, but wearily.

We cut in front of a long line of people entering the grounds, and approached two big fellows in beige uniforms who carried well-worn nightsticks. Their presence inside the heavy gates, and the bullying stares they directed at the equally long line of people leaving the facility, made me wonder if we had arrived at the prison in error. The only difference was the faded Kinshasa General Hospital sign above the doors.

I asked the guards, in French, "Do you need to see our papers?"

The men shook their heads curtly, their eyes still fixed on the flow of locals leaving the hospital.

As Frank and I pushed in through the gate, a stick-thin, elderly gentleman who had been on the other side of the fence attempted to slip out, keeping our bulky forms between him and the guards. The sentries saw him and before I could react, they grabbed the codger. They wrenched open his shirt, popping off all the buttons to reveal a foot-long line of sutures across his flabby abdomen. A great deal of shouting ensued, with numerous bystanders seeming to come to the old man's defense. They all spoke at once, and I couldn't make out their words, but they seemed to be attempting to shame the guards. The elderly patient was slapped around a bit as he tried to push past the gatekeepers, but at least they didn't produce their truncheons. Finally, the downcast patient shuffled back into the wards.

"Why can't he leave?" I asked a woman who witnessed the interaction.

"Those who don't pay don't leave."

Frank smiled when I explained this to him. "How fucked up is that?"

His smile grated on me. "If they produced their night sticks, I would have aerated their skulls for them."

"Saint Stanley rides again."

We crossed an expanse of patchy lawns, where white cattle egrets plucked at drifts of garbage in search of a morsel. Bright clothes hung out to dry between the bushes. Groups of women hustled back and forth, carrying food in battered metal containers for their loved ones inside.

Little of the late afternoon light made it to the crowded corridors. I saw almost nothing that looked like medical equipment. Doors buckled and splintered in the damp heat, and the walls were smeared and stained with generations of God knows what manner of filth. The windows had no screens, and the air was full of mosquitoes.

We pushed through a chaotic mass of civilians, soldiers, men, and women – the healthy and the clearly dying, all adrift in that semi-darkness, as lost as we were.

I struggled to breathe air thick with a stench that seared the nostrils, yet smelled sickly sweet. Infection. The smell of death.

I caught sight of Frank dipping into his bag of pills.

After several fruitless attempts to find medical staff, we went room by room, blindly calling Sheppard's name. I saw no logic to the way in which patients were bunched together. AIDS patients were shoulder-to-shoulder with mothers cradling newborns. Amputees moaned alongside bone-thin, yellow-eyed wraiths.

Frank's potions soon had him chuckling at the nightmares unfolding before our eyes, while I stumbled headlong from ward to ward in a rising panic.

Frank tugged on my sleeve. "What are you moaning about?"

"I wasn't making any sound."

"Uuuuuunh. Oooooh," he said. "Like a fucking ghost."

"I'm fine." My breathing came in shallow sips. My eyes prickled with tears.

"Didn't ask how you were, fucknuts. I asked why you were moaning like you were gut shot."

I clamped my mouth shut, and pushed deeper into that dark hell.

We found Sheppard at last in a nameless ward full of clamoring sickness. It was a stinking, hopeless room just like all the others, but for the presence of a bullet-riddled white man staring at the ceiling.

He squinted at us and smiled. "Aw, shit. I'm well and truly fucked at last."

The nausea I had been fighting nearly overcame me. Not only because of Sheppard's seeping bandages and the bad-meat stink of him, but because it was so clear that he was dying.

The human wreckage before me had once been a brick of a soldier, a compact and highly efficient killing machine. He wasn't tall, perhaps only five feet eight inches in height, but so heavily muscled and broad-chested that until I stood next to him I assumed he was much bigger.

His deep-set blue eyes and sharp features gave him a hawkish appearance. He watched us intently as Frank and I wheeled the dozen or so other protesting patients into the hallway. When the room was empty but for Sheppard, I zip-tied the door shut. Frank took up position four yards from the foot of his bed, and I stood at the same distance to the right of Sheppard's head, my gun trained on his right ear, which was cauliflowered from years of wrestling and martial arts.

Despite his injuries, Sheppard was still one of the most efficient killers I had ever known. He was the kind of man who really could, as the saying goes, kill somebody with just his thumb. Until he drew his last breath, we had to consider him a threat.

Mike smiled at us. "Do I smell that bad? Come over and talk to me."

Frank shook his head. "You're not pulling any fucking Wang Chung bullshit on us, you piece of shit."

Sheppard tried to laugh, but this made him cough weakly, his eyes screwed shut against the pain. He spent some time panting before he could speak again. "Wang Chung," he said between labored breaths, "is a band from the eighties, you stupid wop."

"Under the circumstances," I said, "we're not taking any chances."

Mike pulled the stained sheet down off his chest, revealing a veritable quilt of crudely taped bandages, all soaked with brownish gore. These he pulled off, one by one, to reveal inexpertly stitched, angry red bullet holes, swollen until the puckered skin nearly covered the black cords. "This is what terminal infection looks like, men."

Frank approached him then, and poked one of the wounds. Sheppard winced, but made no sound. Cloudy serum oozed out. Frank nodded, wiped his hand on the sheets, and produced the cigar case we found back at the river house.

I holstered my weapon and dragged two chairs over to Sheppard's bed. "You got bigger issues than infection."

Sheppard smiled, but there was something sad in his eyes. "They didn't fix anything. Didn't dig out the bullets. Just sewed me up. Used a fucking local anesthetic, too. Killing me is gonna be the easiest thing you've done in a while."

My throat constricted, and I didn't trust myself to speak.

Frank, on the other hand, kept up his aggressive façade. "Talk to us, asshole."

Sheppard opened the cigar case and shared the smokes around. I'm not generally one for cigars, but to kill the smells in that hospital I would have gladly puffed on my own burning socks.

Frank produced his lighter and lit Sheppard's cigar for him, handing it back to our old gunny with care that belied his fierce expression.

Sheppard took his first appreciative drags. "Funny how shit works out."

"A fuckin' laugh riot," Frank said.

"This strikes me as more of a tragedy," I said.

It wasn't meant as a joke, but Sheppard and Frank laughed.

Sheppard winced, his laughter cut short. "Chiora got the jump on me. Tactically and psychologically."

Frank rolled his eyes, pretending to be unimpressed.

I said, "That's no mean feat."

Sheppard said, "Day after I got the order to take him down – this was four days ago – he pulled up a seat at my table at the Intercon Hotel. Bunch of heavies with him. Could've taken me out right there, or marched me down an alley and shot me."

"Why didn't he?" I asked.

"He wanted me to work for him." Sheppard chuckled. "He said he needed security for his cooperative diamond mine, which they were taking over from some other outfit. He said he was going to 'subvert the economic paradigm in Africa.' Who says shit like that, right?"

"Stan does," Frank said.

Sheppard grinned. "Goddamn. That's right. Mullens, you and Chiora will get along like a house on fire."

I couldn't tell if this was a compliment or an insult. I said, "I believe circumstances will quash any friendly feelings we might've had for each other."

"I thought so, too," Sheppard said. "But I took to the guy instantly."

Frank pointed to Sheppard's ruined body. "Look at you now."

"Things didn't go according to plan," Sheppard said. "That first day, Chiora worked his way through what had to be a half rack of Primus, talking about how he was going to share the profits equally with everyone who worked with him, and how we would be a model for the whole continent."

"He say anything about the tech he stole from Zhou?" Frank said.

"He said the mine would be five times as efficient as existing operations," Sheppard said. "No mention of tech."

"Zhou said he made off with something extremely valuable," I said.

Sheppard ignored me. "By the time Chiora staggered out of the bar, I was already convinced. The guy is amazing, like a preacher or something. He got me all revved up to be a part of something…I don't know…bigger than myself. I mean shit, I'm forty years old. It's not like I can remain combat effective forever. And frankly, private security work is for assholes. No offense, guys."

"None taken," I said. "But what went wrong?" The air was blue with cigar smoke. I had a knot of nicotine in my chest that felt like panic, or hope.

Sheppard took a long pull on his cigar and blew more smoke at the ceiling. "I took him downtown, walked him through all the bureaucratic shit pretty quick by making it sound like the mine was The Company's business. I bribed the guys that needed bribing and applied necessary force to the ones too stupid to take the money.

"I thought that would be the tough part, but then Chiora told me my crew couldn't be trusted; he said one of my own guys told him how to find me, originally. He couldn't afford to have Zhou's men tracking us, so they would have to be disarmed."

Frank spit on the floor. "You had your whole team whacked?"

Sheppard shook his head. "He told me he would commandeer our safe house and get rid of all the weapons and comms, so we could get out of Kinshasa clean, but he told me he would leave them alive."

"He promise you a fucking unicorn, too?" Frank said.

Sheppard turned to me. "Chiora said he would pick me up at the river gate to our compound the next morning, and we would head to the airport while his men locked down the safe house."

"To go where?" I asked, thrilling at the idea we could finally run Chiora to ground.

"The Kasai River, west of Tshikapa."

My enthusiasm crashed around me. "That's no information at all," I said. "The entire area is laced with tributaries."

"Encyclopedia Stan strikes again," Frank said.

Sheppard continued talking to me. "He said west. Not northwest or southwest. He said it was only a few days walk from Tshikapa."

"But you ain't gonna see this mine now, huh?" Frank said, and his voice was brittle with rage and heartbreak.

Sheppard shook his head. "When I opened the gate, Chiora's men came through with their weapons locked and loaded. I'm pretty sure it was Chiora himself who cracked me over the head with his pistol and knocked me out cold."

"You got fucked," Frank said.

"Damn it!" I said, much louder than I intended. "Unless you have any more tactical analysis, Frank, I would like to hear how this ended."

Frank held up his hands. "Well, excuse the fuck outta me."

Sheppard shifted in his bed, gasping at the pain. "I woke up to a fully engaged battle in the house. I drew my weapon and ran in. A dozen of Chiora's men lay dead outside the front door and in the entryway. My team was pretty much finished, but I went in, hoping to kill Chiora. I took out five men before they put a few rounds in me.

Sheppard paused, smiling. "You know, until then I'd never been shot. Not in Iraq, not in Afghanistan, not even here."

"Hurts like a bitch," Frank said, more to himself than us.

"Not at first. I got out of the house and found Chiora by the river. He squealed at the sight of me, like he'd been shot, and screamed for his men to stand down. They got a few more rounds into my back before they followed orders." Sheppard waved his hand over his ruined body. "That rendered me ineffective."

Sheppard made a fine show of soldierly discipline, even as his body rotted. But tears welled in his eyes.

I nodded for him to continue, not trusting myself to speak through the ache in my throat.

"I was still standing. I wanted to shoot Chiora in the face, but when I tried to lift my arm to fire, it just hung there, dripping blood. Next thing I knew I was on the ground."

"Boo hoo," Frank said, still pretending at disdain despite the tears in his eyes.

Sheppard didn't even glance at him. "Chiora said, 'Ah, Michael, I am sorry! So sorry!' I wanted to spit in his face, but all I did was drool blood. I passed out. Next thing I knew, Marie had me in a car heading for this shithole."

"Did you get any other intel?" I asked. "Geographical coordinates of the mine?"

Sheppard smiled. "No, Mullens, he didn't lay out his whole evil plan while I bled out in front of him. He cried and wrung his hands."

"Is he still in Kinshasa?"

"Negative," Sheppard said. "They had a charter flight out that morning."

"What a fuckup," Frank said.

Sheppard nodded. "That about sums it up."

The smoke, combined with Sheppard's story, had my heart thrumming in my chest. "I don't think it's so simple," I said, my voice rushing out of me as I gestured with my cigar. "Chiora sacrificed Sheppard's men, true, but we can all agree they were extensions of a greater evil. They were killed to protect Sheppard and the rest of the cooperative members. Shep didn't knowingly set up his men for death, either. The only one he intentionally betrayed was Zhou. I, for one, cannot find fault with that."

I smiled, pleased to have proven Sheppard's innocence and to have established his friend, my supposed enemy, worthy of his trust.

"Shut the fuck up," Frank said.

"You think too much, Mullens," Sheppard said, not unkindly.

"I'm trying to shed light on a dark situation," I said. My mind raced with the implications. Sheppard's willingness to trust Chiora put the man in a new light for me. Everyone else we met along our journey painted Chiora in all the colors of myth. What Sheppard described, though, made him sound like someone worth talking to rather than executing. To join forces with him might even offer a new alternative to the chaos of mercenary work, or the drudgery of civilian life.

Both men looked at me like I was the only fool in the room.

With nothing more to say, and Sheppard well on his way to death without our help, Frank and I stood up to leave.

Sheppard said, 'You men got anything that'll move things along for me here?'

Frank produced a single pill from the depths of his supply and put it in Sheppard's hand. "Took it off a psycho missionary upriver. Cyanide. Won't be pretty." He dug around in his pack again and produced four more pills. "Take these first. When you feel good, take the other one."

"Thanks," Sheppard said. Then, casually, "You know Zhou ordered me to take you out, right?"

"We heard some rumblings to that effect," I said.

Frank spit at his feet, but said nothing.

Sheppard nodded, "Chiora did you a favor by taking out my men, but Zhou will send more. You can consider your employment with him terminated."

"No shit," Frank said through clenched teeth.

"Which means," Sheppard said, turning to me, "you don't have to take down Chiora."

"Thanks for the advice, Dad." Frank pulled out his knife and cut the zip-tie on the door. "But we want to do it." A crowd parted as the door swung open, and Frank stalked out of the room.

"Mullens," Sheppard said, "you're a smart guy. Just get the fuck out of here."

"Someone has to point Frank in the right direction," I said.

"Is that what you've been doing all these years?"

The question hit like a body blow. "Why would I still be here, if not to help Frank?"

Sheppard took another long drag on his cigar, his sharp gaze tinged with pity. "Maybe you want to be. Or maybe you're just scared."

"Of what?" The nicotine thrummed in my blood, and my mouth went dry.

"You tell me."

I changed the subject. "I'll get your friend Chiora out of harm's way. I promise." If I couldn't hide from myself any longer, I could at least cast myself as the hero one more time.

Sheppard nodded. "I appreciate that, Mullens, but you can't even save yourself. How are you going to help Chiora?"

"No idea," I said, "but I'd like to try."

Sheppard smiled. "You're a fine soldier, Mullens."

"Thank you, sir." I saluted with a trembling hand and walked out.

I made the mistake of turning back at the doorway to see my C.O. alone in the smoke, with his filthy wounds and a handful of pills. Another friend I couldn't save.

The low moan escaping from me as I turned away was indistinguishable from the cries of the sick and the dying all around.

CHAPTER 31

THE TWIN-ENGINE PLANE bumped twice onto the weed-covered tarmac in Tshikapa and rolled to a stop next to the tin shed they called a terminal.

Frank and I had wasted no time getting out of Kinshasa. After a quiet and somber night at the Intercontinental hotel, re-organizing our gear and cleaning our weapons, we bribed our way onto the first flight of the morning. By midmorning we were approaching the city center of Tshikapa. Looking at the city, one would never know that countless diamonds worth millions of dollars pass through there every day.

It could have been a pleasant place, situated as it was at the confluence of two rivers, in the midst of gentle hills. There were enough trees to offer shade, but not so many as to create the oppressive jungles we had traveled through. Despite the advantages, though, Tshikapa was just another Congolese city full of brick shacks, cratered dirt roads, and European buildings from the colonial era sinking slowly back into the rust-colored earth.

The burning midday sun kept most folks off the street, but I kept my guard up all the same, scanning for threats, and letting my hand drift to my pistol whenever I saw someone loitering in a dark doorway.

A figure rushed out from an alley, and I nearly shot him before realizing it was a little boy, wearing nothing but a blue sweater and chasing the spoke-less rim of a bicycle tire through the streets, his bare feet kicking up dust.

Frank chuckled. "I never took you for the baby-killer type."

"The stick looked like a weapon." My hand shook as I holstered my Glock.

"I'm pretty sure Zhou ain't sending a fucking midget to kill us."

"So you admit there's value in at least one of us remaining vigilant?"

"Fuck you, too."

At an unlit restaurant in a cave-like, colonial-era building, we stopped to consult our maps over Cokes and the greasiest French fries the world has ever known.

We narrowed down our search vector, ruling out the areas without any active mines, and looking for a spot in the midst of known kimberlite pipes. We finally identified an unclaimed area in the midst of several other mines, due west of Tshikapa. It seemed like the most promising place to find Chiora and his crew. We braced ourselves for days of reconnaissance as we scoured the area for our prey.

"We need to move out," I said. "If Zhou's men get there first, all of this will be for nothing."

Frank shook his head, chewing a huge glob of fries. "Once he finds out about Sheppard and the missing team, he'll send his assholes to Kinshasa first. By the time they figure out what happened and trace us or Chiora down here, we'll already have our guy."

"That's no reason to linger," I argued. "The sooner we're out of the Congo and beyond Zhou's reach, the better."

"You got a real bug up your ass about getting out of here all of a sudden."

"There are moments when a timely retreat is the key to victory."

Frank yawned. "Whatever."

Looking at him, his chair tipped back against the wall, guzzling Coke, I tried to convince myself he didn't give a damn whether he made it out of the Congo or not, and that he was no more suited for civilian life than me.

I told myself I'd done him no harm.

A grizzled and foul-smelling panhandler wandered in, leaning on a tall wooden staff and distracting me. He was so covered in red dust he appeared to be made of clay. He had an under thrust jaw, and his top two front teeth were missing, rendering him snaggle-toothed. Frank tried to intimidate the man by glaring, but the old bum was made of tougher stuff than that. He approached us, smelling money.

The beggar gestured to the map. "You hunt for diamonds?" he asked in French.

"We're trying to find a friend," I said.

He grinned like a jack-o-lantern. "A friend."

"Our friend is looking for diamonds."

"What is his name?"

It was my turn to smile. "Are you on a first name basis with all the diamond miners in Tshikapa?"

"I am in the street day and night," the man said. "When I am not too drunk I see everyone who comes and goes."

"How often are you too drunk?"

"Whenever possible. It is my goal to stay entirely drunk at all times, my friend."

I found myself liking yet another unexpected ally.

"Our friend is Tonde Chiora," I said.

The old fellow's face lit up. "The African People's Mine!" he crowed.

"You know it?"

"It is here." The old man thumped his right arm, which ended at the wrist in a puckered stump, on the map.

Frank waited through this exchange with growing impatience. "What're you and Stinky talking about?"

"He's showing us Chiora's mine."

Frank looked at the map. "That ain't even close to where we were looking."

I asked the beggar if he was certain. "They stood in the doorway of this very restaurant, and discussed their plans, thinking I was too drunk to understand. I am certain of their location as I am that Primus is the best beer in all the world," he said solemnly.

"That's a matter of some debate," I said.

"Not to me."

I believed him. Frank was initially hesitant to follow the advice of a homeless man, but eventually he agreed. As usual, he would go where I led him.

I thanked the beggar and slipped him twenty dollars in small bills while Frank paid for our wretched snack. "May I ask how you lost your hand?" I asked the old man.

"I did not lose it. It was taken."

"Fair enough," I said.

"I was a prisoner of Angolan rebels for almost a year, at a mine near the border. I woke one morning in my home, surrounded by them, and that was it for me. They killed my wife and daughter, and made me their slave. All day I worked the shake-shake, and, at night, I slept on the ground next to the pit. When they caught me with a few small stones they cut off my hand as a lesson to the others."

"Why were you in Angola?"

"I was here, in my own country. But they were here, too, for the diamonds."

"These men were UNITA rebels?" I ask, and the man nodded. The Angolan civil war had been over for nine years. "This was a long time back, then."

"Yes. And now I hear those men are politicians in Angola. Sometimes I tell myself that my hand helped end a civil war."

"How did you escape?"

"I was set free. I could no longer mine. They thought I would die in the jungle after they cut off my hand. But, you see, I didn't." He smiled then. "Now, my friend, I hear the Primus calling."

When I wished the man good luck, he looked on me so blankly that I assumed I had somehow botched the translation. Finally, he gestured to the street with pursed lips. "I don't think you are the only ones hunting here."

"We're not hunting anything," I said, trying to look convincing.

"The jungle is full of guns. You must take care, my friend." He patted me on the shoulder with his remaining hand and set out to drink away his memories.

Frank and I shouldered our gear and took the road pointed out by the beggar. Within a quarter mile of the town, it devolved into a root-tangled footpath. I hadn't enjoyed my time in the Congo's cities, but I wasn't thrilled to find myself tramping through the sodden heat of the bush once more. Every twisting vine looked like a snake, and I doused myself with bug repellant every half hour, the chemical smell searing my nostrils.

After several hours on the trail, Frank broke the silence. "We gotta figure out what to do about Chiora."

"Yes, sir."

"And Zhou, who fucked us over."

I tried to explain my theory to him. "The Company played Chiora foul, painting him as a villain so they could claim his new technology as their own."

"It ain't right."

"We agree on that much."

Frank fell into a brooding silence. The only sounds were birdcalls, buzzing insects, and the clank and stomp of our passage. I was impatient to hear what he had to say but knew not to rush him.

"What we could do," Frank said, after fully half an hour's march, "is just whack Chiora, and then do what The Company would've done. Take the shit for ourselves."

The idea was dangerous at best. Zhou would bring all his resources to bear in order to avenge such a betrayal. Also, I needed to convince Frank we could achieve our ends without killing Chiora. Still, I was relieved to hear Frank making some kind of plan for his future. While Frank was being thoughtful, I felt compelled to test his willingness to let Chiora live. "You're suggesting we kill a man who has done us no harm—along with all his men—and make ourselves rich off their labors?"

"Something like that, yeah. Chiora killed Shep and his whole crew."

"That was a friendly fire incident. And Sheppard's last wish was that I try to help Chiora."

Frank dismissed the claim with a wave of his hand. "So, what's the blowback if we do this? You know, if Zhou gets wind of it?"

The words came out before I considered them. "I believe Mister Zhou and The Company would invest whatever amount of money it took to track us down and ensure that we died in the most excruciating way possible. No place on this earth would be a safe haven for us from that day forward. Money would be no object for our pursuers, because The Company would make a lesson of us. Zhou, in particular, would take it all as a personal affront, and would make sure we died slowly, and with a great deal of suffering."

Frank turned back to me, eyes narrowed. "You think he's that pissed?"

"He'd simply be making a point about loyalty."

"There's somethin' you ain't thought of, though."

I answered without hesitation. "We kill Zhou."

Frank laughed. "Atta boy. But do we hire a crew? Launch a full assault? Do we hit him guerilla style, pick off his guys one by one, then pop him while he's trying to bail out? And how do we get out? It ain't like there's just Zhou to deal with."

"The assassination could happen in a number of ways. I'm not sure about the retreat, though. Our renown in certain circles would work against us. For any mercenary worth his salt there would be, in addition to a significant bounty, the added thrill of taking down killers of our stature."

Such was Frank's ego that this fact pleased him. "Yeah, no shit, right? I got half a mind to kill myself just to say I was the guy who took out Frank Giordano."

"That's just plum stupid," I said.

"So. What do we do?"

"We make Zhou's murder look like an accident."

"Like, 'Oops! I accidentally discharged my sidearm in this fat fuck's face?'"

"You're just being perverse now. No. We would have to slip past his security in the early morning hours and suffocate him in his bed. Or perhaps poison his food. Then we slip back into the bush. A few days later we stroll into the compound, acting as though we achieved our mission and are reporting back to our employer. We would act very surprised and upset about the untimely death of our beloved benefactor."

"But then The Company still gets Chiora's whatever-the-fuck-it-is, and you and me did all that shit for nothing."

"You're forgetting something." I tapped the side of my head with my index finger. "We would have Chiora's diamonds. Maybe we could leave The Company and return to Chiora's mine to go into business for ourselves."

Frank laughed out loud, his voice bouncing off the trees.

We labored up a densely-covered slope. Despite the steep pitch, the ground was sopping wet and muddy. The Congo, in its infinite creativity, had birthed a vertical bog.

For some time the only sound was our labored breathing and the squelch of our boots in the mire.

"You're a smart fucking guy, Stan," Frank said at the top of the draw, as his breath returned.

"I try to make the most of what intelligence I possess. Imagine what we could achieve if I could say the same of you."

Frank ignored this. "I gotta ask," he said. "No bullshit. Were you planning on ditching me, like Zhou said?"

"I was going to ask you to work on my cattle ranch," I said.

Frank grimaced. "Cows and shit?"

"Hundreds of cows and a great deal of shit, yes."

"The fuck you were." He shook his head, smiling. "But that's outta the picture?"

I nodded. "But you aren't." The idea of the ranch was easy to give up. I had never fully made it a part of me. If I'd wanted to go back to Texas and buy land, I could've done it at any time. I had the money. But instead of leaving, I'd stayed in the Congo to fight alongside my friend, and to feel alive in a way that only close proximity to death allows. The last few weeks hadn't been enjoyable, really, but the fight to survive had filled me up in a way the peaceful monotony of farming never could. My comfort zone, I now understood, was a war zone. My friendship with Frank, I finally realized, was the closest to home I'd ever get. This wasn't a particularly uplifting thought, but it carried the weight of truth.

Frank put a hand on my shoulder. "Thanks, brother."

"You're impossible to get rid of," I said, "like herpes. I just try to control your outbreaks."

"Wow. I'm fuckin' touched." Frank slapped me on the back and headed down the trail at a brisk pace.

We hiked without talking for some time, our feet slopping in the muck and birds screaming in every direction.

Frank broke the long silence. "We couldn't go into business right away, right?"

"It would be hard to keep that kind of activity secret," I said. "And more than dangerous to stockpile gems."

"Still, it's possible, right?"

"There's a critical dimension of this plan we aren't addressing."

"Ah, shit. You wanna save somebody."

CHAPTER 32

NIGHT FELL BEFORE we arrived at Chiora's mine, so we set up camp in the jungle. After almost a week indoors, I had little stomach for sleeping rough again. I had spent years making my bed in the dirt without question, but now some switch flipped inside me, and I lost patience for the discomforts of military accommodation.

I hung my hammock between two trees so thick of trunk I could scarcely get the rope around them. I lay down on my side at first, thinking to create a less comfortable-looking surface for snakes, but that put a kink in my back. I ended up with my face to the sky like usual.

I lay awake for some time, looking up into the chaotic tangle of branches sitting still in the windless night. Bugs screeched and buzzed their hellish symphony just beyond my mosquito net.

In my anxious state, I worried about the swarming ants I had seen in a bad movie once. In seconds, all that had remained of victims was their shining bones. Images of the swarming creatures pouring into my mouth and nose kept me from sleep for some time.

Somewhere inside of that cacophony, I thought I heard the sound of the river.

In the morning light I discovered we had stopped just a half mile from a branch of the Kasai River, a swift-moving, mustard colored waterway some thirty yards across. After hacking and slipping along the edge of the river for half a day, we finally heard the sound of grinding machinery and men calling back and forth.

It had to be Chiora.

We were exhausted after a day and a half of humping through the awful heat, and made the quick decision to spend one more night out of sight and near the river, that we might be rested and focused for our assault.

We backtracked a few miles downstream and set up camp in the forest gloom some ten yards back from the water. With our camp established, we set out to do recon on Chiora's mine.

They had a perimeter of guards but no understanding of protocol. The men were too widely spaced, and they passed their time in what a military man might call a state of low vigilance. We slipped through their defenses unimpeded and observed the operation at our leisure.

In all my work in the Congo, I had not previously seen an artisanal diamond mine. The Company's interests were in coltan, bauxite, uranium, and gold, as well as diamonds, but all of these operations were highly technical affairs involving a great deal of machinery, large trucks and powerful drills.

Chiora's mine, by contrast, looked like a series of riverside pits.

Two dozen men stood in the bottom of the holes, shoveling gravel onto screens held by other men, who, in turn, swirled the slurry of water and rock in a circle before dumping it onto a conveyor belt. These belts ran up the edge of the pit and dumped the tailings into the river. The ground must have been worked for some time by the previous owners, because there were numerous pits, several of them deeper than the height of a man.

Nowhere in that hive of activity did I see anything that looked like the technology Chiora supposedly stole from Zhou.

Frank and I scanned the camp for some time, searching fruitlessly for the great advance in mining, but we saw nothing but conveyor belts, shovels, screens, some growling generators, and a series of great green hoses, thick around as a man's leg, snaking between the pits.

Chiora himself wasn't in evidence, either. We assumed that he sheltered in one of the large, wooden-floored tents— likely pilfered from the Congolese military—set on a rise overlooking the mine.

As we hunkered in the bushes, a muscle-bound digger broke into song, his deep bass soon joined by the others. The song rose easily over the noise of the generators and transformed the whole scene from one of unmitigated toil to one of physical poetry. The song made sense of the motion somehow, gave it purpose.

A member of the workmen's chorus broke off from the song with a happy cry and held up a gray rock the size of a grape. The other men cheered with him briefly, and then continued with their work and their singing.

Frank and I looked at each other in silent confusion and slunk back to our camp.

"What the hell was that?" Frank said, once we were again deep in the jungle.

"I can't describe it."

"Did you see a single fucking thing that looked like new tech?"

"Perhaps they only use it if they need to follow a vein deeper into the earth. It's also possible they keep it hidden in the daylight to avoid detection." But even I didn't it.

"There's gotta be something more than a bunch of dudes fucking around in a mud puddle, right?"

"Perhaps the shovels were of some unique design?"

"Fuck you."

"Screens made of space metal?"

"Space metal?" Frank said, before noticing my smirk. He punched me in the arm. "Damn it, this is serious. What's the fucking secret?"

My tongue was possessed by some mirthful imp, and I didn't trust myself to speak. I was just as confounded as Frank, but for some reason the apparent pointlessness of our mission struck me as funny, and a fitting end to our time in the Congo. I fairly shuddered with the effort of controlling my laughter. Finally, I failed altogether, giggling and snorting like a fool.

Frank shook his head at my folly, and waited for me to recover my sanity. Soon, though, he smiled. We managed to keep quiet until we got well away from the mine, but by the time we got back to our camp, the forest rang with our laughter.

We puzzled on the mystery of Chiora's camp all afternoon, but arrived at no conclusions. Despite our deepening confusion about our objective, we decided to take the camp the following morning, and see if there was money to be made there before Zhou's men tracked us down. Having settled on our plan of attack, we distracted ourselves by retrieving our long-forgotten fishing lines and hooks. We rigged up some poles, Huck Finn style, and passed an idyllic afternoon on the banks of the river, casting our lines in companionable silence. Despite everything, we were still brothers in arms.

Just before sunset Frank nearly lost his pole when a mighty fish took his bait. He struggled with the beast for almost half an hour, and so great was the fight that we both began to fear he hooked a crocodile. Finally, he dragged the fish to shore, and we stared in shock at the scaly monster.

It was four feet long and more than a foot thick across its humped middle, with a huge mouth full of widely-spaced, spiked teeth.

"Jesus H. Motherfucking Christ," Frank said. "That's one ugly goddamn fish."

"Goliath tigerfish," I said.

Frank sat down in the mud, panting, and smiled up at me. "How the fuck do you do it? All the shit you know? It ain't normal."

"I read things, and they don't go away," I said, taken aback by the question. For years, Frank had mocked me for being relatively bright.

"Everybody reads shit, but they can't spit it back out ten years later."

"My mind takes a picture and files it away for later use."

"And you can always find it when you want it?"

I thought about this a moment. "I suppose so, yes."

"You're a fucking genius, Stanley. I mean, for real. What a fucking waste."

I waited for the cruel punch line, but it never came. When the silence grew uncomfortable, I pointed at the fish by way of distraction. "We should make a fire. We have some serious eating to do."

"Amen to that, motherfucker!" Frank jumped up, and dragged the river monster back into our camp while I set about collecting firewood.

We roasted the fish over a rack of woven branches and flavored it with the burning hot Congolese *pili pili* sauce. I reckon each of us put down no fewer than four pounds of fish that night. Our conversation was of Fallujah and the Korengal, but we didn't speak of the battles. Instead, we remembered the foolishness we got up to in the time between engagements. The good times we enjoyed with our brothers in arms, many of whom were now dead or grievously wounded.

Previous conversations about those days of glory and camaraderie usually ended with Frank drunk and howling about the injustice of his dishonorable discharge, but on this night he held his bitterness at bay. We both knew, I believe, that we were at the end of our run, though it didn't weigh on me at the time. All I knew was that my belly was full, and I was swapping stories with the closest thing to a friend I had in the world, the only person who could understand the strange life I had led.

CHAPTER 33

WE AWOKE BEFORE dawn and ate a huge breakfast of fish before breaking camp and running through our mission plan. We needed to catch Chiora alone and remove him from the camp without engaging his men. From that point, our mission took on what Sheppard used to call "a high degree of *blurocity*," as our strategy went no further than forcing Chiora to explain his technology, or to, at least, tell us where it was hidden.

We figured, I guess, that we would put on a kind of bush trial, and that his explanation would either save or condemn him. I felt certain Frank's idea of leniency for Chiora would be a quick death, but I still wanted to save him if I could.

Just before sunrise, we made our way through the darkness and hunkered down at the perimeter. No men worked at that hour, though we heard a buttery hum of conversation coming from one of the tents. With no one in the mine, it looked more than ever like a dreadful accident, a gray scar in the earth created by concentrated bombing or some such terrible thing.

Brown water stood, mirror-calm, in the pit bottoms, reflecting the brightening sky back at itself in ugliness. I fixated on the idea that so much evil had been perpetrated in the name of pulling shiny rocks out of dirty holes. With me being just another cog in the death works. Were it not so tragic, it would have been worth another great laugh.

I caught movement by a tent at the center of the other dwellings. I glassed it and saw Tonde Chiora step outside to smile at the coming day.

Here was the reason for our whole adventure.

I recognized the wide eyes and friendly set of his face from his photos. He was scrawnier than I expected, though, and his head seemed too big for his body. His mouth moved constantly, and, at first, I assumed he was speaking to someone still inside his tent. Soon, though, the sound reached my ears, and it was a song. Chiora was starting his day with a happy, lilting tune. His singing inspired an odd urge to raise my own voice in harmony.

I might have done so, too, were it not for the voice behind me that said, in English, "If you move, we shoot you."

I looked back and up to see two brawny young men pointing AK-74 sniper rifles at us. "Damn it, Frank," I sighed. "We're losing our edge."

Beside me, Frank smiled as he took his hands off his weapon. "You guys mind if we roll onto our backs?"

"Slowly," the larger of the two said to us.

We rolled over, which may have seemed harmless enough to our two untrained guards, but in fact improved our tactical circumstance a great deal. The move gave us full use of all our limbs, and we could better observe our captors.

They were impressive specimens, large and lean. One of them wore a khaki shirt unbuttoned, the sleeves torn off, and the other went shirtless altogether. I might have, too, were I so cut. Despite the gravity of my situation, I felt a pang of envy for the shirtless man's six-pack abs.

If I live through this, I must lean up.

I pointed to their guns. "You're using sniper rifles for close contact."

The man in the vest said, "They will kill you, no problem."

Frank said, "At two hundred yards, those old Russian babies are fucking lethal. Captive situation, though, you want your basic sidearm."

"Shut up," Six Pack said.

I nodded. "My friend is right. Maneuvering a rifle in close quarters is ungainly."

"If you fellas have pistols, you should switch out now. First you," he pointed to Vest, "then you." He pointed to Six Pack.

I nodded. "That's how I would do it."

"Get up." Six Pack kicked Stan's foot.

It was hard not to smile. Frank and I got our feet under us slowly, as instructed. Then we simply slapped their guns aside and took the men down. Frank kicked Vest in the testicles, while I throat-struck Six Pack. Such a two-finger strike always presents the risk of an accidental kill, but it was a risk I was willing to take in my frustration at having been ambushed. I found the man irritating.

Before Six Pack recovered from my strike, I snatched the little pouch he wore on a string around his neck. I sliced it open with my pig sticker, and a handful of herbs and small stones fell out.

Frank said, "What the fuck, Stan?"

"The marabout made those things," I said, knowing that if I'd found human finger bones as I'd expected, I would've killed the men right there.

We disarmed them while they rolled on the ground, gurgling and whimpering, and strapped their rifles over our shoulders. Then we marched into the camp with them in front of us at gunpoint.

"We got pistols trained on you now," Frank said, concluding the lesson. "And we're staying back far enough so you can't spin on us and knock the barrel away."

"These are basic principles, gentlemen," I said. "If you live through this day, you'll want to get some more training."

"Mai-Mai, my ass," Frank said to me.

"They do seem to lack the swagger of the Mai-Mai. And they speak English."

"We are Tanzanian," Six Pack said.

"Fucking amateurs." Frank glared at our prisoners.

"They're hardly worth killing," I said. The evident harmlessness of Chiora's so-called warriors dampened my murderous urge.

Besides, Chiora was still singing.

Our target made no move to flee as we approached him at the center of the camp, and none of his other men appeared. He didn't seem surprised to see us. Instead, he favored us with a welcoming smile. "Ah," he said, seemingly pleased to have our guns trained on him, "the monster Frankenstein! I have been expecting you."

"Charmed, I'm sure," I said.

"You are bigger than I expected."

"And you're a fucking pipsqueak," Frank said. Chiora was, in fact, no more than five-and-a-half feet tall. Still, he radiated a feverish energy that gave him a substantial presence.

"So, is this to be a battle? Will we fight to the death?" he asked, still smiling.

"That depends on what you do next," I said, disoriented by his refusal to accept the gravity of his situation. Chiora was, all in all, far too happy for a man negotiating for his life.

"Of course it does. Of course! But tell me, how did you find me?"

"Mike Sheppard told us, asshole," Frank said.

Chiora's smile disappeared. He clutched my arm, which I found strangely motherly. "He lives?"

"No. He fuckin' dies," Frank said. "And that's on you, shitwad."

"But you saw him? Did he forgive me?" Chiora teared up. It filled me with equal parts admiration and disgust.

Frank opened his mouth to speak, but I jumped in. "I believe he did, at some level. My impression was that he was more resigned to his fate than anything, and had his mind fixed on the bigger questions."

Frank said, "You're doing that talking thing again, Stanley."

But Chiora wept. He didn't do this half-heartedly. Great rivers of tears poured down his face in quantities I had never before seen produced in real life. I feared he would collapse from dehydration if he stayed sad for too long.

"It was a mistake," he said, his voice steady and calm despite the waterworks. "They were not supposed to shoot him."

"Yeah, well, you fucked up," Frank said. "Now Mike's in the ground, and you're out here getting rich."

This roused Chiora from his sorrow. "All of these men are getting rich," he said. "And it is in part because of Mister Mike Sheppard."

"Mike gettin' whacked helped you?" Frank growled, tightening his grip on his pistol.

"His sacrifice set us free," Chiora said.

I said, "He died for your sins."

Chiora looked at me, his eyes alight with curiosity. "Yes, my friend."

Frank poked Chiora's chest with his pistol. "Stan ain't your friend, asshole. And Sheppard sure as fuck wasn't Jesus."

Chiora kept his eyes on me. "You are not the monster I expected."

"They say a book shouldn't be judged by its cover," I said, flattered to have been recognized that way.

"I believe yours is a violent story."

"That's a painful truth, I admit."

"But there is more to you, all the same." His eyes never left my face.

"*Hey!*" Frank slapped me on the back of the head. "I don't mean to interrupt the book of the fuckin' month club or nothin', but we're in the midst of a situation here."

Chiora blinked and nodded. "Please tell me what you want from me."

"The goddamn blueprints for your mining technology," Frank said. "Or the thing itself if it ain't too big to carry."

"My technology?" Chiora frowned.

"We were told you had a new method of mining," I said, knowing already what the answer would be. "A way of getting more out of the ground, more efficiently. We thought perhaps you had…" I hesitated, not knowing how to avoid sounding foolish. "… I don't know. A special kind of drill or something."

"A drill?" Chiora asked, delightedly. "A *drill?*"

The little man laughed uproariously. I began to wonder if I was witnessing mirth or a mental breakdown. Finally, he said, "There is no miraculous machine, my friends. The great leap in productivity is due to equality."

Frank and I stared at him.

Chiora continued. "I have simply subverted the dominant paradigm. Ever since Cecil Rhodes began mining in South Africa, the trade has been controlled by a single company. The hard labor is done by poor men who are little more than slaves, and the only people who buy their diamonds are functionaries of the global syndicate. The real workers make next to nothing, while De Beers and their subsidiaries make countless billions."

"I'm bored," Frank said. "When I get bored, I wanna shoot somebody."

"How does this relate to our current predicament?" I asked.

"Vertical integration!" Chiora said, spreading his arms to include the whole camp. "These men and I are part of a chain that goes all the way to Antwerp. We have our own transportation, our own cutters. We can sell the diamonds directly to jewelers. The profits we make are all distributed back to the members of the cooperative."

"You gotta be fuckin' kiddin' me," Frank said.

Chiora almost looked sorry for us. "We have no technology. Only hoses, generators, shovels, and shake-shakes."

I didn't know whether to weep or smile. Carrion birds that we were, Frank and I—and Zhou, as well—had been chasing shadows. Our whole mission was built on the understanding that the little Zimbabwean possessed powers worth fearing, and creations worth stealing. But Tonde Chiora had no Mai-Mai horde. No amazing technology. Just vision, energy, and boundless hope. All things I wanted, but lacked.

On the downside, he bullied and intimidated people who stood in his way, surrounded himself with armed flunkies, and aligned himself with whatever foul characters he thought could keep him safe.

Frank and I are foul creatures who could keep him safe.

I smiled, seeing my vague hopes coalesce into what looked like a real plan.

Frank frowned at me. "What's wrong with your fucking face? Are you taking a dump in your pants or something?"

"I think," I said, turning to Chiora, "you should let us join you."

It's hard to say who looked more shocked, Frank or Chiora. Even Six Pack and Vest went bug-eyed.

"Frank and I have cut our ties to The Company," I continued. "After all that has transpired since we first set out to find you, we have no more interest in being Zhou's hired dogs."

To my immense relief, Frank smirked and snapped his teeth. "Woof."

I could tell that he wasn't convinced by my words, but sometimes Frank played along with my ideas just to laugh at how badly things turned out. I considered it a great mercy that this was one of those times.

"It is easy to say you have given up killing, but it I find it hard to believe," Chiora said.

"We came here to learn more about what you're up to," I said, "and make a judgment for ourselves about the long-term prospects of your business."

"You wanted to kill me and steal my diamonds, I think," Chiora answered.

Frank smiled, showing his teeth.

"We're motivated by the promise of profit, just like any man would be," I said. "But mostly we're intrigued by the fairness of your business model and impressed with the moxie you showed by breaking ties with Mister Zhou. We're willing to forgive you sending men against us, since we realize no one is perfect."

"I have not claimed perfection," Chiora said.

"No shit," Frank answered.

I ignored them both. "Frank and I are of a similar mindset. That's why we arrived here in stealth rather than with our guns blazing."

I could see Chiora weighing the risks and rewards of having men like us around. When he finally spoke, though, he said, "I must tell you, Mister Stanley, it's hard to trust murderers who terrify and pillage wherever they go. I don't believe we have a place for you in our cooperative."

"The fuck you talkin' about, pillaging?" Frank said.

"You do not deny being a murderer?"

"Your security situation is unacceptable," I said. "We can protect you."

"Against what enemies?"

"Any that arise," I said. "Zhou will likely be the first."

"But, my friend," Chiora said, "who will protect me from you?"

Frank spit on the ground. "Listen, dickface, are you gonna let us help you, or do we have to fuck you up?"

Chiora looked at me with what I thought was genuine regret. I opened my mouth to beg forgiveness—for Frank, for myself, for all the crimes we had committed together—but I didn't have the chance.

Chiora shouted, "Fire!"

Bullets snapped past my face. I threw myself to the ground.

Frank shot Six Pack and Vest. Their faces blew open, spraying me with gore, and we used their impressive musculature as shields against the shots coming from the tents and the brush to our right. Frank squeezed off a few rounds at Chiora as he scampered away between the tents, but I slapped his arm down. Frank glared murder at me, but turned his attention to our attackers.

Luckily for us, Chiora's men were terrible shots and had no appetite for an assault despite their superior numbers. We dragged our victims' bodies to the lip of a pit, where we were out of the line of fire, and used them to steady their own rifles. It took a moment to accustom myself to the sloppy sighting on Six Pack's AK, but, within a moment, I began picking off attackers. Frank scanned the grounds for Chiora.

"We should go!" I shouted over the snap and buzz of bullets whipping over our heads.

"I'm gonna kill that little shit," Frank said.

"Be that as it may, they have superior firepower and the high ground, as well."

"These assholes don't even know how to shoot."

"If they start lobbing grenades, or firing RPGs at us, their marksmanship won't be a concern."

By way of acknowledgement, Frank shouted, "Smoke out!"

He threw a smoke canister toward the tents, and we ran. As we hustled through the jungle, Frank's face was red with fury, his mouth twisted with hate. I, on the other hand, found the whole experience laughable in a perverse way.

"That didn't go like I had planned," I said. I tried to hold back the chuckle, but failed.

Frank said, "One more word and I'll blow your fucking brains out."

This only tickled me more. Thus we beat our retreat back to the camp, him in a rage, and I beset by merriment. Anyone who chanced upon us then would have seen our faces as the twin masks of comedy and tragedy.

CHAPTER 34

CHIORA'S ASSAULT COULDN'T go without reprisal, and despite my mirth, my intentions hadn't changed. We needed to relieve Chiora of his diamonds and eliminate Zhou.

We spent the night quietly in camp, planning our next moves. We waited through the morning, when the miners would expect us to appear again. In the heat of the afternoon, we took a broad and effortful detour around the mine, avoiding the river and pushing through the low bushes and clinging vines in silence. We kept at least a kilometer between ourselves and the camp at all times and arrived from the north, reasoning that an inexperienced Chiora would concentrate his forces in the direction from which we previously arrived.

The sun dropped into the jungle as we reached our coordinates, one click upriver from the camp. We whiled away a quiet hour waiting for nightfall, buried in the vegetation to avoid detection, practicing our long-ago-perfected art of slapping away mosquitoes without making a sound. Frank lay peacefully in the muck, but I fidgeted and fussed for fear of snakes. The forest steamed and stank of rust and blood. Soon all was darkness.

We put on the night vision goggles I had packed for us back in Kalemie, painting the dark jungle in luminous shades of green, and double-checked the state of our M4s and Glocks before slithering out of the bushes, great deadly serpents in our own right.

We crept through the ferns and creepers in silence, under cover of the whir and whine of millions of bugs. At the edge of the camp we glassed the clearing to confirm the positions of the guards. As we suspected, a ten-man watch was concentrated on the far side of the camp, forming a loose U-shaped perimeter. The closest guards to our position were perhaps thirty meters on either side. I tapped Frank twice on the shoulder, and we retreated to our rendezvous point back in the jungle.

"That's one lame ass attempt at a defensive perimeter." Frank flipped his night vision goggles back up. I did the same. The world blackened briefly, until my eyes adjusted to the moonlight filtering through the thick canopy.

"They're boys playing at being soldiers." I found the beast in me slow to awaken. Defeating Chiora and stealing his diamonds would be like taking a candy from a baby— after killing all the baby's friends.

Frank's teeth flashed in the moonlight. "Let's light 'em up."

"We'll take the guards outside-in," I whispered. "You start on the right, I'll go left. We'll regroup here once we've taken out the flanking guards, and move straight into the camp. Leave Chiora alive if you can."

"Why the fuck can't I kill him?"

"Because…" *I would like to talk to him and find out where he went wrong.* "I want to question him about Zhou, and find out if there are any hidden diamonds."

Frank grunted acceptance. "But I can fuck up the rest of those assholes, right?"

I gave Frank a thumbs-up.

Frank produced his giant knife, and I unsheathed my own blade. The jungle hummed and buzzed in a symphony of scrabbling, blood-sucking life. Despite all my earlier misgivings, my warrior-self finally sprang to life, and, as if to prove his worth, blazed with particular vividness. My heart bounded in my chest. I felt myself grow large and mighty, a giant of a man. My brain became an inferno of bloodlust that burned away all other thought, reducing my sympathies, fears, and doubts to drifting cinders. I felt as though my hands could crush stone, tear apart tanks, as if I was reborn as that other Stanley Mullens who always went into battle on my behalf. This snarling animal exulted at having escaped the prison of conscience. He swaggered into the dark night with the smell of blood in his nostrils and a howl of triumph already in his throat.

I growled low in my throat, and Frank put a hand on my chest, patting me like one might a pet bear.

"Easy, big fella."

Stealth isn't my strong suit, but the insect noise combined with the guards' lack of focus allowed me to approach undetected. The first two men didn't even know they were in danger until their blood sprayed across the leaves and vines. Inflamed by the gore on my hands, I bull rushed the third guard. He turned before I could get a clean cut, and my knife gouged the right side of his neck, severing the gristly muscles there. My blade tip broke off in his skull as he fell backward.

Fortunately, his gun didn't go off, nor did he scream in his agony. I was forced to wrestle with the unfortunate soul as his blood pumped hotly against my face and he thrashed his way into death. When I met up with Frank at the upriver edge of the camp, he looked at me askance.

"What, you slow dance with him before you killed him?" he asked.

"Let's finish this," I whispered hoarsely. I lifted my foot to move out, but Frank sharply grabbed my arm and pulled me back. He silently gestured for us to retreat back into the jungle. I started to question him, but before I could say a word, gunfire broke out on the far side of the mine. Muzzle flashes sparked in the darkness. Bullets whipped past us.

Our night vision goggles revealed twenty soldiers, trained and efficient, pushing toward the pits. Chiora's men retreated before them, firing wildly. Some miners gave up the fight altogether, jumping behind tents and diving into the mud-filled trenches. Others ran toward the fight, taking up defensive positions, but they were utterly disorganized and brainless with fear.

"Zhou's guys?" Frank asked.

I shook my head. "They're firing AKs." Zhou's men either had QBZ-95s or M4s. "These are freelancers."

Frank nodded to me. "You wanna play the hero?"

"I would prefer to see Chiora alive, yes."

"And I'd rather not let those other fuckers take all the diamonds, so let's go save his sorry ass."

Frank and I silently made our way around the edge of the camp, that we might engage the invaders from the flank.

The attackers were more organized than most of the soldiers we had encountered in the Congo, but they lacked night vision goggles, and they didn't so much as turn in our direction as we cut them down. When the last of them fell, the firing from the mine went on for some time. Frank and I moved tree to tree to avoid being struck by bullets fired at random. Finally, a victorious shout rose up from Chiora's men, who believed they eliminated the threat unaided.

"The People's Mine of Africa cannot be defeated!" Chiora's voice slurred over the others.

"That boy is drunk," I said.

"And stupid." Frank moved to the cover of a tree close to the edge of the camp. "You didn't do shit," he shouted at Tonde. "You punched a few holes in the trees, but every one of those dead fuckers took a bullet from either me or Stan."

This ended the celebration. After a moment of sharp whispering in the camp, we heard men stumbling into the bushes far to our left and right.

"Those guys you just sent out to kill us are gonna die now, asshole," Frank said. "Just like the six dumbfucks you put out on the north side of camp."

"Who is speaking?" Chiora called out. "It is the cruel one, am I right? I would prefer to talk to the bigger one."

Frank snarled and gestured for me to enter the conversation. Before I left cover, he indicated that he would eliminate the flanking threats while I provided the distraction. I pushed the night vision goggles back on my head, stepped out of the jungle, and took a few strides toward Chiora and his men, positioning myself next to a kapok tree that I might use as cover if necessary.

I meant to look both confident and harmless, but I ended up moving in a strange and robotic way. Chiora and his men scowled and fidgeted with their weapons as they watched me.

"Good evening," I said, as though greeting friendly strangers on the streets of Huntsville.

"It is the scarred one, yes?" Chiora asked, squinting into the night.

"There's more to me than scars," I said. "But I'm the one you wanted to talk to, yes."

"You are the heavy one?"

"Are you trying to offend me, or is that incidental?"

Chiora threw back his head back and laughed drunkenly. "I am sorry, my friend," he said. "White people look the same to me. I describe the most obvious things."

Despite the circumstance, his words stung me. "I have a name. Stanley Mullens."

"Yes, yes. Sorry, my friend." There was a lengthy silence. Finally, Chiora said, "What is it you wanted to say?"

How intoxicated is he?

"It was you who called me forth to parlay."

"I don't remember it this way."

"Do you have an idea who attacked you?" I asked.

"The men say they look like Banyamulenge, but that is something people here say when they are not sure who to blame." I had seen this attitude, as well. The ethnic Tutsi minority in the Congo often were treated as scapegoats.

"Are there any survivors? It would be good to know how they got to you."

"The same way as you, Mister Stanley. They hunted us. Why they did it is no longer important since they are dead. But tell me, why did you help us? What is it you want?"

"We wanted you to tell us where your diamonds are, and get information on how to run the mine," I said. "We couldn't do that if those men killed you."

Chiora laughed dryly. "You are a strangely honest man."

"Until you shot at us yesterday, we had planned to partner up with you," I said. "I can't speak for Frank, but I at least am still willing to consider working as a team."

Two quick shots rang out in the jungle. Chiora's men grumbled, weapons cocked.

I cleared my throat. "That, uh, will be the men you sent after us."

"And I am to trust a man who murders my comrades?"

"In fairness, you sent them to kill us. And yesterday you opened fire on us after we asked to join your team. Yet we're willing to trust you. Call the others back, and they'll live."

To my surprise, Chiora called his men out of the jungle. They passed right by me, their eyes bulging and hands shaking.

I called Frank.

He arrived, glaring murderously. "What the fuck?"

"I've re-opened the dialogue about joining the mine."

"Are you fucking nuts?" Frank's anger could be heard clear across the camp.

"I thought the same thing, my friend," Chiora said to Frank.

"I ain't your friend!" he snapped. To me he said, "This wasn't the objective."

"Things have changed now that we've saved them from other enemies. We might still be able to find a place in the organization and make our fortune without any more killing."

Frank looked back and forth between me and Chiora. Finally, he put a hand on my shoulder. "The shit I let you talk me into."

I turned back to Chiora. "Every time you oppose us, your men are killed. This isn't our choice, and we've acted until now only in self-defense. I swear to you on my mother's grave that we don't want to kill you or any of your men."

Chiora laughed again. "So you expect to join us as a brother, but if we don't accept you will kill us all? That is not appealing to me."

"We'd earn our place in the company, just like the others. Think of this. If we wanted to kill you, would we have stopped the others from attacking the camp?"

The miners argued, whispering too quietly for me to make out what they said, their voices guttural and harsh. Finally, Chiora said, "My men are confident they killed at least half of the enemy fighters."

"No sir, they didn't. You can check for yourselves in the morning if you feel so inclined."

A lengthy silence followed this. I asked, "Are all of your men all right?"

"Aside from those you killed?" Chiora asked.

"Well, yes. Aside from those."

"Comrade Ngamba has a bullet wound in his shoulder, but it is not bleeding terribly. He says it is very painful though."

"I have a med kit. I know how to treat the wound."

Frank shook his head at this, but I continued. "My partner and I can work the mine with you, as equals. We can also protect you from any other attacks."

"Who says there will be more attacks?" Chiora asked, slurring.

"You've failed at secrecy, I'm afraid."

"Every fucking rebel, mercenary, and homeless guy within two hundred klicks of Tshikapa knows you're out here," Frank said. "You got a target on your back."

I hoped Chiora could see past Frank's tone to appreciate the truth of what he said. In any case, the miners again began to talk amongst themselves. When they stopped, Chiora's sweet baritone voice hummed a slow, familiar tune.

He sang *Amazing Grace*, gathering volume and expression as he walked toward us in the dark. His voice was like maple syrup and buttermilk pancakes, comfort food for the ears. He smiled as he sang.

He stood before Frank, still singing, and offered his hand. Frank reached out and clasped it with a smile of his own, though I could see his eyes were cold and calculating.

The Zimbabwean was really remarkably tiny—not just short, but small of frame besides. His head loomed above his narrow shoulders. He gave off a nostril-prickling body odor redolent of onions and chicken broth. When he turned his gaze to me, my smile was real.

"Welcome," he said. "It is good that we are friends now."

None of us knew quite what to do then.

After standing around for a while, Chiora said, "Let us finish dinner. Then we must bury our friends."

That's not an invitation you hear every day.

CHAPTER 35

IN THE MESS tent, we shared a meal of *fufu* with Thomsons fish and *pili pili* sauce. This put me in mind of Claire back in Kindu, and I felt a pang of regret for my ham-fisted attempt to play the white knight. I wondered if she was spending my money well, or if perhaps she was one of those women who poured all their earnings into frivolities.

My thoughts about Claire devolved until I forgot that I was sitting at a rough table hewn from raw timber, sifting tiny fish bones through my teeth. The psych officer in Jalalabad called my habit of worrying about past mistakes a *meditative exercise*. I saw it as grinding down bad memories into softer stuff.

The mess hall, lit orange with old-fashioned kerosene lamps, showed several empty tables. *Such is our legacy, the empty spaces at the supper table.*

Chiora had only twelve men remaining to him. Frank and I made fourteen, though I wasn't sure any of them would count us among their number any time soon. I probably should have worried about poison in my fish, but those fellows looked more the type to go in for a blade in the throat while I slept. They were all lean and muscle-bound, but not a one stood over five feet eight inches tall. I wondered briefly if Chiora hired only smaller fellows as a way of improving his self-image, but then I remembered that all the men we eliminated were bigger and hardier than this motley bunch.

I swallowed a gluey mouthful of *fufu* and said to Chiora, "You hire different body types for different jobs."

It was the first thing anyone had said during the meal, and it brought the whole room to a halt. The man with the bullet wound, Ngamba, stared at us, unmoving, a handful of *fufu* halfway to his face.

Chiora smiled. "You are observant, Mister Stanley."

"These are the worker bees."

Chiora laughed like someone in a cartoon. *Ha ha ha.* "Exactly." He turned serious again. "Our departed friends were all warriors."

Frank found this amusing. "Yeah, right."

I glared at him. "You don't need to be disrespectful all the damn time."

"What? I'm just sayin'…"

"Leave it be for once in your fool life."

Frank half stood up. "Why you acting like my fucking mother all of a sudden?"

Chiora saved us from our idiotic squabbling. "It is all right. We will miss our fallen comrades, but we pitted ourselves against you, as you said. We opposed The Company, and all of us will bear the cost of that decision in some way. It will do no good to nurture our grievances. That is what is destroying Africa. Hutu killing Tutsi, Lendu killing Hema, on and on. We must realize we are all of the same tribe and work together for peace."

"Cool story, bro." Frank dug into his food again.

I thought Chiora's comments hit the proverbial nail more or less on the head. I was impressed, too, that a man who had just lost numerous friends—and who was drunk as all get-out to boot—could take such a broad view of things and articulate it so well. All the same, something bothered me.

"It seems odd you would go for a class system within the workplace."

"It is not a class system. I simply match the man to his task."

"But you backed right into social stratification. You have Alphas, Betas, and Deltas, just like in that Huxley book, *Brave New World*."

Chiora clapped me on the shoulder. "We are many years from Huxley's land of Soma and mindless pleasure. You truly are a man full of surprises, Mister Stanley. Now, let us get more whiskey and discuss the days ahead."

He popped up from the table to find his bottle.

It occurred to me only much later that he hadn't responded to my observation.

Chiora was gone for some long minutes, and we ate in a tense silence with his men. They snuck glances our way like shy schoolboys visited by a movie star, or like fellows who just sat down to supper with the bogeyman himself. Which may have been, in fact, the case.

I tried to engage them in conversation in English, French, Swahili, and Lingala, but they wouldn't so much as tell me their names. We finished our food and sat at the creaking tables trying not to look at each other.

Chiora finally returned and made a lengthy toast about the importance of forgiveness and the power of putting aside old grievances. From the length of his speech and the drifty way he wove back and forth, waxing Marxist-poetical, I could tell he had availed himself of the bottle freely before returning to the mess tent.

After the rambling soliloquy, Chiora passed around the whiskey, saying that to drink from it was to bind ourselves together for all time. Frank snorted into his sleeve, but he took the bottle and drank all the same. When the bottle made it back around to Chiora, he took an impressively long pull, binding himself doubly, I suppose, to the liquid accord.

Then he screwed the cap back on and looked at the bottle as though gazing into the eyes of a lover.

That's a thirsty man, right there.

I wondered if I had traded clear-eyed tyranny for drunken chaos by forsaking Mister Zhou in favor of Chiora. The *fufu* roiled in my stomach, but I decided that Chiora's good intentions outweighed his flaws. I was willing to bet on him trending toward the good now that his vision had come to life.

Chiora plunked the bottle on the table and looked at us all in turn. "Down to business."

We talked for some time about how things would work. Chiora tended to veer off course once he had the bully pulpit, so while Frank and I waited to hear when and how we would get paid, and how much we could earn, we heard a great deal about vertical integration, colonial history, and distribution of wealth.

For all his double talk, and the dubious steps he took to get by, I could see that Chiora truly believed in his cause. The work fulfilled him on all levels—financially, intellectually, and spiritually—in a way that I had never been satisfied with anything. This realization mixed darkly with the whiskey to leave me sullen and lonely.

Frank watched Chiora closely, as well, but his look was purely calculating. Frank had supplemented his whiskey with a pill from his dwindling supply, and, as the speech wore on, I resented his chemical patience nearly as much as I admired Chiora's conviction.

Finally, we learned that we were each to earn a two percent share of the take. This didn't sound overly generous.

"By my reckoning, we should each get something in the neighborhood of six point sixty-six percent," I said.

Frank chuckled. "The number of the beast."

Chiora smiled. "The African People's Mine takes the first twenty percent to cover expenses. These costs are very substantial, of course."

"But aren't we all the African People's Mine?"

"Someone must administrate the fund."

"And that's you?"

"At our current pace, your share should be twenty thousand dollars per month."

Frank rose to his full height, slowly and a bit unsteadily, tipping the bottle over and scaring the other workers half out of their grubby shorts.

"Deal, motherfucker!" He stuck out his hand to shake, and Chiora gripped that great killing paw with what looked to me like trepidation.

Frank and I decided we'd go back to our camp first thing in the morning to collect our gear, and then begin work immediately upon our return, providing perimeter defense and organizing the company's security strategy. We would also offer support with any heavy lifting that was needed, as our size and strength were great assets to Chiora's diminutive crew.

The question arose about burying the bodies, and for the first time Chiora's men became animated. They were convinced that the men must be taken care of immediately, lest they attract the dark attention of malign spirits. Still, no one cared to touch the bodies for fear of contagion. They demanded Chiora secure a *marabout* to tend to the dead.

Even the word gave me a shudder.

Frank stood up. "I got this."

We all followed Frank into the forest. Several of the men brought kerosene lamps, which cast flickering lights on the night jungle. My partner located the first body and hoisted it onto his shoulder as though it were a bale of hay. Chiora and his twelve followers gasped.

"What's your plan?" I asked.

"Feed the fish," Frank said.

I understood. On our way to the river, we passed another body, which I picked up and cradled in front of me, handling him as respectfully as I could under the circumstances.

We made our way to the river in a procession, and Frank and I dropped the bodies into the muddy current. I expected some outrage from the miners, but they either considered a water burial respectful enough under the circumstances, or they were too frightened to protest. Instead, they offered a song, slow and mournful, as we walked through the steaming night.

They sang their friends into the next life.

After all of the lost men sank into the current, Chiora said, "I am weary of this day." He turned back to the camp, and his men followed, leaving me alone with Frank.

Frank stared into the darkness, and I wanted to ask him what he was thinking. We had made, I thought, a crucial decision in our lives by defying Zhou so blatantly, and working with his arch enemy to make our fortune. It was important to me that Frank approach it with an open mind and a full heart.

In the end, I couldn't get the words out, most likely because I was afraid of what he might say to shatter the fragile hope taking shape inside me. In my exhausted state, I chose to enjoy the illusion of having saved Frank from himself.

CHAPTER 36

WE SLEPT ALONE in one of the camp tents. We didn't ask, and no one told us, who had slept there the night before.

Frank was gone when I woke the next morning. I pulled on my boots and stumbled outside, blinking against the sun, which loomed just above the treetops as if for the sole purpose of blinding my tired eyes.

I held up a hand against the glare and looked about for the others, but the camp appeared empty. The only sound was the gentle lapping of the river against the muddy banks.

I grew nervous, picturing Frank on a nocturnal killing spree. I was greatly relieved then to spy Chiora on a rise at the downriver edge of the clearing, staring into the current. He appeared to be deep in thought. Reflecting, I imagined, on how to improve the lot of men and women across Africa.

As I made my way across the camp, he bent down to pick up a large stone and tossed it in the river. The gesture reminded me of wasting time with my childhood friends in Huntsville, hurling rocks in a pond to see who could make the biggest splash.

When I reached the river's edge, though, I saw the body swirling in an eddy. Chiora picked up another large rock and hurled it toward his former colleague. The rock hit the corpse almost directly in the left buttock, rolling it over to expose the man's terrible death grimace.

Without looking at me, Chiora said, "I cannot make it sink." He levered another rock out of the dirt, but thought better of tossing it. The stone thumped uselessly onto the ground at his side. "This is not the reward I promised him."

"I'm truly sorry about that."

Chiora looked at me, his eyelids heavy with drink and sadness. "As am I. We are all guilty, I think."

"Do you believe in sin and damnation, Mister Chiora?"

"That would require a belief in God, which I do not have. And you, Mister Stanley? Are you a God-fearing man?"

I should never bring up religion until after morning coffee. "It could be awkward for me if there's a reckoning."

Chiora turned back to the body rotating slowly in the current. "That was David Mwanza. He wanted to have at least three wives and a dozen children. Now he is nothing but food for the fish, or perhaps the beginning of a cholera outbreak."

"Where is everyone?"

"I gave the men the morning off to mourn the loss of their friends. Mostly, they are drinking their sadness away."

"And Frank?"

"He went with Ngamba to retrieve your things. They left quite some time ago."

"Ngamba?" I didn't think that stroll would end well for Ngamba.

"Your friend offered to put medicine and bandages on his wound, and in thanks, Ngamba offered to help him. My friends are awestruck by you both. I think Ngamba hoped to protect himself by befriending Mister Frank. An offering to the gods."

"When do you expect them back?"

"Soon, I think."

"Perhaps I should go after them," I said, my effort to sound casual came out pinched. "I can make sure they get everything."

Chiora looked at me sideways, smiling, and swept a hand downriver. "Lead the way, my friend."

We made our way through the jungle. I tried to mask my discomfort. Chiora, on the other hand, proved to be something of an amateur naturalist. He pointed out vines with miraculous healing powers and dragonflies the size of robins with translucent, rainbow-hued wings.

For weeks, I'd viewed the jungle as nothing but the deadliest of adversaries, and his obvious love for its many beauties made me feel I'd missed yet another opportunity for self-improvement. I vowed to remain open to wonder going forward.

Chiora, meanwhile, was slowed by his hangover. After witnessing the way he went at the bottle the previous evening, I could appreciate his predicament. I made every effort to slow my pace despite my growing concern for Ngamba, and pretended not to notice when Chiora hung back to vomit in the bushes.

One would think a man whose senses were so engaged in bearing witness to beauty while suffering through alcohol poisoning wouldn't also be in tune to the subtleties of his companion's mood. It surprised me, then, to hear him chuckling behind me.

"You do not trust your Frank, I think."

This was what one might call a weighty statement, but his eyes were full of mirth. He looked like someone ribbing me about a bad haircut.

I looked away. "Frank is something of a conundrum."

"Yesterday, my men were more terrified of the two of you than they were of all the gods in this forest. But this morning, your Frank dressed wounds and made friends. Why do you think he did this?"

"I couldn't rightly say. It's unique in my experience of him."

"You believe he means to do us further harm?"

"Most likely Frank himself doesn't know what he plans to do next. He's a creature of instinct." I suffered a twinge of guilt at the thought of how I'd guided Frank's instincts over the years.

"You are not used to having him out of your control," Chiora said, teasing.

"I try to keep him safe, and protect others from him."

"By bringing him to the Congo?" Chiora laughed quietly.

Was everyone I spoke to from now on going to suggest our whole miserable time here was my fault? My scalp prickled with a panicky fear that Chiora had it right. "It was the only job suitable for a man like Frank."

"What else did you suggest?" he asked.

"I didn't have time to play career counselor," I snapped. Chiora's reinterpretation of our situation had me feeling cornered and anxious. Like Sheppard before him, Chiora held up a mirror exposing the truth of me, and I couldn't bear to look.

Chiora was silent for a while, breathing shallow as if battling nausea, and frowning at the ground. I thought he had forgotten the topic when he said, "So. You believe he will kill Ngamba."

I shrugged. "I surely hope not." I paused to let him catch his breath. "I'm honestly trying to keep Frank safe," I said, ashamed to hear my pleading tone.

"My friend, you are doing what you do best. I am not sure you are helping your friend."

"You don't sugar coat things, do you."

"Honesty is a sign of great respect, my friend." Chiora pointed to the pistol on my right hip. "You know, we have already put our lives in your hands. We can hope that you don't kill us, but if you choose to we are powerless to stop it."

"We're a unique cast of characters."

"I did not picture myself going into business with the Congolese gods of death." He laughed, and soon I caught the bug as well. I had been laughing a great deal those last few days. I couldn't decide if it was a sign of improved mental health or if I was on the verge of popping my stopper.

A branch snapped downriver, and I turned to see Frank and Ngamba walking toward us. Both men smiled and laughed, and Ngamba carried an enormous tiger fish over his shoulder.

"Look, Mister Chiora!" Ngamba sang out in French, "We caught a great fish!"

Frank said, "Breakfast is served, bitches!"

Chiora smiled at me. "You see, my friend? There is reason for hope."

CHAPTER 37

WHILE FRANK AND the rest of the men prepared the fish, Chiora and I dangled our legs over the edge of the largest trench. My new employer pressed me to talk more about my life, encouraging me to tell him about the many dangers I had passed through to arrive at this point. After his earlier observations about my character, I was afraid of how Chiora might interpret my past actions, and didn't wish to do this. Instead, I turned the conversation to Chiora himself. Unlike me, he was happy to tell his story.

He was born in the black township of Mutare, on the eastern edge of what was then called Rhodesia. His mother was a maid at one of the fine homes in the white neighborhood on the hill. She had to return to work immediately after his birth, but brought her infant along, strapped to her back. This she did for nearly a year before walking away from her job, her marriage, and her son. He found himself, then, in the care of his father.

"I was also left in the care of my father," I said, "after my mother died in a car wreck."

"It is a hard thing for a boy."

"Did you and your father get along?" I thought of the leaden silence in which my father and I spent our time together.

"My father was a brilliant man with vast potential," Chiora said. "But he made money brewing the local beer called *chibuku.*"

The foul, fermented sorghum beverage was very popular in certain parts of Africa, but I couldn't see how its manufacture and sale were the job for a man of ability.

Chiora seemed to see the doubt in my eyes. "He dreamed of working in the Ministry of Education after independence, but the white Rhodesians didn't allow black Africans to hold jobs like that. His frustration drove him to the *chibuku.*"

"He was an alcoholic?" Chiora's own thirst began to make sense.

"I hate the smell of *chibuku.* It is like vinegar and shit. It is the stench of failure." Chiora tossed some small stones into the brown water at the bottom of the pit. He was quiet for some time. "My father's displeasure came out through his fists."

"He beat you."

Chiora shrugged. "He taught me what to expect from life."

"I understand."

"I think, perhaps, you do not, my friend. That kind of childhood is only comprehensible to the man who is forged by it. Be glad, in this case, of your ignorance." He sat lost in thought for a minute, and for once I waited. "When the fight for independence began, my father joined the resistance and left me to take care of myself. I kept myself alive by brewing *chibuku* and serving the old men and women still in the town."

"How old were you?"

"Nine years."

"That's terrible."

"It was the happiest time of my life. When independence finally came, in April of 1980, my father returned. He drank more than ever. And when President Mugabe gave all the ministry jobs to his Shona tribesmen, my father took out his anger and resentment on me."

"How did you get clear of him?"

"Ah! That is the one thing Mugabe's government did for me. My father's complaints about the government attracted the attention of the local authorities. They detained him for several days and returned him to the house unrecognizable with bruises. Shortly after that, I awoke one morning to see him walking out the door with a small satchel in his hand. I knew he was leaving, just as my mother had before him. I can tell you my only feeling was relief. Later, I heard he went to the diamond mines of South Africa."

"Is that how you became interested in mining?" I asked.

Chiora scowled. "I was alone for only two weeks, running the brewery by myself once again, when my mother returned. She was very beautiful, in a dress that showed off her strong shoulders and generous hips. Her shoes, though, caused me great distress. They were terrible, impractical things, all straps and sparkles with high heels. These were not the shoes of a good girl."

"Too fancy?" I asked.

"My mother had become a prostitute," Chiora said. "I did not have the language for this at the time, and I didn't care, anyway. She was home, and that was what mattered. She apologized many times for leaving me, but she was very afraid of my father. He beat her very badly when he was in his *chibuku*, and he threatened to toss her into the minefields on the Mozambique border. She admitted she'd become pregnant when they had been dating only a short time, and marriage was the only way to save herself from becoming homeless. You can imagine, my friend, this news did not make me happy. To know that your life is the result of such an atrocity is a heavy thing. And me, learning this as a young boy! I cried, you know? Oh, I cried a lot. But my mother held me very close, and I began to think things would be all right for me. For us."

"She sounds like a brave woman."

"Yes, that is it exactly. She was brave. I convinced myself that because I was the son of an angel and a devil, I was something exactly in between. This was a great relief for me after having only my father as an example. Things became quite good for me. My mother took over the *chibuku* business and insisted I go to school. I was very happy there. I ate knowledge like most children eat *sadza*, with great hunger and shining eyes. I had an intuition, Mister Stanley, that knowing these things would save me from the life of my parents. My mother and I passed several happy years this way."

Chiora fell silent again, staring into the muddy water. His voice grew soft. "As I grew into a teenage boy, though, it became clear that my father's blood was strong in me. My studies became an addiction, and I didn't want anything in the world but to learn. When my mother tried to coddle me, or take me to play football with the other boys I became terrible with anger. She began calling me *mambo diki*, which means little king. I began to drink the *chibuku* to calm my rage, but it made me even more cruel. My mother saw what I was becoming, and she began to pull away. This was, for both of us, like the tearing of flesh from flesh. In time, she was gone from me entirely, and we were strangers in that small house. To save us both from that terrible sadness, I planned my escape. That is how I came to take the test for the leadership academy in South Africa, and won a scholarship."

"What was that like?" I asked.

"Have you ever been the poorest person in a place full of wealth? Have you, my friend, ever felt yourself so surrounded by privilege that it filled you with disgust and envy?"

I nodded, thinking of Mister Zhou and The Company.

Chiora said, "That was my life in that school. Still, there were books, and there were teachers who actually wanted me to learn things and advance in this world. I think they were excited by my poverty and my skinny arms, and they wanted to make a special case out of poor Chiora from Mutare. I hated them for pitying me, but I saw the advantage of smiling and saying thank you. The results were terrible in the dormitories. I was beaten and subjected to many humiliations until I learned how to protect myself."

"With witchcraft."

Chiora gave a noncommittal shrug. "You do not have to believe in something to use it against your enemies."

"There's a great deal of evil in that art," I said, thinking back to the man in the jungle, and the cabin full of human flesh, and the staff of teeth.

"I did not use the evil. I used their fear of it."

"Isn't that the same?"

"What have you done to survive, Mister Stanley?" Chiora turned to look me in the eye.

I looked away. "Continue your story, please."

"My classmates finished the lesson my father began, showing me how the world treats the weak. They were critical, I think, in my education. When there was nothing more to learn in that place, I left."

"You didn't graduate? That seems like a wasted opportunity, if you don't mind my saying so."

"The degree was of no use to me. I developed an interest in mining technology. That world, I knew, would let me in based on my skills. I created a CV that boasted of great accomplishments, and I presented it to the DBCM Corporation. There was not a thing on that CV I had actually done, but there was also nothing on that paper that I couldn't do if they gave me the opportunity."

I recognized Chiora's habit of stretching the truth to suit his own ends.

Chiora picked up a small stone, casually inspecting it to make sure it was of no value before tossing it into the river. "To keep the company from being too interested in verifying the facts of my history, I offered to work for a salary only slightly higher than the men who dug in the mines," he said. "The company hired me as an engineer at the age of seventeen. I laughed at how easy it had been. I succeeded in that place, not by virtue of my work or my ideas, but by showing people the face they wanted to see. People can be very stupid, my friend, especially the smart ones."

"That's a nonsense statement," I said.

"It is truth. It was hard, though, to work with people I hated. That company controlled ninety percent of the world's diamond trade at the time, and it was run by stupid men whose only qualification was the color of their skin. They called themselves Africans, but they were Dutchmen, Englishmen, and Australians. They were the sons of invaders. I was the only true African in management, and I only had a job because I was willing to work harder than anyone, and for less money."

"It was the same for the mercenaries in Iraq," I said. "The locals were paid one-tenth of what we got."

"It's always this way when the *mzungu* are involved. The men called me *kaffir,* the monkey. The mines were unsafe and inefficient, and I offered many solutions for improving the business. My bosses told me my ideas were foolish and sent me away, then presented the ideas to their bosses and got credit for my work. I tried to drown my hate with alcohol, but this only made the anger worse. I actually planned the murder of my supervisor, but then I stumbled upon a different solution."

His eyes gleamed. "I drank too much one night. Much too much. When I awoke, I was on the floor of one of the vaults. I had security clearance, you see. In my stupor, I had locked myself in a room full of many millions of carats worth of rough diamonds. I saw that all I had to do was take a single small diamond every day, and adjust the records to make the absence disappear."

"You became a thief."

"If you steal from a thief, have you broken the law?"

"You've only carried the crime forward."

"Ah, you are mistaken, my friend. These white men had stolen from Africa. I'm Africa."

"The diamonds are yours, you say?" I couldn't keep from scoffing.

"They are the property of all Africans."

This sounded to me like what my father would call *a bunch of hooey*. Frank would call it bullshit. Yet I was there to listen, not to judge. I didn't care to start an argument with Chiora, so urged him to continue.

"When I had enough, I moved on to another mine. I worked during the day, and at night I made plans to put the power of the mines in the hands of African people. Everywhere I learned something new about mining, about distribution, or about greed and violence and fear."

"And you stole diamonds."

"I repossessed diamonds, gold, coltan, uranium, cobalt, and copper. All in the name of Africa."

"The people thank you, I'm sure."

Chiora grinned. "You have spent too much time with this Frank person. You wear his sarcasm like a bad coat."

I frowned at the stinging remark. "How did you fall afoul of Zhou?"

"I made the mistake of trusting him. My dreams were close to becoming a reality. My plans for the African People's Mine were almost finished, and I had drawn a group of trusted men to my cause. I thought it would be best to tell Mister Zhou that I would leave The Company and pursue my own great dream. But, you see, the dream didn't make money for The Company. Mister Zhou fired me and told me that if I pursued this idea he would make sure I was ruined."

"Tyrants aren't overly fond of sharing. Were you surprised?"

"I should not have been, but I was. Mister Zhou raised his voice and accused me of stealing from the mine, of encouraging rebellion among the men. These were very serious accusations."

"Both of them are true."

Chiora ignored me. "I went to collect my clothes, and he sent men to beat me. Unfortunately for him, those were men I had already won to my side, so I was allowed to escape."

"But these types of men don't work for the hope of future riches. They're focused on the *now*. How did you convince them to come with you?"

"I redistributed some wealth from the mine to help us begin our journey to freedom."

It gave me pause, the way Chiora painted himself in a saintly light at all times. It didn't square with the violence and thievery perpetrated by his men, or the casual way he handed out death. It echoed uncomfortably of my own justifications.

As though reading my thoughts, Chiora said, "We have worked very hard to get this far. We have not always lived up to the ideals I strive to maintain. But look! Here we are, making our dream a reality!"

Look, I did. I saw a ragged collection of tents, gashes in the raw earth, teeming jungle, and a muddy river, which at that very moment rolled the bodies of Chiora's former colleagues slowly toward the sea.

It's hard, at times, to tell a dream from a nightmare.

CHAPTER 38

AFTER LUNCH, AND before the mining began, the men gathered at the edge of the river in the afternoon sun to be exhorted by Chiora. His thin arms flapped and pointed as he spoke of the nobility of labor and the rewards thereof.

The men waited him out. To me, they seemed more focused on gathering strength for the task ahead than on subverting the dominant paradigm. I thought that with me and Frank looking on from the high ground, the model of worker equality in African mines looked indistinguishable from a prison gang in the American South.

There were differences, of course. For one, Chiora insisted everyone have a pull at the Johnny Walker bottle before the work began. He treated it as a kind of sacrament, and in that light his own suckling at the liquor teat was more deeply spiritual than the others.

Another important difference was that Frank and I were invited to drink as well, but only after the others had taken their share.

After the bottle was put away, Chiora shouted, "We work, this time for Africa!"

This tickled me. The man was quoting the theme song from the 2010 World Cup in South Africa, which Africans in even in the most remote corners of the continent had closely followed. A potently sexy Colombian woman sang the song while doing things with her hips that made my imagination soar.

I must've laughed aloud at the silliness of the accidental plagiarism, and received some stern looks from the crew. I had earlier heard some discontented whispers amongst the men during lunch. They read foul portents in the unfortunate fact that one of their number still spun in the current at the edge of camp. It reminded them that though Frank and I were now nominally part of their group, we were also responsible for culling their numbers by nearly fifty percent.

I caught a whiff of emotional flash powder in the muggy air and raised my eyebrows to Frank in silent warning.

He nodded curtly, acknowledging the danger.

While I sweated and nursed my anxieties, the work began.

Ngamba ran about the camp starting up the generators, which spluttered to life and set up their infernal racket. Frank and I again exchanged concerned looks; the noise would make it impossible to hear enemies approaching. For that matter, it would most likely be impossible to hear people firing on our position, so great was the clattering effort of the motors and the gurgle and cough of the hoses vomiting muddy water into the river.

Once the pumps cycled up and the water level in the pools dropped to a reasonable level, the men jumped in and began digging. They worked in teams of three. One man dumped gravel into the shake-shake screens, and the other two swirled the water around and stared into the reddish brown slop in search of precious stones.

The experience wasn't magical. It was men scrabbling about in the mud, hacking at the soil, and swilling muck in a pan. It takes, I guess, a better man than me to see the nobility of such base labor.

Chiora's men, however, began singing. This did much to improve my sense of the moment, mostly because it offered relief from the blattering generators. I found myself wondering whether a baritone voice raised in song could physically eliminate the ugliness of a diesel motor, like two waves canceling each other in the ocean.

The song, in Kiswahili, described the great things these men would do once they made their fortunes—the wives they would have, the changes they would bring to their home villages. These men sang their futures into existence.

I remained mute. What would Stanley Mullens sing about his future? I could muster no words, no tune. I had only the present. My song would always be the rattle of motors and the snap of gunfire.

Ngamba shouted happily and raised his hand in the air.

Even from twenty yards away, I saw the exceptional size of the gray rock in his hand. Frank abandoned his post to rush over for a closer view, and I joined him, dropping into the pit to bear witness to glory.

The men clustered around, jostling to get a closer look and babbling excitedly about how many carats it must be. For me, the look of the thing was a disappointment. There's a reason they call uncut diamonds *rough*. It was shiny enough, I suppose, in the context of the endless miles of mud and green surrounding us, but it was also misshapen and somewhat cloudy.

Something sunk in my belly. So much had been sacrificed in the name of what was ultimately nothing more than a damn rock.

How many people, I wondered, understand the amount of suffering and death that goes into sticking a bauble on their pampered fingers? My excitement, and my hope, were gone. I was mortified to have been dragged into this stupidity.

I turned to Frank to share this minor revelation. His eyes shone with greedy awe.

Chiora waded into the muck and snatched the diamond from Ngamba's hand, laughing even while encouraging everyone to get back to work. I saw that for all his high talk, Chiora stared at the diamond with the same brainless lust Frank did. Only when the diamond disappeared into his pocket was the spell broken, and the song resumed.

That night, as we ate supper, Frank crowed. "Fuck man, we're gonna be rich!" He slapped me on the shoulder, "Cheer up, Stan! You brought us to the goddamn mother lode! This is our stake, brother. We're set for fucking life!"

I tried to echo his enthusiasm, but after all we had been through, all I felt was a bone-deep regret. If this was, as Frank suggested, our crowning achievement, it only emphasized the degree to which my dreams were appallingly misguided.

I produced a facsimile of a smile. "It was a successful day."

"Are you fucking kidding me? We hauled in probably a hundred K worth of rocks." Frank slapped the table. "In half a fuckin' day!"

"But what's our objective, Frank?"

He shrugged. "Get rich or die tryin'."

"That's the name of a rap album. And let me rephrase the question. What is *your* plan?"

Frank's smile went cold. "You're doin' that thinkin' thing again."

"I reckon one of us should make the effort."

"Jesus H fuck, Stanley. Here we're, clear of Zhou, partners in a goddamn diamond mine, and you look like you just found out you've got the fuckin' cancer."

I knew he wouldn't understand, but I told him anyway. "I don't have a song."

Frank stared at me for a long time. "A song."

"These men spend the day singing about their future. Doesn't it bother you that we have nothing in front of us?"

"You want a song?" Frank jumped up from the table and barked out an old rap song about *gettin' rich, or dyin' tryin'.* He accompanied his sad attempt at rap with what he likely considered dance moves. It looked more like a seizure. Chiora and his men stared in quiet horror.

I said, "Whiteness can be a disease."

Frank sat back down, grinning. "That was 50 Cent, bitch."

"You dance like a busted down robot."

Frank's high spirits wouldn't be dampened. "Tomorrow I wanna get my hands dirty. I wanna work in the hole."

"We have a job. We guard the perimeter."

"We stand around like assholes. I could work circles around these guys. And who the fuck is gonna attack us out here in the middle of bumfuck nowhere?"

"Greed has rendered you even more stupid than usual," I said. "Chiora and his men felt the same way until we killed half their number. Zhou sent men after us in Kinshasa, and you know damn well it's only a matter of time before he does so again."

"Fine. You keep standin' in the bushes tomorrow feeling all scared and whatnot. I'm gonna dig me up some fuckin' diamonds."

CHAPTER 39

IN THE MORNING, Frank came out to the pits without his weapons, shirtless like the rest of the men. The sight of his obscene musculature, not to mention the bullet wounds and shrapnel scars, rendered the rest of the men timid. They cowered and snuck furtive, awestruck glances at the damaged giant in their midst.

Chiora came from the edge of the pit to speak with me, bringing a sharp smell of whiskey. "My colleagues think he is Tata Fumbi come to walk among them."

"An evil spirit?"

"He is one of the *nkisi*. You would call him a god of death." Chiora pointed to my ruined face. "They think the same of you, of course."

"This isn't surprising."

"You have an intimidating aspect."

The vile *marabout's* words came back to me. "We were told once that the shadows of our dead follow along behind us," I said.

"I believe that, my friend."

"Our way of life isn't wholesome."

"You can change."

"You think so?" I frowned. My visions of life beyond soldiering had been vague at the best of times. Recently, they had faded almost completely.

"I am African. I must believe in the possibility of change, you see? Otherwise, I would lie down and let the lion take me. But in your case, I am very optimistic. You are a man on the verge of shedding his skin."

I'd already shed my skin. The problem was what would replace it. What shape would I take? "I would like to believe you."

"Then you must!" he said, grinning. "Look at me. I have become a new man completely."

Have you?

The generators coughed to life, and Chiora clapped his hands. "The work begins!"

Frank clawed back dirt like a back hoe. So great was his capacity for work that instead of the normal complement of two men working shake-shakes in front of him, he had four, and still the others couldn't keep pace. He moved with feverish urgency, muscles bunching and flexing.

I suspected he fortified himself with what he called his *Peruvian marching powder*, and worried that he might blow out his heart. I also had the pointlessly maternal thought that he needed sunscreen, but knew better than to say anything about either.

From time to time Frank shouted joyful nonsense, his ragged voice cutting through the men's songs. His intensity seemed to both frighten and inspire the others, and the pace of work became universally manic. Even Chiora climbed down into the pits, as though bent on scraping the soil clean of all its riches in a single day.

There was nothing left for me but to set up my one-man perimeter. Since Tshikapa was on our downriver side, I assumed the greatest risk of attack was from that direction, and so set about pacing the edge of the camp, alone.

The men's song was interrupted with increasing frequency by the discovery of diamonds. Their work shifted, concentrating on the downstream edge of the largest pit, and they were all lost to my view. From their ecstatic shouts, I had to assume things were going extremely well.

By midday, the song broke down completely, and their cheers of wonder and surprise were the only music to be heard. Frank's discordant melody, you might say, became the order of the day.

Eventually, my curiosity got the best of me. I abandoned my post to take a look for myself. In the pit, the entire workforce of the camp clustered around Frank as he hacked away at one wall of dirt and gravel. The other three diggers worked in a straight line beside him at the bottom of the deepening hole. In their greed, they had abandoned the precaution of expanding the outer edge of the pit and working their way down to create a gentle slope. Chiora stood behind the men, holding a canvas sack the size of a grocery bag. It was perhaps a third full of diamonds.

The men gabbled and shouted, and even as I watched they tossed diamonds into the bag several times a minute, in a cascade of unimaginable wealth. I wasn't overly familiar with the rate of success in diamond mining, but even I could tell we were in the midst of a miraculously rich strike.

The smile on Chiora's face could only be described as beatific.

"My friend," he said to me, nearly tearful with joy, "there are so many diamonds. So many!"

I pointed to the walls of the pit, which were more than ten feet high around the men, and increasingly vertical. "I reckon you should ease the slope here."

He nodded distractedly, still smiling. "Yes, yes. We are all rich men now. Very rich."

"Gravity affects wealthy men the same as the rest."

Frank must have heard my voice, if not my warning. Without looking up from his labors, he shouted, "Zhou can suck it, brother!"

It was tempting to drop into the pit and join them. What boy doesn't dream of finding treasure, after all? My imagination soared and my heart raced, but the need to protect Frank—and now Chiora, as well—tugged at my sleeve and bid me back to my patrol.

The men needed to stop for lunch, given the enormous amount of energy they burned. But of course in their mad joy they didn't consider it. The afternoon waxed infernally hot and humid, and still they tunneled deeper into the ground. In time they could no longer muster the energy to shout, or perhaps they were simply numbed by the sight of so many diamonds. All I could hear over the generators was the slice of shovels, effortful grunts, and the sluicing hiss of the shake-shakes.

I took up position at the base of a giant greenheart tree and was staring into the bush when the inevitable happened.

The pit collapsed.

A deep *whump*, like a grunt from the earth. Rending screams.

I sprinted to the pit. One wall had fallen, pouring mud into the hole and smashing a knot of men against the far side. Some were buried up to their necks. They bawled in pain and confusion.

I couldn't see Chiora or Frank.

I leapt into the quagmire, sinking in loose slurry, and began to pull men from the hole. Most came easily, but others had to be rocked out of the sucking mud and gravel. Once free, the men tried to crawl out of the pit, but I bellowed at them to help me, threatening to shoot those who refused.

The last men I uncovered were Chiora and Frank.

Chiora had been thrown to the far wall of the hole and pinned beneath a boulder so large it took three of us to roll it off him. He didn't cry out, but his eyes were huge and vacant. Even after we freed him, he panted in pain.

Frank's weight had kept him near the wall of mud as the collapsing dirt flowed around him. He was almost entirely submerged, with mud and gravel up to his chin. He couldn't speak, but he glared his outrage at the sky.

Using my hands for fear of gouging him with a shovel, I clawed through the muck until I could birth him from the soil and drag him to safety.

The men sprawled at the forest's edge, panting and shaking, fully slimed with mud. Most were simply bruised and terrified. Some had been sliced by rocks or shovels as the slide overtook them.

Chiora wasn't bleeding, and his limbs appeared to be unbroken, but he still took unnatural little gulps of air. I tore back his shirt to find the majority of his torso bruised and misshapen. These were internal injuries, and I had no way of helping him out here in the jungle.

For all his pain, he still clutched the bag of diamonds to his side.

Frank said nothing when I asked if he was hurt. But I saw the pool of blood expanding near his left ankle. He didn't protest when I stooped to get a better look. Something, probably a shovel, had sliced through the back of his leg clear to the bone, severing his Achilles tendon. His calf muscle bunched up at the back of his knee.

"You took a knock there, partner," I said.

"Fuck it. I'm fine." His brow furrowed, and his mouth pulled into a sneer of rage. He didn't seem overly concerned for a man who had nearly chopped off his own foot, and whose wound was now filled with bacteria-ridden mud.

I pulled a bottle of purified water from my pack and doused the wound. Frank inhaled sharply, but made no other sound as I washed the filth out of his leg.

"I can still work," he said.

"I imagine a bit of rest would be in order," I said, as casually as possible.

"Wrap it and get the fuck out of my way."

I didn't rise to the bait. "Do you have any antibiotics left in that bag of yours?"

Rather than digging out a pill, Frank unlatched his entire sack of medical tricks and tossed it to me. This was a first. I took it as an indication of the seriousness of our situation that he would expose his chemical world to me in this way.

I dug through a veritable rainbow of strange pills, powders white and brown, sticky green buds, and several small syringes. Finally, I located a baggie of antibiotics and recognized Cipro, Augmentin, and Doxycycline. I had no clue what a doctor would recommend for a leg wound full of jungle filth. I made Frank take one of each.

"Hand me three Oxy," Frank said, as I began to close the bag.

He chewed them like candy and soon enough, he relaxed somewhat. Still, when I tried to move away to check on Chiora he clutched my arm fiercely. "Wrap the leg, motherfucker."

"You would be best served high-tailing it to the nearest surgical hospital. That'll be septic by morning."

Where most men would have been howling with pain and fright, Frank was merely defiant. "You put me back together, or I will beat your ass."

"Unlikely, seeing as how you would have to catch me first."

"Douchebag."

A wail of despair kept rising in my chest, but I tamped it down. "I will get the med kit, and I will sew you together as best I can. But don't come crying to me when your leg turns green and smells like a dead goat."

"Duly noted, asshat."

We bantered as always, though Frank's eyes glittered feverishly and his chest heaved like a baited bull.

Frank's gaze pierced me, stripping away any illusions I had about our salvation. We'd been in the throes of this disaster for many years. Frank, I knew, had seen it all along, though I was only now waking up to the truth of our slow immolation. For all my supposed cleverness, I'd gotten the wrong end of the stick about the most basic truth of my own life.

So, as always, I acted as though I was saving Frank, while doing nothing meaningful to rescue him.

In the last light, I cleaned out his leg as best I could, dousing it with purified water, then knitting the skin together with the same black fishing line he had used on my face.

We passed a terrible night at the camp, with me shuttling back and forth uselessly from Chiora, who spoke little and struggled to breathe, to Frank. Somehow I ended up as the camp doctor, though all I had to offer was whiskey for Chiora, and pain pills and antibiotics for Frank. Both men seemed content with those ministrations.

All night I went through the empty motions of rescue, arguing with them and the rest of our mud-covered colleagues about the need to take our wounded into Tshikapa at first light. All they could talk about, both the injured and the whole, was getting back into that pit.

The next morning, that is precisely what they did.

Some men simply can't be saved.

CHAPTER 40

CHIORA COULDN'T WORK, of course. He couldn't even move without gasping and crying out. In a first world hospital, he could be put back together. Out in the bush, there was nothing for him to do but die slowly and painfully. His agony and drunkenness released the tyrant in him. He accepted no dissent and demanded to be brought to the mine. At his command, I put him in a folding camp chair and carried him like a baby down into the hole. Propped up on a rickety seat in ten inches of mud, the administrator of the African People's Mine seemed to improve. Though he looked ashy and frail, his eyes shone when he looked upon the site of his great strike. The previous night, at his instruction, I'd put the day's diamonds in a large metal toolbox and buried it next to the latrines. Now, in the early light he sat with the emptied canvas sack on his knees, a look of joyful anticipation etched upon his features.

I have never envied a dying man so much.

All of the men seemed to have succumbed to some kind of hemorrhagic greed; their common sense bled away from every orifice.

Frank could scarcely put weight on his damaged leg, though I wrapped it so tightly I feared he would lose his foot before sundown. The slurry of antibiotics and pain medicines I threw at him would have killed a lesser man, and from time to time Frank turned his head to the side and spewed bile.

Despite all this, he limped and hopped down into the mine and took up one of the shake-shakes not lost in the previous day's slide. He barked at the others to use the few exposed shovels to dig out the rest of the buried equipment. The men complied. The pumps snarled to life. The miners didn't sing as they worked.

I looked on with numb resignation as they all set about re-digging the hole that had very nearly turned into their mass grave just the day before. I had worked with many men who weren't afraid of risk, but never before had I seen a whole group turn their backs on self-preservation so completely. Watching them file into the pit, I thought of suicide cults, driven by some charismatic fool and the dream of eternity. I opened my mouth to share my fear, but said nothing. After ten years of hurling myself at death alongside Frank, I finally understood the futility of standing between men and their true nature.

I felt a dull surprise at my unwillingness to join them in the ground. Having abandoned the illusion of some better future, I believed the noble thing would've been to pick up a shovel and join Frank and Chiora in the pit.

Instead, I chose to remain among the living.

Within minutes the men discovered more diamonds, and the pace of the work picked up. The mood, however, remained dark. At least that's how it appeared to me from my vantage point above the hole.

There was nothing for me to gain by hovering over the mine, but still I looked on as the muddy ghosts clawed at the soil.

I wished I shared their focus. They had moved past all practical concerns, and the petty fears that beset most men. Their road to salvation was set out before them, and they let nothing, not even death, distract them. Their faith was pure, and their reward was here on this earth. These were men exalted, while I alone was left in the realm of minor concerns such as life, death, and maintaining the perimeter.

The attack came later that morning, from upriver, where I didn't expect it.

I was on the other side of camp, watching for attackers from Tshikapa, when an RPG round hissed across the open ground and struck the wall of the pit above the miners. The far tree line erupted with the pop and rattle of small arms fire. I caught glimpses of men I recognized, Zhou's giant Rwandan guards, moving through the trees. The South African bastard I'd hit with a book on my last night in Zhou's compound stepped out of the bush, smiling as he sprayed the pit with an Uzi.

All of my men, trapped in the trench, were helpless to flee. I saw Chiora topple from his chair. Bullets ripped through miners, staining the pit with blood. I couldn't see Frank in the chaos of smoke, gunfire, and shouting, but I knew he was there, unarmed and lame.

My only hope against such a disciplined foe was to pick off Zhou's men one by one. I knew I couldn't do it in time to save my friends, but I could avenge them.

The heat was upon me, and my whole body sang. My goal, if you can apply any real thought to such a state of animal fury, was to save at least a couple of Zhou's men for hand-to-hand combat. Such was my rage that I wanted to feel their bones snapping in my hands and to tear their beating hearts from their chests.

There were twenty or so attackers. Using every skill I learned in my years of military training and experience, I circled through the jungle, hunting them down one after the other, going out of my way to avoid head shots. I planned to come back through with my pig sticker and make them feel the terror and pain they'd caused the miners.

Despite their superior armaments, I quickly had the enemy in disarray. They weren't expecting an ambush. Fear beset them, so they shot wildly and gave away their positions. At that point, I no longer feared anything. I put a bullet or two into each man before I slipped out of range.

They turned their RPGs on the jungle. The trees exploded, peppering me with shrapnel and showering me with shards of hardwood. This only heightened my wrath.

I howled death in their faces, bellowing gibberish in no human language, and shot out their legs. Their battle cries gave way to pleas for salvation as discipline broke down. The wounded begged God for mercy, called for their mothers.

I experienced the purity of battle. Everything that I am flowered in that moment of vengeance. On the hunt, in a rage, I found peace.

I chased stragglers across the jungle, crashing through bushes to catch each of them, and cut them down.

The South African was the last one. I dogged him for half an hour as he stumbled through the underbrush. Unlike the others, he wasn't completely unmanned. Though he was out of ammo, he continued to shout insults as he retreated. I followed behind, stalking effortlessly through the tangled growth, shooting at him occasionally, taking care to just graze his arms and legs.

Finally, he staggered to a stop. In the deep gloom of the trackless jungle he dropped his empty weapon and turned to face me, panting and snarling, hurling curses.

I shot him in the thigh and pulled out my knife. He stank like a soldier, a familiar blend of soupy sweat and the bitter tang of fear. The shock of the leg wound emptied his bowels. I grabbed his throat and dragged him up a tree, level with me. His feet dangled uselessly in the air, his blood *tap-tap-tap*ping on the leaves.

"How could you?" I shouted, tears and snot running down my face.

The man's face was already going gray. His brow furrowed in consternation. "I'm a soldier, *bruh*. Just like you."

With that, my rage abandoned me, replaced by a terrible calm. A vast darkness opened up beneath me. My ears rang. "You are nothing like me," I said. "I'm a good soldier."

I slid the pig sticker across his throat, releasing a hiss of air and a gout of blood. His face went slack, and black gore pumped down his chest. The man seemed to double in weight, and my arms ached. I allowed him to slide down the trunk.

I cleaned my knife on the dead man's sleeve, and turned back toward the mine.

CHAPTER 41

Our mine was now an open grave. Some men had died with their arms outstretched, crawling toward safety. Others curled in on themselves, as though death were a return to infancy. I don't know how long I watched their blood swirl into the mud, before I became aware of the flatulent racket made by the pumps.

I bestirred myself to climb up and switch them off, my limbs leaden and slow. It felt as though the walls of the pit were some huge peak rather than ten feet of gravel slope.

When the pumps stopped, the pipe drooled a slurry of mud and gore back into the pit. An oppressive silence fell over the clearing. I considered turning the generator back on, if only to mask that awful nullity. Even the damn bugs were quiet.

I heard my breath, my heartbeat, the relentless coursing of my blood through my veins. I thought about the men I had killed, and whether Zhou had already replaced them at the compound. I calculated how much time I had before Zhou learned of my survival, and idly wondered how many miles lay between me and the next breathing soul.

When I heard a groan, I flew down into the pit, stumbling in my haste, and dug through the pile of bodies to find the source of the noise, tossing aside the dead like old clothes until I found Chiora blinking at me, his eyes huge and terrified.

I pulled him out and lay him on the grass. Not until I examined his injuries did I see that he still clutched the day's bag of rough diamonds. I tried to take it from him, so that I might see his wounds more clearly. He snatched it back with surprising strength. He was shot in the chest and back, one side of his face gored by shrapnel.

"I cannot sit up," he said.

"You took a few bullets." My voice caught, and I had to look away.

"Ah. That is bad, my friend."

I took a deep breath and turned back to him, trying to arrange my face into a smile. "You just rest here a moment, and I'll see about patching you up."

Chiora didn't respond. He lay on the grass, tears cutting tracks through the mud on his face. I descended into the pit once more.

To my great surprise, Ngamba was also still alive, though just barely. His breath wheezed and gurgled, and blood leaked from his mouth. So thoroughly had he been aerated that the fact he was breathing at all was a kind of miracle. His face was a mask of fear. As a mercy, I went behind him, as though to lift him out of the hole, and snapped his neck.

When this was done, the deadness in my limbs overtook me. I collapsed, still holding Ngamba's body.

Behind me, Frank said, "You're crying like a big, fat, ugly baby."

He lay on his side in the bloody water, a piece of metal the size of a business card lodged in his forehead.

I said, "It's a natural reaction to death."

"Whatever."

We spoke casually. As if I were not holding a dead man in my arms. As if Frank wasn't mangled beyond all repair.

"You look poorly," I said.

"Do I really have a piece of metal stuck in my fucking head?"

"I'm afraid so, yes."

"Fuck me."

I set Ngamba's body down and slid closer to Frank. His entire body was cut up and punctured, as though bullets were magnetically attracted to him. I pictured the scene from the attackers' perspective. Frank had presented the biggest and best target, the trophy animal in our small herd.

"You shouldn't have tried to take on an army with a shovel."

"Is it bad?" he asked.

"I've seen worse."

Frank tried to laugh. He jerked spastically, wincing. "Just haul me outta the goddamn sun. Let me rest a minute. I'm good to go."

I complied, as I always did. Blood pooled around him, soaking the ground as I dragged him out of the pit. As I neared the shade his shoulders went slack, and I nearly lost my grip.

"Damn it, Frank," I said, "You have to help me out a little here."

He didn't answer, nor would he ever again.

I set him down gently in the mud. His eyes were open, though he wasn't breathing.

My mind slipped out of gear, unable to process my failure, after all of this, to keep Frank safe. I dropped into the mud beside him and put a hand on his chest. I sat with my head bowed, tears blurring my vision, my heart a howling emptiness.

Chiora call out, rousing me from my trance.

He looked up at the sky but his eyes darted around, as though tracking the flight of some insect. His chest rose and fell too fast, and his breath huffed unnaturally.

He told me, "I have made some terrible mistakes."

"Most of us have. You shouldn't worry about it just now."

Chiora shook his head. "No. I can do better. Next time, I will do things…differently. I will…be prepared."

"You should rest."

Chiora closed his eyes. When his breathing eased, I thought perhaps he was dying, but then his eyes flew open, finding mine. "The rest of the men, are they well?"

"They are as well as can be expected." I figured the time for brutal truth had passed.

He said, "I would like to apologize to them."

"They want you to regain your strength."

Chiora's breath again came unevenly, as though something was lodged in his throat. I shifted my position, and he turned toward the sound. "Where did you go?"

"I'm still right here."

"I am resting my eyes," he said, though they were wide open. He felt the bag of diamonds in his hands, and his mangled face broke into a smile. "This is a good mine. So many diamonds!"

My throat tightened. "It was quite a strike."

"We will do better tomorrow. This vein, my friend, it is the best one in the Congo."

"We've been lucky." I nearly choked on the falsehood, but Chiora was inside himself now, hardly hearing me.

"And your friend, Frank. He is a hard worker, is he not?"

"He can get up a good head of steam when he's motivated."

"I thought poorly of him, but he has turned out to be a good man."

"The two of you are surprisingly similar."

"What about Stanley? Where is he now?"

I didn't have the heart to correct him. "He's on patrol."

"Keeping us safe from our enemies."

"He's alone in the wilderness."

"I like that man. He has impressed me."

"I know he considered you a friend, as well."

"What did you say?"

"*He likes you, too*," I shouted, louder than I intended, my voice an aching sob.

Chiora shut his eyes, and didn't open them again. His smile remained. "I never thought I would become such a success," he said. "No one did. But here I am, the owner of a great mining interest, surrounded by good men and rich beyond imagination. I am a lucky man, am I not?"

"You are," I said.

"The future…" His chest convulsed, and his spine arched backward. He opened his mouth wide, and a terrible noise issued forth, a heaving groan that guttered out with a sigh. His body went slack.

I put my hand over his stilled heart. The bag of diamonds remained clutched in his hands.

CHAPTER 42

BURYING ALL THOSE men was simply beyond me that evening, so I slept that night in the company of the crowding dead. The *marabout*'s vision proved true at last.

Despite my terrible sadness and the strangeness of being alone in the world for the first time in many years, I slept deeply, exhausted, I suppose, from the day's appalling losses.

Before first light, I set about burying the bodies with businesslike efficiency.

I started with Chiora's men, simply trenching into the pit that was their undoing and laying them out side by side. This was distasteful, but not particularly emotional. There is nothing of nobility in the dead. Fluids leak out willy-nilly, and they give off terrible smells which discourage sympathetic feelings.

I couldn't be so businesslike about Chiora, however.

My desire was to make some grand gesture befitting the scope of his vision. But in the end I knew that the promise contained in the mine was what he loved most, and where he would want to spend eternity. There was nothing for it but to put him in the pit next to his men. I dug a deep shaft at the point of the mine's greatest advance, and I lay Chiora in the bloody water pooling there. While the rest of the men lay flat on their backs with their shovels and shake-shakes across their chests, I wrapped Chiora in the fetal position, curled around the bag with the last day's strike.

I obsessed about arranging him in just the right way. By the time I was satisfied with the job, he was nearly submerged in the slurry of gore and mud. This, too, seemed fitting.

With all that done, I walked to the top edge of the mine to scrape dirt onto the men and their leader. It was excruciating work, and the sun beat down upon me like a punishment. If there were diamonds in the gravel I dumped onto those men, I was blind to them.

Frank, of course, was different. I dragged one of the long tables from the mess tent out into a broad patch of open ground, and hauled Frank's body onto it. This was no small feat, as the dead are unwieldy at best, and Frank was a particularly massive bag of guts. In life he came in at just over two hundred and fifty pounds, but as a dead man he seemed to be built of something heavier than flesh.

The struggle was terribly undignified, but in time I stretched him out properly, his face pointing up at the sky. I placed his M4 across his chest and his absurdly large knife in his right hand. After I culled through his ammo to replenish my own supply, I arranged it, along with the rest of his gear, on top of and around his body. At last I tore down the rest of the mess tent, piling the greenish poles and the broken tables around the base of Frank's pyre.

I hesitated to pour the gasoline from the pump engines over his body, but finally did so, avoiding his face. I paused again with the matches in my hand, feeling the need to say something profound about my fallen friend. But oppressed by exhaustion and heat as I was, I couldn't muster any last sentiments. My attempts to formulate a eulogy sounded childlike and false even in the darkness of my own mind.

I lit the match and threw it, igniting the gasoline which burst into flame with a mighty *whump* that blew me backward and singed my eyebrows.

By the time I recovered from the shock of that mishap, the ammo around Frank's body began to cook off. The clearing came alive with the pop and bang of gunfire. I stumbled for the shelter of a Ceiba tree, cursing my stupidity.

However, after watching the fireworks from a safe distance for a time, I smiled. There was no more appropriate way to send Frank out of this world than in a burst of flame and a hail of gunfire.

It was mid-afternoon by the time I walked out of the mine, laden with my gear, and the diamonds I had unearthed from Chiora's hiding spot near the latrines. The intelligent thing would have been to spend another night under shelter, but I couldn't countenance twelve more hours in the company of ghosts. Also, the bodies of Zhou's men moldered in the woods, befouling the whole area with the stench of death.

I got as far as the last camp Frank and I made prior to joining forces with Chiora. The underbrush we had hacked so thoroughly had already replaced itself, and little evidence of our passage remained aside from the small scorched place where we cooked our giant fish.

My path across the planet will leave nothing but blank spaces where life used to be.

I made a new fire and passed the time putting diamonds into small sachets crudely sewn from swatches of one of Frank's old shirts.

I distributed the parcels across my person, tucking them into pockets, rolling them into socks, even stuffing one into a bag of peanuts I had purchased in Tshikapa before heading into the bush. In a particular stroke of genius, I sewed a long thin strip of cloth into a kind of belt, which I connected to my underpants with a few loose stitches.

I made Tshikapa the next day, and headed straight for the airport. There, I used my diamonds to charter a bush flight to Kalemie.

CHAPTER 43

JUST TWO DAYS after Frank, Tonde, and the rest of the miners were murdered, I hunkered in the bushes outside Zhou's compound at nightfall. My mind was sharp, focused. I felt neither fatigue nor fear. This was, I realized, the first time in many years I felt a real sense of mission. I no longer had to worry about anyone else, there was nobody to blame for my behavior. The enemy, once again, was clear.

I set my watch for one in the morning, the true witching hour, and secreted myself deeper in the underbrush to wait.

When the alarm on my watch buzzed, I felt fresh and clear-eyed. The compound was dark and silent. Just two guards slouched in plastic chairs, one on each side of the gate, asleep. For the sake of convenience, I put the silencer on my Glock, crept to the edge of the clearing, and dispatched them both from fifteen meters away.

I crossed the open ground in a crouch and reached through the wires to pluck the keys from the dead guard's belt. Once inside, I glanced at the building where Yingchun slept. I wondered if she was content, or if that was even possible for her. Her sole motivation in life seemed to be earning money for her family back in Yunnan Province.

I wondered if my actions would shatter that purpose. I pushed her from my mind and approached the old monastery.

I expected to encounter more guards, but our former employer appeared to be understaffed with Sheppard's team gone and the bulk of his security forces off hunting me and Frank. Moving swiftly and quietly, I shot just three more men on the way to the monastery, and snapped the neck of the hapless Chinese fellow in the entryway. I went room to room on the main floor, confirming I'd cleared the building. Finding no other guards, I crept upstairs.

When I slipped into Zhou's rooms I stood in the darkened entry a moment, listening. A bottle clinked on a glass, and Zhou said something in Chinese. No one answered, but I assumed one of the housekeeping staff was somewhere in his apartment. I didn't relish the idea of more collateral damage, but there was nothing for it. I couldn't afford to leave witnesses.

Zhou's voice receded, presumably toward his bedroom. I heard him bump into furniture, drunk. He chuckled quietly. A door slammed.

I moved into his large office, skulking in the shadows. The place was dark but for the low glow of a desk lamp, the air hazy with a pall of cigarette smoke hovering motionless in the humidity. Zhou barked what sounded like an order, and bedsprings creaked under his weight. I wiped the mud off my feet on his white carpet.

I briefly thought of how angry I'd been at Frank the last time I was here, which brought on a falling sensation of loss. I grabbed that feeling and sharpened it, forming a weapon to use against Zhou.

My body crackled with the promise of violence. I kept the silenced Glock in my right hand for the housekeeper. With my left, I slipped my pig sticker out of its sheath.

There should be intimacy to this moment.

I moved through Zhou's opulent living area, with its glaring red silks, black lacquer, and flashes of gold, and put my ear to the door of his inner sanctum. Ice tinkled in a glass. Zhou slurped noisily. He shouted something in

Chinese, and fell quiet. A few minutes later, his breathing slowed and deepened. The son of a bitch was asleep.

I came silently through the door with gun and blade poised, eager to bury my knife in Zhou's body.

The big boss slumped naked on the bed, propped up on pillows, snoring. His prick peeked out from thick black pubic hair, and his left hand precariously balanced a tumbler of whiskey on his blubbery paunch.

No one else was in the room, so I decided to deal with the housekeeper later. I holstered my gun and leapt forward, covering Zhou's mouth with my right hand as I threw my weight on him. My hand muzzled his panicked cry.

Zhou tried to bite me, but his teeth skimmed my fingers without finding purchase. He hit me weakly on the side of the head with his drink, slopping whiskey in my ear and down my back. The smell of booze seared my nostrils as I buried my knife in his neck.

Zhou didn't scream. He merely let out a quiet *ah,* as though he had solved some deep riddle. Black blood spurted from his throat. His survival instinct kicked in, but only limply. He reached to his neck and placed his free hand gently over mine. Blood pumped through our clasped fingers. He looked at me, and I forced myself to look back.

Nothing showed in Zhou's eyes but the fear common to every man, woman, and child as they die. Here was a man who controlled hundreds of millions of dollars of riches, who meted out life and death like a god, now sprawled on a sagging mattress, naked and fat as a baby, slick with his own blood.

Mister Zhou, supposedly my greatest enemy, died. His hand went slack. His drink tumbled to the floor, the glass clunking woodenly and rolling to the far wall. His eyes were blank and already filming over. His mouth gaped open in a permanent state of weak surprise.

I placed a few small bones and bird feathers on Zhou's chest, a calling card to make his men believe the Mai-Mai were responsible for the murder, and then savaged his body with my blade to simulate a bloodlust I no longer felt.

I turned to leave, and saw Yingchun standing in the doorway. She held a tray laden with a bottle of whiskey, a bucket of ice and two tumblers. Her hands shook, and she opened her mouth wide as though to scream, but made no sound.

I had to kill her, of course, or my plan to blame it on the Mai-Mai would fall apart. I didn't want to spend the rest of my life pursued by The Company's thugs.

Yingchun had to die, but I couldn't move.

Finally, I sheathed my knife and holstered my weapon. I walked toward her slowly, with my hands low in front of me, palms down. Keeping my voice gentle, I said, "Put that down, before you drop it."

She didn't respond. I took a few more steps, lifted the tray from her shaking hands, and set it on a coffee table in Zhou's living room.

When I came back to her, Yingchun couldn't meet my eye. Her terror stung me, but I could think of nothing to say that might ease her fear.

I said, "Do you want to sit?" She still didn't react, so I put my hands on her trembling shoulders.

She flinched at my touch but allowed me to settle her on the black couch. I retrieved the tray from Zhou's bedroom and poured her a shot of whiskey on the rocks. She held it, but didn't bring it to her lips. I took a short pull from the bottle. She kept her head down, her hair hanging in her face.

Yingchun waited to die.

I lifted her chin until she had no choice but to look at me.

"It's okay," I said. "It's me, Stanley,"

"Why did you do this?" There was no outrage in the question, though her voice shook.

I shrugged. I didn't want to tell her about Frank. "One of us had to go. I thought it should be him."

She drew herself up, looked me in the eye defiantly. "And now you will kill me."

Whatever she did or didn't feel for me, at that moment I admired her tremendously. "There's nothing to gain from that," I said.

Her shoulders sagged with relief. A tear slipped down her cheek. She continued searching my face, and I forced myself to hold her gaze. I don't know what she saw in my eyes, but at last she nodded. She said, "You are covered in blood."

I looked down, and saw that I was drenched in gore from my throat to my knees. I wanted to tell her I wore the blood of my enemies always, and that their ghosts would trail behind me for the rest of my life, their ranks growing as I pursued my calling. I wished I could tell her I'd made peace with it. Instead, I reached out, took the glass from her, and rested my bloody hand on hers.

Yingchun rose, still holding my hand, and led me to Zhou's bathroom. I followed, docile as a child. She took the ammo, grenades, and GPS out of my flak jacket, put me in the shower fully clothed, and washed me down as best she could. Her hands still trembled, but they were gentle, patient. If you ignored all the blood and the dead man in the next room, the scene was almost domestic. In any case, it was as close as I could come to that kind of thing.

Afterward, at the door to Zhou's rooms, she said, "They will kill you when they find out."

"They won't find out unless you tell them," I said.

Yingchun nodded. "You can trust me."

"You do what you need to take care of yourself. I'll get by regardless." Struck by a sudden inspiration, I handed her one of my larger packets of diamonds.

She opened the bag and stared at the glittering contents in confusion. "What is this?"

"Small consolations."

"Diamonds." Her voice trembled. "It's too much."

"You were always kind to me." I could think of nothing else to say. I kissed her on the cheek and left without saying goodbye.

I strolled across the compound, careless as to whether or not anyone saw me. Despite the fact that my clothes were drenched, my legs felt strong and light, as though gravity pulled on me just a bit less than it used to.

When I got to the gates, though, I hesitated.

I was a man utterly free of the mundane entanglements of life. There was nothing and no one left to escape from, and nobody depending on me. I knew at last who I was, my debts were all paid.

A man so unencumbered is capable of just about anything.

This newfound sense of possibility opened around me in an immense and terrible loneliness that set me clutching at the fence for fear of spinning off into the void. I endured this sensation, sure in the knowledge of its passage.

Then I opened the gates, and stepped into the welcome embrace of the Congo.

Also Available From WildBlue Press

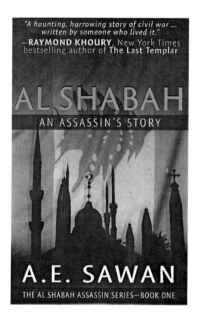

"A haunting, harrowing story of civil war ...
written by someone who lived it."
—RAYMOND KHOURY, New York Times
bestselling author of The Last Templar

AL SHABAH
AN ASSASSIN'S STORY

A.E. SAWAN
THE AL SHABAH ASSASSIN SERIES—BOOK ONE

In this first book of the Al Shabah Assassin Series, Paul ultimately finds himself on the trail of a childhood nemesis who had become the feared charismatic leader of a violent jihadist group. This fast-paced thriller takes Paul around the world in his personal search for truth and justice, and a final showdown with a yellow-eyed terrorist who one violent day ended Paul's childhood and set him on the road to becoming an assassin. *"A haunting, harrowing story of civil war ... written by someone who lived it."* – Raymond Khoury, New York Times Bestselling Author of *The Last Templar*

Read More: **http://wbp.bz/alshabah**

Also Available From WildBlue Press

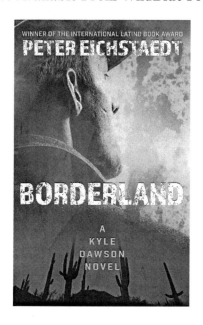

When a prominent land developer is brutally murdered on the U.S.-Mexico border, it's not just another cartel killing to journalist Kyle Dawson. The dead man is his father. Dawson, a veteran war correspondent, uncovers the truth and brings down a man poised to take the White House.

Read More: **http://wbp.bz/borderland**

See even more at:
http://wbp.bz/cf

More Crime Fiction You'll Love From WildBlue Press

HEADLOCK by BURL BARER

A paranoid recluse lures Jeff Reynolds into a complex web of deception, where delusions are deadly, life after death can be hell, and all roads lead to the McFeely Tavern.

Edgar winner Burl Barer spins a unique and wondrous mystery from the opening paragraph to the spectacular cinematic climax featuring one of the best plot twists in PI history.

wbp.bz/headlock

SAVAGE HIGHWAY by Richard Godwin

From an internationally acclaimed author of noir thrillers comes *"the road novel from hell"* (Castle Freeman Jr., author of The Devil In The Valley). Women are disappearing on the highway, a drifter hunts the men who raped her, and a journalist discovers the law has broken down. An *"irresistible hard-boiled read that's reminiscent of old school black and white noir."* (Vincent Zandri, New York Times bestselling author).

wbp.bz/savagehighway

WHEN FALL FADES by Amy Leigh Simpson

A *"Must-Read Romance of 2015"* (USA Today). Hunky FBI Agent Archer Hayes reluctantly enlists the lovely and beguiling Sadie Carson to solve the mystery of her elderly neighbor's death and its connection to a conspiracy dating back to WWII. Results in fiery romance and chilling murder plot. *"Simpson swung for the fences."* (Anthony Flacco, New York Times bestselling author). The first book in up-and-comer Simpson's The Girl Next Door romantic mystery series. Compares to New York Times bestselling romance author Julie Garwood.

wbp.bz/whenfallfades

CPSIA information can be obtained
at www.ICGtesting.com
Printed in the USA
LVOW10s1512170118
563088LV00009B/222/P